'Hammer has confirmed and underlined his reputation as numbering among the very best novelists in detective fiction.'

Sydney Morning Herald

'Complex and nuanced, this intelligent thriller shows why former political journalist Chris Hammer has become one of Australia's best-loved authors.'

The Australian

'Well-written and powerful, *The Valley* confirms Hammer's place as a master of bush crime.'

Canberra Weekly

'Will satisfy Chris Hammer fans and those who enjoy an Aussie murder mystery.'

Glam Adelaide

'Hammer nails it again with his latest crime thriller. Taking the template of a rip-roaring western and fashioning it around an historic homicide and a current killing, *The Valley* is resplendent with the greed feeding lust for gold, street shootouts, kidnappings and grave robbing.'

Sydney Arts Guide

'Chris Hammer is at his very best when immersed in small town life, politics, quirks and secrets—and all of these feature large in this book. But it's the pursuit of gold, the rare sound of running water, and the pure Australian-ness of it all that makes this one an absolute winner.'

DeathBecomesHer, *Crime Fiction Lover*

'Chris Hammer continues to create stories and people about whom we care, brimful of issues about which we sometimes tear out our hair in the real world. It's writing with both style and substance.'

Living Arts Canberra

PRAISE FOR
THE TILT

'Richly layered . . . the characters are drawn robustly and definitively. Hammer has confirmed and underlined his reputation as numbering among the very best novelists in detective fiction.'

Sydney Morning Herald

'Chris Hammer has surpassed himself . . . It is constantly intriguing, shocking and moving . . . I doubt I'll read a better novel this year.'

The Times

'It would be unfair to say Chris Hammer is at the top of the crime writing game. Chris Hammer IS the game. *Full Tilt* may be a better title, given the speed with which readers will devour Chris Hammer's exceptional novel.'

Benjamin Stevenson, author of
Everyone in My Family Has Killed Someone

'Ominous, pacy and intricately plotted, *The Tilt* hits the ground running and never lets up. Hammer's best yet!'

Emma Viskic, author of *Those Who Perish*

'Chris has another absolute cracker on his hands here . . . A new book from him is always an unmissable event . . . The way Chris weaves three different timelines without ever losing focus, and creates such a broad cast of compelling and emotionally complex characters is truly impressive.'

Shelley Burr, author of *Wake*

'Chris Hammer at the height of his powers . . . absolutely not to be missed!'

Hayley Scrivenor, author of *Dirt Town*

'A darkly simmering mystery, gorgeously told . . . Utterly brilliant.'

Dervla McTiernan, author of
The Rúin **and** *The Murder Rule*

PRAISE FOR
TRUST

'A tightly constructed and well-paced crime thriller that smoothly moves to a suitably surprising and bloody finale . . . The descriptions of Sydney are vivid and evocative and there are also sharp-eyed comments on politics, corruption and the modern media . . . a terrific read.'

Jeff Popple, *Canberra Weekly*

'Chris Hammer has excelled himself with *Trust* . . . a thriller strong on character development, social insights, ethical issues and dramatic action.'

Robyn Walton, *Weekend Australian*

'A dark and gritty Sydney, superb character work and a fast-paced mystery to keep you on your toes . . . This thrill ride of a story is everything we have come to expect and more. Perfect for those looking for a fright this October!'

Better Reading

'Immersive, pacy . . . one of Australia's best new crime authors.'

Irish Independent

'With Corris and Temple departed, Chris Hammer almost makes up for the hole they left in Australian crime fiction. Wickedly well-written, a phrase turner that powers a page turner, trust me: *Trust* is a rip-roaring read.'

Richard Cotter, *Sydney Arts Guide*

'Another twisting and turning thriller from the author of *Scrublands* and *Silver*. Australian crime writing at its best.'

Village Observer

'This is Hammer's most elegant plot thus far.'

Sydney Morning Herald/The Age

PRAISE FOR
SILVER

'Chris Hammer is a great writer—a leader in Australian noir.'

Michael Connelly

'A terrific story . . . an excellent sequel; the best Australian crime novel since Peter Temple's *The Broken Shore*.'

The Times

'Elegantly executed on all fronts, *Silver* has a beautifully realised sense of place . . . There's a lot going on in Port Silver, but it's well worth a visit.'

Sydney Morning Herald/The Age

'The immediacy of the writing makes for heightened tension, and the book is as heavy on the detail as it is on conveying Scarsden's emotional state. *Silver* is a dramatic blood-pumper of a book for lovers of Sarah Bailey and Dave Warner.'

Books + Publishing

'Hammer has shown in *Silver* that *Scrublands* was no fluke. He has taken what he learnt in that novel and built on it to create a deeper, richer experience. He has delivered a real sense of place and uses the crime genre to explore some very real current social issues and character types.'

PS News

'A taut and relentless thriller—just jump into the rapids and hold on.'

Readings Monthly

'The action unfolds at the same breathless pace as it did in *Scrublands* . . . Hammer's prose brings the coastal setting vividly to life. An engrossing read, perfect for the summer holidays.'

The Advertiser

'An enthralling, atmospheric thriller that fans of Aussie crime won't be able to put down.'

New Idea

PRAISE FOR
SCRUBLANDS

'One of the finest novels of the year.'

Peter Pierce, *The Australian*

'Vivid and mesmerising . . . Stunning . . . *Scrublands* is that rare combination, a page-turner that stays long in the memory.'

Sunday Times **Crime Book of the Month**

'So does *Scrublands* earn its Thriller of the Year tag? Absolutely . . . It's relentless, it's compulsive, it's a book you simply can't put down.'

Written by Sime

'A superbly drawn, utterly compelling evocation of a small town riven by a shocking crime.'

Mark Brandi, author of *Wimmera*

'An almost perfect crime novel . . . I loved it.'

Ann Cleeves

'A heatwave of a novel, scorching and powerful . . . Extraordinary.'

A.J. Finn, author *The Woman in the Window*

'Stellar . . . Richly descriptive writing coupled with deeply developed characters, relentless pacing, and a bombshell-laden plot make this whodunit virtually impossible to put down.'

Publishers Weekly **(USA), starred review**

'*Scrublands* kidnapped me for 48 hours . . . This book is a force of nature. A must-read for all crime fiction fans.'

Sarah Bailey, author of *The Housemate*

'Immersive and convincing . . . This will be the novel that all crime fiction fans will want . . . a terrific read that has "bestseller" written all over it.'

Australian Crime Fiction

Chris Hammer is a leading Australian author of crime fiction. His first novel, *Scrublands*, was an instant bestseller when it was published in mid-2018. It won the prestigious UK Crime Writers Association John Creasey Award for best debut crime novel in 2019 and was shortlisted for various awards in Australia and the United States. *Scrublands* and subsequent books have been sold into translation in multiple languages, and made into a hit television series. His follow-up books—*Silver* (2019), *Trust* (2020), *Treasure & Dirt* (2021), *The Tilt* (2022), *The Seven* (2023) and *The Valley* (2024)—are also bestsellers, and all have been shortlisted for major literary prizes. *Legacy* is Chris's eighth book.

Before turning to fiction, Chris was a journalist for more than thirty years, dividing his career between covering Australian federal politics and international affairs. He reported from more than thirty countries on six continents with SBS TV, while in Canberra his roles included chief political correspondent for *The Bulletin*, senior writer for *The Age* and online political editor for the *Sydney Morning Herald*.

Chris has also written two non-fiction books, *The River* (2010; 2025) and *The Coast* (2012). He holds a bachelor's degree in journalism from Charles Sturt University and a master's degree in international relations from the Australian National University.

LEGACY

CHRIS HAMMER

ALLEN&UNWIN

SYDNEY • MELBOURNE • AUCKLAND • LONDON

First published in 2025

Copyright © Chris Hammer 2025

Allen & Unwin
Cammeraygal Country
83 Alexander Street
Crows Nest NSW 2065
Australia
Phone: (61 2) 8425 0100
Email: info@allenandunwin.com
Web: www.allenandunwin.com

Allen & Unwin acknowledges the Traditional Owners of the Country on which we live and work. We pay our respects to all Aboriginal and Torres Strait Islander Elders, past and present.

EU Authorised Representative: Easy Access System Europe, Mustamäe tee 50, 10621 Tallinn, Estonia, gpsr.requests@easproject.com

A catalogue record for this book is available from the National Library of Australia

ISBN 978 1 76147 102 5

Map by Aleksander J. Potočnik
Set in 13/18 pt Granjon by Bookhouse, Sydney
Printed and bound in Australia by the Opus Group

10 9 8 7 6 5 4 3 2 1

MIX
Paper | Supporting
responsible forestry
FSC® C001695

The paper in this book is FSC® certified.
FSC® promotes environmentally responsible, socially beneficial and economically viable management of the world's forests.

FOR THE MAGNIFICENT TEAM AT ALLEN & UNWIN

With blighted eyes and blistered feet,
With stomachs out of order,
Half mad with flies and dust and heat
We'd crossed the Queensland Border.
I longed to hear a stream go by
And see the circles quiver;
I longed to lay me down and die
That night on Paroo River.

—Henry Lawson, 'The Paroo' (1893)

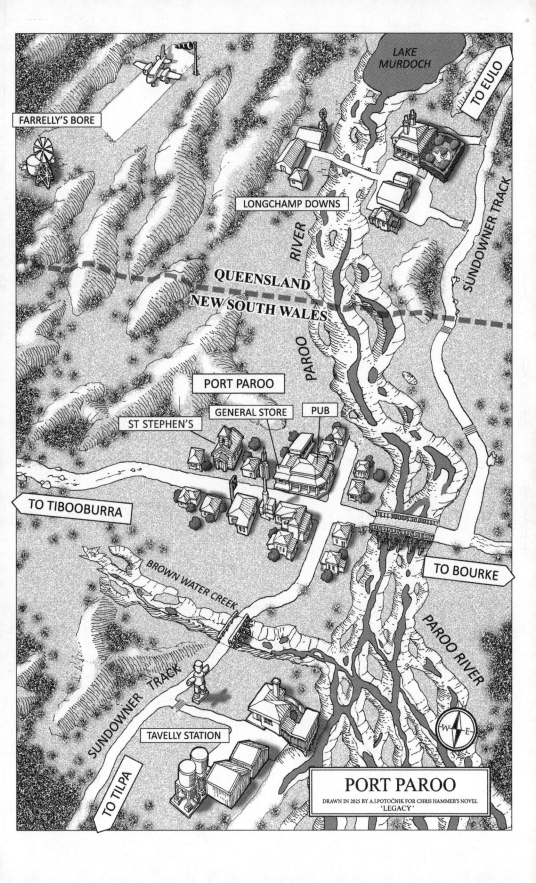

PORT PAROO

DRAWN IN 2025 BY A.I.POTOČNIK FOR CHRIS HAMMER'S NOVEL
'LEGACY'

MONDAY

chapter one
MARTIN

MARTIN IS LAUGHING, MANDY IS LAUGHING, LIAM IS LAUGHING. HE'LL REMEMBER it later, the joy in the car that night, the sense that all was right with the world, that they were on a trajectory safe and true, the frailties of fate not apparent. Now, in the moment, the whole family is celebrating. They're in the Subaru, heading into Port Silver for the launch of Martin's latest book, a true-crime exposé: *Melbourne Mobster: The Vivid Life and Violent Death of Enzo Marelli.*

Martin himself feels a sense of anticipation, the work done, that hiatus between the last edit and publication over at last. It has been a difficult gestation, plagued with lawyers, every sentence checked and double-checked, eliminating anything defamatory, anything actionable, eradicating the risk of sub judice and contempt, purging anything that might betray sources or expose innocents to potential harm. Write an exposé on organised crime and that's what you can expect. That and the death threats.

'How you feeling?' asks Mandy from the driver's seat, even as she concentrates on navigating their crumbling track of a driveway.

'Relieved. Wasn't sure it would see the light of day.' He recalls other projects, one book in particular, where the threat of legal action was too much, the weight of money too intimidating, when the publisher had buckled. A lot of work wasted, a lot of stress for nothing. Not this time. Enzo Marelli was gone, the godfather, the threat of defamation evaporating with his assassination. His heirs, the younger generation, were intent on moving on, evolving towards the corporate and away from the criminal, presenting a more polished and professional and benign image.

'It's already making quite the splash,' says Mandy, pulling out onto the main road leading into town.

'Hope so. After all we've endured.' He reaches across, hand lightly brushing her shoulder. 'Thank you. For everything.' In the back seat, seven-year-old Liam is listening intently.

Martin basks in the moment, watches the world ease by. Across the bridge, into town, the sunset flaring above the escarpment. No matter the sense of accomplishment the book gives him, he knows it's nothing compared to what he has found here in Port Silver with Mandy and Liam. This life. Surrounded by family and friends, a community. He thinks back to the man he once was, the anchorless foreign correspondent, the lone wolf, the lost soul. That younger man would have been so impressed by the book, by the other books, but would have been oblivious to the real achievement of this older self.

Having the launch in Port Silver means he has been able to invite some of the locals, the friends he and Mandy have made since moving to the coastal town six years ago—his uncle Vern and family, the lawyer Nick Poulos, their neighbours Bede and Alexander—before he hits the big city events, the TV and radio interviews, the bookshop signings and writers' festivals.

They park on the roof of the supermarket and walk down towards the surf club, to the small community hall out the back, a converted boatshed sheltering in the lee of the new clubhouse.

Jack Goffing is waiting for them outside the hall, the ASIO man in casual clothes—city casual in neatly pressed trousers and a sports jacket, not the cheesecloth casual of the coast.

He and Martin shake hands. 'Thanks for coming, Jack. Means a lot.'

'Wouldn't miss it.'

Goffing leans across, pats Liam on the head, exchanges an air kiss with Mandy.

She pulls back abruptly, frowning. 'Jack? Are you armed?'

'Oh yeah. Sorry about that.' He pats his jacket to the left of his chest. 'Regulations.'

Martin's ingrained scepticism kicks in. 'Regulations?'

'I didn't think ASIO carried weapons,' Mandy says. 'All cloak, no dagger.'

'I'm on secondment. Federal police. We're required to carry.'

'On your day off?' says Mandy.

Martin shares her puzzlement. They're in a country town, a coastal backwater. Nothing ever happens here. Well, not since the dramatic events when they first arrived. But before Martin can pursue it, they're joined by Ivan Lucic and Nell Buchanan, the Homicide detectives whose investigations linked the Riverina town of Yuwonderie to the Melbourne underworld, the catalyst for Martin's book. They all greet each other.

'Nice to be back,' says Ivan. 'Place seems to be booming.'

'Maybe too much,' says Mandy. 'We'll end up like Byron before we know it.'

5

Mandy's tone is light, but Martin recognises her unease. The two Homicide detectives are also wearing jackets despite the warmth of the evening. It's the New South Wales north coast; no one wears jackets at this time of year. At any time of year.

Instinctively he glances around for Liam, sees him playing chase with another boy his own age. Martin chastises himself: he's always overthinking. He needs to go with the flow, to enjoy the evening. What the police do is their business.

The guests are gathering inside, a buzz growing as people make their way to the bar for free drinks. The local bookseller, down from Longton, has set up next to the drinks, piles of books on a trestle table. Martin pushes across, thanks her for making the effort, promises to stick around to sign copies afterwards. He picks up the book, holds it for a moment, savours it. The designer has done a great job with the cover: it's sinister but not too confronting, more intriguing than blood-soaked.

Martin sees his publisher standing by herself, juggling a glass of champagne while making last-minute corrections to her speech. He greets her warmly, appreciative of the fact she has flown from Melbourne.

'You only want me to speak for five minutes, right?' she says.

'Yeah, just an intro, then Nick and I will take over.'

'Excellent,' says the publisher. 'Drinks and dinner afterwards?'

'All booked,' says Martin.

It's still ten minutes to kick-off, but the hall is almost full.

'Told you so,' says Mandy, sidling up.

Martin had worried no one would come. 'No sport on telly,' he says. 'Cricket's washed out.'

'Excuse me! Excuse me!'

It's the booming voice of Sergeant Nathaniel Jones, the new policeman in town, still in uniform, standing in front of the bar, arms raised. The murmur fades but doesn't die completely.

'Shut the fuck up and listen!' shouts Jones and suddenly there's quiet, all eyes on him.

Martin watches the crowd, an old journalistic trait, focusing on the reaction rather than the person speaking. He sees Goffing is doing the same, one hand inside his jacket. Martin swivels: Ivan Lucic and Nell Buchanan are also scanning the audience. He has a bad feeling, hair on his neck rising, some latent nerve switching on. Fight or flight. All he wants to know is that Liam is nearby, that the boy is safe.

'I'm sorry,' booms Jones. 'We've had a bomb threat. Nothing to worry about, I'm sure, but I'm going to have to ask everyone to exit quickly and make your way across the road while we check it out.'

There's a collective groan from the throng.

The lawyer Nick Poulos yells above the muttering: 'Everyone to the pub. Back here in forty-five minutes.'

People shuffle out, conversation stepping up a notch. Something new to talk about; jokes about Martin being a trouble magnet. He's relieved to see Mandy has Liam and his friend in tow. 'I'm going to get them some food,' she says. 'I'll see you back here.'

'No problem.' Martin gives Liam a kiss as the seven-year-old squirms.

People wander towards the pub. Martin spies Jack Goffing across the road from the hall, talking with Ivan and Nell.

'Bit of excitement,' says Martin, joining them. 'Lucky you lot are here.'

'Glad to be of service,' says Nell, but there is something in her manner that unsettles him. She's tense, on guard.

'What is it?' Martin asks. 'What do you know?'

Goffing gives him a weary look. 'Just some chatter. Nothing to worry about.'

'Jealous local,' says Nell.

'Kids,' says Ivan.

Sergeant Jones and his constable come across the road. 'All clear,' he says. 'No one left inside.' He looks at his watch. Jack Goffing echoes the gesture.

Martin looks from one face to another, sees the apprehension. 'Why aren't you searching the premises?' he asks.

Jones looks uncertain.

'Protocol,' says Goffing, filling the gap.

Martin is about to ask something else, he's sure he is, when the night is rent by a massive orange flash. He's facing the other way, his back to the hall, but he feels the heat on his neck, sees the glow reflected from walls and windows lining the opposite side of the street. The blast hits them, a shock wave. Debris begins to rain down and he crouches instinctively, arms above his head. The noise of glass smashing, of car alarms, of dogs barking, fragments of wood and glass clattering down onto the tin roofs of the shopping strip. Somewhere a woman screams.

A second explosion, and Martin looks towards the hall, what's left of it, flames roaring and smoke pouring skywards. Next to him, he can see Ivan has a cut to his head, hit by wreckage, wiping it off, staring at the red glaze. Martin experiences a sort of flashback: somewhere foreign, the Middle East, the smell of burning, the orange glow of destruction, wonders what it is doing here, in Port Silver. In his home.

He turns to Goffing. The agent has his gun out, tensed.

'What the hell?' Martin manages, just as the first bullet ploughs into a road sign behind him.

'Down,' Ivan Lucic orders, cut forgotten, dragging Martin behind a parked car, pushing him to the pavement.

'Up there, above the car park,' says Nell, crouching beside them, firing off a shot. Actually firing a gun into the night. A small voice in Martin's mind is protesting: not guns, not here.

'I see them,' says Ivan. Another bullet smacks into the side of the car and Ivan returns fire.

'They're on the move,' says Nell. 'Getting away.'

'Good,' says Goffing tersely. 'Let them go. Not worth getting killed for. Give it three, then get Martin the fuck out of here.'

'Mandy,' Martin says. 'Liam.'

'We'll look after them,' says Ivan.

As he heads off in a crouching run, a Homicide detective on each side of him, Martin looks back at the hall, now reduced to nothing more than a flaming ruin, the night filled with sirens. He can't make sense of it; it makes no sense. Bombs and bullets in his home town, the world turned awry. He runs, his mind trying desperately to catch up. How can this be? Is this his doing, has he brought this violence down upon his friends and family?

WEDNESDAY

chapter two
ECCO

I STAND IN MY BRAND-SPANKING APARTMENT, MY EYRIE ABOVE THE BRISBANE River, unable to move, frozen by fate. Unable to believe what has befallen me, the casual cruelty of the world.

This was meant to be the best day of my life. I'd been savouring it for weeks, anticipating it: the launching pad, the pivot upon which my luck would turn, the moment when I shucked off my old skin and replaced it with a newer, shinier, successful me. The moment I would finally leave my ex-husband behind for good, and my old life with him. But I should have known that isn't how the world works: not for the likes of me. Karma was still after its pound of flesh—insatiable and relentless—no matter how I struggled to free myself from its debt. Foolish to think I could get off so lightly. I was too determined to make the leap, too confident, too focused. I never saw it coming.

The apartment was testament to my resilience, my determination. Smaller than I could have afforded elsewhere, but I wanted it, that view, that elevation, looking down. I no longer dreamt of dilapidated Queenslanders and joyous renovation. This had zero character, nothing worn, nothing tainted: no memories, no legacy; none of mine, none of anyone else's. It shone with glass and engineered stone, hermetically sealed behind double-glazed windows. The stainless steel on the fridge, the stovetop, the oven, the range hood, the kettle and the toaster: all glowed in uniform splendour. The coffee machine represented a new and better world.

I should have waited for the deposit to lodge in my account, but I was eager. Any delay seemed unnecessary; the money would be there soon enough. I'd submitted the manuscript, the publishers had gushed with gratitude, the deadline met, the book out in time for Christmas. Not my book, of course. Ghostwriters don't get our names on the cover, or not often. Sometimes we score a mention, the name of the film star or sporting hero or politician in huge letters, with an acknowledgement in a font a fraction of the size: *with Ekaterina Boland.* I had that once on the autobiography of a female footballer, as generous and humble off the field as she was aggressive and talented on it. Despite my notoriety, she'd insisted I be acknowledged, even though it wasn't stipulated in the contract. She said no one would believe she could write a book. Which says something, as she was definitely among the smartest and most articulate of my subjects.

There was no way Reilly Sloane would ever make such a concession. He was convinced of his own brilliance; he told me in all seriousness he could have written the book himself, done a better job, in a third of the time, but the task was menial, beneath him. And yet it would be his name on the cover and his alone. And he insisted on the title, *My Way,* and on the photo, his face, up close and personal, those beautiful eyes of his dancing. Writing the book, I was glad I wouldn't be credited. Not because I had any inkling of what was about to come down, but because of how he bad-mouthed his fellow actors, how he was forever seeking out mirrors, how he propositioned me. How he groped me, exposed himself, and just laughed when I told him to fuck off, knowing his power, assured in his privilege. The guy was a prick, but that was his problem: I was being paid handsomely to tolerate his ego—more than my last three commissions combined. It was the pay-off, the start of it. I had served my apprenticeship, demonstrated my ability and my discipline, and the publishers were ready to trust me with bigger names, not just the 'celebrities' but the 'icons'. My agent, Emma, had explained it to me: if a publisher pays some dude twenty grand for their autobiography, they don't care if the guy's uncle writes it, but if they shell out six or seven figures, they want someone who knows what they're doing. They'll pay for an accomplished ghostwriter, a professional they know will deliver. That was me, the professional, and for Reilly Sloane they were paying enough for the deposit on my apartment.

The real estate agent was already here waiting with the paper-work when I arrived, his Audi waxed and gleaming in the sun, as shiny as his product-lathered hair, which he'd elevated into a priapic tuft. He'd brought along a bottle of champagne to celebrate the occasion, but I could see the impression on his ring finger where he'd removed his wedding band. One of those. We signed the papers, and the apartment was all but mine. He left, taking his champagne with him, but I lingered, gazing down at the sparkling river. I'd done it. I was replete with pride, with accomplishment. Euphoric.

It lasted five minutes.

Then came a text came from Emma. She must have been a telegraph operator in another life: she never uses two words when one will do. *Reilly Sloane arrested.*

I rang.

She answered immediately. 'Ecco.'

'How bad?' I asked.

'Bad as it gets,' she answered.

'Tell me.'

'Predator. Child abuse. Goes back decades.'

'Fuck.'

'There's no coming back for him. Even if he gets off.'

My heart sat in my throat.

'I delivered on Monday,' I said, referring to the manuscript.

'I'm sorry. The publishers no longer want it.'

'But I gave them exactly what they asked for.'

'Ecco, you know they can't sell it. They won't even print it.'

'That's their problem. We have a contract.'

Silence.

I filled it. 'Twenty-five per cent on signing, fifty per cent on delivery, twenty-five on publication. They don't publish, I'll wear the final twenty-five per cent, but I've delivered.' And then, almost as an afterthought, the apartment wavering before my eyes: 'I need the money.'

Another silence, then Emma explained, 'It's not just delivery. The contract says fifty per cent on delivery *and acceptance*. You've delivered, but they haven't accepted.' Trying to sound calm, but I could hear a tremor in her voice I'd never heard before.

And now it was my turn to be silent. Emma was more than an agent; she was my friend, my champion, one of the few who hadn't deserted me. She wouldn't hesitate to go into battle for me if she thought we stood a chance. I knew right then that she didn't.

She waited a beat before speaking again. 'They might be interested in an exposé. Your name on the cover. Nowhere near the same money, but some. Reveal him as the arsehole that he is.'

Hope flared and died within a breath. 'How can I? I thought he was a sleaze, not a pedo. I'm not a journalist; the papers will be all over it before the day's out. They'll have wrung every drop from the story before the end of the week.'

Emma tried to console me. 'I'll get you something else. I promise I will.'

That was twenty minutes ago. And so, here I am. In the apartment that should be mine, knowing I will never live here. Outside, the day is as clear as ever, the sun bouncing off the river, turning it blue. Even if I rent the flat out, I don't see how I can keep it. I can't make the numbers stack up. A bridging loan is out of the question; I've already borrowed the maximum, and that was dependent on the advance I was due. Now I don't have a job. I don't even have a place to live beyond the end of the month. My husband is gone, my parents have disowned me, my friends have abandoned me. I look around one last time; I'll never get to use those gleaming appliances, smudge the stainless steel.

And then Emma calls back. God bless her.

chapter three
MARTIN

THE SEALED HIGHWAY FINISHES AT BOURKE AND THE DIRT BEGINS, THE OUTBACK proper. Martin drives through town without stopping, crossing the Darling River, an opaque brown gutter, the water motionless. He passes through North Bourke: a pub, an oval, an airstrip, a spattering of houses—the edge of the connected world. The last vestiges of irrigation slip past, leaving only mulga and red dirt. The horizon expands and the surface beneath the Subaru's wheels turns from dirt to dust. There is no traffic on the road, no clouds in the sky, the world split in half: blue above, red earth below, his car caught between.

Fifty kilometres on, Martin slows, one eye on the rear-view mirror, one on the way ahead. Nothing. No cars, no trucks, no telltale swirl of distant dust, just a willy-willy raising a russet spiral off through the scrub. He watches it pass, sputter into nothing, another taking its place, rising further away, gathering strength before it too loses momentum and wafts into the sun-blasted void. He finds a side track, dead straight, some sort of survey line running off to nowhere, and eases the four-wheel drive down it a kilometre or so. He brings the car to a halt, and climbs out.

The heat hits him, pushes down on him like a physical object. It's eleven in the morning and the temperature is already in the mid-thirties. Another couple of hours and it will be into the forties. February hot; desert hot, where the air temperature doesn't come close to explaining the force of the sun. Mad dogs and journalists. And fugitives. The light is too sharp out here, the red dirt road too saturated with colour, the contrast to the blue sky too vibrant. There is no wind, no moisture, no airborne dust to soften the blue, just the sun, bleeding the colour from the firmament as it fades to white at the horizon.

A trickle of sweat descends from his hairline; he wipes his brow, checks again that he's alone, then sets to work. He removes the fake licence plates with a Phillips head screwdriver, the rear plate still coastal clean, the front caked with the desiccated remains of insects embedded in red dirt. He takes the plates, walks into the scrub, uses a stick to scrape away at the dirt. A pair of feral goats watch curiously, unperturbed by his presence, chewing on a spiky bush. He places the plates in the shallow hole, pushes the earth back over them with his boot, stamps it flat, pulls a dead branch across to disguise the spot. It takes him five minutes, no more, a rough and ready effort, yet his t-shirt is soaked and sticking to his back. He knows it's not a convincing job, but the chances of the plates being found out here are minimal. This will all be over before anyone finds them. Whatever this is.

Summer. Challenging enough out here in winter, but summer. He cocks an ear. No sound at all. High in the sky, there's a wedge-tail eagle, and its mate, circling. He'd be lucky to last until nightfall without a car. Without water. Back at the Subaru, he fetches his drinking bottle, drains half of it, pours the rest over his head. It brings scant relief. Then he crouches by the car and screws another set of plates into place: the set Jack Goffing had given him.

Goffing. Protector, enabler, source. And friend, hopefully. The intelligence operative had shepherded them out of Port Silver, driving his rental, Martin and Mandy and their boy Liam following in Mandy's Subaru, driving through the night, arriving at a hastily arranged safe house west of the coastal divide as dawn was breaking. An Airbnb, booked under a false name, an anonymous account, an untraceable credit card. A converted farmhouse, high on a hill, approaches visible, the key in a lock box.

Goffing had taken them through it, speaking in that low voice of his, honed by years of confidential conversation. He'd explained in dot points; Martin and Mandy struggling to comprehend. It was less than twelve hours since they'd fled Port Silver.

'There is an app. Encrypted. Anonymous. Used by the worst of the worst. Airtasker for the underworld. Armed robberies. Abductions. Murders.'

'You've hacked it?' Mandy asked.

'Unhackable,' said Goffing. 'We have human intelligence. A source with access.'

'You're saying that attack last night was outsourced?' asked Martin.

Goffing looked him in the eye, expression hard. 'Not sure about last night. I'm talking about the next one.'

'Next one?' Mandy was on the couch, face alive with trepidation. Liam was asleep, his head on her lap. Martin was glad the boy couldn't hear their conversation.

The ASIO man's face was so serious he looked sorrowful.

'A contract. Taken out on you, Martin. In the early hours.' Goffing's tone was professional but his eyes were brimming with disquiet.

'A *contract*?' Mandy gasped, appalled; it was a word from a gangster movie, from Chicago and New York, not rural New South Wales.

Goffing didn't respond. The word spoke for itself.

'Who?' asked Martin, mind reeling. He'd run up against some tough people before. As a correspondent, it had been dangerous at times, always with the risk of becoming collateral damage, caught in the wrong place at the wrong time. Even in Australia, there were plenty of people unhappy with his reporting, who would wish him ill: scumbags and killers and conmen and ruthless tycoons, financial fraudsters and psychopaths. That was the problem with the old journo creed of speaking truth to power: power didn't always like it. True crime, his stock in trade, was an entertainment, a diversion—until they wanted you dead. And were willing to pay for it.

'Don't know,' Goffing said. 'That's the defining characteristic of this app. Total anonymity, people hiding behind fake names. Don't know who's commissioning the hit, who's bid on it, who's won the contract.' He let that sink in. 'All I can tell you, all our sources can tell us, is that the job was advertised, there were bids, and the job was taken by someone calling themselves the B-team. It's live.'

'Fuck,' Martin said.

'We need to go,' said Mandy. 'Hide.'

'Exactly,' said Goffing.

'Protective custody?' asked Martin. He looked about the farmhouse. Good for a few hours, maybe overnight, but not more than that.

The ASIO man shook his head. 'Not so easy.'

'Why not?' Mandy asked, an edge of confrontation in her tone.

Goffing met her gaze with his steady look. 'Not my call. Management doesn't want to risk it.'

'Risk what?' asked Martin.

Goffing looked grim. 'Anyone learning that we have intel on the app.'

'What? That's more important than my son's safety?' said Mandy, anger flaring. Liam stirred in his sleep.

The agent examined the ceiling, avoiding eye contact. 'There was a suggestion of using you as bait. Putting you in a safe house, staking out the place. Seeing who turned up. Putting the heat on them.'

Martin could see Mandy was fighting to control her emotions. 'And were you planning to capture the assassin before or after they'd fulfilled their mission?'

Goffing had smiled then, a wan and fatigued expression. 'There was some debate.'

But Mandy wasn't finished. 'They blew up the community hall. Gunshots in the street. Isn't that reason enough for protective custody? You don't need an app to justify it.'

Goffing said nothing, just wore it. Martin wondered if he was sharing all he knew.

'You're here now, with us,' Martin said to him. 'Thank you.'

Mandy looked from one man to the other, then her shoulders dropped, the fight going out of her. 'Yes. Thank you, Jack.' She took another breath. 'I hope we aren't putting you in any jeopardy. Career-wise, I mean.'

'I think that ship sailed long ago.'

'So are you here as ASIO, or the federal police?' asked Martin.

'Might be handy if I'm neither. Not sure any of them want to know me right now.'

Martin laughed at that. The first rule of the bureaucracy: cover your arse. Didn't matter if it was the town council or counter-espionage. 'So what's the plan?'

'Split up. Mandy should take Liam and go somewhere far away.' The ASIO man looked about, as if searching the shadows, before turning back to her. 'I doubt you or your son are in any direct danger. But if you are with Martin, there's always the risk you could get caught in the crossfire. And even if you aren't with him, there's the risk someone could abduct you, use you to flush out Martin.'

Martin and Mandy exchanged a long look then. No words were spoken, but Martin nodded his concurrence, and Mandy eventually signalled her own assent.

Goffing spoke directly to Mandy. 'My suggestion would be overseas. Hawaii would be good. Put it on social media once you're there, so people know. Then bounce out again. The Americans can help cover your tracks. I'll request their help. They're good at that: whisking family members of various tyrants in and out of their country when it suits their diplomatic game.'

'I hear we're not too shabby at that ourselves,' said Martin.

Goffing offered his wan smile again. 'Is that what you hear?'

'What about Martin?' Mandy asked.

Goffing addressed him directly. 'Take your car. Leave today. I'll drive the first little way with you. Mandy can take my rental. We'll get you a burner phone and fake licence plates in Moree. I'll take your real phone with me when we split. Leave a false trail.'

'You're not telling us everything,' Mandy said, eyes narrowed. 'How could they possibly track his phone?'

'We don't know if they can or they can't,' Goffing said. 'That's the point. We don't know anything about them.'

'Bullshit,' said Mandy. 'It's obvious. It's the fucking mafia. Out to punish Martin, retribution for his book.'

'Maybe, maybe not,' said Goffing with a shrug.

'Surely it has to be them,' Martin said.

'Not necessarily,' said Goffing. 'Think about it. Bombing a community hall, shooting up the main street. Sales of your book will go through the roof. Why would the mafia want that?'

'A warning against prospective informants, then,' Mandy suggested.

'That makes more sense.'

The conversation lagged then as they each considered the implications, Liam snuffling in his sleep.

'You think they have someone on the inside, in the police, don't you?' whispered Mandy.

'What makes you think that?' asked Goffing.

'You said management thought about using us as bait in a safe house. See who turned up. How could assassins possibly learn the location of a safe house?' Her gaze was unwavering. 'That's got nothing to do with any underworld app.'

Martin gave Goffing a sharp look. 'You think your own organisation has been compromised, Jack?'

Goffing sighed heavily. 'It's possible.'

There wasn't a lot to say to that. Martin turned off his phone, handed it over. 'All yours.'

'Thanks.'

Now, a full day later and seven hundred kilometres further west, Martin is back in Mandy's Subaru, white and ubiquitous, the aircon struggling but arctic cold compared to the burning desert. He negotiates a three-point turn, carefully makes his way back to the main road, weaving through the sandy drifts of the survey line. Back on surer ground, he checks the burner phone. It's a new iPhone, not a cheap service station throwaway; something to do with encryption and security. Untraceable and untrackable. But despite the latest tech, there's not a single bar. Nothing. Only spitting distance back to Bourke, and he's already off-grid. Like a medieval sailor heading off the edge of the world. He opens Signal, types a last message to Mandy, phrasing vague. *Safe for now. Love you*. He adds a heart emoji, then another, then hits send. Somewhere, sometime, the phone might pick up a connection, send it off through the ether.

He's about to drive on when he notices a message. It must have arrived as he was passing through Bourke. He thinks it might be Mandy, but it's from Goffing, the only other person with the number.

Careful. B-team in country.

He stares at the phone. *In country.* A shiver runs through him despite the heat.

Whoever it is who wants him dead, they're not mucking about. He sends a thumbs-up emoji, knowing the symbol is an empty gesture, going nowhere. Around him the landscape shimmers: a hellscape of reds and oranges and yellows.

chapter four

PORT PAROO MUST BE SOME SORT OF JOKE, MARTIN THINKS, AS HE DRIVES across a single-lane bridge into the fly-speck settlement. There is no port; there is no water. The Paroo River is a dry bed, bespeckled with intermittent waterholes too choked with dirt and weeds to reflect the sky. There's a sign next to the bridge warning of once-in-a-hundred-year floods. Maybe it's a once-in-a-century port.

There's a pub. Of course there's a pub, the defining characteristic of every self-respecting outpost. The Port Paroo Hotel. And not much else. There's no school, no cafe, no stock and station agent. Just the pub, and attached to it, as if unable to stand on its own, a general store cum post office cum petrol station, with one bowser for petrol and another for diesel. The only other buildings of note are a CWA hall opposite the pub; a wooden church, paint peeling, looking more like an oversized kennel than a place of worship; and a shuttered police station, cream weatherboard smeared orange with dust, yard gone to seed behind a steel-framed fence. A smattering of houses gather round in various states of disrepair, placed seemingly at random, outnumbered two to one by vacant blocks,

26

like teeth in a pauper's jaw. None of the houses are new, none of them pretend at a garden. A stray dog limps past, thinks better of it, turns back, circling to a standstill and slumping down in a rare piece of shade.

Martin thinks yet again of Mandy and Liam, wonders where they might be. Perhaps transiting Hawaii. It doesn't seem possible that Honolulu shares the same planet as this place. He looks about, seeking green, failing, the colour banished from Port Paroo. He hopes they're safe, somewhere they can start to relax, where the boy can make friends, where Mandy can stop worrying. He wonders how Goffing is doing, if there is any progress in neutralising the threat. It rankles Martin, his inability to do anything, to be so reliant on others.

He stops the car, considers the town's location. It sits at a crossroad, where the east–west road between Bourke and Tibooburra meets the Sundowner Track running north–south from nowhere to nowhere, tracking the ephemeral river. A crossroad and a here-again-gone-again river. Barely enough reason to justify a settlement.

But there is a mobile phone tower opposite the pub, evidence that Martin remains in the twenty-first century. He checks his burner phone: nothing. He looks across at the tower. There's a cherry picker, a worker in a high-vis vest and a hard hat lounging next to it, drinking from a can and smoking a cigarette. Old school. The tower is closed off behind a series of orange witches hats and plastic web fencing. DANGER—NO ENTRY. Martin checks the phone again. Nothing. It's the reason why Goffing suggested the town: it's a telecommunications black hole, at least for now. Martin restarts the car, rolls it down to the worker.

He lowers his window, waves his handset. 'Hi, mate. What's with the signal?'

'On the fritz.'

'Sounds technical.'

The bloke cracks a smile. 'Cockatoos. Chew through the wiring. Bastards.'

'How long's it out?'

'Another couple of days.'

'Must be big cockies.'

The worker laughs, sounding grateful for the distraction. 'Easy enough to fix. Just waiting for the spares.'

'Thanks, mate.'

'Pub's got a landline if it's urgent.'

Martin thanks him again and drives on. The pub sounds inviting. Goffing had advised him to flee beyond mobile range— not because of his own phone, but because of those of strangers, and the possibility that his pursuers might deploy bots to scrape the internet, married to facial recognition software. All it would take was some tourist's Insta-moment and the killers would be on to him.

He wonders if cockatoos really are responsible, or whether Goffing has somehow arranged for the tower to be sabotaged. It wouldn't surprise Martin; his spook mate conjured the licence plates and camping gear and the burner phone and fake IDs in next to no time.

He still has two-thirds of a tank of petrol in the car but decides he should take the opportunity to fill it and pulls in outside the general store. He has the fuel cap open and is reaching for the hose before realising it's not self-serve. It must be the last full-service bowser in the country. Maybe the southern hemisphere.

An old geezer limps out, a grey beard of spun steel wool speckled with what might be egg or might be congealed nicotine.

The man has bleary eyes, a blue singlet struggling to contain rolls of flesh. Small flies cloud about; he seems inured to them, giving a cursory wave of his hand, more of a salute than a discouragement.

'Fill her up, thanks,' says Martin. He's wearing wraparound sunglasses, a baseball cap pulled low, his hair shaved short. Still, he feels vulnerable.

'Beaut little car,' says the geezer, nodding at the Subaru as he slips the nozzle into the fuel inlet. 'All-wheel drive, right?' He sounds ready for a chat. Given the dearth of customers, Martin can understand why.

'Yeah. Good for out here.'

'Good, but not good enough,' the man says matter-of-factly. 'Not if you want to go deeper.'

'Why not?' asks Martin.

'Clearance too low, no winch, tyres aren't suitable. You need two spares out here, not just one.'

Martin smiles. 'Anything else?'

'No roo bar.'

'Lot of roos?' asks Martin.

'Roos. Pigs. Goats. A whole fucking menagerie. Camels. Emus. Snakes. Like Noah drank a skinful and rolled the Ark.'

'Godforsaken place for a God-fearing man,' says Martin, laughing at the colourful imagery.

The old man looks around the unforgiving vista. 'I reckon.' The bowser clicks off, the tank is full. The man rehangs the hose, becoming serious. 'Where you headed, mate?'

'West,' says Martin, on guard.

The old geezer stops moving, looks hard at Martin and shakes his head. 'Out here, specially this time of year, you need to tell people where you're going. Give 'em a timetable. Expected arrival times.' He regards the car, looks back at Martin. 'West doesn't cut it. People die.' He flicks his head in the direction of the Port Paroo Hotel. 'Publican knew this country like the back of his hand. Didn't save him.'

Martin feels chastised. 'Sure. Of course. Heading towards Tibooburra. Camping along the way.'

'Camping? Out there? What the fuck for?'

'Night photography. The stars. My hobby.'

The man frowns. 'Strange timing.'

'How do you mean?' asks Martin.

'Coming into a full moon. Shit for stargazing.'

'Annual meteorite shower,' Martin counters, grateful for his research. 'Next few days. Might get a shot or two in either side of the moon.'

'You got water? Extra fuel? Food? Enough to last at least a fortnight? A spade, hessian sacks, in case you get bogged?'

Martin can see the old bloke is unsettled, wonders at what he might have witnessed, what corpses discovered too late. Maybe the publican. 'Yeah. Well supplied.'

'You got one of them Apple phones? The ones with the emergency satellite messaging?'

'I do,' says Martin. He's not sure the phone Goffing gave him has such a feature, or if it's been disabled to prevent tracking. 'And an EPIRB,' he lies for good measure.

'All right, your funeral,' says the geezer. 'That'll be forty-three bucks—forty if you have cash.'

'Suits me,' says Martin, handing over a couple of twenties, the same colour as the town's streets.

'Mind if I give you some advice?' the old bloke says.

He reminds Martin of the bush flies: persistent. 'I'm all ears.'

'Stay in the pub tonight. Heard the cops might be closing the roads.'

'Why would they do that?'

'Rain's forecast. Been coming for a week. The last gasp of a monsoonal front. Floods in the Territory, hit Mount Isa last night. Heading our way.'

Martin squints up at the cloudless sky. Rain seems as likely as a river steamer. 'The roads are that unreliable?'

'Too right. Doesn't take much. A few specks and the bulldust turns into the slipperiest, gooiest, bog-happy sludge you ever saw. Stop a road train, the gnarliest farm trucks, let alone a city crate like this one.' The old man chews his lip. 'No one ever told you that?'

'No. But thanks.'

'You'll be right at the pub,' says the geezer. 'Always have vacancies there. They'll be getting updates from the coppers.'

——

The Port Paroo Hotel is dark and deserted, a couple of ceiling fans turning lethargically, no other movement. There are windows in front, but they're shuttered against the heat of the day. The bar itself is fronted with corrugated iron, its burgundy laminate top lined with worn wood. Nothing fancy; nothing new. The place has the smell of old bars the world over: stale beer, stale bodies, not enough air. There's a big open fireplace that looks like it hasn't been used for months, maybe years.

'Hello!' Martin yells. 'Anyone?'

A woman's voice responds, dry and nasal. 'Hold your horses. Give me five.'

While he waits, Martin looks about. Mounted along the walls are a series of framed images, a metre and a half wide, a metre high, not recent. Underneath each image, in separate frames, explanatory notes are printed. Martin walks around, taking them in one by one. There's a sepia photograph of a camel train, the handlers swathed in exotic robes, the Afghan drivers who carried the wool clip to Bourke before the advent of trucks. There's a shot of men behind a horse-drawn plough, looking as if they're ploughing a field, with the portrait of a man inset, his face engulfed in whiskers. Henry Wallace Tollisker, the accompanying note explains, was a visionary, the man who proposed a wharf to gazump Bourke and carry the wool clip south. *No wool was ever successfully shipped from Port Paroo*, the note ends without further explanation. Martin is beginning to enjoy himself. He wonders if it's the posters, or the lack of people, or the lack of phone signal. All of the above, he decides.

The next poster in faded Kodachrome shows an opal miner, squinting at the camera, beside his shaft. *The Legend of the Hidden Road Hoard*, reads the caption. This was an opal seam somewhere to the west, apparently, a treasure rivalling Lasseter's Reef. Next is an artist's impression of the min min lights, mysterious hovering illuminations said to have extraterrestrial origins. The description claims that Port Paroo is a hotspot for *psychic phenomena and extraterrestrial sightings*, an Australian Area 51.

Next is another sepia photo, a group of men, faces shaded by hats, one identified as the bush poet Henry Lawson, face angular, moustachioed, holding a pipe. His poem 'The Paroo' is quoted in full. Martin squints in the gloom, the photo too blurry to make out anything much beyond the sparest detail. The next poster is another nineteenth-century image: the doomed explorer Ludwig Leichhardt, lost in the desert without a trace, the explanatory note recounting a rumour the expedition might have travelled south, following the Paroo, instead of west or north-west as originally planned. The posters continue: a colour photo of a Variety Bash rally, then another nineteenth-century image of men on horse-back, wielding guns, participants in a cross-border feud sparked by an argument over land claims and accusations of cattle duffing. According to the caption the feud lasted well into the twentieth century, pitting two grazing families against each other. The last poster is the blurry image of a bird: the elusive and much-sought-after Night Parrot. No confirmed sightings, but rumours persist that the call can be heard on a still night. Martin concludes the pub has more wall space than the district has facts to fill it.

'Sorry about the wait, darl,' says a cheery-looking woman, hair a messy dark bob, skin tanned. She looks about forty, a few years younger than Martin. He can see evidence of Asian heritage, but the voice is all Australian: the same treble twang as roofing metal. 'What can I get you? Beer? After a feed?'

'A room.'

'The rain?'

'Yeah, old bloke next door told me. The petrol guy.'

'Ah, Perry. Good man.' The woman hauls a huge register out from under the bar, an old-fashioned ledger bound in cloth, leather on the corners and spine, and takes Martin's details: *Jacob Solander* says the fake ID Jack Goffing has supplied. 'Jacob?' she asks.

'Jake,' he replies. 'How long since it's rained?'

'Months. But when it does, it does.'

'This time?'

'Dunno. Should hit about midnight, if the bureau's to be believed. Cops will call through well before then, let us know the situation with the roads, but I reckon they'll close them in advance. Precautionary.' She identifies a space in the register. 'You're in luck. One of our best rooms is available.'

'Presidential suite.'

'Ha,' she responds. 'Hope you like it. If it really pisses down, you might be here for a while.'

'Any other guests?'

'A couple of grey nomads, the Telstra guys, a bunch of backpackers all jammed into one room. You'll probably see everyone tonight. We're putting on a spread. Six o'clock. All welcome. Rain lifts the spirits; gives people something to talk about. We'll have 'em in from the properties.'

'Properties? People farm out here?'

She scrutinises him, as if trying to work him out. 'Not cropping. Graziers. The flood plain. Cattle.'

'Sounds marginal.'

'Sounds desperate,' says the woman. 'I'm Maureen, darl. Everyone calls me Maz. Maz Gingelly.' She reaches across and shakes Martin's hand. 'What about a beer before I show you the room? On the house. Cut the dust.'

'Sure,' says Martin. 'Not like I'm going anywhere.'

chapter five
ECCO

EVERY KILOMETRE FURTHER WEST FROM BRISBANE IS A KILOMETRE FURTHER from the apartment and the river, and there are a lot of kilometres. There's probably something profound in that: in order to keep something I love, maybe the only thing I love, I need to remove myself from it completely; the further I go, the safer it is. Without me to tarnish it, the apartment remains a gleaming promise, beckoning from over the horizon, a lighthouse to guide me home.

I fly from Brisbane in a cramped twin-prop plane, hopscotching to Toowoomba, on to St George, and through to Cunnamulla, just three passengers left by the time we arrive, the land having moved from green to brown to bone to red, from ranges to hills to pan-flat, from rainforest to broadacre to semi-desert. And after three hours of flying, on I go, driven into the setting sun, the taciturn farmhand saying nothing, me grateful for his reserve. Hour by hour the sureties of the coast are being stripped away: elevation, vegetation, civilisation. I'd always imagined hell as hot and claustrophobic, but I was only half right. The thermometer on the dash of the twin-cab says thirty-eight degrees; the horizon keeps expanding, as if the fabric of the world is being stretched.

'Hot,' I offer, my first word in a hundred kilometres.

'You reckon?'

The road is good, sealed, but vehicles are rare enough to elicit a raised finger of acknowledgement.

'What's your name?' I ask.

'Jamie Stubbs.'

'Hi, Jamie. I'm Ecco.'

'Yeah. I know who you are.' And that's it, end of conversation. Fine by me. Better than being hit on.

My mind drifts back to Emma's call. She'd explained the deal, and I'd clutched at it like I was drowning, agreeing before knowing what I was agreeing to. I'd tried to sound sceptical, maintaining the pretence that I had a choice when Emma and I both knew that I had none.

'It's not vanity publishing, nothing as bad as that,' she'd said.

'What then?' I had no problem with vanity publishing, provided it paid. Reilly Sloane had swamped me with vanity; I could tolerate anything.

'Bespoke,' Emma said.

'Bespoke?'

'An old man. Wants the history of his family written. A grazing property out west. Way out. Something for his grandkids.'

'How much?'

'One hundred and twenty thousand, plus food and board.'

'How long?'

'Up to you.'

I'd worked the sums even as we spoke. Food and board meant no out-of-pocket costs, the apartment could be rented. Maybe it was possible to keep it. Emma was offering to take just ten per cent instead of her standard fifteen, leaving me with one hundred and eight thousand. Shit money if it took me two years to write; outstanding money if I knocked it over in six months.

'I'll take it,' I said. 'An advance?'

'I reckon I could get you twenty-five per cent up front. I'll push for forty.'

'Do your best.'

'He wants photos included, from the family album. Some documents. A family tree, a timeline. Glossy paper, hardback, full-colour printing. Wants you to curate the images, but he'll pay for the designer. You just have to choose them and write the captions.'

That sounded promising. 'How many words?'

'Sixty thousand. Seventy tops.'

I'd assumed ninety or a hundred; in my mind six months contracted to four. Four months, more than a hundred thousand dollars. Sweet. And stuck in the middle of nowhere, no distractions. Nothing to spend it on except sunscreen, fly spray and booze.

'Your name will be on the cover. He doesn't want a ghost-writer; just the opposite. He wants the prestige of a real author. But it'll never make it into a bookstore; he'll print enough to get an ISBN and that's it.'

'Suits me,' I said, astounded that my name could be associated with prestige. Maybe the old coot had been out in the sun too long.

Back in the present, Jamie stops the truck unannounced, pulling off the side of the road. We're in the middle of nowhere, nothing but scrub and a fence line and power poles. He gets out, takes a few steps, turns his back to me, unzips and pisses where he stands.

He gets back in. 'That's better,' he says, and then we're moving once more.

As we head further and further west, I begin to harbour my first doubts. I'm checking my phone, watching the reception drift in and out, and still we drive. We reach Eulo, the last town, the end of the bitumen, nothing more than a pub and a hall and a shop and a petrol bowser, notable for nothing except that it exists. We don't stop. Instead we turn south, onto the dirt, the Sundowner Track, with a sign warning that the next fuel is at Port Paroo, two hundred and thirty kilometres distant. On and on we go. Jamie is unfazed by the unmade road, steering with one hand even as the truck drifts this way and that on the shifting surface. Rocks kick up, thumping into the floor beneath our feet. To our right is a straggly line of trees, advancing and retreating. The Paroo River, bone-dry. The thermometer hits forty degrees, even with the sun easing towards the horizon. I glance across at Jamie, caught in the glare of the sun, see the bead of sweat on his lip despite the air-conditioning.

It's taken all day, sustained by airport sandwiches and bad coffee, but finally I arrive at Longchamp Downs, an hour before sunset. The driveway is a track, three kilometres long. The main house and its outbuildings rise out of a mirage, its coterie of trees growing from a green dot to a promise of water. The homestead isn't as large as I had imagined: single-storey, wide verandah, raked roof of corrugated iron, two brick chimneys and two satellite dishes. The trees, the rosebushes, the glowing green lawn, the wisteria on the verandah are so much more impressive than the house itself.

Jamie pulls up outside the gate. All around is red dust, only inside the steel fence is green, like a portal to another world. I go to collect my suitcase from the back seat, but he stops me. 'Not for the likes of us,' he says. 'This is the boss's place. He'll want to meet you, but you can't stay here.' He looks almost apologetic as he explains. 'People would talk.'

I look about the wasteland. 'What people?'

Jamie cracks a smile, the first in a couple of hundred kilometres. It makes him almost handsome. 'Come on. He'll be waiting.' He opens the gate for me, like a gentleman, but stands back. 'I'll wait out here.'

I walk along the path towards the house, and I feel myself intimidated. The homestead, which I initially thought small, now looms much larger. It's the garden, I think; the display of wealth, water used for ornamentation not production. I swallow nervously as I approach the steps to the verandah. Jamie will be watching me, though; I won't give him the satisfaction of seeing me hesitate.

As I take the first step, the door to the house opens and an old man emerges, scarecrow-thin. He's slightly stooped, stomach concave beneath an impressive belt buckle, blue eyes watery. He's clean-shaven and well dressed: moleskins, a blue linen shirt, socked feet.

'Here you are,' he says, running his eyes over me, unabashed. Like I'm livestock. 'I'm Clayborne Carmichael. Call me Clay.'

'Ekaterina Boland,' I say. 'Ecco. Nice house.'

'It is. Come in out of the heat.'

Inside, the house is cooler. Darker. The ceilings are high. There's an absence of noise, the hum of the exterior excluded. Clay shows me into a hallway, twice as wide as seems necessary, the broad floorboards dark and twisted by age. I can smell furniture polish. The light diminishes as he closes the front door behind me then leads me through, opening the first door to the right. It's a beautiful room, spacious, the light from the verandah filtered through leadlight windows. There is a large fireplace behind a brass screen, already set for a winter still months away. Paintings adorn the walls, original oils of the desert landscape. There are framed photographs on the mantelpiece: family images, kids laughing at a beach, a boy wearing Mickey Mouse ears.

'Told you're a good writer,' Clay says, after showing me to a seat.

'I am,' I say.

'Written some impressive books.' He reels off some of my titles.

'That's me.'

He appraises me again before continuing. 'I don't give a shit what you've done or haven't done. Just do a good job.' And he smiles, as if satisfied he has said what he needs to say.

'I intend to. Just tell me what you want and I'll deliver it.'

He squints. 'I don't want any bullshit. No gloss, no lies. The truth. Warts and all.' Then, having settled that, he rises and walks past me, pausing at the door to the hallway. 'Forgive me. You've come a long way. You'll need a cuppa.'

'Thanks,' I say.

While he's gone, I examine the room. The photos on the mantelpiece tell the story in faded film: he and his wife, a wedding, the two of them with children, a boy and a girl. They look like twins. As children, as teenagers, as young adults. Graduation pictures—the son, not the girl. Unblemished skin. None of the images seem recent.

I hear the sound of something being wheeled down the corridor and hurry back to my seat. Clay is followed into the room by a woman of a similar age. She's pushing a trolley bearing a bone china teapot with a pair of matching cups and saucers, silver spoons, a milk jug and sugar bowl of cut glass. A plate of homemade slices, a lemon cake.

'Milk's long-life, but it's not so bad,' Clay says, sitting. 'This is our housekeeper, Mrs Enright. Don't get on the wrong side of her.'

'How do you do?' I ask, standing up, sounding overly formal, falling into my assigned role.

Mrs Enright grunts. 'You're welcome, I'm sure.'

I sit again. She pours the tea without speaking, then leaves.

'Jolly old stick, isn't she?' says Clay, and I'm not sure, but I think I spy a hint of mischief in his watery blue eyes.

I sip some tea, take a slice, compliment him on its quality. Then I cut to the chase. 'The book. My agent gave me the brief, but best I hear it from you, to avoid misunderstandings.'

He looks relieved that I have spared him the burden of small talk. He considers me a moment over the rim of his cup, before setting it on an occasional table by his side. 'Hundred and twenty years we've been here. My family arrived at the birth of the twentieth century, once the dust had settled. The mob before us were here for forty years; they got it from the original settler. But I'm the last Carmichael. My kids aren't interested. I'm going to sell. My son lives on the Gold Coast, wants the money, not the land. So I'm moving on. The book's for them. For their kids. To know where they come from. What has paid for their overseas holidays and private schools and waterside house.'

He says this with no apparent rancour, voice flat and matter-of-fact, but the words themselves suggest some subterranean resentment: that his life's work, the work of his father and grandfather, will be sold to the highest bidder.

'Will you move to the coast to be with them?' I ask, my voice just as neutral.

'That's my business,' he says. Then he shakes his head, as if reprimanding himself. 'Not the coast. Not for me. Too many people. Too claustrophobic. Too . . .' He searches for the words, finds them: 'Too far away.' And then he stands, rather abruptly.

'But plenty of time to discuss all of this. You'll be tired. Want to get settled. Jamie will show you to your quarters.' And he walks out of the room to the front door, and I have little choice but to follow him, tea and slice left behind.

Jamie is waiting for me in the twin-cab, engine idling, air-conditioning subduing the heat.

'All good?' he asks as I climb onto the passenger seat.

'All good,' I say.

He drives me towards a group of buildings several hundred metres south of the homestead along the banks of the dry river. Most of them look like storage sheds and silos and machinery sheds. There is one house, a modest dwelling of brick and wood, its yard small and confined by a wire fence. There's a single tree, a patchy lawn, brown and brittle-looking, a windmill turning slowly behind the house. There's no wraparound verandah, just a porch big enough for a couple of chairs and a table.

'This it?' I ask.

'Manager's house,' says Jamie. 'Mine now.'

'Where's the manager?'

'Gone. Him and everyone else. Most of the cattle sold. Just Clay, Mrs Enright and me left. Waiting for the sale to come through.'

'So what's your job?' I ask.

'Manager. Caretaker. Dogsbody. Take your pick.'

Past the manager's house, we veer west, following a newly made track across the ill-defined riverbed, bereft of water as it is, spreading out from the collection of buildings. It's a good two hundred metres wide, the land too flat to constrain it within a more defined channel. The shearers' quarters sit on the western side of the dry waterway. It's hard to determine where the water might flow: the falling sun is in our eyes as Jamie drives me across.

The quarters lie at the end of this track, a half-kilometre from the manager's house, further from the homestead, sitting beneath a low ridge of red rocks, running north–south, marking the boundary of the flood plain. Further down, near a low point in the ridge, is a shearing shed and animal yards, dilapidated, wood and steel and ancient. Another windmill, blades fallen, no longer working. The shearers' quarters are made of stone and cement and mud bricks, and next to them is a small, self-contained cottage, no garden but solar panels on the roof. Jamie stops outside.

'Foreman's cottage,' he announces.

'Foreman gone too?'

'I told you: everyone's gone.' He fetches my bag, drops it on the threshold. 'There's food in the fridge. In the cupboards. Let me know if you need anything else.'

'Shearing shed,' I say, pointing. 'Is it still used?'

'Not for decades,' he says. 'It's all cattle now.' He looks about him, then takes his leave. 'Pick you up in the morning,' he says. 'Early.'

'Thanks.'

He doesn't respond, just gets back in the vehicle and drives off.

I'm alone in the great expanse, the sun dipping behind the ridge. My home. A new tin roof, signs of upkeep. The door is unlocked. Inside, there's no mains electricity, the place powered by the solar panels, a newly installed battery, instructions on the kitchen bench. There's an office. A desk, a chair. A lamp. But no phone, no wi-fi, no TV. I check my mobile: no signal. I make myself some pasta and wish I'd brought something to read.

——

I sleep fitfully this first night. There's scurrying in the ceiling and I imagine rats, and then I imagine snakes coming to feed on them.

I'm not keen on snakes. And then, sometime around midnight, the rain comes through. At first I think I must be imagining it, the tapping on the tin roof: rain out here. But the staccato increases, demanding investigation. Outside, wearing little more than a large t-shirt, I spread my arms, the drops falling fat and ripe and weighted. I can smell it, the approaching storm, the air full of it, bristling with it. Lightning arcs and a peal of thunder cannons across the desert, nature's fusillade. The drops become a sheet, stinging my face as I scan the sky. I head to the stony ridge, using the torch on my phone, climb up a way. Lightning careens about me: by its strobing revelations, I can make out the plain, the track across to the farm buildings, a light in the manager's house, nothing at the homestead. The rain moderates, the first wave passing, the wind starting to whip up instead, insisting this is all real, this landscape, my existence within it. It occurs to me I might like it here, out here by myself, on the edge of the great nothing. And for a moment, I think I may have found a new centre, a new balance.

I hear a squall of rain belting towards me along the ridge, announcing its imminent arrival. I think of running for the shelter of the cottage but choose to stand instead, take the full brunt, getting soaked to the skin, the rocks steaming about me.

chapter six
MARTIN

THE ROOM IS NOT ATTACHED TO THE HOTEL PROPER BUT IN A CONCRETE BLOCK annexe behind the main building, a long rectangle split into six motel rooms with parking outside the doors. Martin eyes the tin roof with misgivings; inside, his suspicions are confirmed: the air is dead and oppressive, the heat stifling. He tries the air-conditioner and is surprised to find it quiet and effective, the temperature immediately beginning to drop towards something more tolerable. Next to that, everything else is secondary, forgivable: the sagging bed, the line of ants on the wall, the clunking bar fridge, the discoloured water in the bathroom. There's a rust-stained notice above the rust-stained basin: *Non-potable—don't drink*. And another: *Filtered water available in hotel*. He checks his phone; there's no wi-fi. No phone, no internet: perfect. He's stayed in worse places; he's certainly stayed in better, but he can hold out here provided the air-conditioner does the same.

He sits on the bed, feeling it slump under him, even as the fatigue hits. It's been a long drive, full of anxious tension and fearful speculations of what might have befallen Mandy and Liam.

Goffing's last text keeps imposing itself onto his consciousness: *Careful. B-team in country.* The hit squad. *In country.* An international team? Martin doesn't like the sound of that: it suggests expertise, a large budget. A slow fear has been building ever since he read the text, gathering in the recesses of his mind. He'd been wrong to conclude that the death of Enzo Marelli would usher in a new era, the new godfathers keen to become more corporate, less visible. Instead, it appears they're determined to assert their authority, suppress any dissent, intimidate anyone emboldened by Martin's book. Not payback, but an attempt to shape the future. Yet killing one of the actual informants, even if their identities were known, could trigger a civil war at a time when the new leadership is still establishing its authority. Who knows what sort of internecine power struggles might be underway? But killing a journalist—no one is going to complain about that. And they'll all still get the message. The attempt at Port Silver was bungled, so now they've imported the pros. *Shit.*

He stands, looks about. The room has no back door, just the bathroom. Only one way in and out. He wonders if he could scramble out the bathroom window if worst came to worst. Probably not. He feels he's in a movie, some American gangster film, the location scouts attracted by the outback charm of the Port Paroo Hotel and the austere shabbiness of its motel annexe.

There's a print above the bed, a mass-produced image of a large cactus, native to the US and Mexico. It irritates him for some reason: all the way out here, on the edge of Australia's nowhere, and the owners have installed an imported image. He lies on the bed, imagines it a hammock, and falls asleep, only to jolt awake sometime later, alerted by a noise, disturbed by a dream of gunmen.

He doesn't want to stay inside, not in this room. He has his portable gas stove and supplies in the back of his car in preparation for camping, but it would appear strange to be cooking canned food down by the river when everyone else is gathering at the pub. Drawing attention to himself is the last thing he wants. And he doesn't want to cower in the room, wait for fate to come to him. He can go out and mix, seek out information, learn the lay of the land. Do it now, before it's too late. That has always been his way, his life, his answer: gather intelligence, discover facts, work out what is going on.

He waits until almost half past six before leaving his room. When he opens the door, he realises just how effective the aircon has been; the heat is an affront, the glare an assault, a battalion of flies waiting for him, engulfing him as he emerges. He puts on his wraparound sunglasses, oversized to thwart facial recognition software. He knows the real risk isn't anyone recognising him; the chances of that are slight. If anyone thinks of Martin Scarsden nowadays, they think of the actor who plays him on TV, the good-looking rooster with the curly black hair, not him. Sure, his author photo is in the back of his books, but whoever looks at those? It's social media that remains a threat, as explained by Jack Goffing. A single photo might be enough. While there is no immediate danger—the phone tower is down and there is no wi-fi—photos can sit on phones indefinitely, to be uploaded at some future time. Martin adjusts his sunnies and walks across to the main building, unsure if he is doing the right thing, until the smell of barbecuing meat convinces him he is.

The town's population is meant to be twelve, but there are more than twenty people gathered in the pub's courtyard. There is shade cloth strung out above them, curbing the solar assault but trapping the air, stifling any breeze, and confining flies beneath it. They buzz about lethargically. All of the men still wear their hats, everything from sweat-sculpted akubras, through a bucket hat or two, to a couple of mesh baseball caps bearing the insignias of farm machinery and fertiliser brands. The outsiders are obvious. A retired couple, husband and wife, the man in chinos and a polo shirt, the woman in a shapeless cotton frock, too old and too bland to be killers. Too Australian. A group of three backpackers are drinking enthusiastically, accents European, surely too young and fresh-faced to be killers. Enjoying themselves far too much. Across from them, a young roustabout, a local by the looks, with dusty jeans and a worn cowboy hat, is trying to insert himself into their conversation but seems to be struggling to keep up with the flow of their patois. He's clutching what looks like a Bundy and Coke and is surely too soused to be an assassin; lucky if he could piss straight, let alone shoot a moving target. There's a truck driver with a basketball gut under his blue singlet, having pulled his rig up behind the hotel, reluctant to try for Bourke. The Telstra linesmen sit together, studiously drinking beer, skins so leathery they could be borrowed from lizards. Martin recognises the man he spoke to by the tower earlier.

Perry from the petrol station is manning the barbecue, seemingly impervious to the heat coming off the steel plate, happily curating sausages, chops and chicken breasts, a couple of steaks waiting to one side, ready to go. Next to the barbecue is a table with plates and cutlery, a salad of iceberg lettuce hiding under a fly-proof lattice, white sliced bread, tomatoes that look hard enough to play cricket with, canned beetroot slices, lumps of processed cheese. Bottles of shop-bought dressings are arrayed in a row, together with jars of insipid mustard, four-litre bottles of tomato sauce. Pineapple pieces impaled with toothpicks.

'Hello, young fellow,' says Perry, greeting him cheerfully. 'Pay at the bar. Thirty bucks, all you can eat. Get yourself a beer while you're there.'

'Sure. You want one?'

'Good on you, son. But none of that mid-strength shit.'

Inside, there are a dozen or so women chatting happily in groups of three or four: the familiar gender segregation of Australia. At least the women are smart enough to seek the cool and shade of the interior. Martin assumes they're married to the graziers in the beer garden. Maz is behind the bar, pulling beers with practised expertise, chiacking with her customers.

'Quite the celebration,' says Martin when it's his turn, paying his thirty bucks and ordering schooners for himself and Perry.

'It is. People are up for this.'

'The rain?' asks Martin.

'Not just the rain, the flood,' she says.

'Flood?' asks Martin. 'It's going to flood?'

She laughs at his consternation. 'Yeah, this rain that's coming through tonight, it's just an afterthought. Tail end of the monsoon. A big lick came through about three weeks ago. Missed us, but dumped hard in Queensland, up past Charleville, on the tin-roof country. It's on its way. Give it another week and it'll be with us.'

'Four weeks? World's slowest flood.'

'And getting slower by the day. One-legged man could walk in front of it by the time it gets past here.'

Martin looks around the room, hears the undertone of excitement, before returning his attention to Maz. 'So it's welcome? A flood?'

She laughs again. 'Too right. Without the floods, we wouldn't even exist.'

Outside, sunglasses back in place, Martin delivers the beer to Perry before joining the queue for food behind a couple of the Telstra linesmen.

'What's the prognosis?' he asks. 'The tower?'

'Hey?' says the bloke.

'The mobile tower. You're fixing it, right?'

'Yeah. Sourced a spare inductor in Adelaide. Be in Bourke tomorrow. After that, it depends on the roads.'

'Inductor?' asks Martin.

'Yeah. Damnedest thing. They never break. First time I've heard of it.'

'Must've been a big fucker,' says Martin, wondering if he's laying on the blue-collar accent a bit thick.

'Hey?' asks the bloke, confused.

'The cockatoo that ate through the wiring. Isn't that what happened?'

The bloke looks at him more closely. 'Yeah. That's what we reckon.' He takes a slug of his beer. 'A big fucker.'

'Long as you know how to fix it,' says Martin, privately relieved. Closed roads and a mobile black spot. He looks around: not a phone in sight. He feels the tension in his shoulders ease.

He gets a plate, gathers a little salad, and a sausage and a small steak. He sees an older bloke eating by himself at the end of a table, face like cured parchment under a bird's-nest mop of greying hair. 'Mind if I join you?' he asks.

'Free country,' says the man.

Martin sits, quaffs some of his beer and starts on his meal before initiating conversation. 'Grazier?' he asks.

'Bees,' says the man. 'Bees and opals.'

'Bees? Out here?'

'Hedging my bets,' the man says before chomping down on his steak sandwich. 'Fuck me,' he says, reinserting his dentures, loosened by the meat. He sighs. 'Man's falling apart.' He wipes his hand on a napkin and extends it. 'Fergus,' he says. 'Fergus White.'

Martin shakes the bloke's hand, feels the tomato sauce smear, pretends not to notice. 'Jake.'

'Good to meet you, Jake. What brings you out here?'

'Photography. The night sky. Stars. Just my luck to get here in time for rain.'

Fergus chuckles at that and takes a more considered, more successful bite of his steak sandwich.

'This flood—good for the bees?' asks Martin.

'Absolutely fucking terrific. I'll be in clover.' And he chuckles again.

'And that's why everyone is here? Celebrating?' Martin gestures to the men standing, their voices growing louder as the beer seeps into their parched throats.

'More like planning. Comparing strategies. They've all been trying to figure out how much water is coming down, how far it will spread, how long it will last, how long after it evaporates that the new growth will be at its peak. They've already been ordering new stock, knowing them, scheduling its arrival for when the grass is at its richest. They'll fatten the cattle, get 'em in prime condition, then sell 'em off by the time the heat kills off the pasture.'

'And the roads? They'll stay closed?' asks Martin. He's not sure he wants to be marooned here, even if that would make it difficult for his pursuers to reach him.

'No. Not down here. They're raised above the flood plain.'

'They are?' Martin thinks back, can't remember any great difference in height.

'Not by much. Half a metre. But that's all you need.' Fergus bites off more of his sandwich, takes his time chewing it. 'Sooner or later we'll cop a really big flood, and we'll be isolated for weeks, but not this time.'

'And opals. There's opals out here?'

The old bloke, who was happy to talk bees, just shrugs.

Martin smiles, familiar with the compulsive secrecy of opal fossickers. 'The Hidden Road Hoard. Read about it on the pub walls.'

'Scoff if you like, but it's out there all right.'

'Well, I hope you're the bloke to find it, 'cos I sure won't.'

Fergus seems mollified by that. 'Prefer the honey anyway. Lot less work.'

Martin hasn't finished his meal, although he seems to have drained his beer. At the next table, one of the laughing backpackers has her phone out and is taking selfies in front of Perry's gourmet smorgasbord. Martin makes his excuses, bins the rest of his meal, and retreats indoors.

A trio of graziers have also made the move inside. They're standing around a bar table, talking enthusiastically. Martin removes his sunglasses. He buys himself another beer and, feeling the sense of wellbeing growing and his inhibitions falling, approaches them. 'Mind if I join you?'

He's met with silence, the three men studying him intently, before one of them speaks, an older man with a face seared by years in the sun.

'Who are you?' There's no hostility in his voice, but there is a wariness that surprises Martin.

'Jake Solander. On my way west. Astrophotography.'

'From the city?' asks one of the younger men, a bloke about the same age as Martin, early to mid-forties, with a thick mop of dark hair threaded with grey.

Martin holds out his hands, palms up for inspection, as if that's evidence enough.

The third man laughs at the sight. 'City hands all right. Soft as a baby's bum.'

The older man smiles, the edge coming off his voice. 'Sorry, Jake, but we've got business to discuss. Once we're through, I'll come find you. Buy you a beer.'

'Fair enough,' says Martin, figuring he's not the only one in the pub with secrets to protect.

'No offence,' says the man with the mop of dark hair.

'None taken.'

Martin carries his beer over to a side table. One of the women sashays over, trim and fit-looking, blonde hair up in a bun. Late thirties or early forties. 'Hello, handsome. Haven't seen you about before.'

'Just passing through,' says Martin. 'You?'

'Down the track. Floodplain graziers.' The woman is swirling a large wineglass, a virtual balloon, containing plenty of white wine topped up with ice. 'Gloria,' she says, holding out a wine-cooled hand, and Martin shakes it.

'Jake,' he says.

She flicks her head towards the three men. 'Don't mind them. A few more beers and they'll be your best mates. That's my husband over there, the one wearing the Beatles wig.' She laughs and Martin can't help grinning. 'Call him Ringo if you want to give him the shits,' she says.

He wonders if she might be coming on to him. Boredom must be rampant out here, even for those married to a rock star. 'Hear the weather's been kind,' he says.

'Shaping up nicely for once. Last few years've been pretty ordinary. Last five, really.'

'So the whole enterprise—grazing—it all depends on these floods?'

'Not completely. We can tick over most years, provided we get a bit of rain, bit of water down the river. Keep stock levels sustainable and don't spend any money. But we need a flood every now and then to soak the plain, bring down the water and the silt, renew the pasture. Get a lot of stock in, get it off, make enough to see us through to next time.'

'And this is just on the flood plain?'

Gloria shrugs. 'It's big. Thousands of square kilometres. Plus a bit of channel country out west, in among the ridges.'

'I'm glad I'll get to see it,' says Martin.

'Good for the community,' says Gloria. 'Gets us together. Gets us excited.'

'Good for the pub,' says Martin. Over at the bar, Maz is starting to struggle to keep up with demand. The thirst is building, like the storm outside.

'She deserves it, poor thing,' says Gloria.

'How's that?'

Gloria looks at him, sips at her wine balloon and grows momentarily serious. 'Tough life. Dad died in the desert. Mum drank herself to death. Best friend turned out to be a killer.'

Martin regards the woman behind the bar, laughing with one of the graziers even as she fills a jug. 'Looks like she's doing okay now.'

Gloria laughs, seriousness gone. 'Tonight she is.'

Just then the wiry young bloke, the cowboy who'd been sitting with the backpackers, staggers in. He's smaller when he stands, with bowed legs. He sees the line at the bar, thinks better of it and weaves his way unsteadily towards the three graziers.

Gloria stops laughing, glass suspended halfway to her mouth. 'Shit,' she says.

'What is it?' asks Martin.

Around them, a hush is moving across the bar, like air pressure dropping.

'Northerner,' says Gloria, and places her glass down on the table.

Martin watches closely. He can't hear what is said, but the body language is easy to read. The young man seems overly friendly, or overly drunk, waving his arms in greeting. The graziers bristle. One takes a step backwards, another stays where he is, the elder statesman steps forward, hands raised, trying to calm the situation.

The interloper makes a huge, dismissive gesture, and Martin can see the scowl envelope the grazier's face. From out of the crowd, now completely silent, two young men join their elders, looking no older than the interloper, in their early twenties at most, lean and muscled, tanned faces turned pink by alcohol. Five against one.

Through the fog of his intoxication the young man seems to realise that he has become the centre of attention. He sneers at the newcomers. Breaking the impasse, the jukebox kicks into life. Hunters & Collectors singing 'When the River Runs Dry'. Gloria glances sideways at Martin, raises her eyebrows.

'Just leave,' instructs the elder statesman, voice clear. 'Long drive. Rain's coming.'

From outside, people are filtering in. The linesmen, the backpackers, Fergus the beekeeper and Perry. A couple more young rural workers step forward, backing up the cowboy. Five against three.

Perry and Fergus start making their way towards the confrontation, community leaders preparing to soothe tempers.

But it's too late.

'Fuck youse,' spits the young man at the old grazier, the patriarch. 'And fuck youse,' he snaps, gesticulating at the others, before turning to the whole bar. 'And fuck youse all, you fucking cockroaches!'

The two younger graziers nod to each other and step forward, hands raised in a non-threatening manner. 'C'mon, mate. You're not welcome here. Time to go.'

They take another step towards him. The confrontation teeters on the edge, and then it topples over. A shove, a shove back, the swearing, the first punch. And then it's on. For young and old, for love or money. An all-in, only the elder statesman stepping back. A stool is broken, there's the sound of glass breaking, the air saturated with swearwords. Martin sees blood, hears a shriek amid the swearing. A woman screaming.

A deafening roar. Silence. People freeze where they are. Maz behind the bar, shotgun smoking, barrel pointing at the ceiling. Martin can see the residue flaking down from above. A blank cartridge, but effective enough. Loud enough. There's quiet, all eyes on her, the fight stopped in mid skirmish, the combatants still.

'Weather report,' states Maz. 'Front's about an hour away. So you should all fuck off home while you still can.' And then, for emphasis, 'All of you. We're closed.'

The old grazier, the patriarch, addresses the young cowboy, who is tenderly touching his lips, assessing the damage. 'You heard what the lady said.'

The young man gazes about him with disdain, suddenly sober, contemptuous of the gathered audience, voice a snarl. 'I was fucking trying. To be fucking friendly.'

Martin turns to Gloria, who has regathered her glass and is taking a huge slug of wine. 'What just happened?' he asks.

'Northerner.' She adds, by way of explanation, 'Queenslander.'

'And?'

She smiles—not a real smile, more a knowing sort of expression. 'Goes way back. Generations. Like the Hatfields and McCoys.'

'The feud?' He turns around, looks at the poster of the armed cowboys. 'Says it's a distant memory.'

'Don't believe everything you read.' Gloria sculls the last of her wine. 'Surprised Maz let him in. Should've known better.'

After that, the graziers drift away, their wives driving, getting ahead of the rain. The grey nomads retire, and Fergus heads off, limping towards a nearby house. It's just the hotel guests left: Martin and the linesmen and the backpackers. Maz keeps the bar open for them. Martin loses track of time. Before he knows it, it's approaching midnight and she's closing the bar.

He steps outside as the first rain starts to fall, large drops, splattering, audible. Out on the horizon, the lightning plays like the backdrop of a theatre stage, and the thunder rolls in. He holds his hands out, raises his face to the sky. Maybe when this is all over, when Goffing and the federal police have caught the killers and life has returned to normal, he should come back out here. The feud might make a good story.

Instead of continuing on to his room, he does the right thing, carrying a bunch of empty glasses back to the bar. The mix of the beer in his stomach and the rain on his face fills him with a warm contentment; for the first time in days he feels himself relaxing, enjoying the moment rather than worrying about the future. The road is closed, the phone tower is down.

'Goodnight,' he says to Maz. 'That was pretty impressive.'

'I've been watching you,' she says, studying his face.

'And?'

'You're Martin Scarsden, aren't you?'

2001

THURSDAY, 12 JULY

So boring!! So unimaginably, utterly, irredeemably, brain-stewingly boring!! There's no water in the river, not even at the waterhole, so there's no swimming, even if it was warm enough. Clancy is lame, so there's no riding. There is no internet, of course, and not even any television, because Dad has somehow allowed the satellite subscription to lapse. Apparently, Mum used to look after it. So we've got the dish, installed on the roof, ready to go, but nothing to watch until Dad gets into Cunnamulla and sees the Retravision guy. Which will be no time soon. I'm surprised the electricity is still connected.

What does he do all these evenings here by himself? Read books? Talk to Mrs Enright? Wallow?

I used to love it here. But I was a kid then. Didn't know any better. Not anymore, though. I've read three books in four days, and I'm no bloody reader. And even that is making me frustrated, because in books things happen. They have a plot. There is fuck-all chance of anything happening out here. There is no plot. The sun comes up, loiters all day, *warming the place up, and then goes down again, leaving every-thing cold and dark. And then it does it again. And again. And again.*

Dad has become a misery guts since Mum died. He's practically given up talking. The drought's eating away at him, or the effects of it: no cattle, no sheep, no stockmen. Just Dad, the manager and a worse-than-useless jackeroo. And Mrs Enright, hovering like a black crow, judging me, judging him, judging everyone except Vincent, the old witch. Money's tight, I know that, but I'm not sure it would make any difference if Dad was loaded. He's decided to be miserable and, as we all know, when he sets his mind on something there is no shifting him. I reckon the only reason he gets out of bed in the morning is to save himself from the tongue-lashing he'd give himself if he didn't.

He misses Mum. I know that. We all miss her. Every day. But it's been more than three years and I reckon he's getting more morose. He's worse now than he was two years ago, and he was worse then than when it actually happened. Like he's becoming fossilised. I've tried talking to him, tried geeing him up. He's not interested. Vincent and I wanted him to take a holiday with us this coming summer, maybe down to the Sunshine Coast, where we used to go as a family, but he refuses to leave Longchamp. Says we can't afford it. You'd think the place would collapse if he left it for a week or two. I reckon with no rain and no stock, it's the perfect time to take a break. The topsoil is going to dry up and blow away no matter where he is. I wouldn't mind if Mrs Enright withered up and blew away with it, the way she bosses me around, as if I was her employee and she was the employer, and not vice versa.

I mentioned global warming to Dad, suggested it might be causing the drought, this theory that Al Gore is pushing, but he didn't say anything. Then I added that our cows could be making it worse, farting methane. Dad got angry then, started swearing under his breath. I didn't mention it again. He never ever used to get angry; he never used to swear. He used to smile and laugh and tell lame jokes. I miss that version of him.

And now I miss school as well. I never thought I'd say that, and yet here I am, eager to get back there. To see my friends. To see my enemies. To see anyone! Two more weeks. I'll have run out of reading well before then. I'll be into the library, reading Dickens and Shakespeare and bloody Becky Sharp, the way I'm going. Honestly, I can see how people become religious.

And it's all made worse knowing Vincent is at the snow, skiing. Stupid me. Stupid, stupid, stupid me. Why didn't I organise something?

SATURDAY, 14 JULY

Ha ha! There is a god. Vincent is on his way back. His mate Eric got sick and Eric's dad buggered his back and the snow's lousy anyway. Brilliant. It will make purgatory so much better, sharing it with someone. I know I should feel bad for him, but desperate times make for desperate people.

SUNDAY, 15 JULY

Oh, the best of days. First up, Vincent arrived home. Reckons he loves it out here, that it's 'authentic', that the snow is full of wankers. Whatever. Then, even better, Maz rang and invited us down to stay with her. Her mum owns the pub at Port Paroo. How cool is that? A pub! And Dad said he'll let us drive down in one of the farm trucks. I never would have believed it. Vincent has his Ps, and I've got my learners, but even so, I didn't think Dad would agree. Maybe he realises what a dick he's been lately.

TUESDAY, 17 JULY

We got the farm truck, all right, an old Toyota, drove it down the Sundowner Track. Two hundred kays of bleak. The cassette player carked it years ago and there's no radio, so I plugged my boom box into the cigarette lighter and we compared mix tapes. Vincent got so enthusiastic, caterwauling along and smashing out the beat on the steering wheel, that he almost stacked it a couple of times. I insisted he give me a drive. It was such fun. He taught me how to double-declutch. It took me a while, and a lot of grinding gears, but by the time we got to Port Paroo I was right on top of it. Vincent reckons it's handy if you need to change down descending a steep hill. I guess I just have to believe him; the nearest proper hill is hundreds of kays away. It's pancake flat out here.

There was one grim encounter. We came across a dead steer. A wedge-tail was at him, ripping out the guts, crows circling, waiting their turn, flies so thick they formed a dark cloud. A blowfly murmuration. The carcass was smack bang dead centre of the track, blocking the way.

'Drought,' said Vincent. 'Poor fucker. No water in the river along this stretch.'

'Middle of winter,' I said. 'Imagine what it's going to be like in summer.'

We swapped back, so he could drive. When we got out to change places, the smell was appalling, the air too still to blow it away. Back in the car, Vincent edged us around the rotting mess, taking the truck off road, pushing through dead bushes. I was thinking of Dad, how tough it can be out here.

'And to think, someday all this will be yours,' I said, a feeble attempt to lighten the mood.

'Ha-de-ha-ha,' said Vincent.

'At least it's authentic.'

'Sure is.'

Maz has given us a room each out in the annexe. Pretty shit to be honest. The place used to be accommodation when her dad was still alive, but her mum hasn't been able to keep it up, so the annexe isn't used anymore. We need to send Mrs Enright to sort it out. Chuck all the garbage and give it a proper vacuum. But we've got our two rooms halfway liveable. At least the toilets flush, even if the showers run cold and the tap water is a murky brown.

THURSDAY, 19 JULY

Jesus. I knew Maz had it bad, but nothing like this. Her mother's a full-blown pisshead, and barking mad with it. Maz had told me at school, but I always thought she was exaggerating. Now I'm thinking she's understated it. The mornings are best, when Mrs Gingelly is still comatose. She doesn't get out of bed until lunchtime. Then she's okay until about four or five, drinking steadily but still keeping it together, before accelerating into oblivion as night falls. It's up to Maz to open up at eleven and serve any early customers. Vincent and I are happy to help. It's kind of fun, at least when Mrs Gingelly is off the scene. I don't know what happens when Maz is at school. I guess the pub just doesn't open until her mum gets up. There's an Aboriginal bloke, Perry, who runs the general store and lives across the way. He gives her a hand.

The best bit is serving the customers. It's freezing at night, so we get a big fire roaring in the front bar. Word's got about and the locals love it. Vincent and I are seventeen and Maz is still sixteen and we're running a pub. But no one gives a shit. Not out here. As long as we keep the bar warm and the beer cold and can fix them a feed of steak or burgers or shnitty. A cop came in yesterday and didn't even bother to ID us, he just wanted to make sure we were okay. He gave us his number, just in case. The cop shop here has shut down, so the constable was out from Bourke, running welfare checks.

Maz, Vincent and I have made a pact: we don't drink before the sun sets. I think it's very adult of us.

Tonight, the Stanton boys came in: Roman and Merry. I swear, Roman is seriously hot, three years older than us, halfway through ag college. Merry's a year younger than his brother, taking a gap year. I reckon he's keen on Maz, the way he looks at her. Sort of awkward and tongue-tied and endearing, like a big chocolate lab, with his thick brown hair. I reckon it's good for her, a bit of attention, after all the shit she has to put up with. Roman isn't at all awkward, just the opposite. If anything, he's maybe a bit aloof.

I reckon they're good guys, not interested in perpetuating the feud. The way Dad craps on, you'd think it was World War III, us and the Stantons. The only reason it lingers on is because people have got nothing better to do. It's the boredom and the heat; it makes you want to hate someone, even if there is no good reason for it.

They've invited us out to their place, Tavelly Station, this Saturday, for a barbecue by the river. For some reason, they seem to have water down on their property. How does that work? We've got fuck-all at Longchamp.

SATURDAY, 21 JULY

We went out to Tavelly Station, left Maz's mum propping up the bar, Perry keeping an eye on her. It's a proper spread, all right, easily as big as Longchamp Downs. Similar setup, with the house by the river, almost a small lake, just before the river fractures and the giant flood plain opens up. Strange thing is how there's water down here. Not flowing, but not stagnant either. You can see where it's shrunken back, that it was higher not so long ago. Roman says there is a kind of natural weir that holds back some of the water, that it's the reason Tavelly was established where it is. I could see Vincent looking at it. He was thinking the same as me, how it would be good if Dad had some of this at home. We have Lake Murdoch, but that empties out when the river drops. It's been dry for four or five years.

To play it safe, Vincent and I went incognito, called ourselves Cobain instead of Carmichael, in honour of Kurt Cobain. I wanted Gallagher, after Oasis, but Vincent won out. Apparently Roman and Merry's parents are still hung up on the feud, same as Dad. Pathetic really, these old people.

It was still a bit weird when Roman introduced us. His mum seemed really nice, but his dad is crook as shit. Fucked lungs. Emphysema, from smoking all his life. Neither Roman nor Merry smoke and you don't need to be Einstein to work out why. Mr Stanton has trouble getting enough air to speak, and he wheezes when he breathes, and kind of drools. It's a bit disgusting, but we tried not to react. Maz reckons her mum should meet him, it might make her realise how lucky she is. Or they could drool together. Sometimes I think Maz has a very dark view of the world.

Still, it was nice to be there, with people our own age. There was Vincent and me and Maz, Roman and Merry, and another mate of

Merry's from school, Alan, and his little sister Gloria. Alan and Gloria live on a place over on the Darling. They reckon it's even worse than here, that what little water is left is tainted with blue-green algae, even in the middle of winter. They blame the chemicals from the cotton, but we all know the real reason is the lack of rain. It'll be a disaster come summer.

At one point, I found myself talking to Roman, just the two of us, laughing about Vincent and me calling ourselves Cobain. The feud gave us something in common, something to talk about, this shared knowledge that the two of us meeting was somehow illicit. And that we were different from our parents, that the ancient quarrel held no power over us. I like Roman. He's lots of fun when he wants to be, but he definitely has a serious side to him. I guess that's inevitable given how sick his father is. Roman says he and Merry are already doing all the physical work around the property. His dad is still totally with it mentally but can no longer be hands-on. Roman said that sooner or later he'll have to go into care. There is no cure; it just gets worse and worse. They're thinking of Dubbo or maybe Moree. Their mum will need to go with him. She wants to. So the brothers will kind of inherit while their dad is still alive, which seems cruel. I told him Clay was still fit and healthy, just miserable. Vincent will inherit, but that's so far in the future it's not worth talking about. It's not set down on paper, not that I know of, but I'm okay with it. I love the place and all that, but I don't want to run it. Not in the middle of a drought, when there's no money and no water and cattle dropping dead in the middle of the road and having their guts ripped out by eagles. I certainly don't want to spend the rest of my life out there.

I told Roman I wanted to live in London. I'm not sure why; it just came to mind, maybe because of all those old English books in the library at Longchamp that got me through the first week of the *holidays. I spun him quite the story; said I wanted to go to uni and study art, work as a curator or a conservationist. Work at the British Museum. I was making it up on the go, but it was kind of liberating, like daydreaming out loud. To pretend that such things are possible, even when you know that they're not. But Roman seemed really impressed. He said I was lucky, that he would need to look after the property, look after his parents. But he said he wouldn't mind visiting me in London and I said I wouldn't mind if he came to see me.*

THURSDAY

chapter seven
ECCO

THE MORNING IS BRIGHT AND HOT, MY SUNGLASSES NOT A FASHION STATEMENT but a necessity. In the distance, I can see the last of the clouds receding over the horizon. Water has pooled on the ground and the flies are in a celebratory mood. There's a stillness to the air, a lack of wind, that I find unnerving: the implicit threat of extreme heat turned swampy by the rain.

I'm not sure what I'm expected to do. I'm stranded out at the foreman's cottage, no phone, no internet. I want to get started on the project, but I have nothing to work on. My laptop is taunting me: all powered up, but nothing to feed into it. Are they expecting me to walk across? To the homestead, or to the manager's house? I wonder if that's even possible, after the overnight rain, or if the way will be too muddy. I return inside, make a second cup of tea. Before long I hear an engine.

It's Jamie Stubbs, on a quad bike, mud-spattered.

'Jump on,' he says, not bothering with a greeting. 'Old man wants to see you.'

'Where's the four-wheel drive?' I ask.

'Bike's better in the mud.'

'Give me a moment.' I return inside, change out of my sun dress and sandals, put on jeans, a t-shirt and boots. I place my laptop and notebooks into my backpack.

'No hat?' he asks when I emerge from the cottage.

'Sunscreen,' I say. 'We'll be inside, won't we?'

'Suit yourself.'

I climb onto the back of the quad bike.

'Hang on,' says Jamie, and the bike lurches forward, spraying mud. I grab his waist; I don't have much choice, it's either that or fall off. I wonder if he's done it on purpose, trying to get a rise out of me. As soon as I can, I grip the handles on each side of the pillion position instead. But the memory lingers a moment, the feel of his torso through his fabric shirt. Lithe and muscly. It makes me reflect on how long it's been since I touched a man beyond the formalities of a handshake. Not since before. An eternity.

We pass over the creek bed, still empty despite the rain, pass the manager's cottage and continue on to the homestead. The track is passable—just. Jamie drops me at the entrance to the garden but doesn't dismount, doesn't come with me, as if the gate is an invisible dividing line between the owner and the staff. I thank him, and he tips his head, gives the bike a throaty rev and leaves in a cloud of exhaust.

Either side of the path, the lawn is still wet, looking all the better for it, and the roses look relieved. I sit on a bench on the verandah, remove my boots and set them alongside a well-worn pair of RMs and some smaller hiking boots. There's a jug of water; I use some to wash dirt from my hands.

I use the brass knocker, hear it reverberate through the interior, wonder if I should let myself in. I hear footsteps approach and the door opens, revealing Mrs Enright, hair pulled back into a tight bun, mouth pursed and eyebrows arched. She assesses me and sniffs.

'I'm Ekaterina,' I say. 'I didn't get to introduce myself properly last night. You can call me Ecco.' I try a smile.

'I'm Mrs Enright,' she says. 'You can call me Mrs Enright.' And she turns on her heel and leads me through the sitting room and into a formal dining room.

Clay is seated at the head of the table. It's a big table, made of cedar, Victorian in its solidity. On its surface are two piles of books. They look old. Ledgers and accounting books and journals. A couple of photo albums, dated by their faux leather covers, made of pressed cardboard rather than post-war vinyl. He has one of the albums open and is examining its contents with the aid of a magnifying glass. He doesn't look up immediately, seemingly lost in the pages, but when Mrs Enright clears her throat he comes back to himself and rises to his feet. He seems more nimble than he was last night.

'I'm sorry,' he says by way of greeting. 'Sleep well?'

'The rain was very peaceful.'

He smiles. 'I'm glad. But don't expect more.' He turns to Mrs Enright. 'Tea, please, Mrs Enright.' He turns back to me. 'Some toast? Fruit?'

I haven't eaten. 'Yes, please,' I say to Mrs Enright. 'Both would be lovely.'

She frowns. 'As you wish.'

'I've fetched some of the journals for you. Ledgers, that sort of thing. There's plenty more in the library, plenty to delve into. They go back a hundred and eighty years, near enough.'

I cast my eyes over the books. They seem large, their bulk intimidating, and I realise how much work the project might require, not in the writing but in the research. Ploughing through thousands of pages of records is quite a different proposition from burnishing the reputation of some self-important poseur with a paper-thin record of achievements. Ghostwritten biographies are all about optics, about the story, the imagery; they have little to do with research.

'Let me show you,' says Clay, apparently oblivious to my discomfort. He leads me back down the central corridor to the sitting room. Along the way, I see the walls adorned with portraits of stuffy men wearing stuffy clothes, but also more recent portraits. A colour photograph of a handsome young man, a beautiful young woman. I pause to look. Their skin is flawless, their teeth perfect, their smiles warm and genuine.

'Who are they?' I ask.

Clay looks unhappy to be impeded. 'My children. The twins: Vincent and Chloe.'

'Very good-looking,' I say.

Clay harrumphs, and leads me into a library, fitted bookshelves reaching to the ceiling, an imposing desk under the window looking out across the verandah. Part reading room, part study.

'It's beautiful,' I say, running my hand over the surface of the desk. It's made of oak, an antique, the top inlaid with green leather.

'I've cleared out,' says Clay. 'Working out of the manager's office. So it's all yours. Phone in the hallway.'

'Internet?' I ask, daring to hope.

'Of course. Wireless.'

'Password?'

'Out here?' He laughs. 'No need.'

I'm feeling better by the minute, buoyed by the setup. I can work here just fine. Nobody to disturb me, no one to remind me.

I can cocoon myself away, let the world keep spinning, emerge in a month or two, butterfly-like.

'I'll be off,' says Clay. 'You should have everything you need.'

'Not everything.'

'How's that?'

'You, Clay. I need to interview you.'

He says nothing, but the way he shifts his weight from one foot to the other, I can see he's unsettled.

I gesture around the walls. 'It's all great, all the details, all the background. All the facts. But I need context, I need a story. Your story. The story of you and your family. That's what I need.' I point to the bookshelves again. 'That way, we can be sure I get the best out of these.'

He remains stoically noncommittal.

I try a different tack. 'When your grandkids read the book, it should be your voice they hear, not mine,' I say.

I can see that sinking in, the way he considers the bookshelves, looking beyond them.

'I'll think about it,' he says at last. 'I'll let you set up. Mrs Enright can bring you your breakfast in here. I'll be back later.'

I set up my laptop, connect it to the wi-fi. It's surprisingly speedy: the satellite, I guess. I try a news site, but it all seems too far away: politics, floods, America unravelling. There's an email from Emma: a copy of a receipt. Forty thousand dollars. I check my account, disbelieving, but it's true. Deposited by Clay at 5 am. I feel a weight lifting. I look about the room, this beautiful room, finding reassurance: I can do this.

Mrs Enright knocks at the door with my breakfast tray, which she places on the desk.

'Thank you,' I say, beaming.

'You're welcome,' she replies, her tone suggesting that I'm not.

A half-hour later, another knock at the door. Clay. He doesn't enter, as if the library is now my domain. 'I thought about what you said, about interviewing me,' he says, almost reluctantly, before delivering his verdict. 'Makes sense.'

'Thank you,' I reply, trying not to betray my relief. Having his through line, his personal take, will help me find the story that he wants told. The alternative—trawling through all those books, all those generations—doesn't bear thinking about. His input could save me months of grind while making for a much better story.

'Let's talk in the dining room,' he says.

I agree and follow him, bringing my laptop and notebooks with me. The books he was studying when I arrived are still spread out on the table.

He resumes his seat at the head of the table, and I sit to his left. I open a fresh notebook and am about to request an overview, but he starts without me, anticipating what I need.

'Us Carmichaels, we're not the original settlers. We came here in 1905, bought it from a family called Abbott. English, had no idea what they were letting themselves in for. They purchased it from the estate of a man called Patrick Murdoch. He was the original settler, the one who staked his claim, who started clearing the mulga and putting in fences. Nothing like we have today, of course, but the start. His journals are there in the library. You should write a chapter on him. Doesn't have to be long, but our story here doesn't make sense, won't have the correct perspective, without him.'

'The Abbotts bought it from his estate? He died out here?'

'Killed by the blacks.'

'That's awful.'

'Probably deserved it.'

'Seriously?'

Clay cracks a sardonic grin. 'That's for you to find out. Should all be there. Different world back then. Didn't try to hide it, not for the most part. Some were murderous, some were sympathetic, most fell somewhere in the middle: callous and indifferent. And all of them superior.'

I'm taken aback. I'd had Clay pegged as a conservative old cocky, card-carrying National Party. A redneck with money. I wasn't expecting this. 'And you want this in your book?' I ask.

'Of course. No blood on our hands. Not that I know of, at least. It was over by then. But we're the beneficiaries, no doubt about it. Then again, the whole country is the beneficiary. Sydney and Melbourne and Brisbane as much as Eulo and Port Paroo.'

I'm not sure what to say, even though I'm pretty sure what he's alluding to. 'Blood? Over?'

He smiles, a knowing sort of smile. 'What they refer to as the Frontier Wars. That's the modern term. Depends on your definition of a war, though. There were skirmishes, there was resistance, there was murder, there were reprisals. No frontline, no regular armies, but a kind of war nevertheless. Settlers, the blacks, the native police.' He indicates the books on the table, the leather-bound journals and ledgers. 'All in there, and those in the library. Written by Murdoch in those first years of Longchamp Downs.' He doesn't take his eyes off me, those watery blue eyes shrewd and calculating, making their assessment. 'They called it "dispersion". Drove the blacks off, to the missions back along the Darling. If they were lucky.'

I don't know how to respond, puzzled by his eagerness to tell me all this, for it to be the first subject he covers, and it makes me wonder at his claim not to have read the diaries. 'Sounds brutal,' I say. There's emotion running through him, but I'm having trouble identifying it. His manner is matter-of-fact, as if he's disconnected from what he is saying. 'Why include it?' I ask. 'Your family wasn't here then.'

'Vincent should know the truth. That the money coming his way isn't from winning lotto. It's hard-earned. Hard work, hard decisions.'

'If you say so.' And I look to the journals and ledgers, wonder at what cruel truths they might contain, what ugliness. I think of Reilly Sloane, so desperate to varnish the truth or bury it altogether, and compare him to Clay Carmichael, so eager to expose it. To impose it on his heirs, to flagellate himself. 'I'll read the material, see what's there. But I agree, it makes sense to write a preliminary chapter. The coming of the white man.'

Satisfied, Clay settles back into his chair. 'As far as I know, Patrick Murdoch came here very early in the piece, years ahead of others, attracted by the river, the flood plain, the lake. It must have been full when he got here. He was a freed convict. Came in the 1840s, staked his claim, lived here for twenty years or so before he was speared. His diaries are there on the table.'

I look at them. Reach out and touch them. Covers of cloth and leather, appearing almost new, the pages marble-edged, preserved more or less untouched for posterity on the shelves of the library. And at that moment, instead of intimidating, they become intriguing. 'But you've never read them?' I ask.

'Not me. Not much point, really.' He indicates another stack of books. 'The Abbotts lasted two generations, until they got taken out by the Federation Drought in the 1890s and sold out to us in 1905. It was still pretty wild out here, still the frontier, but the railway had been put through to Cunnamulla by then, so we could get the clip to market, especially once we got trucks. Not like the old days with bullock trays and camel trains and floating it down the river from Bourke. Our timing was perfect. The weather came good, the floods returned, and the First World War massively boosted demand for wool. We increased the flock, bought out neighbouring properties. And that was that. We were set. By the time the next drought rolled around, and the Depression, we had a big enough buffer to see it through.'

'So 1905, who was that? Your grandparents? Great-grandparents?'

'Grandparents. The real driving force, the one who built the empire, was my grandfather Ernest. He was in his early twenties when they moved here.'

'You remember him?'

'Very well. Lived to a ripe old age. Outlived my father.'

'Oh. I'm sorry.'

'Don't be. I was already in my twenties. Dad died at forty-seven. Shot himself.'

'What?'

'This country. It can get to you. It was the sixties, there was another big drought. We were on the edge. You have to be the right type. Resilient. My grandfather, Ernest, was. Made of ironbark. So am I. Skipped a generation.'

'Might be a good thing your kids have gone to the coast then.'

He says nothing, just stares hard into my eyes, before standing. 'You got enough to get you going?'

I stand as well, the old-fashioned room demanding old-fashioned courtesies. 'Yes. Thank you. But I'll want to talk again, if that's okay.'

'Of course,' he says. 'Right now I need to get moving; the place doesn't run itself.'

As he leaves, I wonder what I've signed up for. I'd thought it was going to be a puff piece, like all my other ghostwriting projects, the task to make the subject unambiguously good, the story not so much the truth as truth-adjacent. But clearly that's not what Clay Carmichael wants. It's almost as if he wants to rebuke his children, to teach them a lesson. And that's not all. It's as if he wants to punish himself for the sins of the first settlers, to acknowledge them, and pass that sense of obligation on to his children, a twisted birthright.

I carry the books back to the library where my toast and tea sit lukewarm. As I eat some apple, I look through a family photo album. They all seemed so happy, but the pictures were taken long ago; from the past decade or two there's just the one of Clay on a beach with his son and grandchildren, similar to the one on the mantelpiece in the sitting room.

I wonder again why Clay has hired me. Is it despite my reputation, or because of it? Another jibe at his children, their history written by a scarlet woman.

And I find myself smiling. If that's the case, I don't mind at all. If he wants to suffer, let him suffer. As long as I finish the work, as long as I collect the money. And I find myself relishing the idea: writing a book where I actually get to tell the truth.

chapter eight
MARTIN

MARTIN SLEEPS FITFULLY, DREAMS MERGING WITH REALITY AS THE RAIN COMES in waves, surging in tandem with his subconscious. And within the dreams, threading through them, an underlying anxiety, prompting him in and out of wakeful consternation. Images from a Scorsese movie wash over him, heavy-set men with Homburg hats, overcoats and Brooklyn accents, the rain on the roof melding with the rat-a-tat of tommy guns, even as part of his subconscious fights back: who would wear a well-tailored overcoat out here? He wakes suddenly: the sound of thunder; the sound of an explosion. Lightning flares outside. Maz the publican has identified him; has anyone else? She's promised to keep his secret, but why should she? The bush runs on gossip; he knows that well enough. He lies still as death, listening to the rain beating down, normally such a comforting sound. Not here; not now. He wonders where Mandy and Liam are, hopes they're safe, that the boy is sleeping well. He tries to plan his next move but falls asleep before making progress.

By the time first light is penetrating the curtains, he feels more tired than when he went to bed. There's a heaviness to his bones and a minor headache is chasing itself around the interior of his skull: too much drink, too little sleep, too much tension. The closed roads and broken telephone tower no longer seem so reassuring: a team of assassins has arrived in Australia and is hunting him. He's failed to fool a country publican; how can he expect to evade professional killers? He sits up, swallows some painkillers, remembering at the last moment to use the filtered water from the fridge. It has a chemical taste. He tells himself he should feel reassured by Goffing's last communication: the ASIO man is across the movements of the hit men. And yet, if the authorities are so competent, why weren't the killers stopped at the border?

Emerging from his room, he can see the cloud cover is retreating; it's now just a thin band of cloud to the south-east, glowing pink and gold, heralding the sunrise. As he watches, the sun breaks through, and already he feels its potency, the promise of another baking day. All around, the ground is red mud and gravel, colour enhanced by the overnight soaking, dotted with ochre puddles. The place has been saturated, yet he wonders how long the water will persist under the solar bombardment.

He finds Maz in the hotel's kitchen, pulling breakfast ingredients from an industrial fridge.

'Morning,' she says. 'Early in the day for a journo.'

He grimaces at the mention of his profession. 'It is.' He looks about, making sure they're alone. 'But please, I'd be incredibly grateful if you didn't let on who I was.'

'So you kept saying last night.' She lifts her attention from a cryovacked packet of bacon and looks him in the eye. 'What's the big deal?'

'I'd rather not say.'

'Big assignment, is it? One of your investigations?'

Martin sees the opportunity, takes it, finds it easy to lie. 'Something like that. Undercover. Best if people don't know who I am. At least, not at first.'

Maureen examines him, perhaps considering his motives, then appears to accept his claim. 'Secret's safe with me,' she says. 'What is it then? Water theft? The feud? Cattle duffing? Rorting carbon credits? Maybe I can steer you in the right direction.'

He blinks, decides that if he has to play into the role, he should make it convincing. 'This feud. Is that what I witnessed last night?'

She cracks a sardonic smile. 'Yeah. The latest chapter.' She hauls the bacon off the bench. 'Goes back generations. The Carmichaels and the Stantons.'

Martin can't help it; his interest is piqued. 'Those blokes fighting last night were Carmichaels and Stantons?'

'The young bloke, the Queenslander, wasn't a Carmichael. But yeah, the Stantons were there, among that group he pissed off.'

'They're neighbours?'

'No. The Carmichaels own Longchamp Downs, two hundred kilometres north, over the border in Queensland. The Stantons are down past here at Tavelly Station; big spread on the flood plain.'

'Same river, though?'

'Yeah. The Paroo.'

'I'm guessing you side with the Stantons?'

'Bad for business if I didn't.' Maureen starts grilling bacon and frying eggs.

'Right.' He looks at the eggs and bacon. 'How long before the roads open, you think?'

'This time of year? No clouds, temperatures touching forty degrees. Possibly passable by sunset, but the cops will wait until tomorrow at the earliest. Drive through in the morning to make sure before they give it the all clear.' She studies him. 'You leaving?'

'Can I drive up there? Along the river into Queensland?'

'Not now. Maybe tomorrow. That road isn't so good. More of a track.' She studies him. 'So you are interested? For a story, I mean?'

'Sounds like a great yarn,' he says, and he's only half bullshitting.

— —

Martin walks down to the river, picking his way across the red dirt, crusting under the sun, then following the road, its surface more compressed. He sees the phone tower, not a worker in sight. They're still awaiting the spares, the roads closed. He walks along to the bridge, the flies insistent and incessant. From the roadway he can glean a better idea of the subtle variations in elevation. The bare earth of the channel is about two metres below where he is standing, the earth grey instead of red, with a thin smattering of dead grass. He attempts to visualise the coming flood. It will rise steadily but not reach the level of the road. Before that it would top the banks, spread out. There is no valley to contain the stream, but Martin can determine where the water will flow by following the grey silt left by previous flows. He sees the buildings are subtly elevated, the pub on a level with the bridge. There must be a metre in it at most from high point to flood plain, but from the bridge the delineation is clear: the grey silt is where the water will flow, the red dirt, slightly higher, will remain dry. Just how high, or how far, the flood might reach will depend on the flow. If it's gentle enough it will continue further down the channel before breaking apart. From what Gloria told him, there mustn't be any channel at all further south, just one almighty plain, levelled over the years from the silt of a hundred floods.

He walks further, off the far side of the bridge, the elevation in the road all but imperceptible. He comes to a shallow gully branching off the main channel, a culvert under the road. He realises the night's rain will not flow into the river; the land is too flat. The river is fed from the north, not from the surrounding land. He thinks he understands the location of the town better now: the east–west road passes through here because it's the most southerly place where a bridge can cross a defined channel.

Returning to his room, he notices a sodden sheet of paper resting beneath his car. He gently prises it from the ground. It's a receipt from Pudding Motors in Port Silver for the servicing of the Subaru. It bears his real name and address. He checks the Subaru's door. It's unlocked. Inside, he opens the glove compartment. There is no telling from its messy contents whether it's been rifled through or not, but that's where he would have left the receipt. He searches through. There are rego papers, also in his and Mandy's names. He swears softly to himself. So much for changing licence plates. Why hadn't he ditched the identifying papers? How could he be so negligent?

He sits in the driver's seat for a moment, thinking. He's convinced he locked the car. He remembers feeling awkward, a touch paranoid, knowing well enough that locals this far west wouldn't lock anything, cars or houses. And yet, if someone had broken into it, they would have triggered the car alarm, surely waking him from his fitful sleep. The other possibility is that someone had entered his room, found the key fob and used it to open the car. While he was sleeping. No, he'd barricaded the door. So it must have been before: during the evening he'd spent eating and drinking and talking in the pub. Someone had entered his room. He gets out of the car, goes to his room. There is no sign of forced entry. So it was someone with a spare key. Maz? Or with the place so busy, Maz at the bar, it would have been easy enough to access a key. Where did she keep them? In the office, behind the bar? It would have been simple to lift it unnoticed during the brawl.

Inside his room, he inspects his belongings. His keys are where he left them, on the bench by the kettle and microwave. Nothing is missing, including his laptop. He sits on the unmade bed, thinking it through. Why didn't the intruders relock the car before replacing the key fob? Was the invoice deliberately dropped, placed under the car to keep it out of the rain, to let him know he was discovered? By whom? And what would be the point?

It puts him on edge. Someone has entered his room, his locked room, taken the keys, used them to open the car, then replaced them. He picks them up now, walks to the window and points them out at the car. The indicators flash and the side mirrors retract, demonstrating the fob's signal is strong enough to lock the vehicle. Maybe that's what the interlopers did: entered the room, unlocked the car, replaced the keys and left the room, not bothering to return. Like someone was sending him a message, someone with unfettered access to his room.

——

This time he finds Maz in the bar, chatting to the linesmen who, having finished their breakfast, have moved directly to day drinking.

'Any news on the tower?' he asks the same worker he spoke to the day before.

'Depends on the road,' says the leathery bloke. 'They've got the spare, can get it to Bourke, but no further. Not yet.'

'Thanks,' says Martin. 'Good luck with it.'

He waits until the man has rejoined his coworkers and Maz is by herself. 'Mind if I ask you something?'

'What's that?'

'Who else knows I'm Martin Scarsden?'

Maz looks perplexed. 'Beats me.'

'How did you work out who I am?'

She smiles then. 'Read all your books. I'm a big fan. Hoping you might sign them for me.'

He studies her, wonders if she's having a lend of him.

'Like the TV shows too,' she adds. 'Bloke who plays you is a hunk.'

'Someone broke into my car last night. Rifled through the glove compartment. I'd like to know who it was.'

She frowns. 'Are you accusing me?'

'No.'

She's still frowning. 'You locked your car?'

'Yeah.'

'Only person this side of Bourke who does. Maybe someone thought there was something valuable inside.'

'Maybe.'

Maz looks about; now she's the one who seems to be checking they can't be overheard. 'I saw what happened back on the coast. The book launch. They said the explosion was a gas leak.'

Martin says nothing but feels himself become very still, eyes locked on the publican.

'Not sure anyone believes it, though. Lot of speculation on the forums.' Maz, too, has become serious. 'People are saying it was a bomb, that it's this new book of yours, *Melbourne Mobster.*

They reckon you've upset some powerful people. Reports there were gunshots.'

Still Martin says nothing, wondering if he would be better off enlisting Maz's help, telling her the truth.

She gets there first. 'If you're out here to lie low, I'll keep it to myself.' And she smiles. 'For what it's worth.'

'I'd appreciate that,' he says. 'I'd appreciate it very much.'

'But if you are looking for a story, you could do a lot of good out here.'

'How's that?'

'The Paroo. Doesn't look like much right now. An empty gutter. But it's the last wild river in the whole Murray–Darling. No dams, no irrigation. If you're still here when the flood comes, it's magnificent.'

Martin reconsiders her. 'Worth saving?'

'Future generations will thank you.'

'Not sure that's a story, though. Not my sort.'

'You need a bit of spice, eh? A bit of skulduggery?'

'Wouldn't hurt.'

'As I said, there's no irrigation. Not legally. If there's water in the river, you can pump for domestic and stock, but not for pasture.'

'You sound pretty sure of that.'

'I am. People have light planes, access to satellite imagery, every man and his dog has a drone. Try diverting water and someone would spot it within a day or two.'

'So where's the skulduggery?'

'The graziers run cattle on the flood plain, feeding on native vegetation, a couple of head per square kilometre. They depend on floods. South of the town the land is so flat it fractures into smaller and smaller channels until the floodwaters push out across the land, an uninterrupted sheet of water. It can cover thousands of square kilometres before it soaks into the earth or evaporates. Land's so flat that any bank at all, even one just a few centimetres high, has the ability to divert megalitres of water.'

Martin considers this. 'And there's a flood coming.'

'There is. It'll be up at Carmichael's soon enough. Another week and it'll get down here.'

'You think someone might risk it?'

'This summer? This drought? There are rumours.'

'Such as?'

'If I hear anything concrete, I'll let you know.' Maz looks about to turn away when she raises her index finger and eyebrows in unison, as if just this moment recalling something. 'Oh. While I remember. A bloke called for you, said his name was Jack. Said it was important. Wants you to ring him.'

'A call?' Martin immediately thinks of Mandy and Liam, mind racing. Where are they? Are they safe? 'So you do have a landline.'

'Same thing. Comes through the internet.'

'The internet?'

'Yeah. Starlink. Just in the office and my apartment.'

'Not for guests?'

'No. Not set up for it.' She's looking at him intently. 'The phone's in the office. You can use it if it's an emergency.'

'Yes. It's vital.'

Maz shows him through. And sure enough, there are copies of his true-crime books on the shelf above her desk. She leaves him, and he uses the desk phone, which looks for all the world like an old-fashioned landline. The call goes through, rings once, twice, a third time.

'Yes?' The voice on the other end is noncommittal.

'Jack? It's Martin.'

'Martin. Good to hear your voice.'

'Mandy. Liam. They're safe?'

'Yes. Beyond reach.'

The relief is so strong, for a moment Martin is lost for words.

'You're still at Port Paroo,' says Goffing. It's a statement, not a question.

'Yeah. Roads have been closed by overnight rain.' He looks around, wonders if there is any way he is being monitored. 'Safe for now. Telephone tower is down.'

'Cockatoos,' says Goffing.

'I thought we were maintaining radio silence,' says Martin. 'What's so urgent?'

'Good news. Threat's been downgraded.'

'Downgraded?'

'The killers are in Melbourne. The B-team.'

'Melbourne?'

'Surveillance all over them. Won't be able to clean their teeth without us knowing the brand of toothpaste.'

'Why there?' asks Martin.

'Not for you, that's for sure. Intel reckons a gang war might be about to kick off.'

'But the app. It listed me as the target, right?'

'Sure. But once the contract was accepted, they would have opened up direct lines of communication. Telegraph or Signal or WhatsApp. You and Mandy have vanished, so my guess is they've been redirected.'

Martin scans the office, as if seeking an indication of how he should take this news. There's a calendar displaying earth-moving equipment, a map of the district, a list of local phone

90

numbers. Another map, the potential extent of flood waters shaded in deepening tones of blue. He no longer feels any sense of relief; instead he remains wary, on edge. 'Is the contract still live?'

'We don't know,' says Goffing, voice clear on the line. 'Once it was accepted, the job left the app. So you need to stay out of sight, but this should at least give you some breathing space.'

Martin frowns. 'Jack, my presence here has been compromised.'

'How?'

Martin tells him about Maz, then recounts the Subaru break-in.

Goffing takes his time before delivering his assessment. 'Not good.'

'What do you advise?'

'No immediate concern. Wait until the roads open, then get moving. Ring me before you do. I'll get you a rental car, set up a rendezvous.'

'Thanks, Jack.'

Call ended, Martin stands there for a long moment. The hit squad has been redirected, but they're still in country, still on the payroll. Jack Goffing is still taking the threat seriously. It's not over.

chapter nine
ECCO

MRS ENRIGHT BRINGS ME MY LUNCH, UNBIDDEN. A WHITE BREAD SANDWICH, curried egg, and a second with some sort of processed meat and tomato relish, plus another pot of tea.

'Thank you,' I say.

She says nothing, just grunts and leaves.

'Suit yourself,' I say to myself. But the food tastes surprisingly good, and I wolf it down.

I'm starting to map out a possible structure for the book. A preliminary chapter on the first settlers: Murdoch and the next family, the Abbotts. Some photos to pad it out. Maybe an old map. No need to go into any great depth, I figure. Clay shouldn't care too much about the details, as I already have an inkling of the narrative that will appeal to him: settling the land was hard, and ultimately Murdoch and the Abbotts weren't up to the challenge. They failed, but the Carmichaels were made of sterner stuff. They tamed the land, stared down war and depressions, saw off droughts and fires and adversity, and emerged victorious. A story of resilience and sacrifice and survival.

So, a first chapter on Murdoch, and possibly I'll give the Abbotts their own if I can sustain it. Then a chapter on the coming of the Carmichaels in 1905, followed by chapters based on each generation. The grandparents, then Clay's father and mother, and finally Clay. Maybe a summary chapter to wrap it up.

I think about that. So maybe six principal chapters, eight thousand words each. It will be a coffee-table book, so maybe I could incorporate small breakout boxes with historical context, or things that don't fit the main narrative. The Frontier Wars, the Federation Drought, the coming of the motor car, the last of the sheep, that sort of thing, all dressed up with images. I eye the photograph albums. Yes. Lots of images. Every page I fill with illustrations would be one less page requiring words. Perfect.

Clay would see his family's history through male eyes, chapters divided by generations, the patriarchal line. That should appeal to him. I wonder about his daughter, Chloe. Might not she care to know something about the lives of the women? Perhaps, but I would have to find that story in among the books. Again, the idea of breakout boxes, image-rich, with their own self-contained stories. I wonder about Mrs Enright and how long she has served the family, what knowledge she must possess. Could I persuade her to talk to me? Perhaps if Clay requested it. Or maybe not. I should stick to the family. Maybe a breakout box on the employees. There must have been plenty of them, especially back in the early days, before mechanisation really took hold.

I sort the books, the diaries and the ledgers. Photo albums. I remember Emma mentioned a family tree. That seems like a good idea, and as if by providence, I find one in the back of a Bible, running from the first Carmichaels to Clay. I copy it. I'll just need to add the kids and their kids, and I'll be set. I'm making progress, feeling happy.

I flick through an album. Pictures of this and pictures of that. They're not exciting or in any way out of the ordinary, but interesting enough. I'm licensed to pry, to peel back the layers of an entire family, to sniff out the scandals and relive the exhilarations and disappointments. An escape from the confines of my own limited and limiting experience.

I return to the journals of Patrick Murdoch, the first settler. There are three of them, covering the decades he lived here, from the early 1840s through to the 1860s. I recall what Clay told me, that Murdoch had been speared. I open the last of the books. The leather spine is dusty, the cloth cover parched, the thick pages brittle, but the ink is clear.

I turn to the last entry, and find it mundane.

Hot weather continues. No let-up in sight. The home bore level has dropped. Will take the horse and head out for a couple of days and check all the bores.

That's it. No premonition: all normal one day, dead the next, with no opportunity to write a final summation. I close the diary. Murdoch had been killed, and yet his journals remained, most likely because there was no one to pass them on to. Or perhaps the Abbotts had kept them, thinking they might contain valuable insights into rainfalls and river flows and good soil. Perhaps they did. And so they were kept on the shelf and rarely, if ever, left it. I should suggest to Clay that he or the new owner donate them to the State Library, or even the National Library. The first-hand account of an original settler must be of some value.

I turn back to the beginning of the first diary, start moving through, not in any deliberate way, simply seeking an impression. The entries are haphazard: an entry a day for a week or more, then nothing for a month. There are occasional drawings, but Murdoch was even less capable as an artist than he was as a diarist. Nevertheless, I find myself handling the journal with a kind of reverence: the paper dry, the swirl of copperplate, ink on paper; this man, here alone, trying to retain some semblance of civilisation. Perhaps I feel some connection with him: trying to forge a new life. Maybe he was running from something. What had Clay said? That Murdoch was a former convict? I wonder how he knows that. I plough on. Maybe a breakout box: *Convict made good.*

I have found a new well. Extraordinary. How can it be, out here where there is nothing, this water pushing to the surface, clear and clean and free of salt? Providence. God has scattered them about, an invitation to the pastoralist, his grand plan made obvious. The blacks know all of this, of course, as do the animals. But I'm the first white man to discover it, the first to understand its divine purpose. This well lies out past the fourth ridge line. If I take sheep out there, then they could drink. But I would need to amend it, push the water down a channel, spread it, establish some pasture, fence it off from the wild beasts. I have christened it Farrelly's Bore, after the magistrate who set me free.

I pause for a bit, google on the laptop. The Great Artesian Basin. It runs beneath all this land, a massive subterranean reservoir, and occasionally springs to the surface. Capped for the most part nowadays, particularly the old bores, depleted by centuries of exploitation, but there nevertheless. Even now, this property out on the edge of nowhere isn't totally dependent on rainfall and what comes down the river.

I return to the diary feeling a little smug, in possession of knowledge that Murdoch could only guess at.

And then I find the entry. The life-changing entry. I almost miss it. I only see it because the names are underlined in pencil. That and the exclamation marks, neatly circled, in the margin.

A strange passing. Two white men calling themselves <u>Hentig and Stuart</u> heading south-west, down the river line—searching, they said, for a border, the line between east and west, a hidden road. They were peculiar men, captured by a kind of zealotry, well-fed but with a hunger in their eyes. I told them I knew of no such border, that the land was featureless, just the ridges running north to south, folding away into the west, becoming more and more arid the further you travel, the land less and less hospitable. They asked where they might find <u>the camel's head</u>; I told them I had never heard of such a place. I suggested if they were looking for camel skulls there were plenty to be found scattered about, the remains of the wild herds that have escaped their handlers. They accepted it, or they seemed to have done so. I let them camp by the river, offered them some meat and flour, and that seemed to satisfy them. But when I went to pay my respects the next day, they were gone. I presume they were prospectors. If so, they are deluded: there is no gold out here. I wish them luck, but this is no country in which to wander aimlessly. That was my advice to these adventurers. Go with purpose, don't linger, and be glad if you survive the journey.

The underlined names mean nothing to me—'Hentig and Stuart'—and nor does 'the camel's head'. I almost leave it there, but the three exclamation marks pencilled into the margin, a circle around them, suggest there is something significant about the entry. So I google the names, Hentig and Stuart. And feel my breath taken from me.

Arthur Hentig and Donald Stuart. Members of the ill-fated expedition led by Ludwig Leichhardt. The great enduring mystery of outback Australia: Leichhardt and his men, endeavouring to cross the continent from east to west, swallowed by the interior, never to be seen again, their fate unknown.

I search Wikipedia and read: *The party was last seen on 3 April 1848 at Allan Macpherson's Cogoon run, an outlying part of Mount Abundance Station, west of Roma on the Darling Downs.*

I return to Murdoch's diary entry. *July 1848.* July: three months after the last recorded sighting of Leichhardt and his party. And now I have this, Hentig and Stuart, heading south-west, following the Paroo. Leichhardt was trying to traverse the continent, trying to reach Perth. So heading west, surely. I read more online theories of his fate, finding speculation that he might have attempted an arc, heading north-west to avoid the central deserts. Nowhere is the suggestion that the party might have split, nor is there any indication of an intention to head south or south-west. Had these two men followed the Paroo at Leichhardt's direction? Or was it some sort of defection, a mutiny? Following the Paroo was no way to cross the continent, unless they believed the Paroo turned westwards. I recall stories of inland seas. What were they looking for? Longchamp Downs is hundreds of kilometres south of their last known location. This was no diversion; they had come this way deliberately. But why? I re-read Murdoch's diary entry: they were searching for a line, the border between east and west. What could that possibly refer to? A mythical route from Australia's east to its west? A hidden road . . . What was that? And what was the camel's head?

I sit back, exhilarated, overwhelmed by the possibilities, my pulse alive in the stillness of the old house. Even if I find nothing more, this one diary entry is explosive. Just a paragraph, but enough. Enough to construct an award-winning article. A podcast. A reputation. The foundations for redemption. Not ghostwriting, not repackaging some other person's story, but writing one of my own: my discovery.

And suddenly more thoughts are coming to me, tumbling over one another, vying for attention. What if I could actually discover the fate of Hentig and Stuart? Learn what it was they were looking for?

Ludwig Leichhardt. I'd been assigned Patrick White's novel *Voss* at high school, a fictionalised version of the adventurer's expedition. I never finished it, relying on crib notes and internet searches instead. But is my memory playing tricks on me, or does White's version include a survivor? Was that a narrative necessity, an invention, someone to recount what had passed? I wonder, sitting here in the Longchamp Downs library, whether White's masterpiece was pure invention after all, or had the Nobel Prize winner himself heard a whisper, the rumour of a survivor, and decided to fictionalise it? Was that what inspired him to write his novel? Or had he borrowed from that other ill-fated expedition, Burke and Wills, pushing from Melbourne to the Gulf of Carpentaria, travelling north–south while Leichhardt had ventured east–west?

I return to Wikipedia. Yes, Burke and Wills: they both died, together with nearly all of their companions, with the exception of a sole survivor, John King, who endured with the assistance of the Yandruwandha people.

I seek *Voss* on Wikipedia, read the plot line. And I dream of the accolades, the redemption, if I can track down more on the two men, Hentig and Stuart. Is it possible one or both of them survived and, ashamed at abandoning the main party, lived out their lives in the exile of anonymity? What a story that would be.

And then I realise. I return my gaze to the diary and accept I am not the first. Sometime in the past one hundred and seventy-seven years, someone else has read the entry and recognised the significance of the names, enough to underline them, enough to place three exclamation marks in the margins.

Who was it? Did they know something I didn't? Or go on to discover something more? What happened to this earlier reader?

My thoughts are interrupted by a call from the front door. 'Hello? Anyone there?'

chapter ten
MARTIN

THAT SAME AFTERNOON, MARTIN IS BACK IN HIS ROOM, SHELTERING BENEATH the air-conditioner, the day outside grown torrid, the post-rain humidity making it even more unbearable. He's studying maps, trying to determine his next destination, when there's a knock at the door. He closes the computer's lid and stows it under a layer of clothes in his suitcase. He takes a deep breath.

A second knock.

If it's an assassin, it's an awfully polite one.

He opens the door a crack. The beekeeper Fergus White stands there in a cloud of flies and, behind him, one of the three graziers from the night before, the men who'd brushed Martin off, the ones involved in the brawl with the Queenslander. Martin recognises him as Gloria's husband, distinguished by his thick mop of hair. Ringo. The men appear to be unarmed.

Martin opens the door a touch wider. 'Help you?'

'Talk inside?' says the grazier, half question, half statement. He's carrying a leather satchel, old and battered.

'Maybe the bar?' suggests Martin.

'No,' says the man, adding, by way of explanation, 'A bit of privacy would be useful.'

'Might have a story for you, young fellow,' says Fergus.

A story. They know who he is. Momentarily lost for words, he concedes, standing to one side and ushering them in, trying to shoo away the flies as the men enter.

He remains standing; so do they. It feels crowded in his room; he can smell the sweat on them. The beekeeper, he suspects; the grazier looks freshly showered, his blue cotton shirt neatly pressed.

'Live nearby?' Martin asks him.

'Why do you ask?'

'Roads are closed.'

'Close enough,' says the man, with an unconvincing smile. It doesn't fit as well as his shirt. 'I'm Merriman Stanton,' he says. 'Didn't properly introduce myself last night.' And then, rather brusquely, 'Sorry about that.'

'Did you break into my car?' asks Martin, looking from one man to the other.

Stanton looks affronted; Fergus looks puzzled. The grazier speaks for both of them. 'Not us.'

'Someone did,' says Martin. 'Found my rego papers. Now they know who I am. Just like you.'

'Heard a whisper at the bar,' says Fergus. 'Went home, checked online. Found your photo. Martin Scarsden.'

'A whisper?' asks Martin. 'Who from?'

'Does it matter?' asks Stanton. 'The whole district will know by now. What's the problem, anyway?'

'No problem. Just trying to keep a low profile.'

Fergus laughs. 'I read about the explosion at your book launch, exposing the mafia. I presume that's why you want to lay low.'

Martin says nothing; there is nothing to say. He takes a seat on the bed, trying to work out the best way to proceed. Fergus follows his cue, sits on the only available chair.

'So here's the deal,' says Merriman Stanton, who remains standing. 'We'll look after you, if you look after us. No one will get anywhere near you without us knowing first.'

'How do I look after you?' asks Martin.

'A story,' says Fergus. 'A cracker.'

'We hear you're interested in the river,' says Stanton. 'The flood that's coming down.'

Martin blinks. The river? That's what this is all about? 'Yeah. Maz explained it to me. Rain in Queensland a few weeks back, lot of water making its way slowly south.'

Stanton nods. 'Let me show you.' He opens the satchel, extracts a laptop that looks almost as battered, fires it up. 'Here, look. Satellite images.'

Martin looks at the screen.

Stanton alternates between two images showing the same terrain. 'Aerials of the upper river. Three weeks ago, and yesterday.'

'You have internet?' Martin asks.

'We all do. Satellite. Starlink or Sky Muster.'

'Of course,' says Martin. He studies the two images, can't see any great disparity. 'What am I looking for?'

'Change in river height.'

'I can't see any difference.'

'That's because the river is still running in its channels. Up there, where it rises, they call it the tin-roof country. Rocky as hell. Water doesn't soak in. Also hilly, so it flows into creeks, and from there into the river proper. So you need to look over here, at these numbers. River height.' Stanton pulls up a spreadsheet.

Martin sees a line of figures.

'Here's the chart,' says Stanton, changing pages. There's a red line rising dramatically. 'The tributaries up there run between ridges, like small valleys, and there's enough elevation to give the flow impetus. But when it gets further south, the land flattens and the water will flow over the banks and start to spread out. Property called Longchamp Downs has an ephemeral lake. Lake Murdoch. After that, the channel splits, then forms again until it gets down near here. Past Port Paroo it really opens up, becomes completely flat. No inclination, no gravity, nothing to guide the water, it just spreads out over thousands of square kilometres. The flood plain.'

'Right.'

'So, we can take the river heights and flow figures up in the tributaries and use past floods to project how much water is coming down and how far it will spread.'

The grazier clicks through a few more screens. There is a satellite image of the river, Port Paroo on the top of the image. Day one, there is no water. Day two, it starts spreading as it comes south. Day three there is more yet, and by day seven the image is a sheet of water stretching out like an inland sea, only the town and the road and some homesteads and a few other islands of high ground remaining above the tide.

'Not the largest flood by a long shot,' says Stanton. 'But not the smallest either.'

'And the road won't be affected?' asks Martin, concerned he may become marooned here indefinitely.

'No. Not on these projections.'

'And this flood, this lake, how long will it last?'

Stanton keeps clicking. Day eight, day nine, day ten. By day nine the water is receding, by day eleven it has vanished altogether.

Martin is impressed. 'How accurate are these projections?'

'Accurate enough. Refined over years. Margin of error is only a day or so. Depends a little on air temperature, wind speed and cloud cover. But there's no cloud cover expected, so this will happen.' He smiles, and this time the expression seems less forced, as if he is relishing his explanation. He keeps clicking. 'Now watch.' Stanton clicks ahead a few more days, and by day sixteen, the earth has taken on a bright green colouring. 'Grass. Feed. We'll give it another week, then put the cattle on it.'

'And it's really that predictable?'

'Like clockwork—unless someone interferes with the flow.'

Another image, another satellite photograph. 'Here. See it?'

Martin does. 'That line . . . Looks like a track.'

'It is. A new road, stretching right across the flood plain, heading out to the western ridges.'

'What's out there?'

'Nothing. Derelict shearing shed and a couple of unused outbuildings. An airstrip on the other side of the ridge.'

'So why build it?'

Stanton smiles. 'What do you think?'

'You're claiming it's a dam, pretending to be a road.'

'Not claiming. Stating. See how it's not straight across but angles down to the west? It will divert millions of litres down into this area here, running out behind the ridge. Look at the dark soil there. Left by floods, but big ones, much bigger than this. Without the road, our projections predict no water would spill from the channel.'

'Really? How raised is this road?'

'Probably half a metre or less. That's all it takes.'

'And this is in Queensland?'

'Yeah. Property called Longchamp Downs.'

'So you want me to write an exposé?'

'That's the idea.'

Martin stands, looks the grazier in the eye. 'They're Carmichaels and you're a Stanton.'

'Theft is theft.' Stanton's gaze is unwavering.

'And you'll protect me from all comers?' says Martin.

'That's the offer.'

'Deal,' says Martin, and shakes their hands. Goffing advised him to flee, but to where? And with what guarantees? This way he gets protection and a story. Win-win.

chapter eleven
ECCO

'HELLO?'

The voice comes from the front door. I think of leaving it to Mrs Enright, but the knock comes again, so I go myself.

It's Jamie, standing on the threshold, holding his akubra in his hands, a gesture of subservience. He's spattered with mud, and his boots are caked with it.

'Got something for you,' he says.

'What?'

'See for yourself.'

I walk out onto the verandah. There's nothing to see, just a red quad bike sitting outside the gate.

'What am I looking at?' I demand.

'The bike. Clay reckons you should have it while you're here. Save me being your taxi driver.'

The proposal appeals to me: being able to get back and forth to my accommodation at the foreman's cottage independently. 'Excellent,' I say.

'Ridden one before?' he asks.

'No.'

'Okay, I'll guide you through it.' He turns, replaces his hat and walks down the path.

I sit on the verandah seat and put my boots on. He waits at the gate and opens it for me. His gentlemanly manners are starting to grind.

'Show me,' I say, approaching the bike.

'Pretty basic. Key's in the ignition. Won't start unless it's in neutral and you've got the brake engaged.' He climbs on, makes a show of depressing the brake lever, shows me how to put it into and out of neutral, then the throttle. Points out the starter button. Then he kicks the engine over. It starts first time. 'Remember: brake on the left, throttle on the right.'

'Gears?' I ask.

'Not this one. Automatic. Brake on, revs down to idle, engage it here.' He demonstrates. I can hear the engine change pitch but continue to idle as he holds the brake lever in.

'Dangerous?' I recall reading about quad-bike fatalities.

'Can be. If they roll over on you. More likely on hills, steep inclines. Not much danger of that out here. Just don't turn too tight at speed and you'll be okay.'

'What about on the ridges? The country out past my cottage?'

Jamie looks doubtful. 'Why would you want to go there?'

I shrug.

'If you do, leave the quad at the bottom, take it on foot.' He cuts the engine, climbs off the bike, looks serious. 'You have a phone?'

'Yeah.' I take out my iPhone.

'Show me,' he says. 'Could save your life.'

I unlock the handset and pass it to him, moving closer to see what he's doing, ensure he isn't invading my privacy. I can smell him: earthy and real. He takes me to the compass app.

'Gives you your exact location. Doesn't need wi-fi or network coverage.' He takes a screenshot. 'Okay, that'll be in your photo library—our location here.'

'Got it,' I say.

'Also, before you head out, set up your phone for emergency satellite calls. There's a guide online, and there are explainers on YouTube. You'll need an emergency contact pre-loaded. You should put me in.'

'You?'

'Not much point contacting someone in Brisbane. Also, if you crash or fall and the phone detects you're unresponsive it can send me a text via satellite.'

I laugh; he seems overly serious. But then I look around, and remember where I am. Sun and flies and dirt and not much else. And I imagine myself marooned out there, the bike broken down or run out of petrol. Or me thrown off, unconscious. I stop laughing. 'Yes. Good idea.'

He takes out his own phone. 'What's your number?'

I hesitate, I'm not sure why, then tell myself I'm an idiot and give it to him.

He enters it into his contacts. 'I've sent you mine,' he says. 'You can pick it up next time you connect to the homestead wi-fi.'

'Sure,' I say.

'Now jump on the back,' he says, 'and I'll take you over to the machinery shed. I left my bike there.'

He climbs onto the bike, starts it up, waits expectantly. I hesitate again. It's not the bike, or riding pillion, I realise; it's the ever-present question: can I trust him? I consider declining, walking over to the shed after him to collect the bike. But it seems churlish; yesterday he was monosyllabic, borderline surly, but today he seems to be going out of his way to be polite. And he's displaying none of the telltale lechery I know so well.

'Let me drive,' I say. 'That way you can tell me if I'm getting it wrong.'

'Fair call,' he says, getting off.

I clamber on, and I feel him brushing up against my back as he eases on behind me. He puts his hands on my waist, just for a second, then removes them. I half turn to see; he's gripping the rails alongside him.

The bike starts without effort. I put it into gear, give it a small rev, brake still on, feeling it straining to move forward. I drop it back to an idle, release the brake, and then accelerate slowly. It feels very responsive. Seductively easy. Fun even.

At the machinery shed there's another bike. I pull up beside it, cut the engine.

'Not much to it,' Jamie says.

'It's good,' I say. 'Thank you.'

'Let me know when it's getting low on petrol. Don't head out anywhere without a full tank.' Again, that note of concern. 'Can I show you something?' he asks.

'What's that?'

'The flood. Not far away now.'

'Really?'

He nods at the other quad bike. 'You can follow me.'

'I thought the roads were closed. The rain.'

'We won't be on the roads. These go where a car can't.'

I almost reject his offer. I think of Murdoch's diaries, the mystery of Leichhardt and his men. But the books are going nowhere, and the prospect of seeing this flood intrigues me. It seems as if the whole grazing enterprise depends on these periodic inundations. I'll need to know about them for the book: they play a critical role in the fortunes and misfortunes of Longchamp. When the floods came, and when they didn't.

Before we leave, Jamie enters the machinery shed and returns with water and goggles and a trucker cap for me. 'Try these for size.'

I put the cap on, thread my hair out the back in a ponytail.

'And this.' It's a tube of sunscreen.

'Thanks. Thoughtful of you.' I smear it on, then try the goggles. They're more like sunglasses, with leather seals on the sides and an elasticised strap. They make me feel a little steampunk.

We get moving, heading north, the channel of the empty river to our left, a low ridge, stone-tipped, to our right. The land is flat, the sun unrelenting, but the momentum of the bikes creates its own breeze. The air is dry on my skin despite the sunscreen. I'll need half a bucket of moisturiser tonight.

We reach a couple of low trees, anomalies in the landscape, a group of cattle lounging underneath. They regard us as we pass. A little further on we come to a windmill, a trough of water, more cattle loitering nearby. Ahead of me, Jamie stops, checking something.

'Where's this water from?' I ask.

'A bore. An aquifer.'

'The Great Artesian Basin?' I ask. 'Still pumping?'

'You're well informed. There are bores about the place, even a few natural springs. Come a proper drought, when there's no rain and no floods, it's the water of last resort. The difference between survival and ruin.' He scoops a little water into his hands, tastes it. 'Not bad. Bit salty, but that's probably the cows.'

I can hear the challenge: will I taste it, or does the idea of sharing a trough with the livestock put me off? It does, of course, but I'm not going to let him know that. I get off the bike, dip my own cupped hands in the trough, take a tentative sip. He's right. It doesn't taste so bad. I splash more water over my head; it feels good.

In front of me, unabashed, he strips off his shirt, dunks it in the trough, puts it back on. I can see his sleek torso. He catches me looking, but I'm not about to apologise. I gave that up long ago. 'If you like, I can turn my back,' he offers, glancing at the trough.

I smile at that. I'm not sure if it's another challenge, if he's being pervy, or if he's being polite. 'That's okay.'

I go to the trough, use the trucker cap as a ladle and splash myself thoroughly, until I'm as drenched as him, glad of my bra's utilitarian styling.

Back on the bikes, the wind is almost cold for the few minutes it takes my shirt to dry.

We reach a gate in a fence line that runs off into the shimmering horizon. It's the first fence I recall seeing since we left those circling the homestead and outbuildings. I wonder if there are paddocks out here. There must be. I make a mental note to ask.

The riverbed is ill defined, more a series of channels, but as we make our way north they combine into a single distinct channel. Off to the west is a vast clay pan, sand gathered at its edges. An ephemeral lake. Past the lake, the ground begins to rise ever so slightly, and the blur of the horizon has diminished, defined by ridges of red stone, similar to the one backing onto my foreman's cottage.

Jamie eases his quad bike into the dried riverbed itself. He rides the bike like he might a horse, standing in the stirrups. There's nothing but coarse gravel and fine sand in the channel, and I find it a challenge to imagine any water in it. While Jamie waits for me to follow, he checks his phone. 'Not far,' he yells, and heads off again. I wait for him to get a hundred metres or so ahead and round a bend before following. Now we need to travel in single file, I refuse to eat his dust.

A few kilometres further, and I brake; Jamie is heading back towards me. He pulls up. 'It's almost here.' He points. 'Time to get the bikes out of harm's way.'

We ride them up, then walk back into the riverbed. The water comes frothing towards us, and we jog ahead of it. It's moving at not much more than walking pace and is just a few centimetres deep. It looks dirty and dark, pushing debris before it, straw and sticks and leaf litter.

We clamber up a bank, ankle high, then move up onto some rocks to watch it pass.

'Amazing,' I say. 'How long until it gets to Longchamp?'

'Be there by tonight, I'd reckon. It'll slow down a bit first, start filling Lake Murdoch, and slow again after passing the station. That's where the country flattens, where the water will spread. It'll be quite the sight.'

We sit in wonder, watching it. The heat is as fundamental as ever, but there's something in the sight of the moving water that is cooling. Now the initial surge has passed, the water looks a little clearer. Jamie steps forward, fills his hat, drenches himself. This time I don't follow his example.

He returns to sit beside me. I'm enjoying the quiet, experiencing the passing water, when he speaks. 'Is it true? What they say about you?'

I can't believe it. Not this, not now. I stare at him, and I feel the old anger. Just when I was living in the moment; just when I wasn't thinking about myself. Or them. I search his face, then I look away, back to the water. 'You watched the video,' I say.

He says nothing, and I turn to him once again. He's looking at his shoes, snapping a twig into pieces. Perhaps he's embarrassed, or perhaps it's just the sun and the dry wind reddening his face.

'I wish it wasn't, but yeah, it's true,' I say. I'm not about to lie.

'Why?' It's almost a whisper, barely audible. Only after he asks the question does he look me in the eye.

I sigh, but I don't avert my gaze. 'Another time, Jamie.' I don't owe him an explanation; I don't owe anyone an explanation. I stand up, brush the dirt from my bum. 'Thanks for showing me this. We should be getting back. I've got a book to write.'

chapter twelve
MARTIN

MARTIN IS FEELING TRAPPED, FRUSTRATED. THE SUN IS DOWN, AND NIGHT IS
falling. He eats a lonely hamburger in the pub. Unlike the previous
night, the place is all but empty. The grey nomads are nowhere to
be seen and the Telstra crew have drunk themselves into oblivion.
He's grateful for the quiet. But back in his room, there is nothing.
No phone, no internet. Just the television, with nothing on. He
leaves it on ABC News 24, volume low, pretending he's staying
informed but really just for the company. He's relieved news of
the 'gas leak explosion' at Port Silver has washed through the
news cycle.

Restless, he walks down to the river. It's hard to believe it
will actually fill. The ground, muddy and waterlogged just this
morning, has miraculously dried, as if the rain had never been.
With nightfall almost complete, the heat is starting to leach out
of the land and the flies have finally dispersed. A full moon is on
the rise, full and shimmering, the golden glow transitioning to
silver as it lifts clear of the horizon. Somewhere, Mandy will be
able to see the same moon. He hopes for the hundredth time she

is all right, she and Liam. He feels a pang of guilt for bringing this down upon them.

Returning to his room, he studies his maps. The road will open tomorrow and the parts for the telephone tower will arrive soon enough. Is he really better off here, protected by the locals? He's not sure how much faith he can place in that, not if they're up against a professional hit squad. Maybe he'd be better served following Jack Goffing's advice: get in his car and start driving.

He must have drowsed off; the next thing he knows, he's woken by knocking on the door, soft at first but insistent. Coming fully awake, Martin looks about him: he's trapped. The knocking persists; he has little option. He cracks the door open.

A figure dressed in black, face in the shadows. 'Evening.'

For just a moment, panic wells, as the man takes a step forward into the light spilling from the room. Merriman Stanton.

'What do you want?' asks Martin.

'Let's go.'

'Where?'

'Get your boots on. We're in the truck.'

Martin closes the door. Wonders if he has a choice. Not much of one. He dons his boots. Stanton is a local, a landowner. Not mafia, not a killer. Not likely to be delivering Martin to an assassin. They've offered him a story: is that what this is about?

Outside the moon is high in the sky, a glowing sphere, the brightest silver-white, bathing the landscape in a milky translucence. There is no wind, yet it's pleasantly cool. The moon's position, almost overhead, suggests it must be approaching midnight.

Merriman is leaning against a large four-wheel drive, a Nissan Patrol, with a roo bar that could ram a battleship and a pair of

VHF antennas that could broadcast to Jupiter. Merriman shakes his hand, bone-crusher grip.

'Ride in the front with me,' instructs the grazier.

'The roads?' asks Martin.

'Dry enough,' says Merriman. 'We know the country.'

'Where we going?'

'You'll see.'

Martin climbs in. The cabin lights are off, but he sees two men in the back seat. 'G'day,' says one; the other merely lifts his chin in acknowledgement.

'My boys,' explains Merriman. 'Lachie and Punt.'

They head east out of town, across the bridge, then turn left onto what Martin knows is called the Sundowner Track, heading north towards the Queensland border. The track is graded, but that's all, and not for some time judging from the periodic corrugations that rattle the vehicle. It's not wide or smooth like the road from Bourke: more of a track. Yet the massive four-wheel drive makes easy work of it, the driving lights flooding the way. Small animals scurry away or freeze, eyes catching the lights like silver dollars. Merriman takes it easy, as if there is no hurry.

'How far?' asks Martin.

'Skip and a jump,' says the grazier, before adding, 'Not quite two hundred clicks. Two and a half hours.'

They cross over a cattle grid, through a fence line. This must be someone's property, but there is no fencing alongside the road. Sure enough, Martin sees cattle, standing like cardboard cut-outs perhaps sleeping. There are goats and there are kangaroos, western reds. Lizards. A bat. They pass over another grid, through another fence line. There is no traffic, no tracks to indicate anyone has passed this way since the rain. The road carves across a clay pan; the harsh contrast of the driving lights makes it look like the lunar surface.

There is a sat nav map on the console. It shows the road and the car and nothing else. According to the display, the landscape is featureless, but from the windows he can see stunted trees and sand dunes, a low ridge of sandstone to their right, and to their left the riverbed, every now and then the lights catching the gleam of a waterhole or a grouping of trees, as if they have come together for an after-dark natter. There are low rises, a single-lane bridge, dips. A rusted sign bearing a coat of arms, tilting precariously, punctuated by bullet holes: ROADS TO RECOVERY—A FEDERAL GOVERN-MENT INITIATIVE.

They traverse a sharp dip in the track and Merriman, silent for the past half-hour, speaks: 'These gullies, they're dry creeks. Channels. A day or two they'll be full of water. Impassable if the flood is big enough. That's why we need to get up and back tonight.'

'The flood?'

'Aye, the flood.'

They come to a stop and Merriman cuts the driving lights, then the engine. Martin gets one last look at the sat nav—still nothing. They are alone in the darkness of the plain. The doors open. They're in the middle of nowhere. Again the panic in his chest, but he pushes through it. If they want to kill him, there's nothing he can do about it.

'Why are we stopping?' he asks.

'Don't want to get too close. They'll see the lights, hear the engine. It's just over the next rise.'

Martin looks ahead of him. He can't see a rise, although the horizon seems closer. To the left is a fence, a corner post, the barbed wire running off in one direction towards the river and in another beside the road. The start of someone's property. He can't help but feel admiration for the people who live here: they know the landscape so well, see things he struggles to perceive even when they're pointed out to him.

Merriman hands him a torch. 'Don't use it unless you have to.'

They move forward on foot, following the track, Martin's eyes growing more accustomed to the moonlight. On some other night, it would be magical, the landscape bathed in the lunar glow. He imagines what it might be like to live his alibi on a moonless night, the Milky Way sprayed across the dome: to camp beneath the stars, capture them with a camera. As it is, the moonlight is so bright he believes he can make out colours: the red of the earth, the blue of Merriman Stanton's shirt.

They walk along a little way, up, then along, then up again. They reach a gate in the fence, left open, above a cattle grid. There's a sign, black lettering on white. In the clarity of the moonlight it's not difficult to read: LONGCHAMP DOWNS.

'Southern entrance,' says Merriman. 'Not used much. Main drive is further north, leads out to Eulo.'

They scramble across the grid, Martin concentrating hard, the steel bars slippery, and keep going along a low ridge.

Merriman stops, points. 'Look.'

Martin follows the direction of his arm. Ahead, to the left, water is rippling in the moonlight, moving slowly south.

'We won't get trapped here?' asks Martin.

The grazier doesn't answer for a beat, as if calculating. 'No. We'll be okay. See what we need to see, witness what we need to witness, then get out. Take us no time.'

They walk on and, from out of the night like a constellation that has dipped below the horizon, Martin sees lights in the distance. 'What is it?' he asks.

'Longchamp Downs. The manager's house and farm sheds. Not far now.'

They keep moving and Martin sees the point of their venture, opening up before him. Spreading out across the plain is a veritable lake, shimmering in the moonlight.

'You see it?' asks Punt.

'Couldn't miss it,' says Martin.

'There's your story,' says the father. 'Illegal. Harvesting the flood plain. Stealing the water, denying us our due.'

'Cunts,' says the other boy, Lachie, who spits into the dust.

'Explain it to me,' says Martin. 'What's wrong here. Where the water should be going.'

'It's coming down from the north, contained in a channel. Gets to a bit north of here, land flattens, a few ephemeral lakes form. Lake Murdoch. Water spreads out into them, onto the flood plain. Nothing to complain about there; it's the natural landscape. It's why Longchamp is here, why it was settled in the first place. Those buildings over there, where you can see the lights, they're on higher ground, above even a record-breaking flood. This is nowhere near record-breaking. But that water you can see there, that's not natural. It's been held back and diverted by the new road I showed you on the laptop. That old bastard Clay Carmichael has bulldozed it across the flood plain.'

Martin stares hard, can just make out the road, a hard line bisecting the plain, the glimmering water to the north, the dark earth to the south.

'Where's the road going?' he asks. 'Could there be a bona fide reason?'

Merriman laughs, a bitter guffaw. 'There'll be some excuse, no doubt. But he's lived here his entire life and hasn't needed such a road before. He knows the impact. Knows the law. He could build the road, put culverts in the channel, let the water flow uninterrupted. But see for yourself. The water is backing up, getting diverted.'

'Surely you can complain to the authorities?'

'He'll only hold the water for a day or two, long enough to thoroughly soak the soil. By the time any official gets out here, the culverts will be open again.'

While they've talked, Lachie has been assembling something, guided by the subdued light of his phone. A drone.

'We'll take it up,' says Merriman. 'Give you a much better insight into the lay of the land. And get you some photos. Evidence, images to go with your scoop.'

Martin feels a thrill, the pulse of an exclusive. The man is right: this will make a great article. Not just the images and the underlying issues, but recounting the clandestine journey through the night, on an undercover mission to expose malfeasance. It'll make a bloody good magazine piece if the pictures are as good as he hopes. For a moment, all thoughts of assassins, of being on the run, are forgotten.

Lachie gets the drone airborne, its rotors whirring noisily in the quiet of the night. The young man is guiding it with his phone and quickly sends it skywards; soon it is barely audible. Any lights have been disabled, and it's invisible against the night sky. Martin moves next to the lad, peering at the phone screen, which shows the images from the drone's camera. It must be extremely light-sensitive, as the land glows.

'I'll take it right up, get as high as I can, widest angle of view,' says the pilot, not looking at the others but concentrating on the screen. His fingers flick at the controls, spinning the machine. 'I'll take it back a bit, so we get the moon on the water.' He does what he says, reversing the drone, tilting the camera down as he goes, and suddenly the landscape is revealed, the extent of the water, spreading out to the west, filling the frame to the north, a lake.

'Fucking gigalitres,' says the father.

'Here,' says Lachie. 'Over there. Those lights, that's the farm buildings. The water coming down the riverbed. And here's the road.'

Martin can see it perfectly, glowing light on the top half of the frame, blackness in the lower half, like the sky floating above the earth.

There is a clicking sound from the phone as Lachie takes photographs. 'I'll get some video in a moment.'

'Let's see where the road leads,' suggests Martin. 'See if there's any excuse for it. Might come in handy when I challenge him.'

'Got it,' says Lachie.

'Don't want to stay here any longer than we have to,' cautions Merriman.

Lachie takes the drone along the line between road and water. As the lake leaves the frame, the sensitivity of the camera intensifies and, although grainy, the moonlight is powerful enough to discern a few details. The road leads to a cluster of outbuildings.

'What are they?' he asks.

'Old shearers' quarters—abandoned,' says Merriman, peering at the screen.

But even as he speaks, the camera picks up a light. As they watch, a shape moves into view, a person, a thin illumination in front of them, torchlight.

'Someone's out there,' Lachie says.

'Makes no difference,' Merriman says. 'But bring it back. We've got enough.'

'Video?'

'Okay. Just one pass. Keep it high.'

Martin averts his gaze from the screen, letting the pilot do his job. Instead, he stares out across the glowing land to the shimmering water. He can just make out the buildings in the distance, the old shearing shed looming large. He can see the rocky ridge, black against the moon-washed sky. Does he imagine it, or just for an instant, does he see a flickering light on the ridge?

So he's looking in the right direction when the first explosion rips through the road, a flash of orange light, bright against the monochrome, followed by the crump of the shock wave, followed by a second detonation a little further along.

'What the fuck?' says Lachie.

'Get it down!' his father barks. 'We've got to get out of here.'

Martin is caught staring, staring at the water rushing down through the gaps in the road, released from the dam.

'Not so quick, cunts.'

The voice comes from behind. Martin turns to look. But he's blinded by floodlights directed straight into his eyes. His hands come up to shield them, even as he hears the rifle shot.

chapter thirteen

MARTIN KEEPS HIS HANDS UP, SHIELDING HIS EYES, BUT IT'S NO GOOD—HE still can't make out much against the glare of the lights, just the vague outlines of two or three men. Beside him, Merriman and Punt are standing with their hands raised. The sound of the gunshot is still ringing in his ears.

'You,' says a disembodied voice. 'You with the drone. Bring it in. Land it.'

Lachie says nothing, but in the silence, Martin can hear the telltale buzz of the approaching drone. It drops down to a metre above the ground, then eases to rest, rotors falling silent.

'Those explosions are nothing to do with us,' says Merriman, defiance in his voice.

'Tell it to the judge.'

A man emerges from the lights, a young man, sandy hair. Wearing gloves. He picks up the drone without a word, returns behind the dazzling lights.

'Get it all on camera then, did you?' asks the voice.

'Is that you, Clay, you old bastard?' asks Merriman.

The man laughs, doesn't answer, addressing Lachie instead. 'Stand with the others. Hands on your heads, all of you.' Another rifle shot into the night. Martin sees the muzzle flash. There is no echo; there is nothing for sounds to bounce off out here. He puts his hands on his head.

'Tell us your names.'

'What? Why?' demands Merriman.

'Then we let you go.'

'You filming us?' asks Punt.

'Names,' says the voice.

'Richard Stanton,' says Punt, earning a glare from his father. Nevertheless, the older man follows suit. 'Merriman Stanton.'

'Lachlan Stanton,' says the other son, voice surly.

Martin stares into the light. He considers giving the false name he used to check into the Port Paroo Hotel: Jake Solander. But if the men are filming, they might be gathering evidence, building a case to present to the police. And giving a false name would only dig his hole deeper. 'Martin Scarsden. And it's important that—'

Another gunshot, as effective a punctuation mark as possible.

'Okay, now fuck off,' says the man with the rifle.

'You haven't heard the last of this,' spits Merriman.

'Let's go, Dad,' says Punt. 'The water. The creeks.'

Merriman grunts but starts moving, the others following.

'We'll get the truck,' says Lachie, he and his brother sprinting ahead, Martin and Merriman jogging behind. Martin's eyes are readjusting to the darkness, the moonlight again taking hold after the glaring spotlights. He can see water off to the right, the pent-up pressure of the artificial dam propelling it.

'That wasn't you, was it?' he asks Merriman. 'The explosion?'

'Fuck no. Why would I bring you if I was going to do that?' says the southerner breathing hard.

'Knew we were coming?' asks Martin.

'Must have done.'

They get to the cattle grid, the gate out of Longchamp Downs, clamber quickly across. Lights appear, the sound of the truck. It roars up to them, the driver swinging close.

'In the back,' says Merriman.

Martin clambers in next to Punt, the father in the front, Lachie driving, the truck moving before Martin has the door closed.

They drive hard and fast, lights carving away the darkness. Martin gets his seatbelt on, feels a surge of nausea as the truck drifts and brakes and lurches through the night. They get to a creek line, cross through the gathering water, still shallow enough for easy passage.

Merriman has his window open, assessing the flow. 'Good lad, we're getting ahead of it.'

Another couple of kilometres and they reach another crossing, still parched. Lachie eases off the accelerator. The tension inside the cab notches down.

'Everyone okay?' Merriman asks. 'Martin? Punt?'

'All good,' says Punt.

'No problem,' says Martin, cracking hardy.

Lachie continues on at a much more moderate pace. Now they're ahead of the flood, there's no longer any need to rush.

'What just happened?' Martin asks.

'A setup,' says Merriman. 'Payback.'

'So I gathered,' says Martin. 'But why?'

'History,' says Merriman.

'The feud?'

'Got it in one. Back in the day—after the Second World War—the Carmichaels built a dam, a turkey nest dam. Stantons blew it up. Dynamite.'

'Jesus,' says Martin. 'Did the cops get involved?'

'No. There was no proof it was us. And besides, the dam was illegal.'

'But they knew it was you?'

Merriman says nothing for a while, and then, 'Every grazier south of the border benefitted.'

'So this time, tonight, why didn't you blow it up? What's changed?'

'You. We thought media exposure might achieve what dynamite couldn't.'

'Last night, in the pub, you and your sons were roughing up that lad from Queensland.'

'He was boasting. Some shit about the river course being diverted.'

'Goading you?'

'Yeah. Baiting the hook.'

Martin stares out into the night, the moon impassive. 'If the dam is illegal, what do they gain? Why would they call the police?' But the men don't answer, and Martin is left with his thoughts and the uneasy feeling he is missing something.

chapter fourteen
ECCO

I'M NOT SURE HOW I KNOW THE WATER HAS COME. I'D BROUGHT PATRICK Murdoch's three diaries back from the homestead with me, plus a couple of ledgers from his time at Longchamp, intending to delve further into the coming of Hentig and Stuart. But I was too exhausted, drained by the heat of the day, the trip up the river with Jamie. So I went to bed early.

And then, suddenly, I'm awake. Something has changed.

Outside, the night is perfectly still. A full moon hangs unmoving in the sky, a giant lantern, so bright it's almost fizzing, flooding the landscape with light. And there, before me, the water, spreading silently, filling the plain, the moonlight playing on its surface like a spell. I stand for a moment, bewitched.

I climb the low ridge behind the foreman's cottage, scrambling up over the rocks, still warm from the heat of the day. The outcrop is not high, just a few metres at most, but high enough to present a panorama: the foreman's cottage before me, the darkened shearers' quarters behind it, and the looming bulk of the shearing shed. In the distance, the homestead and manager's house sit under the next ridge, connected to me by the thread of the newly constructed road. And backing up behind the connection, illuminated by the glowing moon, the water's stealthy ink. Black and silver. The flood, come to Longchamp Downs. I watch, mesmerised by the gentle inundation. I see a duck land, its wake delineated by silver-black ripples, followed by two more. Ducks, in the desert, in the night. How could they possibly know this would be? And still the silence persists, as if the world is in awe.

The vista is somehow fragrant, the scent elusive in the cooling night. I sit on the outcrop, watching, my eyes becoming more and more accustomed to the half-light.

I hear something, some sound carrying across the water, every little thing amplified in the darkened quiet. On the far side of the water I can just make out the shapes of people walking beside the new lake, near where the road crosses the river course. It must be Clay and Jamie. I think of standing, yelling, shining my phone, but why should I? It's better to be alone, to witness this by myself, to cherish the experience. So I sit and observe, words forming themselves in my head, rehearsing the descriptive passage I can use in the book. The arrival of the water will breathe life into the narrative, just as it's breathing life into the land, just as it's breathing life into my time here.

The men are still there, walking the road. I wonder what they're doing: perhaps supervising the flood, admiring its progress.

The water has reached the bottom of the ridge now, lapping at its base. I know I'm safe up here, the path to the outbuilding elevated enough, a sheet of steel over a tiny gully, feeding the water off beyond the ridge. There is nothing threatening about this newborn lake. The road seems unaffected, high enough to avoid inundation. I am again amazed at the clarity of the night.

The air is growing cooler, but I don't want to return to the cottage. This is something special, a once-in-a-decade occurrence for those who live here, once in a lifetime for me. So I sit and watch, mesmerised by the slow-motion drama. And fall asleep, nestled into the warmth of the rocks, cushioned by their residual heat. How long do I sleep? I can't be sure. A few minutes? An hour? Enough for a chill to enter my bones, the heat draining off into the cloudless sky. I stretch, stiff from my awkward position. The moon is higher, past its zenith, heading west. I check the time on my phone. Past two in the morning. It was almost midnight when Martin left Port Paroo. Below me, the lake has filled out. I stand and try to photograph it. In the noiseless night, I hear a buzzing. It sounds like it's coming from above me, but I can detect nothing in the night sky. I see the ducks floating. More of them now. A flotilla. I wonder if the buzzing sound is insects, beetles perhaps, attracted by the water.

And then the night erupts. It's so abrupt, I almost fall—not from the blast, but from the surprise. An explosion, caught by the corner of my eye, an intense flash, a flume of dirt and water, and the sound, deafening in its intensity, thundering across the plain. And then a second, flaring orange and red against the monochrome of the night. There is the sound of debris landing in the water, like rain, sending ripples. And on the far side of the newborn lake, downstream, driving lights, like small suns, spreading out, reflecting from the surface. I crouch down, as if they might be searching for me. A gunshot, staccato in the night. A gunshot— what could that mean? There are three men, no four, silhouetted in the driving lights. They're tiny. I can't tell if they're facing me or have their backs to me. Another gunshot. I watch with mounting horror as three of them place their hands on their heads.

The other one is doing something I can't see, and then I catch a glimpse of an object in the driving lights. A bird? And then the buzzing stops, and I realise it must be a drone landing. A person walking out of the darkness to retrieve it. It's almost a kilometre away, I can see no detail, the men mainly backlit, but there is something familiar in the movement: is that Jamie, walking into the light, retrieving the drone?

What am I witnessing? I can't comprehend it, my ears still ringing with the sound of the detonations, my retinas still flaring from staring into the driving lights. Interlopers destroying the road, freeing the waters, then caught in the act? By whom? Clay and Jamie? Who else could it be?

And then, as I'm still trying to catch up, a third gunshot. A minute more and the lights go out, like the curtain falling at the end of a play. I peer into the darkness, unsettled, as my eyes, still dazzled by the lights, struggle to adapt to the moonlight.

I can see lights on at the homestead now, some movement there. I can't remember if that's a new development or not. A distant crackle; I wonder if it's the VHF radio.

Back where the confrontation took place, I can just make out dark shapes hurrying south. It's the four men. So they've been let go. I breathe easier: after the gunshots, when they were standing with their hands on their heads, I'd feared the worst, that I was witnessing something terrifying, something from a foreign war. Behind the men, I can discern a vehicle parked where the men were illuminated. It must have been the source of the lights. Now it drives back towards the homestead, headlights low, maybe just the parking lights. No, not towards the homestead. It turns onto the road across the lake, my road, moving ever so slowly. I don't know why, but again I lower myself, squatting amid the rocks, not wanting to be seen. I don't want to be a witness, don't want to be involved in things I don't understand. That's not why I'm here. The truck inches along the road, then stops. A man gets out, holding a torch, and examines the damage wrought by the explosions. He's caught in the lights. No doubt this time: it's Jamie. He gets back in the truck. For a moment I fear they will drive on, through the breach in the road, seeking me. Instead, the truck gradually reverses back the way it came. It reaches the beginning of the road, then turns and drives towards the manager's house.

Only then do I descend from the ridge, past the cottage, along the road. Already the water is receding, pouring down through the holes in the track. I stand watching, wondering again what has happened here. Then I return to the cottage. I make sure the curtains are drawn before switching on the lights. Not that it matters. I'm already concocting my story: minimising what I have seen. If Clay and Jamie want to tell me, that's fine. Maybe I can use it to add colour to the book. A breakout box. But I don't want it to distract me; I want to concentrate on the fate of Arthur Hentig and Donald Stuart.

2001

FRIDAY, 21 DECEMBER

*I'm going to write it all down, every moment, every little thing,
because I never want to forget what happened. I want to remember
it all. Even the shit bits.*

*When summer came, Vincent and I were forced to come home.
Not literally forced, but it's coming up to Christmas, and we couldn't
leave Dad alone at Longchamp. Even Mrs Enright will be off to visit
her sister in Sydney.*

*Vincent had the shits. He'd been invited to go sailing in Vanuatu
with the Strath Mortons, but Dad had vetoed it, saying we couldn't
afford it, that the drought is getting worse and worse, so bad he might
have to let the manager go. I thought Vincent was a bit petulant,
although I can understand his frustration. I wish I had a rich friend
like Eric Strath Morton.*

'Can't we just sell a few cows?' Vincent suggested.

*'They're skin and bones,' Dad said. 'Everyone's selling, arse has fallen
out of the market. And we've already destocked as much as I dare.'*

'Maybe sell options on them then,' Vincent proposed. 'Like pork bellies. Hamburger futures.'

Dad gave him a withering look, the sort he reserves for vermin like dingoes, rabbits and politicians. 'Things are bad enough. I'm not going to start gambling with your future.'

I remembered the dead steer blocking the road to Port Paroo and I wondered who'd be mad enough to stump up money for a half-starved cow. There's no feed at all, and the river by the homestead has been reduced to nothing more than a series of fetid waterholes. Lake Murdoch is a massive clay pan, more like the surface of a frying pan than a potential body of water.

Vincent and I decided that, come January, we'd escape to the beach. Pay for the tickets out of our savings. Find work, waiting tables or washing dishes. Or in a store selling t-shirts and tea towels and souvenir spoons. Stay in a backpackers and enjoy ourselves a bit before heading back to school. I thought I'd returned home prepared this holiday: books to read, sketching, box sets of DVDs borrowed from the school library. Diary-keeping and plans on riding. But just one week back, I still hadn't written a thing in this diary because there was nothing to write about. Boredom was setting in, like concrete curing in the sun.

When I'm at school down at Southport, I always imagine Longchamp is better: no uniforms, no teachers, no homework, no one to boss you around. No hierarchy, no pecking order, no bitches. No shit food, Mrs Enright even asking us what we might like to eat. But when I get home, school suddenly seems like the more attractive option: friends, gossip, the beach. The beach, the beach, the beach. Sneaking out. Cigarettes and booze. Parties. Boys.

Still, I do appreciate Longchamp. Maybe because I know I won't end up here. One more year and school will be done with and I'll head to uni. Or take a gap year: live in Brisbane, save money, go overseas.

Go to London. Not Madame Tussauds and the Tower of London and Cats, *but the Tate and the British Museum and the V & A during the day, and pubs and nightclubs and parties at night. I daydream about it constantly. It's different for Vincent: his future is all laid out for him. He'll do ag college, then come back and help Dad. On-the-job training. And at some point, he'll take over. Strictly speaking, being eight minutes older than him, I should have a prior claim, but everyone knows that isn't how it works. He's a bloke. Not that I'm complaining. I love the place: I love the landscape, the light, the smell of it after rain. But livestock? If I ever see another sheep or cow it will be too soon. Or however that saying goes.*

So I was here, boredom creeping, when I got the call from Maz. Come down, she said. Bring Vincent. She reckoned her mum was sober, the place was semi-functional. I was all for it. It had been such fun last time, despite Maz's crazy mother. At least the pub would have people passing through, even in the middle of summer, tourists and a few locals. Maz told us to get down as soon as we could; there was a party that weekend down near Nyngan, an eighteenth birthday, out at a property called Sunderby. A boy named Michael Ferguson, but everyone called him Massey, like the tractors.

Dad said it was okay, provided we were back for Christmas. I suspect he's feeling guilty for making us spend the holidays at home.

Anyway, Vincent and I both have our Ps now, and we drove the Sundowner Track to Port Paroo. The country is looking utterly cooked. We got to where the steer had died in the middle of the road. There was no sign of it, of course. I was just about to say something, make a joke, when I saw a dead wedge-tail, a mess of feathers beside the road, just a single crow pecking.

'Fucking hell,' said Vincent.

'They're calling it the Millennium Drought,' I said.

Vincent laughed, a kind of scoffing sound. 'I tell the guys at school we're on sixty thousand acres. Impresses the hell out of them. Same size property as the Strath Mortons.'

The Strath Mortons are on the Liverpool Plains. Beautiful country. Deep volcanic soil and plenty of rain or, failing that, plenty of groundwater. Must be worth fifty times as much as Longchamp Downs. Even in a good year, we're two-thirds desert and one third dependent on the Paroo.

'Not worth shit, is it?' Vincent said, flicking his head out towards the empty river and beyond. I guess we were still on our land; it's hard to know sometimes.

'It will be when it floods,' I said.

'Sure,' he said, unconvinced.

I looked out the window of the old Toyota for some sign of hope, but found nothing. I started counting skulls for something to do.

But the pub was fun. Maz's mum was on the wagon, so we didn't have to run the place like last time. We still pitched in, though. We're helping do up the annexe so it can take guests again.

The day of the party, we drove down to Nyngan in our faithful truck, three abreast in the front. A four-hour drive, but it went quickly. We were lucky, the weather wasn't so bad. Dry, of course, but probably not much above thirty. We talked most of the way, and occasionally played music. We had the boom box plugged in, sitting on the shelf behind us, and every now and then we'd fire it up, playing our mix tapes, singing along. It was good to have Maz with us. I think she's rather taken with Vincent, or possibly the other way round. She was squeezed in between the two of us, but didn't seem to mind at all.

The party seemed pretty low-key when we got there. It was still late afternoon and many of the locals were leaving it until later to show up. Massey had a bunch of mates out from school, so it was kind of a pre-party. He was a Kings boy. Strange how country kids in New South Wales go to school in Sydney and we head to the Gold Coast or Brisbane. Vincent knew someone, but Maz and I were on the outer. Not that it mattered, everyone was super friendly.

We were out at the shearing shed. It still stank a bit from the spring, but that was okay. Most of us were from the bush anyway and weren't bothered. There was a band, but it was just Massey's big brother and some of his mates, not a proper group. They only knew about five songs, and the singer couldn't hold a tune. But once the band had finished mangling its limited repertoire, it turned into a raucous karaoke, which was more fun.

Vincent was standing by a keg, drinking beer and talking about the markets with a couple of like-minded nerds. I can't do either; day drinking does my head in, and so does economics. Normally, he's such a quiet guy, but he was really fired up, getting enthusiastic. Good for him. One thing about Vincent, he's a happy drunk. I like that about him. Not picking fights and showing off, like half the blokes our age, full of piss and wind.

I wandered off to sit by the creek. I wasn't upset or anything like that; I just needed a break. It had already been a big day, with the long drive, all that talking and singing, and then the effort of making small talk with strangers.

I was sitting by the creek—which actually had water in it, a real creek, with willows and other trees, not just a gully eroded through a paddock—when Roman Stanton walked up to me. Just like that. I didn't even know he was at the party.

'Chloe? Is that you?'

'Roman, hi.'

'You all right?'

'Fine. Just having a breather.'

I felt his eyes on me and my heart fluttered. Seriously, it was like a butterfly trapped inside my rib cage.

'Mind if I join you?' he asked. He wasn't drunk like some of the others. Then again, he wasn't a schoolboy.

'Sure,' I said, and my heart fluttered some more.

He sat down, not too close, and we just stayed like that for a while, looking out across this creek. The sun was beginning to set, catching a band of clouds above the horizon, flaring their edges gold. I was fiddling with a straw, and he picked up a pebble and tried to skim it on the water while sitting down. It kind of plopped in and didn't skim at all.

'Nice try,' I said.

'Years of practice,' he said.

And I laughed, and he laughed, and the tension eased a little.

I'm not sure how long we sat there without speaking, side by side, but it was probably only a minute or two. And then we were talking, innocuous stuff, just making conversation. He told me one of his mates from uni in Armidale was Massey's big brother, the one in the band, and that's how he ended up here. I talked about my school, he recollected his: teachers, the good ones, the bastards and the creeps. Pranks kids play. The cliques: the jocks and the swots and the nerds and the goths and the druggies. And soon we were laughing, and the longer we talked, the more comfortable I was feeling, and the more we were looking at each other and the less we were looking into the creek or across it to where the sun was turning the clouds all sorts of hues. I liked his eyes. Mine are blue and boring, regular, like Dad's, and Vincent's are brown, like Mum's, but I saw that Roman's are kind of hazel, flecked with darker shades and lighter shades, little shards of green. Amazing eyes. And beside them, smile lines. Not just from squinting, but smiling, I could tell by the way they compressed when he laughed. *I always like people with smile lines, particularly young people, because you know they're not just wrinkles from getting old.*

And then, for no reason I can put my finger on, we were quiet again. Maybe we'd just run out of anecdotes, or I was too busy studying his eyes to think of anything new to say. But just as it was getting awkward, two black cockatoos came wheeling past, following the creek line.

'God, I love them,' I said. 'My favourite birds.'

'Me too,' he said. 'Rare to see them so far west.'

We watched them go past, squealing as they went, sounding as prehistoric as they looked.

'In Native American culture, everyone has their own totem animal,' Roman said, his voice kind of faraway. 'I think if I had one, it would be the black cockatoo.'

I kissed him then. I didn't plan to, didn't think about it, it just happened. There was no lingering gaze, no hesitant move towards each other. I just leant across and kissed him. On the mouth. Not just brushing lips, but a proper kiss. Then I sat back and looked at him, to see his reaction.

His eyes were wide, like twin sunsets. He looked away to the creek, and then immediately looked back. And he smiled. 'Wow,' he said.

So I kissed him again. And this time he kissed me back.

Sitting there with him, in that moment, I felt the pulse of life.

Nyngan. Massey Ferguson's eighteenth birthday party. I'll never forget it.

FRIDAY

chapter fifteen
ECCO

I CAN'T BELIEVE IT; I'VE SLEPT IN, ONLY AWOKEN BY THE SOUND OF A MACHINE revving outside my cottage. I put on a robe, walk out. The sun is like a scalpel, the coolness of the night long burnt off.

Jamie is there, sitting on his quad bike, engine idling.

'You okay?' he asks.

'Fine. What is it?' And I remember the events of last night, and suddenly I'm fully awake.

He takes a breath before responding, and I can sense him scrutinising my face. 'We had a bit of drama in the early hours.'

'I know. I saw.'

'Right.' He's squinting, expression stern. 'What did you see?' he asks.

Something about his attitude puts me on edge, like he's quizzing me.

I shrug, trying to act nonchalant. A small voice inside my head is warning me to tread carefully. 'I was asleep. Got woken up by two loud bangs. Really loud bangs. I thought it was thunder, like

Wednesday night. So I came outside to see if there was another storm, but there were no clouds, just the moon. It was really bright.' I'm keeping my voice hazy, as if this is inconsequential. 'That's right. Now I remember. I thought I heard gunshots. I think they were gunshots. Over there somewhere?' I wave vaguely towards the homestead and the manager's house. 'I thought it must be a roo shooter, taking advantage of the moon. Then I went back to bed. Why? What's the drama?'

Jamie is still regarding me intently, but his posture has lost some of its stiffness. I think he believes me.

'Some men came from the south, blew up the road between the homestead and here.' He turns and points.

'What? Why would they do that?'

'That's what we're trying to work out. Come on. Clay wants to see you.'

'Sure. Let me get dressed.'

I go back inside and splash water on my face, clean my teeth, get dressed, and all the while I'm wondering how I should play this. My gut is telling me to act ignorant, stick to the version I've just recounted. Whatever is going on, it's got nothing to do with me. I think of the Murdoch diaries, the tale of Hentig and Stuart. I don't want to do or say anything that might jeopardise my access to the diaries.

Back outside, Jamie has climbed off his bike and is standing in the shade of the building. I feel a little guilty; I should have invited him in out of the sun.

'The way across is a mess,' he says. 'We'll need to go the long way.'

'The long way?'

'Follow me,' and he climbs on his bike, starts it up.

I return inside to fetch the goggles he gave me yesterday and the trucker cap and some gloves. Only then do I climb on my own bike. He watches me, his sunglasses rendering him inscrutable.

Instead of turning east towards the homestead, he leads me the other way, heading west. We cross the low bridge made from steel sheets over the small gully I crossed during the night. I can see where water has flowed through a natural gap in the ridge. There's a family of goats, attracted by the smell of water.

Past the bridge, the road continues, an extension of the track between the homestead and my cottage, but an older road, not recently repaired. We move past the ridge line, emerging onto a wide plain of red dirt and saltbush, a few mulga trees dotted here and there. In the distance I can see what appears to be another ridge, running north to south, parallel to the one we've just passed. Jamie pauses for a moment, then gives a thumbs-up. I reciprocate the gesture, and he turns, following the road where it swings north, the ridge line now on our right.

Ahead I can see a tin shed, like a suburban garage, green steel, sitting in the middle of nowhere. And next to it, a wind sock, fluttering in the breeze. An airstrip. Jamie increases his speed and soon enough we get to the building and past it, and then we're on the runway itself, red dirt and orange pebbles, cleared from the scrub. Jamie doesn't pause, opening his throttle, racing ahead. I give him a few seconds and then follow, accelerating until I am going as fast as I dare, the wind whipping at my t-shirt and grabbing at my cap. It's exhilarating.

I take care slowing down, easing to a stop where Jamie is waiting for me at the end of the strip.

'That was such fun!' I say.

He smiles. 'Good. But we need to take it easy now. No more roads.'

He moves off, following what I think might be a remnant track, or maybe not. It's hard to tell. But the land is flat and stony, interspersed with wide expanses of red sand, held firm in places by saltbush. I see no cattle, no more man-made structures. I know the homestead and the other buildings, and the flowing Paroo, are on the far side of the ridge to our right, but there is no sign of them. We could be in the wilderness; lost in the deep desert. It's only our knowledge, our sense of place, tethering us to the built environment. On the edge of the great expanse, the empty heart of the country.

Eventually, we come to another lowering of the ridge, another natural gap, a fence line threading through it. I can see it this time, make sense of it, as if my eyes are learning to appreciate the incremental changes in the land, the subtle differences in elevation. We leave the sand, climb onto the red sandstone. Jamie is riding at a walking pace. I concentrate on moving forward, the bike handling easily enough, responding well to the brakes and the throttle and a turn of the handlebars. I see a fence pole, an old car wheel, the signs of a rudimentary track. I realise the ridge is a natural barrier, the gaps access points. But access to where? Does the flood ever reach beyond the ridge? We pass through it, and the home valley opens up. On this side the track is more evident, running before us.

Jamie stops, cuts his engine. I pull up next to him. He points further north. 'See the water up there?'

I can, shimmering like a mirage, made real by a phalanx of pelicans swooping in to land.

'Lake Murdoch. The whole reason Longchamp is here. Ephemeral. Fills when there's a flood. Turns into beautiful pasture.'

'I remember. Yesterday. The clay pan.'

'Filling up now.'

'And then dust for another few years.'

'You got it.'

'Natural?' I ask.

'Undeniably,' says Jamie, and I think I catch a smile.

'You like this, don't you?' I say. 'Getting out on the bikes. Into the middle of nowhere.'

'Shit yeah.'

He revs his engine, starts off, moving more quickly now we're on the track's firmer surface. We cross the plain, come to a proper bridge, made of solid wood, spanning the river. Beneath it the Paroo is flowing, looking like a real river, where only yesterday there was nothing. I stop, just to witness it. I climb off, take a photo with my phone, wish I'd taken more out beyond the ridge.

Past the bridge, we join a proper road, the driveway that leads from the Sundowner Track into Longchamp Downs. We turn right and travel at a steady speed towards the homestead, taking mere minutes where the journey up the far valley had taken an hour. Beside us, the river continues on its way. There is nothing green, not yet, but I can sense the promise. The air still smells of dust, but a new note has joined the outback fragrance.

We reach the homestead. The field beyond the river is a dark quagmire, the water from last night gone, the grey silt turned to black mud. I wonder how much has soaked in, whether it's enough, whether just a few hours of inundation will conjure much-needed pasture. Down along the track leading to the foreman's cottage, I can see a bobcat working, pushing earth, repairing the track.

Hopefully it will be fixed by the end of the day and the journey back to the foreman's cottage will be straightforward.

We leave the bikes and sit on the verandah to remove our boots.

'How serious is it?' I ask Jamie. 'The explosions?'

'Serious enough. Depends on how far Clay wants to take it.'

'Police?'

'I guess.'

We're about to go inside, when the man himself pulls up in a farm truck.

'Got across okay, then?' Clay asks Jamie.

'Came the long way, up past the airstrip.'

'Good call.'

'How's the track?' I ask. 'Much damage?'

'We're in luck. Bloke with the bobcat was already in Eulo. Should have it patched up by this evening. Jamie can go and give him a hand.'

'Goodo,' says Jamie, putting his boots back on.

'Thanks for fetching me,' I say to him.

'No sweat,' he says. Out here, the expression takes on a new significance.

Inside the homestead, Clay is eager to talk, wanting to know what I saw in the night, the detonation of the track.

I repeat my version of events, the same as I recounted to Jamie back at my cottage.

'And that's it? You saw nothing more? Heard nothing more?' demands Clay. He's on edge, unable to sit still.

'No. That's it. Jamie says it was southerners, that they came up here. Blew up the road.'

'So I believe,' says Clay.

'But why?' I ask. 'It seems so extreme.'

'Spreading lies. Claiming the track to your cottage is really a dam designed to harvest water and push it across the flood plain.'

'Really?' I ask, playing dumb. Because that's exactly the effect I witnessed from up on the ridge: the road impeding the flow, diverting the water. The evidence remains not far from where we sit, the muddy aftermath spread across Longchamp's land. 'Could it do that? Unintentionally?'

'It could. But when I upgraded the track, made it all-weather, I put culverts in under the road to ensure the flow. That's what they blew up, the culverts. Destroying the evidence. So they could continue making their fake claims against me.'

He's lying; I know he's lying. He must know that I know. And yet he sounds so convincing I almost believe him. I'm not about to challenge him, not directly, but I do encourage him to talk. 'Why would they do that? Why blow up the road if the water was making its way south anyway?'

Clay sighs, holds his hands wide, walks one way then another, powered by nervous energy. And then he comes to a halt, as if reaching some decision. Looks me in the eye. 'I'm planning to sell the property. You know that; everyone knows that. The Carmichaels will be gone. It will bring a hundred-year-old feud to an end between the Carmichaels and the Stantons, owners of Tavelly Station, south of the border.'

He spreads his arms. 'I've got to be honest. After I upgraded the road, I saw the opportunity to get in one last win before I sold. We'd put in the culverts to let the water pass through, as the law requires, but when I heard of the rain up north, the approaching flood, I was tempted to block the culverts, harvest the water. Not because it would do me any good; I've already sold most of my cattle. I don't have time to restock, fatten the calves and get them to market. Still, I was tempted to land one last blow. But in the end, I decided it was time to leave the feud behind, put it to rest.'

'So you didn't block the pipes under the track?'

'No.'

'If you're selling, why upgrade the road at all?'

He looks at me, studying my face, before answering: 'To guarantee all-weather access to the airfield. Agent thought it would make the place more attractive to a prospective buyer.'

I'm getting an inkling that there are things being left unsaid, that Clay is struggling with something, but I don't know what. 'So someone blocks the culverts without your knowledge. And then the Stantons come north, see what's happening and blow up the track.' I pause, trying to catch up with my own theorising. 'Such a quick response. Rather than demanding the culverts be cleared. Give you a chance.'

Clay laughs. 'It was them that blocked the culverts in the first place. Don't you see? Once it was dark and we were inside. They waited for the water to back up and photographed it, then they blew up the evidence.'

I can't help myself; I'm shaking my head, engaging. 'Even when they know you're planning to sell? What's the point?'

Clay looks into my eyes, seeing and unseeing, as if working through how to respond. And then he turns away, relenting. 'There's something you should know. Something I should have told you right from the start. I thought you would have found it out for yourself by now.' He draws breath, as if giving me the opportunity to respond, but I'm clueless. 'Or Jamie. Jamie should have told you.'

I have no idea what he's talking about.

He continues. 'The man who I suspect was responsible, his name is Merriman Stanton. He hates me. Utterly loathes me. He knows I'm leaving; this is his send-off.'

My mind is trying to make sense of what he's saying. What does he mean, the man he *suspects* is behind it? I remember what I saw, the four men silhouetted in the floodlights, hands on their heads. So either Clay is lying, or he wasn't there. I recall the lights coming on at the homestead. I'd assumed it was Mrs Enright, but maybe it was Clay. I'd supposed he was one of the men behind the floodlights, but maybe he wasn't part of the drama. I'm sure Jamie was, but he wouldn't have been acting without Clay's knowledge, would he? And yet I can't ask that, not after delivering my redacted version, not once but twice, first to Jamie, then to Clay. So instead I ask the simple question: 'Why does Merriman Stanton hate you so much?'

'His brother, Roman, was engaged to my daughter, Chloe.'

I look past him towards the hallway, the photograph hanging on the wall. 'Those pictures. Taken that long ago?'

'Yes. Beautiful, isn't she?' I can see the distress in the old man's eyes, some deep-seated pain.

'Very. So what happened?'

'It's my opinion Roman tried to rape her. Maybe he did. I don't know.'

I'm horrified. 'When was this?'

'In 2005. On or around the sixteenth of March.'

'What? More than twenty years ago?'

'Yes. This year was the anniversary.'

I think again of the photograph and imagine I see something in the face I didn't notice before, a cloud behind the sunny disposition and smiling eyes.

'Where is she now?' I ask, a whisper. Twenty years.

He lowers his head. 'I don't know. Wherever she is, I pray she's safe.' He looks back up, meets my gaze. 'It's one reason I never want to leave here, even after I've sold. Why I'll move to your cottage, if the new owner lets me. In case she ever comes back.'

I'm speechless. Twenty years. I look at Clay, but his head is bowed. I think of my first day at Longchamp, Clay's instructions, telling me the book would be for his kids. Vincent and Chloe. And their kids. 'You haven't heard from her in all that time?' I probe.

He doesn't speak. His eyes are focused elsewhere, off into the distance.

What am I missing? I wonder, before responding. 'This man, Roman. He assaults your daughter. She flees. I get it. But twenty years without contact? Why?'

'She killed him.'

'Roman Stanton?'

'Shot him dead. Put a bullet through him. She wanted to break it off, and he assaulted her. Then she went on the run.'

'You're sure about this?'

'Yes. She acted in self-defence; evidence to the inquest said as much. Then she took her stuff and fled. Her car was found in Dubbo.'

'What stuff?'

'Clothes. Money. Her diary. She took it everywhere.'

My reaction is instantaneous: it can't be true. If it really was self-defence or justifiable homicide, and accepted by an inquest as such, she would have given herself up long ago. Fought it. But I can't say that, not to her father, not when he is denying it so vehemently. So I prompt Clay in another direction instead. 'This man who blew up the track, Roman's brother—is that why he still has it in for you?'

'He thinks we're protecting her. Hiding her. Sending her money. He can't accept that I have no idea where she is.'

'And last night?'

'One last shot at me. To send me on my way.'

chapter sixteen
MARTIN

MARTIN STILL CAN'T QUITE BELIEVE IT'S COME TO THIS. HE SITS IN HIS MOTEL room, bag packed, head in hands. Outside, it's still dark, but the inevitability of the dawn weighs on him. If his cover wasn't blown before, it certainly is now. The adrenaline has worn off, leaving him simultaneously fatigued and on edge. He needs to get out, get away from here. Maybe he should just leave, risk it. Maz had said the police wouldn't open the road to Bourke until late morning at the earliest; they'll need to drive through to make sure there are no choke points, low-lying, where bogging is still likely. But surely if Merriman Stanton had been able to negotiate the Sundowner Track—albeit in his brute of a four-wheel drive—then Martin's Subaru could handle the graded and relatively well-maintained road to Bourke.

He imagines it. Driving east, encountering the police, trying to plead ignorant. But would he use his bogus ID or his real one? Jacob Solander or Martin Scarsden? And what would their computer say about his fake licence plates? He wishes now he'd kept his real ones. He'd ditched them when he really should have ditched the papers from the glove compartment. The current plates were from Goffing, though, so maybe they would present as legitimate. And would the New South Wales police be aware, at this early stage, of what transpired across the border just a few hours ago? Probably not, but all the more reason to get going before they're alerted. What a shitshow.

Should he head east, or should he keep going? To Tibooburra? Or into the desert, to lie low for a week or so? That was the original plan. But no, not yet. Off road would be too treacherous.

He lies down, suddenly exhausted, fatigue winning. He's been in far more dangerous situations in his time as a foreign correspondent, he reminds himself. It seems a lifetime ago. Back then he could sleep through anything short of a mortar attack. But that was a different Martin Scarsden, full of himself, believing himself bulletproof, the star of his own movie. Now it's different. There's Mandy and there's Liam. There is no physical danger from last night, there is no immediate threat, but he no longer has the licence of the correspondent and the insouciance that came with it.

He wonders at the wisdom of coming here to Port Paroo in the first place, to the outback, where every stranger is noteworthy. He would have been better off in Sydney, hidden away in an apartment, ordering in Uber Eats, binge-watching Netflix, catching up on his reading, trying his hand at that novel he's always wanted to write. Instead of listening to Jack Goffing, agreeing to strand himself in the middle of nowhere. Not that he can blame Goffing for his predicament; instead of lying low, he'd been tempted to chase the story. The men had cajoled him, promised to protect him. Was that what had persuaded him to go north with them, or had it been the same old lure: the front page, the exposé, the truth? The adrenaline rush, the competitive spirit. The ego. Maybe he hasn't changed that much after all.

He dozes. And the next moment the dawn has come and the day has started without him. The sun is above the horizon when he walks across to the pub. Inside he finds Maz.

'You really are an early riser for a journo,' she says by way of greeting.

It sounds as if she knows nothing of the raid on Longchamp Downs. Not yet. 'Thought I might get going. Any news on the roads?'

'Which way you heading?'

'Not sure.'

'The Bourke–Tibooburra road will open first. The Sundowner Track south—don't go that way. It's not the same standard of road. And don't head north.'

'Why's that?'

'The flood. It crossed the Queensland border yesterday. Might creep up over the road in parts.'

'Right.' A memory passes through Martin's mind: him and the Stantons just a few hours earlier, racing south before the flood cut the track, driving through water. 'So closed for the foreseeable future?'

'I'd reckon.'

'So when will the Bourke road open?'

'Should get the all clear later today. Blazing hot yesterday, no clouds forecast. But wait for the cops to give the green light. They get pretty shitty with anyone flouting the rules. Particularly non-locals.'

'I was thinking of checking out.'

'No hurry. Keep your room. No additional charge if you're out before sunset.'

'Thanks. That's good of you.'

'How'd you go with your research? Your big story?'

'Yeah, good.' He changes the subject. 'Maz, how many people do you think know who I am?'

She smiles. 'Probably half the district. Fergus knows. Thought he was telling me something new. And if Fergus knows, Perry will know, and if Perry knows, everyone will know before long.'

'Great.'

She laughs. 'Breakfast starts at seven.'

Martin is returning to his room when Maz calls him back. 'Phone call for you.'

In her office, he takes up the handset. 'Yes?' he asks warily.

'Martin, it's Jack.'

Martin's thoughts again leap to Mandy and Liam, a pulse of concern pushing through his veins. 'What is it?'

'What is it? You serious? You're meant to be keeping your head down.'

'What do you mean?'

'I mean your little escapade up on the Queensland border last night. That's what I mean.'

Martin is impressed; the ASIO man's network of sources is astounding. 'How'd you know about that?'

There's only the slightest pause, perhaps Goffing mentally recalibrating. 'It's in the papers, Martin.'

'*What?* What papers?' He looks instinctively at his watch. It's six thirty in the morning; he only got back to Port Paroo two hours ago.

'The *Daily Mail* for a start.'

'That shit sheet? What's it say?'

'You have internet access? Have a look. Then call me back. We need a plan B.'

Martin seeks out Maz. 'Listen, can I connect to the internet? It's important.'

She seems puzzled, maybe more by his sense of urgency than the request itself. 'Big story?'

'Something like that.'

'In the office. Password on the whiteboard. Bottom right corner.'

'I'll get my laptop.'

He goes to his room, fetches his computer, returns to the office. He engages his VPN and logs on to the only wireless network, PP Hotel, and keys in the password: PPH2021. Hopefully, the virtual network will offer him some protection against tracking. But thoughts of assassins are quickly forgotten once he sees the *Daily Mail*.

There it is, splashed across the home page, flanked by bikini girls and C-list celebrities and stories stolen from more reputable outlets. CELEBRITY JOURNO SPRUNG RED-HANDED. There's a close-up of him taken last night, a still from a video, an expression on his face that shouts guilty.

He reads the copy:

Bestselling author and notorious newshound Martin Scarsden stands accused of a serious breach of journalistic ethics, alleg- edly breaking the law and inflicting criminal damage in pursuit of his next big story.

Scarsden, who hasn't been seen since his book launch on Monday night was cancelled in spectacular style, appears to have become so desperate for his next adrenaline hit that he's participated in the brazen destruction of private property, allegedly involving the illegal use of prohibited explosives.

It's alleged Scarsden joined an outlaw gang that crossed a state border, wreaking widespread destruction, destroying valuable farm infrastructure.

His accusers have compiled a compelling brief of evidence, including photographs and video footage. One video, taken from a drone, shows at least two powerful explosions ripping through culverts installed to enable the free flow of flood waters as mandated by interstate laws and agreements. In another video, reproduced here, Scarsden admits his guilt after being caught red-handed and restrained in a citizen's arrest.

Professor of Psychology at Bond University Noam Malinsky says: 'I wouldn't believe a word this bloke writes from now on. He's become a sensation-monger. I feel sorry for him; I think he needs help. There's a name for it: relevance deprivation syndrome.'

Martin sits back, mouth open, unable to believe that someone has published this alternative reality. He reads on.

Scarsden has been silent since an explosion ripped through a low-key book launch in his home town of Port Silver on Monday. There is speculation that the blast was not caused by a gas leak, as originally claimed, but was part of an elaborate publicity stunt to promote his latest book, *Melbourne Mobster*.

'I've seen this phenomenon before,' says Professor Malinsky. 'People become so addicted to the limelight they will do anything to attract attention. Scarsden is a textbook narcissist.'

Industry sources describe the book itself as 'highly contentious', including 'unsubstantiated and defamatory claims' against
respected members of Melbourne's Italian community.

Mr Scarsden's publishers would not comment on the record,
but confirm they have been unable to contact Mr Scarsden.

Martin scans the videos. One must have been lifted from the
captured drone's SD card: the explosions caught as they punch
one hole then another in the track at Longchamp Downs. Part of
him, the journo part, can't help but admire the presentation with
its attention-grabbing visuals. The sort that will make the story
irresistible to network television: he'll feature on every channel
this evening. Another video has the four of them, hands on their
heads, squinting into the light, reciting their names: *Richard
Stanton. Merriman Stanton. Lachlan Stanton.*' And then him:
'Martin Scarsden.'

He's speechless. Accused of being 'a sensation-monger', of
'a serious breach of journalistic ethics', by the *Daily Mail*. If it
wasn't so serious, it would be funny.

He searches online, and it's as if he can see the story spreading
before his eyes. It's on news.com, the most popular free site in the
country, which has considerately included a map: Port Paroo, Eulo,
the border, Longchamp Downs. The ABC, scared of being left
behind, but also scared of getting it wrong, repeats the same story,
albeit inserting even more 'allegeds' and 'it's reported' and so on,
the two videos spliced together. It's there on the home pages of the
News Corp tabloids—Sydney's *Daily Telegraph* and Brisbane's
Courier-Mail—altered only to emphasise Martin's identity as 'a
prominent *Sydney Morning Herald* journalist'. Martin can imagine
the tabloid editors' howls of glee: the detonation of the dam is a

good story, no doubt about it, made great by the vision. But the cherry on top—catching a journalist for a rival organisation in the wrong—guaranteed elevation to the front page. Once the right-wing columnists climb out of bed and recover from their hangovers, they'll be putting the slipper in as well. And not only the right: *The Guardian* won't spare him, *Media Watch* will crucify him.

He dares a quick search on social media. The videos are every-where. Going viral. Going pandemic. The image of him with his hands on his head, stating his name, has been turned into a GIF, playing on an endless loop, and a still version is spreading as a meme.

He sits, just staring at the flickering screen. And finds himself laughing, laughing at the absurdity of it all, of coming all the way out here to escape detection, only to achieve the exact opposite. He wallows in it for a moment. Even wonders if the rent-a-comment psychology professor might have a point: what seized him to pursue a story when he was meant to have disappeared? But he doesn't dwell on it for long. The roads will open later today and any would-be assassins only need to read a newspaper to know where he is. He's no good to Mandy and Liam dead; he needs to get the hell out of Port Paroo.

chapter seventeen

concerned about detection.

'So?' says Goffing. 'Kind of spectacular, I must say. What were you thinking?'

'Not sure I was.' Martin breathes. 'Sorry, Jack. Stupid of me.'

'You okay?'

'For the moment. But I'm a sitting duck out here.' He tries to keep his voice light, to conceal his growing trepidation. 'Any news on the contract? Any killers headed my way?'

'Not that I'm aware of. The B-team is still holed up in Melbourne. And we've got direct access to the app now, the one they used first time around. There's no sign of the contract being readvertised, although there's no guarantee that whoever commissioned it before would use the app again, not if they've brought in the team from overseas. We're also monitoring the cameras at Bourke and have tasked the police at Tibooburra to report the licence plates of everyone passing through. Not exactly foolproof, but best we can do at short notice. I'll let you know if we detect anything untoward.'

'Right, thanks.' Martin feels a little better, reassured that he has some breathing space.

Goffing continues. 'Now take me through what happened last night. Leave nothing out.'

And so Martin recounts everything he believes is relevant, from the brawl in the bar the night he arrived to the drive north, including Fergus White and Merriman Stanton's offer to protect him and his identity.

Goffing lets him finish, then takes him back through it, asking questions. The final one: 'So you don't believe Stanton and his sons blew up this road?'

'Doesn't make any sense. If they were going to do that, why take a journalist? The whole point was to expose the illegal damming of the flood plain. Now they're all over the net, smeared alongside me.'

'So it was a trap?' asks Goffing.

'Absolutely,' says Martin. 'Whoever filmed us knew we were coming.'

'I agree,' says Goffing. 'The only question is whether they knew in advance that you'd be with the Stantons.'

'You think it's possible?'

'The speed of it worries me,' says Goffing. 'If it was just this fellow Carmichael trying to entrap the Stantons, would it really be in the papers already? Is that how the mind of some flyblown cocky from outback Queensland works? And even if it did, wouldn't he go to the local papers, not the metropolitan press?'

'Okay,' says Martin. 'Is it possible the Stantons were in on it? That they let this Carmichael guy know in advance?'

'No. You know all about this feud, I take it? They hate each other's guts. Fever pitch since 2005.'

'What happened in 2005?'

'The murder.'

A pit opens in Martin's stomach. 'What murder?'

'You don't know?' There's concern evident in Goffing's voice. 'Right,' he says, sounding like he's gathering himself. 'There's a warrant out for the arrest of Clayborne Carmichael's daughter, Chloe. She's wanted for the murder twenty years ago of Roman Stanton, Merriman's brother.'

Martin is too stunned to speak.

'You really didn't know?' asks Goffing.

'I didn't. No.' He thinks of the poster on the pub wall, of what Maz told him of the feud. Neither referred to murder.

Goffing sighs. 'If I had to guess, the Stantons played you. They went up there, blocked the culverts under the track. They wanted you to put Clay Carmichael's water theft on the front page. But Carmichael got wind of it and outflanked them. Planted the explosives himself. Waited until you and the Stantons were there, then blew it himself. And caught the Stantons, and you, in the so-called act.'

Martin mulls it over, mortified by the possibility he's been so easily manipulated. 'So maybe not just a flyblown cocky after all. I guess that might explain how the news hit the press so quickly. But Carmichael's plan didn't play out in the way he intended. I ended up the focus, not the Stantons. Has it been reported to the Queensland police?'

'Not yet. Which is another reason to suspect Carmichael detonated his own road. If the Stantons were responsible, why wouldn't Carmichael report them?'

Martin weighs it up. It doesn't seem all that convincing to him, but he can't assemble a better theory. 'So the Stantons were always going to travel up, block the drains, film it. I was just a last-minute addition.'

'You can understand their reasoning.'

'I guess.' He looks about the office. The calendar, copies of his books, the flood plain map. 'What should I do, Jack?'

'Leave, Martin. As soon as possible. Don't tell anyone where you're going.'

chapter eighteen
ECCO

I'M ALONE IN THE HOMESTEAD, CLAY AND JAMIE ARE OUT REPAIRING THE TRACK.
I suspect they're not telling me everything about last night's events,
but I'm not sure exactly what to make of it. Clay is probably right:
the southerners were trying to write the last chapter in the feud
before Clay sells and the Carmichaels lose control of Longchamp
Downs forever. At most, it will be a footnote in my book.

The death of Roman Stanton is another matter. Chloe
Carmichael is a fugitive, her father unable or unwilling to leave
the property in case she returns, twenty years later. I consider what
this might mean for my history of Longchamp Downs. How will
Clay want me to address it? Would he prefer I dispense with it in
one sentence or make it the focus of a whole chapter? Or maybe
he wants me to ignore it altogether.

It prompts me to ponder again why he has hired me, despite
my notoriety. I'd thought perhaps he was making some sort of
statement, trying to embarrass his children, rub their noses in their
privilege. Wanting them to realise the hard graft of generations
past. But now I wonder if it is something else entirely. Maybe he

is giving me a second chance, an opportunity to redeem myself, just as he must desire for his fugitive daughter. He's a crusty old bloke, taciturn, but there's no doubt he loves Chloe, no matter what her crimes.

Intrigued, I search for references to her online and find news reports by the bucket load, all focused on the shooting death of Roman Stanton.

I pull one up: the ABC.

Police in four states are hunting for alleged killer Chloe Frances Carmichael, a week after she allegedly shot dead her fiancé Roman Stanton.

Police allege she shot her lover beside a dry creek south of Port Paroo and left him for dead.

The funeral for Mr Stanton will be held in Bourke later this week, followed by a private burial on the family property, Tavelly Station.

The crime is the talk of the western district. It is the latest episode in a longstanding feud between the Carmichael and Stanton families reaching back decades and fuelled by disagreements over land, water and cattle.

I search on, establish that Chloe Carmichael has never been apprehended, that her trail ran cold in Adelaide some weeks after the murder.

Next I turn to reports of the inquest. I learn the coroner entertained few doubts about Chloe Carmichael's guilt. She found that on the day of the murder, Roman was killed by a single shot fired at close range on the Sundowner Track, between Tavelly Station and Port Paroo, by the bridge over Brown Water Creek.

A reliable witness claimed to have seen Chloe driving at speed through Port Paroo, heading east. She was later seen in Nyngan, and withdrew money from ATMs in Nyngan and Dubbo, before her car was discovered abandoned near the town's railway station.

The coroner explored possible motives. She cited evidence that the shooting was preceded by a lover's quarrel. The court heard that Roman and Chloe were engaged, but she'd suspected him of having an affair, which might have led her to end the engagement. The court also heard testimony of violence, perhaps sexual violence, perpetrated by the deceased against Ms Carmichael and that she might have killed in self-defence, the result of an abusive and controlling relationship. The coroner was unable to determine the motive with any certainty. She urged the police to redouble their efforts to capture the perpetrator.

My mind is swimming with questions and I don't like it. It's not why I'm here. I remind myself I don't care who is right and who is wrong in the Stanton–Carmichael feud: my only concern is how to write about it. I don't care if Chloe Carmichael was justified in shooting her fiancé, whether he harmed her or not. I'm not an investigative journalist; I'm a hired hand, a hagiographer.

Except I'm not. Not entirely. If Roman Stanton was the arsehole he seems to have been, I can't help but feel for Chloe, especially after what I've been through. And again I wonder if that has played some part in Clay's decision to commission me: knowing I would empathise with his own daughter's ordeal and her decision to fight back. Fine by me: if that's how he wants the story told, that's what I'll give him.

It's different with the story of Ludwig Leichhardt and his wayward lieutenants Hentig and Stuart. It's imperative that's as accurate as possible, as factual as I can make it. No doubt it will require embellishment, will involve lots of speculation, but I have to avoid including anything demonstrably wrong.

I need to learn all I can about Hentig and Stuart, everything on the public record and, more importantly, find any additional references to them in the diaries and ledgers and notes of nineteenth-century Longchamp Downs. I regard the bookshelves, packed with well over a century of records, most of them irrelevant. It's all so frustratingly analogue, no way to do a quick word search. I have no one to spin me the narrative; with Leichhardt and his party, I'm on my own.

I take Murdoch's diary, turn again to the mention of the two men. I can safely ignore anything before that date, at least for now, but I need to scrutinise every word from then on. I take a deep breath and begin. I've barely got underway when a message lights up on my laptop screen. It's from Emma.

Holy shit! You okay? What drama!

I blink, not sure what she's referring to. Last night's events? So soon? I use WhatsApp to make a video call to my friend and protector.

'Hey, champion—getting a bit of colour up your way,' is Emma's breezy greeting.

'You heard?'

'Hard to miss. It's all over the papers.'

'Seriously?'

'Yeah, take a gander. Martin Scarsden, up to his neck in it.'

'Okay,' I say. The name seems familiar, but I can't place it. 'Anything else I should know?'

'No. Just checking you're okay. How's it going?'

'Good. The client has set out what he wants. I'll need to inter-view him some more, but I've got all I need to flesh it out. Plenty of records, diaries, letters. No distractions. Piece of piss.'

'Better you than me,' says Emma. 'All those dusty old tomes.'

'True,' I reply. 'Although you never know what I might turn up.' I consider telling her about the murder, but decide I don't want to get into a debate about what is wise to include and what isn't.

'That's the spirit.'

Ending the call, I wonder if I should have told Emma about the lost explorers but figure I've done the right thing in keeping it to myself. After all, I have a solitary diary entry, nothing more.

Instead, I do what she suggested, go online and search the web. The response is instantaneous: the internet is engorged with reports about the midnight raid on Longchamp Downs.

The name Scarsden dominates, and I realise I know who he is: the celebrated journalist, the one who wrote a true-crime bestseller about a homicidal priest. *Unburied Pasts.* That's it. I experience an internal glow, an inner delight, at his current predicament. I hate journalists, the conniving, vindictive bastards. After what they did to me, how they crucified me on the altar of their front-page scoops and exclusive by-lines and clicks and newspaper sales and television ratings and bullshit speculation and their holier-than-thou condemnations. I feel an urge to leave the library, ride the quad bike down to the work site, and personally thank Clay and Jamie for exposing him. Even out here, in the middle of nowhere, journos are sniffing about for stories, like rodents. Like post-apocalypse cockroaches. Imagine if he'd realised I was here, what malicious shit he could have fabricated.

And now, he's been hoist with his own petard, caught breaking the law and all sorts of ethical codes in a desperate attempt to gain a front page. Well, he got that all right. Schadenfreude runs through my veins like ice water.

But as I read on, my relish starts to diminish and something begins to nag at me. All that time in the media spotlight has sensitised me to the rhythms and patterns of hype and clickbait journalism. What it feels like to be targeted, to be a scapegoat, a whipping boy. How could this be appearing in the papers so quickly? Sure, Clay would have wanted to make the most of it, but it seems too fast. Where did the news outlets source their information?

I recall Clay's conversation this morning. Was he actually out there when it happened? It sounded like he was still trying to work out for himself what had occurred. The news coverage contains no quotes; surely if Clay was behind it, he'd be directing condemnation towards the Stantons, not Scarsden.

I waste a full hour trawling the internet for more information, but I conclude the different mastheads and blogs and social media posts are regurgitating and repackaging the same line and the same sparse facts: Scarsden was caught red-handed participating in an illegal raid, driven by his insatiable need for a headline. Pushing back a little further, it gets more interesting. Just a few days ago, a community hall next to the Port Silver Surf Life Saving Club was destroyed at the launch of his new book. There's speculation it was a bombing, that the mafia is after him. The book is called *Melbourne Mobster*, an exposé on organised crime in Victoria. Who would be stupid enough to poke that hornet's nest? Scarsden must have a death wish.

I find myself laughing. He most likely headed out here to hide but couldn't resist the lure of a story. Typical journalist. What an idiot.

When Clay comes back to the homestead for lunch, we eat together in the kitchen, a large airy affair, remodelled in the final years of the last century.

'Seen the news?' I ask.

'I have. Gotta feel sorry for that reporter chap, Scarsden.'

'How's that?'

'Collateral damage,' he says, devouring a sandwich. It's the same choice as yesterday: white bread with curried egg, or white bread with processed meat and tomato relish.

'Who gave it to the papers?' I ask. 'You?'

Clay shifts uncomfortably. 'Not me. But I'm not complaining. Tell the world about those bastards.'

'The Stantons?'

'Yeah.'

I press the point. I'm not sure why. Maybe it's his reluctance to talk, as if this doesn't concern me. 'You see the footage? It's everywhere. Media says it's from the Stantons' drone.'

Clay frowns. 'What of it?'

'There's a few seconds before the first explosion when you can see all the water banked up behind the road, reflecting the moonlight.'

Clay stares at me, eyes unflinching. 'What's your point?'

'Doesn't it show they were right? That you were harvesting the flood water?'

Anger flashes in the old grazier's eyes. 'Not me. The Stantons. I told you. They blocked the culverts themselves. Trying to frame me.'

'But if that was the case, then they wouldn't have blown up the road? Either you were damming the river so they blew it up, or they dammed the river to frame you, and someone else blew it up.'

Clay looks troubled, as if the curried egg has turned. 'All I know is that it wasn't me.'

Mrs Enright comes through with a fresh pot of tea and some fruitcake and an apple each, and I drop the subject. But I can't help observing that Clay seems more certain of the chain of events than he did when I spoke to him earlier. Even so, I refrain from questioning him further, reminding myself I don't have a dog in that particular fight. I think of what I saw this morning: the waterlogged flood plain, the cloying mud. I recognise the metaphor: I don't want to be anywhere near that. Already, I regret reopening the conversation.

chapter nineteen

BACK IN THE LIBRARY, I RETURN TO PATRICK MURDOCH'S DIARY. PAGES OF
tedium: rain, no rain, supplies arriving, a newspaper. A snake in
the outhouse. A local tribe passing through. A comet, hanging
in the sky like an omen. Then, dated April 1850, near the end of
that first journal, a new entry.

> *Flannery came through with the supplies, including my back copies
> of* The Bulletin. *It reports that the government is mounting a new
> expedition to find Ludwig Leichhardt, that brave and gallant fool.
> I wish I could help them, wish I could go back in time and warn him,
> inform him of the impossibility of his quest, for to enter the central
> deserts is to enter the great maw of this country. It is a nothingness,
> a desolation, dry and hot and merciless, that feeds on the life of any
> man foolish enough to enter it. I was thinking this as I read, when
> I came across, at the very end of the report, a full list of Leichhardt's
> complement, the poor souls he had taken with him, the names Arthur
> Hentig and Donald Stuart among them. I remember those two well,
> the gleam in their eyes, and their talk of <u>treasure</u>.*

I stare. *Treasure*. And again, in the margin, the same pencil, the same circled exclamation mark, another circle enclosing two question marks, and the word 'treasure' underlined in the text. I feel like scribbling my own question marks—if Murdoch had now learnt that the men he'd encountered two years before were part of the Leichhardt expedition, why didn't he alert the authorities? Did he try? I already know from Wikipedia the last known sighting of Leichhardt and his party was in April 1848. Surely Murdoch knew the same, and now realised he had encountered Hentig and Stuart months after that last official sighting. Yet if he had notified the government in 1850 or at any time after that, it's impossible to believe that there would be no mention of it, no record. I conduct an online search: nowhere can I find the name Patrick Murdoch mentioned in connection with Ludwig Leichhardt. All the accounts of Leichhardt's disappearance, all the conjecture about what happened to him, agree on one fact: he and his expedition were last seen on 3 April 1848. His fate has been a matter of conjecture for more than a century and a half; books have been written, documentaries made.

I'm certain that if Murdoch had done the right thing, had notified the authorities, the world would know about it. So he must have kept the secret to himself. And I suspect I know the reason why: the underlined word 'treasure'.

He mentions it now, in this new entry, but he didn't initially, just the vague assumption the men were prospectors. I wonder why. Because he wanted to keep it secret? This solitary settler on the edge of civilisation? But what other possibility could there be? And so I must conclude only the long-dead founder of Longchamp Downs, myself and one other knows any different—

the one other being whoever it was that wrote in the margins of Murdoch's diary.

I'm disturbed by the sound of the front door. It's Jamie.

'All good?' he asks, coming through to the library. 'Thought I should check.'

'All good. You've fixed the causeway?'

'Getting there. You'll be able to get across this evening if you take it easy.'

'Thank you.'

He lingers, seems to want something. 'See the news?' he asks.

'I did. Quite the drama. And to think I missed it all.'

'Right,' he says. 'I'd better get back to it then.'

I take the opportunity. 'Were you there, Jamie? Last night? Did you see what happened?'

'Me?'

'Yeah. You. Were you there when they were caught? The Stantons and the journalist?'

He smiles, a wry sort of expression. 'Yeah, I was there. Helped catch them. Helped expose them.'

'Job well done then,' I say. 'And no doubt it was them who blew up the culverts?'

His smile has gone. 'No doubt. It was them.' I can't tell what he is thinking.

'Thanks for dropping over,' I say. 'But I need to get back to work. I might have found something intriguing in one of the old journals.'

'Excellent,' he says. I might be imagining it, but he sounds relieved.

Time passes. I'm deep into Murdoch's diaries, trying to find some further mention of Hentig and Stuart. Eventually, I find it, dated August 1850, some four months after their last mention.

I am determined to find the men. Their remains. Imagine the kudos that might bring. Maybe some much-needed money. A reward. But even more, imagine if I could find the treasure of which they spoke. And so I have taken to exploring myself, heading further west, away from the river, into the heartland, across the ridges.

I have asked passing swagmen, I have enquired of the local blacks, I have written to explorers and geographical societies. And finally I received information that might help: the Camel's Head is a distinctive rock formation, found deep in the desert west of here. It is not much, but it is enough.

And so I set out, with a local tracker for a guide. Two horses, provisions for a week to ten days. A first foray. I did not wish, in searching for a lost expedition, to become one myself. So my intention was to travel some distance, assess my equipment, determine what I lacked and what I possessed in surplus. And to test the way, to see if I might locate a viable route, if not find the destination itself.

I always believed I was the first white man to venture so far, discounting the two explorers themselves. That was before I found the most remarkable thing, the most remarkable person. On the second day, as the wind howled, lifting dust about us so I struggled to see, guided more by compass bearing than line of sight, I stumbled across a man camped at Farrelly's Bore. A white man, although so scorched by years of sun that his skin was as dark as many a native. I had encountered this man before, passing through, catching yabbies and clams in the river, dressed in rags. I always thought that was his domain, trudging down through the flood plains to Tilpa and up the Darling to Bourke. So to find him out there, beyond the ridges, emerging from the dust like a spectre, came as a great surprise.

He gave his name as John. He must have a surname, but no one knows what it might be. If he knows himself, he shows no sign of it. I have heard him called John the Baptist, and out there in the wilderness the sobriquet was fitting. He was harmless enough. For every comprehensible sentence he muttered two of nonsense, but there was no dismissing his skill or his knowledge, demonstrated by his ability to survive in those most hostile of lands. He knows the blacks, speaks their language, knows the seasons and the unseen paths, the way the sands come and go, building multi-hued dunes only to flatten them again. I happened upon him not because I was looking, but simply by chance. Providence. Farrelly's was at the limit of my explorations, but he told me he'd come to it from the west, from the deep desert. We sat, and I gave him food and a little taste of brandy, which he liked very much. Maybe it was the liquor, but he became most talkative. I asked him about Hentig and Stuart, the two men I had encountered at Longchamp. He'd not met them, he said, but told me he had heard of two men, two Europeans, wandering the never-never with two natives as guides, men not from the local tribes. I asked about the Camel's Head, a rock formation, and he nodded sagely, saying he'd heard tell of such a place, heard it as a whisper on the wind, in the mumble of the drifting sands, but could not point me in the correct direction, for the wind and the sands did not recognise the meaning of north, south, east and west. I enquired of paths and borders, a line between east and west, a hidden road. But he knew nothing of these, only the Camel's Head. Then his mind started to wander, and he informed me that it is easier for a camel to pass through the eye of a needle than a rich man to enter the kingdom of heaven. I thanked him and promised him flour and sugar the next time he came by the house. The poor chap, he was so gaunt when I left him, he would slip through a needle's eye without even brushing its sides.

I'm elated, of course. What a story. Cinematic. I mean, John the Baptist, wandering the desert? You couldn't make that shit up. And again, the pencil marks in the margin. No notes, no underlined text, but the same three exclamation marks, their dots small circles, childlike. Maybe there is a story in that as well, the mystery of my predecessor. I can really feel a sense of momentum. There is no way this is just a magazine article. It will be a book, a hefty hardback; it will be the making of me.

The discovery, after hours of meticulous scrutiny, makes me restless. I walk out onto the verandah. The boards are dusty underfoot, the air oven-hot. Down by the river, the men are still working at their repairs. A truck arrives with a new culvert and they gather round.

I gaze past them, out at the self-same view Murdoch himself must have once contemplated, the inhospitable landscape stretching to the horizon, empty and arid, the same red stone ridges. The stage for my story, my magnum opus. I wonder if Murdoch became infected with the same disease as Hentig and Stuart: the allure of a treasure, somewhere out there in no-man's-land, like Lasseter's Reef, that other enduring mystery of the colonial frontier. Is that how Murdoch met his death: speared out in the desert, searching for the treasure, swallowed by the great maw, as he described it?

What a strange place it is that I have found myself. Out on the very end of the world, where history itself risks falling off the edge and becoming lost. I return inside, pace the corridor, the pictures on the walls returning me to the present day. Now it makes sense, how dated the portraits are. It wasn't the death of the mother that put an end to them, but the disappearance of the daughter, Chloe, wanted for murder. Just that one recent image, Clay on the beach with his son, Vincent, still handsome, with a pretty wife and two kids. That's all.

Walking further down the corridor I pass Clay's room. Then a spare. And another, door open, furnished with the clothes and teenage memorabilia of Vincent. And a fourth, the door closed. Locked. I return outside, walk around the verandah, peer in through the window. The curtains are drawn, but they're thin, diaphanous. Enough for me to make out a bedroom. A single bed. Chloe's room? Still waiting for her return, all these years later. Does Clay know something he hasn't shared with me?

chapter twenty

MARTIN

MARTIN SITS IN THE OFFICE OF THE PORT PAROO HOTEL, AS A LOW SWELL OF anger builds. He knows he should ignore Goffing's suggestion that he's been manipulated by the Stantons. But it rankles; he can't shake it off. The graziers used him in their vendetta against the Carmichaels, their desire to avenge the murder of Roman Stanton. They'd blocked the pipes under the road, then brought him up there to frame Carmichael. He could hardly blame Clay Carmichael for outmanoeuvring them. How had Martin been so stupid? Because Merriman Stanton had offered to protect him, to safeguard his identity. Maybe he'd meant it, maybe he hadn't. It's not worth dwelling on.

Martin leaves the hotel through the beer garden, avoiding Maz, and unlocks his car. He sits behind the wheel, contemplating his next move. Decision made, he starts the engine and drives the short distance to the front of the hotel and the general store. He finds Perry sitting outside, puffing on a cigarette in the morning cool.

'Hi, Jake,' says the old-timer. 'Or Martin, whatever your name is. Good work, though. Showed those thieving bastards.'

'Yeah, thanks,' Martin replies. 'Police might not see it that way.'

'Possibly not. But free tank of petrol next time you're passing through.'

Martin can't help smiling. 'Generous of you. But do me a favour. Where do I find Merriman Stanton? I take it he lives close by?'

'Yeah, only about fifteen kay south, down the Sundowner Track. Tavelly Station.'

'Road okay?'

Perry casts an eye to the sky. 'Should be all right by now. Just don't go any further south. The road down there runs out across the flood plain. Boggy after rain, impassable during a flood. But Tavelly will be fine. Can't miss it. There's a robot guarding the entrance.'

'Robot?'

'Sculpture. Welded out of scrap metal. Twenty feet tall. You'll know it when you see it.'

—-—

Martin feels somewhat better driving, on the move. He wishes he could drive further, feels the urge to keep going and not stop. But his resentment remains, the wounded pride at being used. So he heads south, the Sundowner Track running along the right bank of the expectant Paroo riverbed. He takes it slowly: the surface is similar to the road north, but the Subaru is nowhere near as capable as Stanton's Nissan Patrol.

He crosses a low bridge, a sign beside it identifying Brown Water Creek. It's bone-dry. He wonders if the creek flows into the river or the river flows up the creek: the land is so flat it's hard to tell. He recalls the maps Merriman Stanton and Fergus White

showed him the day before in his motel room, the projections.
The graziers know exactly where the flood will reach, and when.

He arrives at the entry to Tavelly Station, and there's the huge
robot Perry described, with a couple of forty-four-gallon drums for a
torso and smaller cans for a head and limbs. It's been spray-painted
green and blue, a contrast to the orange dirt of the surrounding
land. The robot is waving, a smile painted on his oil-can head,
red highway reflectors for eyes.

Merriman Stanton and his sons are in a machinery shed, loading
a flatbed truck with fencing materials, when Martin pulls up.

'Wasn't expecting you,' says Merriman, forgoing any sort of
formal greeting.

'You've seen the news coverage?'

'Yeah, that fucker Carmichael. What an idiot.'

'Idiot?' asks Martin.

Merriman blinks. 'It'll attract the attention of the cops. Last
thing we need. But it'll come back on him.'

'How do you figure that?' asks Martin, impressed by the
man's confidence.

'We did nothing wrong. And we have a reliable witness. You.'

'Me?'

'Yeah. You saw. We never had time to plant explosives. We
were collecting evidence.' He peers at Martin with a calculating
eye. 'He set us up, but he wasn't counting on you being there.' He
grins. 'You're still going to write your article, right? You don't strike
me as the sort who'd kowtow to some low-life like Carmichael.'

Martin feels disconcerted, the anger leaving him. He'd come
here to accuse Merriman Stanton of duplicity, yet now he realises
he and Goffing may have interpreted the previous night's events

incorrectly. He's conscious of the sons, Lachie and Punt, assessing him silently. 'Well, I'm still keen to write something,' he says. Which is the truth, although he doubts the *Herald* will be interested in his original story. He probes Merriman further. 'So it was a setup?'

'Of course it was.'

'Targeting you?' asks Martin.

The grazier scoffs at the question. 'Who else? You? Why would Carmichael give a shit about you? He wouldn't have known you were there until they sprung us.'

'He mightn't give a shit, but the Sydney papers do.'

The grazier chuckles. 'Yeah, that must piss him off.'

Martin cuts to the chase. 'They knew we were coming. They were waiting for us. You say they had the explosives planted, waited until just the right time. Agreed?'

'Absolutely.' But now the man has stopped chuckling. 'What are you driving at?'

'How did they know you were coming? Who else knew you were going to Longchamp last night, at that hour?'

Merriman says nothing, but his good humour has subsided. Martin can see he's working through the question.

'And when did you decide to take me along? That must have been pretty last-minute.'

The flies have found him, small and irritating, seeking his eyes. He swats them, wonders if Perry sells repellent, reminds himself to check.

Merriman takes his time before answering. 'Two ways of looking at it, I guess. Who knew what we were planning? My wife, the boys, Fergus White. Perry, maybe. Possibly Maz at the pub. That's all I could say for sure. But this place, it's so small. If we woke anyone up with our car, and they saw us heading north, then they could easily guess where we were heading. Bugger all else between Port Paroo and Eulo. It's two and a half hours to get up to Longchamp Downs, so the Carmichaels would have had time to prep.'

'They'd have explosives on hand, just like that?'

'Yeah. We all do. Clearing tree stumps, that sort of thing.'

Martin nods. 'Nevertheless, I'm intrigued. You and Fergus White, when you came to see me yesterday, you'd worked out who I was. Who else knew I wasn't really Jake Solander?'

'Does it matter? Everyone knows now.' And some of the humour has returned to Merriman Stanton.

'No, probably not,' says Martin, accepting he's exhausted this line of questioning. 'You know, when I do write about this, I'm going to have to set out the whole background of the feud between your family and the Carmichaels.'

'Is that necessary?'

'Yeah, it is. Otherwise I'll be accused of bias, or a cover-up. It will allow the Carmichaels to attack me and the credibility of the article.'

Merriman's mouth curls with distaste. 'You want to know about Roman's murder. That entitled bitch Chloe Carmichael gunning him down. That's what you mean, isn't it?'

'I need to know what happened, yes.'

The grazier stares at him for a long time before responding. 'Okay. Come up on the verandah. We can have a cuppa.'

Merriman turns to his boys, issuing instructions, before leading Martin to the house.

The place is not the original homestead; it's modern, made of cream bricks, like it's been teleported in from the suburbs, along with a lush lawn and flower beds. It has a long patio extending along the front, enclosed in flyscreens; Martin doesn't know what's more welcome, the shade or the relief from the insects. Merriman's wife Gloria comes out to greet Martin, wearing an apron. She has a copy of his book, *Unburied Pasts*, and asks him to sign it. He grimaces at his author picture on the back cover. He recalls her at the pub on the night of the brawl. Had she already recognised him, even then? Was she the first? So much for his stubble and short hair.

Merriman waits until Gloria has returned inside to organise morning tea before speaking. 'Roman was a great guy. Best big brother a kid could have, best friend a man could have. He and Chloe were on and off for a couple of years. They could be a bit tempestuous at times. Her, not him. She was high maintenance, scatty, banging on about getting out of here, living the grand life overseas. It was a while before we found out they were back together. Roman kept it from us for a while.'

'Because of the feud?'

'I guess. He knew how Mum and Dad felt about the Carmichaels.'

'But there's no doubt they were an item?'

'No doubt. They were engaged. Dad wasn't keen on him marrying a Carmichael, but I think he was coming round to it.'

'What about your mother?'

'She didn't think it was a problem. You can ask her if you like. She's living down in Dubbo.'

'And you?'

'I was fine with it. Roman and me, we were the next generation. We reckoned Chloe and Vincent were the same. Over it. I recall thinking if we all got together, if Roman and Chloe were married, it might put an end to the feud.' He looks up at Martin, eyes sad. 'I reckon my parents were beginning to think it was a good thing, the two of them, when it happened. Not sure how her old man felt about it, though. Clayborne was part of the feud, that generation, like Mum and Dad.'

'How old were Roman and Chloe?' Martin asks.

'Young. Roman was just twenty-three when he died; she would have been twenty.'

'What were the implications if they'd gone on and got married? Would it have affected inheritance or anything like that?' asks Martin.

Merriman Stanton shakes his head. 'No. Roman was older than me, so this place would have come to him. If he and Chloe were married, she'd be here with him. She has a twin brother, Vincent. He always would have inherited Longchamp Downs, no matter what happened.'

'She wouldn't have any share, given she was her brother's twin?' says Martin.

'She's a girl. A woman. And women don't inherit if they have a brother. Not back then. Who knows, maybe I'm wrong; maybe old Clay Carmichael was more enlightened, intended to split the property. I doubt he'd be so generous if she was married to a Stanton, though. But none of that matters now.'

There's a break in the conversation as Gloria emerges once more and enlists her husband to help her bring out the morning tea: a large pot, mugs, milk and sugar, and a selection of biscuits, slices and teacake.

Martin waits until she has poured before he continues his questioning. 'And you two?'

'Us?'

'If Roman had lived, he would have inherited Tavelly, right?'

'We would have been fine. We have a second holding further south, bottom of the flood plain. Dad always said that would be mine if I wanted it. He'd carve it off, help us finance it. Roman and I even talked about it, how we would run the properties together.'

'So why did she shoot him?' asks Martin.

Gloria starts, her teacup rattling on the saucer. He realises she's walked into the middle of the conversation.

'Sorry,' says Martin. 'I didn't mean to be so blunt.'

For a moment, the Stantons say nothing, leaving only a chilled silence, Gloria holding a hand to her chest.

'I don't know for sure,' says Merriman at last. 'Nobody does. The allegation was that she'd found him cheating on her with some other woman.'

'Who? Do you know?'

'No. Lots of rumours, lots of scuttlebutt, but no obvious candidate. People thought it might have been someone from the city.'

'You think it's possible that he was unfaithful?'

Merriman looks to Gloria, then back to Martin. 'Look, he was my brother, and I loved him dearly. But yeah, it's possible he was having a bit on the side. It's understandable. As I said, Chloe was high maintenance and they'd only just gotten back together. He was a very good-looking guy; the women loved him. Mum used to joke: I got the brains, he got the looks.'

'So not overly bright?'

'He was smart, all right. It's just that he never needed to be. He was charismatic. Full of swagger. Knew he had the inheritance coming to him.'

'Can you think of any other reason why she would shoot him?'

'No. None.' Merriman looks grim, lips squeezed together.

'What do you think happened to her?' Martin asks.

'Chloe? No idea.'

'I hope she's dead,' says Gloria. 'Honestly, after what she did, she doesn't deserve to live. That wouldn't be right.'

'Why are you so interested in her?' asks Merriman. 'I get that you want to reference the feud, but that's all a very long time ago.'

'Because people will say you're motivated by revenge and that's why you blew up Clay Carmichael's road.'

'They can say whatever they like. You were there. You saw how it unfolded.'

Martin thinks again of what Jack Goffing suggested. 'People will also say that you were the one who blocked the culverts in the first place, then took me up there so I'd do a hatchet job on Clay Carmichael.'

Merriman looks dismissive. 'I've told the truth. You have your story. Make of it what you will.'

'Don't let the Carmichaels fool you,' adds Gloria, voice steely. 'They don't deserve to get away with this.'

chapter twenty-one

MARTIN DRIVES BACK ALONG THE SUNDOWNER TRACK INTO PORT PAROO. Sure enough, there is a police car pulled up outside the pub. Hopefully they've just driven through from Bourke to check the road before reopening it. But no point in pushing his luck by going inside. Instead, he keeps going, crossing the bridge over the empty river. He goes a few kilometres, makes sure no one is tailing him, and then heads back and, before regaining the bridge, turns north onto the Sundowner Track, the same route Merriman Stanton drove the night before. In the monochrome night it had seemed like the surface of the moon; now it feels like the plains of Mars, heat lifting from the red soil, distorting the air. It's only mid-morning, but already the temperature is into the thirties.

He makes good progress, the Subaru no match for the stride of the Stantons' twin-cab but handling the road well enough. Evidence of the rain has mostly disappeared, just the occasional, rapidly diminishing roadside puddle. He recalls what Maz told him, that cropping this far west simply isn't possible. By the look of the land, even grazing a few head of cattle must be barely viable.

At one point, to his left, as the road winds back closer to the river, he sees water beginning to run past him within the channel. The coming flood. Already he can see where it's spreading out, filling billabongs and anabranches. He appreciates once more the subtle contours of the land—the difference between the black soil and the red, where the water flows and where it doesn't.

He recalls the urgency of the Stantons on the return journey south last night, desperate to get ahead of the flood, and wonders if he has come too late and will find the way impassable. He reaches a dip, the floodwater pooling across the road. There's a flood marker, indicating the water is barely twenty centimetres deep. He drives through it, makes it easily, but realises how treacherous it might be if the water were deeper; if he'd lost momentum, lost traction, become stuck, then the all-wheel drive wouldn't have been enough. He recalls the words of Perry that first day at the petrol station, the observation he has no winch.

He drives on. After another ten kilometres or so, he reaches another incursion. This time, there is no flood marker. He stops, walks down. He removes his shoes and socks, wades in. The water is flowing gently, there's no threat of the vehicle being swept away, but it's too deep to risk. Back in the car, he engages the off-road setting and leaves the track, heading east alongside the creek. He drives at walking pace; breaking down here would be disastrous. Half a kilometre along, the creek spreads out into a shallow clay pan, a couple of hundred metres around. He's tempted to drive through it, knows it's probably safe, but takes the time to circumvent it, working his way back to the road on the far side. It's probably added an extra half-hour or forty minutes to the trip. Not so bad, but he fears the next encounter. And the return journey: how much more water will have encroached onto the road by then? Perhaps he could drive back the long way, via Cunnamulla and Bourke. Best part of six hours, but the roads would be sealed, all-weather. Maybe he shouldn't think of driving back to Port Paroo at all: get to Cunnamulla and keep going east.

But he's in luck: there are no more water crossings. And suddenly he's at Longchamp Downs, the southern gate, with the sign and the cattle grid. It looks totally different in the daylight. He drives through. No point delaying now he's come all this way. He crests the low rise, barely discernible, and the farm buildings are laid out before him. The water is flowing slowly to his left, men working with a bobcat, reconstructing the causeway, the river no longer dammed but moving freely.

He thinks of approaching the workmen but decides the homestead is the better option. He drives up to it, gets out, looks around. Apart from the men working on the track, there is no movement.

He walks through the gate, along the path, across the verandah. The garden looks outlandishly green.

The front door opens. It's a young woman, the shock of recognition on her face. 'You?' she manages.

He doesn't recognise her. 'Yeah. Martin Scarsden. Nice to meet you.'

'What the hell are you doing here?' There is contempt in her voice.

Martin is taken aback by her aggression. 'Trying to work out what happened last night. And who's dropped me in it.' He pauses; she doesn't respond. 'Can I come in?' he ventures. 'Kind of hot out here.'

'No,' she says. 'I don't entertain journalists.'

Martin can hear antagonism, resentment. 'I'm just trying to find out what took place. Then I'll leave.'

He can see her think it through, reach a conclusion. 'Okay. We'll stay out here.'

They sit on the verandah. Martin would love a drink, some water, and to be inside. But at least the verandah has shade.

'What's your name?' he asks.

'You can call me Ecco.'

'Cool name.'

'If you say so.'

It sounds like a nickname. He wants to ask her full name but thinks better of it. 'You seen the newspapers?' he asks. 'The internet?'

'Yeah. You're everywhere. That's how I recognised you.'

Instead of asking questions, Martin decides to tell his own story. It's an old journo technique, to be giving rather than taking, to build empathy, to tempt the interviewee into contributing, offering their own perspective. Their corrections. So he recounts how he was driven up here by the Stantons, the explosion, the video. But she just lets him talk uninterrupted, doesn't seek to add anything of her own. And yet she's clearly interested, maybe even intrigued, listening intently.

'So why are you upset?' she asks when he has exhausted his narrative.

'I was blindsided. I want to find out why.'

She laughs at him, not trying to disguise her contempt. 'So it's all about you, is it?'

'It is for me.'

'You're asking the wrong person. I'm just visiting. A hired hand. Only been here a few days.'

'What are you doing?'

She frowns, her answer vague. 'Just helping with a few things before they leave.'

'The Carmichaels? They're leaving?'

'Apparently. Trying to sell Longchamp Downs. Clay wants me to write the family history.'

'You're a writer?'

'A ghostwriter.'

Martin takes that on board, still unsure why she seems so hostile. 'They have a buyer?'

'Don't know.' Ecco shrugs. 'Hopefully I'll be long gone by the time any new owners get here.'

'But you'll need to know who they are for the family history, won't you? Round the story off?'

'Just a footnote. Can write that from anywhere.'

'Here's what I'm trying to figure out,' says Martin, attempting to elicit a more informative response. 'I reckon the Stantons didn't blow up the road—the Carmichaels did. They wanted to smear the southerners. But somehow I got caught up in it. Someone latched on to what took place, someone who wanted to damage me. To advertise the fact that I was out here, working undercover.'

She laughs again. 'Bullshit. It's not about you. It's about the Stantons and the Carmichaels. The feud goes back decades, even before Chloe Stanton murdered Roman Stanton. I assume you know all about that?'

'The basics, yes.'

She smiles as if she's enjoying herself now. 'You're not important. Mere collateral.'

'I'm just exploring all possibilities,' says Martin. He doesn't want to tell her about the contract killers, his attempts to keep his presence here a secret.

'Happens all the time,' she says. 'Innocent people get done over. The media doesn't care; victims are just clickbait to them. You've got a dose of your own medicine, that's all.'

He sighs. He can see he's getting nowhere fast. He scrabbles around, gets one of his useless business cards with its redundant phone numbers. He writes out his burner number on the back, hands it to her. 'Just in case you hear something. Keep it close; only two other people have that number.'

'Here comes Clay now. You can ask him,' says Ecco.

Martin looks, see the red cloud of dust and the vehicle beneath it. 'This will be interesting,' he says to himself.

chapter twenty-two
ECCO

AS SOON AS I'M INSIDE, I DROP MY PRETENCE OF DISINTEREST. I CREEP INTO
the sitting room and position myself on an armchair next to a
window opening onto the verandah. Clay and Jamie are coming,
and I'm keen to eavesdrop on their encounter with Martin
Scarsden. I'm hoping I can learn more, but also that they give
him the bagging he deserves. I can see out through the gauze
curtains and, fortunately for me, Mrs Enright has lifted the sash
window a touch to let air flow through. I reason that I will be
practically invisible, given the brightness of the day outside and
the relative darkness inside. Fortunately, Scarsden seems sun shy
and remains on the verandah, making Jamie and Clay come to
him, the arrogant prick. Imagine turning up here, playing the
victim, trying to alter the narrative. Typical journalist.

Nevertheless, I can't help but wonder if there's a grain of truth
in what he's claiming. All the online coverage, whether it's on news
sites or social media, is indeed targeting him. The longstanding
feud between the Carmichaels and the Stantons has been reduced
to nothing more than a backstory, slotted in at the end of articles

to add context, or colour, and left out altogether on the viral whirlwind of the socials. Which strikes me as strange: surely this latest chapter in a century-old saga is far more interesting than some desperate hack crossing the line in pursuit of a story? Scarsden must indeed be a tall poppy to invite that, one who has plenty of enemies among his colleagues. Maybe he's an arsehole and deserves to be run over by the karma bus. Still, reluctant as I am to admit it, showing up here takes guts. I'm curious to know what he hopes to achieve by it.

Clay and Jamie step up onto the verandah, Clay taking the lead, Jamie hanging back. I stretch out on the armchair so my head is just out of sight below the windowsill.

'You've got a hide. Returning to the scene of the crime.' Clay's voice.

'I'm trying to work out what happened.' Scarsden, sounding conciliatory. I can hear him clearly: he must still be sitting, or is standing just to one side of the window, back to the wall. 'I'd like to hear your version of it,' he says, voice honey-smooth.

'You're trespassing,' says Clay.

'You should fuck off now, mate. Cut your losses.' That's Jamie, acting the tough guy.

'Trespassing? You should press charges then,' says Scarsden, still measured. 'Let it play out in court.' I kind of admire the way he says it: the words challenging but the manner relaxed, unbothered.

'Maybe I will,' says Clay. 'Sue you for blowing up my road. Malicious damage.'

'You won't, though, will you?' says Scarsden.

Clay laughs. 'And why's that?'

'Two reasons. The evidence—the drone vision. It shows you were illegally damming the river.'

'Doesn't excuse blowing it up. Or trespassing to do it.'

'No, it doesn't. But the cops don't have to pick sides. They can charge Merriman Stanton with trespass and blowing up the road, *and* they can charge you with water theft. The police would like that, and the prosecutors, and their politician bosses: demonstrate how even-handed they are. Of course, they'd probably succeed in convicting you; the case against Stanton is more circumstantial. They'd have to establish he or his proxies were the ones who laid the explosives. Could go pear-shaped in court for you if they can't.'

Jamie again, sounding just a touch worried. 'You said two reasons would stop us pressing charges. What's the other one?'

'I hear you're trying to sell Longchamp Downs. Prospective buyers might not like hearing allegations of water theft. Might see you as less than trustworthy. Might get spooked by the possibility of ongoing litigation and prosecutions. Might worry that people will think you were flooding the land at their behest. Lots not to like.'

I reckon Scarsden is bluffing and again find myself admiring his chutzpah, his attempt to get Clay talking.

'So you say,' says Clay. He's sounding a little less sure of himself.

'Here's what I think,' says the journalist coolly. 'You either instigated the sting, or went along with it, flooding your property then blowing the road, because it gave you an opportunity to score one back against Stanton. I can understand the temptation, given the feud, and what happened between his son and your daughter. A last victory.'

Clay says nothing.

'Time you left, mate,' says Jamie.

'What's your name?' asks Scarsden. He must be addressing Jamie.

'None of your business.'

196

I can't resist; I risk another look. Scarsden is standing, his back to me; Clay has turned to look at Jamie, who is shifting weight from one leg to another, looking uncomfortable.

'I remember you from last night,' says Scarsden. 'You were the one who stepped into the lights and confiscated the drone.'

This time, Jamie doesn't respond.

'You paying this joker's wages, Clay?'

More silence. I don't like Scarsden, but I like his front.

'Yeah, I pay Jamie's wages,' Clay says. 'What are you implying?'

'As I said. You wanted to get back at the Stantons. Understandable. But the effect was to damage me. Discredit me. It's my face all over the internet.'

Now Jamie does respond. 'Why would we give a shit about you?'

'Exactly,' says Scarsden. 'Why would you care about me?'

'I don't follow,' says Clay.

'Who planted the story in the media? You? Or was it you, Jamie?'

'It wasn't me,' says Clay.

'I don't know any media,' says Jamie.

'Someone did, and got on to them very quickly,' says Scarsden. He lets that sink in before continuing. 'So whose idea was it to blow up the road? Was it you two? Or was it the same person who alerted the media? Just tell me, and I'll be off.'

'We don't take orders from you,' is Jamie's comeback, which sounds lame to me.

Clay remains silent.

Scarsden persists. 'Is it possible the new owners are involved?'

Clay laughs. 'No chance. It's a big agribusiness. Scotland-based. Dozens of properties around the globe, totally impersonal.'

Now it's Scarsden who seems unsettled. 'You sure?'

'That's what the agent tells me,' says Clay. He sounds genuine.

The journalist appears to accept that. 'So, if it's not the new owner, who is it? Who suggested building the road out to the ridge, who suggested harvesting the floodwaters, who suggested entrapping the Stantons by blowing it up?'

'Building the road was my idea,' says Clay. 'When I heard of the rain up north. It's all-weather, to get to the airstrip.'

'So it's new?'

'Finished it last week.'

'The new owners want that?'

'Agent thought it was a good idea. In case they flew in for an inspection.'

Scarsden doesn't speak for a moment. I have the impression he's searching for a new line of inquiry. 'What if the agent is misleading you? What if it's the Stantons who are buying? Airstrip makes sense—cut the time between here and Tavelly Station. Clever of them. Manipulating you into flooding the land, prepping it for their takeover. A double bluff, the ultimate payback.'

I have to stop myself from bursting into laughter, the journalist's play is so audacious. Yet when I steal another look, Clay is definitely looking less resolute: part concern, part irritation. Even so, he offers the journalist nothing new. 'My business is my business.'

'We're done here,' says Jamie. He's sounding rattled as well.

'Have it your own way,' says Scarsden. 'But when I get to the bottom of this, I hope you two find yourselves on the right side of the story.'

He brushes past them, leaving them standing alone. I lower my head, waiting to hear what happens next. There is no sound of movement, no footsteps on the verandah, but no speaking either. Then I hear an engine kick over; it must be the journalist starting his car. I hear it drive off.

It's Clay who speaks first. 'So whose idea was it, Jamie, to block the flow, entrap the Stantons?'

'Does it matter? I know how much you hate those cockroaches.'

'Is that right? And you didn't think to run it past me?'

'I didn't want to incriminate you. If it went balls up.'

'And if Stanton takes it to court, or this punk journo, you'll testify to that?'

'Of course.' And Jamie laughs. 'Scarsden is full of hot air. It had nothing to do with him. We didn't even know he was here until he named himself. It was all about the Stantons.'

'We? Who helped you? You can't have done it all yourself.'

'Dermott Brick from town. Him and his offsider. The three of us.'

'Brick? The buyer's agent?'

'Thought greening up the place would sweeten the deal. It wasn't designed to trap the Stantons. Who cares about them? We only planted the explosives at the last moment when we heard they were on their way here.'

'That was Brick's idea?'

'Yeah.'

'You idiot,' says Clay. 'You heard what Scarsden said. This could cruel the deal. Or give the buyers leverage. Brick works for them, not us, remember.'

Now Jamie is sounding contrite. 'I'm sorry, boss. I thought I was doing the right thing. Making the place more attractive.'

'And alerting the media?'

'Not me. I swear. Must have been Brick.'

I'm left wondering what was really motivating Jamie. And why this real estate guy called Brick would be so keen to alert the media if he was the one who set the explosives.

chapter twenty-three

ONCE THE MEN HAVE GONE, THEIR FOOTSTEPS RECEDING UP THE PATH, I recline in the armchair for a moment, trying to make sense of what I've heard while simultaneously trying to convince myself that I don't care. Why should I? It makes no difference to me if the events were orchestrated to smear the Stantons or the Stantons are planning to buy out Clay or if Scarsden ends up as collateral damage. There's been no mention of me in the media, and that's all I care about. They can do whatever they like to Scarsden; given how those reporters treated me, little doubt he has it coming. Like cannibals, eating their own. All I want to do is finish the book on the Carmichaels of Longchamp Downs, get my money and get cracking on Hentig, Stuart and the tragic Ludwig Leichhardt.

Nevertheless, something is troubling me. I can't help but feel that Scarsden is on to something. Not who was behind it, but that it was a setup. The Stantons stand accused in the media of blowing up the road, but Jamie has admitted that they're innocent. So much for the great feud. When I think back on the previous night, that matches my own recollections. Standing on the ridge, I saw the lake spreading with my own eyes; the pipes under the track were definitely blocked. And then the explosions. All being filmed. Out on the verandah just now, Clay had protested his ignorance. And that also matches my recollection, the lights coming on at the homestead after the explosions. It must have been Clay, not Mrs Enright. He would have believed the media reports stating that the Stantons were behind it. As I had believed. Instead, it was Jamie, following the lead of Dermott Brick. Were there other men, standing out of sight behind the driving lights? Who had fired the gun? This man Dermott Brick, the buyer's agent? Maybe I should ask Clay about him. But I shelve the idea and remind myself once again: I don't care about Martin Scarsden, I don't care about Clayborne Carmichael, I don't care about Jamie Stubbs. It's not my responsibility to correct injustices; no one ever bothered correcting those perpetrated against me.

I return to the library and try to concentrate on my research. Then I hear footsteps, too heavy to be Mrs Enright's.

It's Clay. 'That journo. What'd he want?'

'He confirmed he was here last night with the blokes who blew up the road. Claimed it was trap.'

'What'd you say?'

'I said there was no point in asking me, I knew nothing about it.'

'So why did he come talking to you instead of us?'

'You'd have to ask him.'

'What else did he want to know?'

'Nothing else. Just proclaimed his innocence.'

But instead of accepting my rebuttal and leaving, Clay sits down, looks around. 'You hear any of our conversation with him after you came inside?'

'No. I was in here. Why? What'd he say?'

Clay glares at me, but if he thinks I'll crack under his gaze, he's got another think coming: I've stared down too many people to be intimidated by some hayseed cocky. Instead, I take the opportunity to take the initiative while he's distracted.

'I found your daughter's room.'

'What?' He stands again, angry, distressed. 'Who said you could do that? You have no right to go nosing around.'

'None whatsoever,' I agree. 'The door's locked. I didn't go inside.'

He looks lost for words, wrong-footed by my candour. 'So why mention it?'

'After you recounted what happened between her and Roman Stanton, how she vanished, I googled her. Found the reports. The warrant for her arrest.'

'And?'

'I'm wondering how you want me to treat it in the book.'

He stares at me and then looks about him, as if the walls might instruct him. 'Treat her well,' he says. 'Include the facts, but don't judge her.'

'You mentioned she kept a diary. That she took it with her.'

'That's right.'

'You ever keep a diary?' I ask him. 'Put down in writing the daily events out here, your thoughts, your feelings?'

Now he really does look bewildered. 'What? No.'

'Patrick Murdoch did. So did the Abbotts. And your grandfather. They're all here.' I gesture at Murdoch's journals, spread out on the oak desk. 'You said you never read Murdoch's diaries.'

'That's right.'

'Someone has, though. There are annotations in the margins.'

'Not me.'

'The diaries are interesting. Source material for the book. The personal insights that will make it come alive. But you've never kept one?'

'There are records. Stock numbers, rainfall, floods, income and expenditure.'

'Not the same. Not the human touch.'

'I've told you my story. Said you could ask me what you like.' He frowns. 'What are you driving at?'

'You told me that Chloe took her current diary with her, but what about the ones from earlier years? Are they still there, in her room? I could use them. Make her human. A girl's perspective.' I lower my voice, aiming at empathy. 'A tribute to her.'

He looks tormented. 'A tribute? She's not dead.'

I realise my mistake. 'No, but people think she's a killer. Some sort of monster. You say I should recount the facts but treat her well. How can I? The facts are damning. But the diaries could humanise her. Rehabilitate her.'

He turns away from me, but I can sense him weighing up pros and cons.

'You would get to vet the extracts I select, of course. You'd have the right of veto.'

'Let me think about it. Leave them be for now.'

'And what about when you die?' I press. 'What happens to her diaries then?'

He glowers. 'I'll keep them for her. Of course. Vincent and I. His children. For when she returns. She's family.'

I hesitate, still thrown by his conviction, twenty years on, that

203

his daughter will eventually return. But I realise I might not get another opportunity.

'I can't see how else I might get to know her.'

'You can talk to me. To Vincent. We understand her as well as she understands herself.'

chapter twenty-four
MARTIN

LEAVING LONGCHAMP DOWNS, MARTIN FACES A CHOICE. HE CAN RETURN THE way he came, south along the Sundowner Track to Port Paroo, or he can head north to Eulo, where the bitumen starts. From there, he could go east, keep going for one thousand kilometres until he gets home to Port Silver. It's tempting, to be back there when Mandy and Liam return. He could leave the defamatory slurs of the *Daily Mail* and the rest out in the middle of nowhere where they belong.

But he can't. The threat of assassination remains, and he won't expose Mandy and Liam to that danger. He knows he should leave the district, go somewhere else altogether, become Jacob Solander once more, merging into the background, his stubble thickening, wraparound sunglasses a permanent fixture. So why doesn't he? What is holding him back?

Is it just his native obstinacy, his resistance to being pushed around, manipulated, kept in the dark? And that's what this feels like to him. That things are happening to him, that he has been denied agency. It's an unfamiliar feeling. He's used to driving investigations, being in control. Now the roles are reversed.

He finds himself retracing his steps, leaving Longchamp Downs through its southern entrance, driving across the cattle grid and onto the Sundowner Track. Goffing advised him to leave, but he also said the killers were holed up in Melbourne, that the authorities had eyes on them, that the police were monitoring the roads from Bourke and from the west. For the time being Martin is relatively safe; maybe he's better off here, working through what's happening. Because once the threat from the killers has passed, he will need to restore his name, his reputation. And he has to believe that: the threat will pass, he will survive, he will be reunited with Mandy and Liam. The belief equips him with a new perspective, a new determination. It's as if he has already embarked on the correct trajectory without even realising.

So as he drives, he tries to unpack the sequence of events, starting with the explosion in Port Silver, the gunshots. The memory provokes a physical reaction, a distress, the danger to Mandy and Liam causing his fears to resurface. He tries to calm down, slowing the car as if this might flow through to him. It's important he re-examine the incident dispassionately. Rationally. Was the explosion designed to kill him, or designed to get him out of Port Silver? He concludes that the explosion can't have been meant to kill him. There were far simpler and effective ways to achieve that. And the bombers had phoned, warned people to get out of the hall. It was risky: the place was destroyed. Nevertheless, no one was killed or even injured. Then there were the gunshots, as scary as hell, but again no one was injured, let alone killed, the shooters melting away. So it probably wasn't an attempt on his life after all; it was an attempt to intimidate him. To what end?

To stop publication of the book? Too late for that: it was out in the stores, no doubt selling its socks off, benefitting from all the free publicity. So what then? To frighten potential informants? That still made the most sense. And perhaps to prevent him speaking out about the insidious influence of organised crime on his planned two-week press tour? It had achieved that, but only because he'd agreed to flee.

He thinks of that now. Why had he been so ready to run, instead of standing his ground? Because Jack Goffing had encouraged them to leave, to hide. And with good reason: a contract had been taken out on him on an anonymous criminal recruitment app, a contract accepted by a group of killers calling themselves the B-team. But he only had Goffing's word for that. Could Goffing himself be sure? He's trustworthy, Martin is confident of that. They've been through too much together for him to believe the ASIO agent is manipulating him.

And yet, something doesn't make sense; there's some inconsistency, some part of the narrative that doesn't quite follow. He runs the timeline through his mind again, scratching away at the details. And then he has it. The bomb detonated, and that very night he and Mandy and Liam fled Port Silver in the company of Goffing. Yet it wasn't until they were west of the mountains, safe in the Airbnb, that Goffing revealed the existence of the underworld app and the contract taken out with the B-team 'in the early hours'. Meaning they had fled *after* the explosion in Port Silver but *before* the existence of the contract became known to Goffing. So who had decided they should run? Goffing? One of his superiors? The federal police? Was Goffing himself being misled?

Martin's professional scepticism kicks in. This is fanciful, he tells himself. Influencing an ASIO officer in such a way, or the federal police, is hard to contemplate, hard to imagine. Not impossible, but implausible. And for what? To get Martin out of town, out of circulation? To render him unable to champion his book, his meticulous examination of organised crime? Surely, there would be easier ways to achieve the same goal. He considers the book. It's true: it names names, describes networks, details methodologies. But the existence of organised crime syndicates and their insidious influence is hardly new. Embarrassing for those identified, to be sure, perhaps increasing pressure on the political class to clamp down with new laws and resources. But contemplating it now, the greater part of the book is sourced from police and law enforcement and a couple of insiders, informants. They were the brave ones, talking. Yet if they were talking to Martin, he was certain many of them were talking to the authorities as well. And threatening journalists, blowing up buildings, firing guns in a tourist town was a strange way for the mafia to get law enforcement off their backs.

Martin thinks of the young woman he met up at Longchamp Downs. Ecco, the ghostwriter, making her pointed accusations, lampooning his self-obsession, accusing him of thinking it was all about him. Reluctantly, he concedes she has a point: it's not about him, it's about scaring off informants. And the assassination contract, the one on the app, subsequently rescinded: was it genuine, or just another shot across the bows of would-be grasses? The contract would be discussed widely in the underworld, a powerful deterrent. Jack advised him to leave town, but also assessed the threat as diminished, the hit squad located in Melbourne.

And yet, Martin's still not satisfied. Something still nags at him.

He reaches the crossing where the creek covers the road, the place he circumvented on the way north. The water has stopped flowing and is sitting quietly, respectfully, the front of the flood having moved further south. Even so, it's too deep to risk driving through. He starts to manoeuvre around it again, edging across the wilderness, winding through sparse bushes, reaching the inundated clay pan, the small lake to his right, water rippling under a soft breeze. He pulls up near a couple of shrunken trees, remembers the camping equipment he has in the back of the car. When he opens the door, he finds the breeze coming off the water is cooling, and the flies are less persistent for once. He decides to camp. After all, he's not in a rush to get anywhere.

While he sets up the tent, his thoughts keep evolving.

Goffing had wanted Martin and Mandy to split up, and had rejected the idea of a safe house. He hadn't dismissed Mandy's suggestion that ASIO had been compromised, that it was leaking, that protective custody wasn't secure. And yet here Martin is, camping in the outback, at the suggestion of ASIO. The implication is that only Goffing and one or two others would know where he was going, whereas a wider group would have known the location of a safe house.

Martin finishes with the tent, laying out the self-inflating mattress, unfolding his sleeping bag. He sets up a portable chair, drinks some water. Down on the impermanent lake, some gulls are splashing, and a group of ducks is floating with apparent contentment. It won't be long until sunset. Off to his left, he can see a small mob of western reds tripoding to the edge of the clay pan to drink. An emu joins them.

He walks about, gathering twigs and sticks and dead branches. The wood is dry and brittle despite the recent rain. Back at his camp site, he organises some stones into a rough circle, sets a fire. It's still too hot to light it, but he knows that once the sun has set the temperature will plunge. Besides, the idea of a camp fire appeals to him.

It was Goffing who suggested Port Paroo, the town off grid due to its faulty phone tower. But had Port Paroo suggested itself because the phone tower was down, or had the tower been taken down to suggest Port Paroo? Martin recalls the linesman talking about how unusual the fault was, blaming cockatoos. Martin thinks it through. The tower had been out of service for some days when he got there, so it had gone off the grid before the explosion in Port Silver. Which means it can't have been Goffing or the authorities sabotaging the tower in order to make it safe for Martin. But that doesn't mean it couldn't have been planned by the same people who bombed the community hall in Port Silver.

And yet that doesn't make sense either. If the objective was to force Martin into hiding, why would the mafia care where he went?

Why would anyone, inside ASIO or out of it, direct him towards Port Paroo? Certainly no one forced him to travel with the Stantons to Longchamp Downs, no one timed the flood to coincide with his visit; no one could have anticipated that. The idea that organised crime had blown up the Port Silver community hall and infiltrated law enforcement all for the purpose of sending him west strikes Martin as ridiculous.

And as he watches the sun dip, the reputational damage to Martin from the Longchamp fiasco comes into clearer focus. Yes, it's embarrassing, but at worst people would believe that he was overly enthusiastic, that he was chasing a story and crossed a line, accompanying a group of disgruntled graziers as they blew up an illegal dam. Poor judgement, sure, but not career-ending.

A thin layer of clouds has settled above the horizon, and now the sinking sun is setting it ablaze. He lights the fire, but he won't cook on it. Instead, he gets his gas stove from the back of the car. Some pasta with pre-made sauce will do him.

By the time he finishes cooking his dinner, he's decided he's completely over-baked the events of the past few days. The feud between the Stantons and the Carmichaels had been going for more than a century before he stumbled into the middle of it. As a war correspondent, he'd never thought the battle was about him. Why should he think this was any different?

He eats his pasta. In the western sky, the sun down, Venus has emerged, like a glowing beacon, and for the first time in days, he feels a sense of peace. It's been a long day, the heat sapping his energy, the fatigue from the previous night bearing down on him. He'll sleep well. And at some point in the future, he'll have a good story to tell.

2002–2003

THURSDAY, 5 SEPTEMBER

I just can't wait. We've been writing to each other constantly, Roman in Armidale and me in Southport. I'm dead scared the form mistress will open them, censor me, censure us. But so far so good. He's suggested email, but I don't have my own computer in the dorm, and storing messages on the library computers is not allowed. So letters it is. I don't tell him, but I prefer them. They're more considered. More durable. More romantic. I keep all of his, re-read them constantly. This diary is similar: like a series of letters to myself.

Now the holidays are almost with us, the term almost ended. When school returns, it will be full on prepping for the exams. I should already be studying, but it's so difficult; I keep drifting off into daydreams about our future. Roman is far more pragmatic. He tells me the secret is to compartmentalise, keep the different parts of your life discrete. His theory is that it makes the best parts of your life even better, because if you're not thinking about them all the time, then they feel all the more special when you do *think about them. And that way, they don't become tainted by the more mundane responsibilities and the bad things. He says that's how he thinks of me, as something special, something precious. It is so sweet of him.*

I wish I had his mental rigour. I'm the opposite: all the different elements of my life seep one into another, so nothing is straightforward and I'm constantly distracted. Emotionally incontinent. Like right now: I'm meant to be studying, but how can I concentrate when life lies just out of reach, just beyond the exams, close enough to touch? How can I not imagine what that freedom might taste like? To see him, to hold him? He's different: he will be buckling down, convincing himself to focus one hundred per cent on university, knowing it's the necessary step, the entry price to our adult lives. I dare say he'll do better at uni than I will at my finals.

THURSDAY, 5 SEPTEMBER, LATER

Well, I surprised myself. Having struggled for half the day to achieve the most cursory of work, once I'd vented here in my diary, I was able to study with a clearer head and spent a good three hours uninterrupted. Three hours! Not just art history, but history and even some maths. Maths! In some ways, art history is the most difficult, simply because I do love it so. I'm forever chasing down rabbit holes, lured by interesting stories, whereas I need to be disciplined, more focused. But today I was good at maths, and history, and art.

I'm going to dinner now, feeling very proud of myself. I'm almost looking forward to getting back to swotting this evening!

THURSDAY, 5 SEPTEMBER, MUCH LATER

No study, no swotting. I was heading back to my books after dinner when I came across Maz moping. She seemed really down, so I suggested we study together, even though I knew that would be a disaster: all we do is chatter and gossip. Part of the problem is that I want to go to university, and so I need the marks. Maz plans to work at the pub, save up, then go travelling. She hasn't really thought much beyond that. Or that's what she'd always told me; I learnt different when we got to the dorm.

'Aren't you interested in uni?' I asked her. 'You're so smart. Smarter than me. Your marks are twice as good, with half the effort.'

'It's not for me,' she said.

'But why not? Wouldn't you enjoy it? We could go together. Stay in the same residential college. Maybe Brisbane, or Sydney?'

I was babbling away, all thoughts of preparing for the exams forgotten, when I noticed Maz was sitting very still. It was unlike her; she's normally such a livewire. And then a solitary tear, rolling down her cheek. 'What is it, Maz? What's wrong?'

'I'm turning eighteen next month.'

'I know. Amazing. Will you have a party?'

She said nothing. Wouldn't look at me. I could tell that something was going on, something important. Like she was trying to tell me but didn't know how. She seemed to be fighting back more tears.

'Maz, what is it?'

'My allowance ends when I turn eighteen. My financial support.'

'What support?'

She smiled then, despite her obvious distress. 'Oh, Chloe. It's never occurred to you to wonder, has it?'

'Wonder about what?'

'How I could possibly afford to come here, to a posh boarding school on the coast.'

I felt unsure of myself. 'Isn't there a government subsidy or something, for remote kids like us? Plus I've always assumed you have a scholarship—you're smart enough.'

'There is no scholarship. And the subsidy's less than half the school fees.'

'So where is the money from?' I asked, because I already knew for sure it wasn't from her mother, drinking away her life in the Port Paroo Hotel.

'My father. Until I'm eighteen.'

That threw me. 'Your father? But he died, out in the desert,' I said.

Maz takes a deep breath, fractured and tremulous. 'He was my stepfather. My real father, my biological father, has been supporting me.'

'Who's your real father?'

'I don't know.'

'Your mother won't tell you?'

Maz shook her head. 'It's part of the settlement they reached back when I was a kid. He would pay for everything I need—my school fees, dental and medical bills, clothes and food and so on—on the condition she never revealed his identity to me or anyone else. That was their deal.'

I wasn't sure what to make of that; it sounded horrible. 'Why would he do that?'

'Why? Because he doesn't want anything to do with me.' She almost broke down then, and it took her a moment to regain control. 'He signed the cheque, ruled a line under it. I know I should be grateful, but . . .' And that was about as far as she got before the tears did come.

I held her close and tried to comfort her. Poor Maz.

'So, no,' she said eventually. 'I'm not going to university. I'm on my own.'

FRIDAY, 20 NOVEMBER

Free, baby, free! The exams are over and I've finished school for good. Until February, at least, when I'll be going to Queensland University to study art history and conservation. Provided my marks are up to scratch.

I'm heading home tomorrow. And then, I'll drive down to Port Paroo to see Roman. I'll need to spend time with Dad during the holidays, try and cheer him up. Maz's situation has made me realise how much he has sacrificed for Vincent and me. The least I can do is hang around for a while. But not too long. Roman will be back first week of December. That'll give us a couple of weeks before I return to Longchamp for Christmas.

THURSDAY, 28 NOVEMBER

Maz and Vincent and I caught the train to Charleville together, then continued by bus to Cunnamulla. We were such a contrast, us three. Vincent was sullen; not celebrating the end of school. He'd liked it there, hobnobbing with his rich mates. Although half of them will be heading to Armidale to study ag with him, so I didn't see what the big deal was. By contrast, I was practically bursting out of my skin, excited to see Roman, while Maz seemed full of trepidation about the future. But she put on a good show, talking about working and saving, where she might head on her backpacker odyssey. She reminded me of Roman a bit, that ability to compartmentalise.

Dad picked us up in Cunnamulla, drove the three of us back to Longchamp. The land was even worse than last summer, if that's possible. There had been no rain, there was no residual spring green. Everything seemed dead and the air was choking with fine dust, turning the edges of the sky orange and apocalyptic; the sort of dust that gets into everything, no matter how hard you try to keep it out. The river was nothing but dirt, just a shallow depression, so devoid of moisture nothing was growing, not even weeds. I'd never seen it like that before, not in all my life. The rain tanks are empty and we're on bore water; bottled stuff to drink.

Maz stayed overnight, and then Vincent and I drove her home the next day, down the Sundowner Track, the three of us in the old Toyota, but this time there wasn't a lot of talking and there was no singing. The land looked defeated, beaten into submission by the endless drought. Vincent kept shaking his head in disbelief, or maybe despair. Whatever it was, he looked as miserable as Maz. So I kept my excitement to myself: it was two hundred kay to Port Paroo, but from there only another fifteen or twenty to Tavelly Station and Roman.

The pub was a mess. Maz's mum was a mess. She was back on the piss, worse than ever, one massive never-ending bender that only paused when she passed out. She'd get so drunk she'd piss herself. Perry was doing his best, keeping the place open and tending the regulars, but nothing had been cleaned and the kitchen was unholy, a stinking health hazard. Maz was heartbroken.

Vincent and I set about trying to restore some order: cleaning the kitchen, mopping the floors, scrubbing the front bar, hauling garbage to the town tip. It was the only way we could think of helping Maz.

At one stage, I found Vincent in the kitchen, just standing there, leaning on a mop, staring off into some imagined distance beyond the walls.

'What is it?' I asked.

'You're a good person, aren't you, Chloe?' he asked.

It was such a strange thing to say, I can still remember it, the sort of vacant look on his face.

'So are you,' I said.

'I don't know,' he said. 'Sometimes I wonder.'

'What is it?' I asked. 'You've had the shits ever since we got back.'

'Poor Maz. She has to put up with so much. Compared to her, we're well off. I know I shouldn't feel resentful, but sometimes it grates.'

'What are you talking about?' I asked. 'What grates?'

'The Strath Mortons. Eric invited me to go heliskiing with them in Canada.'

I laughed, not in a mean way, but just at the absurdity of such a proposal. Mountains. Snow. Money. These were things from another planet. The Strath Mortons might just as well have invited him to go dwarf spotting in Middle Earth.

'I didn't bother asking Dad,' he said. 'Would only cause him grief.'

I thought of the drought. The manager at Longchamp was away. Dad said he was using up his leave, which I took to be a euphemism for looking for another job. There was only Dad and Mrs Enright left.

'I'm thinking I might not go to ag college,' said Vincent. 'Might do business instead.' He looked me in the eye. 'Something with a future.'

I didn't know what to say. It would break Dad's heart; we both knew that. And yet I was in no position to criticise my brother: I was free of the burden of inheritance. And there was no way I was going to volunteer to take his place.

One evening, maybe our third night there, as the three of us ate microwaved food rescued from a freezer, Maz's mum staggered out in search of more booze, the bottle in her hand almost empty.

'Chin up,' she said to her daughter. 'He cut me off as well, the bastard. We're on our own now.' She drained her bottle. 'We'll show the cunt.'

The three of us said nothing, just watched her stagger through.

TUESDAY, 3 DECEMBER

Now I'm miserable, just like Maz and Vincent. No. I'm more miserable. Definitely more pathetic.

This morning, I drove to Tavelly Station. I should have rung first, but in my eagerness, my stupidity, I didn't. Roman was due back yesterday, so I thought I would give him a night with his family before I'd surprise him. I'd imagined a thousand times how he'd wrap me up in those strong arms, like we were in some sappy movie.

I pulled up in the yard just as a bloke stepped out from the machinery shed. I thought it was Roman, and I was already out of the truck and running towards him when I realised it wasn't Roman, but his brother Merriman.

I was so embarrassed. To make matters worse, a pretty young girl emerged from the shed, walked up beside Merriman and took his hand, like she was claiming possession.

'Hi, I'm Gloria,' she said. 'We met before.' She smiled. It was a nice smile.

'Yes. I remember. Lovely to see you.'

I asked Merry if Roman was back from college yet.

'He didn't tell you?' Merry seemed puzzled.

'Tell me what?'

'He's got a placement. An internship. He's in Melbourne for the summer.'

'Melbourne?' He might as well have said Reykjavik. I felt so stupid, just standing there with my make-up and my brushed hair and my new shirt, all dressed up for his brother's benefit.

'I'm sorry,' Merry said. 'He can be like that.'

'Yes. Yes, he can,' I said, realising I'd been compartmentalised. Compartmentalised out of his summer. Out of his life.

'Look, I'm sorry, but you'd better go,' said Merriman. He wasn't being rude, or unkind, just matter-of-fact. 'Roman told Mum and Dad about you and they were pretty hostile.'

'The feud?'

'You'd reckon they'd be over it by now.'

Maz was weeping when I got back to the pub and I joined in. I poured it all out: how foolish and small I'd felt, rolling up to Tavelly Station to find that Roman wasn't there; how he hadn't bothered telling me about the internship; how humiliating it was to have Merry and Gloria take pity on the stupid girl from Queensland. Only when I'd finished moaning about my own problems did I ask Maz why she was upset, and that put my troubles into perspective.

It was much worse than she'd thought. Not only had her money been cut off, Perry revealed that her mother had run up a lot of debts. That she was in danger of losing the pub.

So tonight we went through the books. The paperwork was a mess, but between Vincent and Maz, they worked it out. Vincent is a gun at financial stuff. There were bills piled up, bills due. Bank interest. The pub was mortgaged so much, it was worth less than her mother owed. Vincent called it negative equity. He was shaking his head, a look of horror on his face.

They found the combination to the safe written on the desk blotter. Got it open. It was all ancient history, nothing new, but they did find Maz's birth certificate, with her stepfather listed as her parent. And then, when Maz was six, paperwork paying off the mortgage on the pub, ownership passing to Maz's mother outright. This was about three months after Maz's stepfather died.

'Who paid the mortgage?' I asked.

'Doesn't say,' Vincent said.

'My father,' said Maz. 'My real father.'

And then, about four years later, a new mortgage.

'I would have been about ten, then. It's when Mum did up the annexe, bought a new car. I guess this explains it. It wasn't his money, it wasn't her money, she'd borrowed it. She was trying to make a go of it.'

'And has been going deeper into debt ever since,' said Vincent.

'The more debt, the more she drinks,' said Maz. 'Downward spiral.'

'Jesus,' said Vincent, and he looked at me, and I could see the anguish in his eyes.

MONDAY, 9 DECEMBER

Vincent has gone back to Longchamp. With the manager on 'leave', Dad needs my brother's help on the property. They have Mrs Enright to cook and clean, so Dad doesn't really need me. Vincent got a lift up with the mail truck, so I can hang on to the Toyota. I'd decided to stay with Maz a bit longer, help her out. I didn't feel I could just abandon her. But that all changed this morning, two days after Vincent left.

'Do you have any money you can spare me?' Maz asked.

'I could,' I said. 'But what about your allowance? I thought you were saving it up, before you were cut off.'

'It's all gone. I needed it to keep the pub open, keep the bank at bay for a few months.'

She'd given up what little she had to help her mum. It made me feel guilty, having a father who wasn't a drunken deadbeat, who'd set aside enough in the good times to pay for me and Vincent to go to uni.

'What are you going to do?' I asked.

She was still emotional, but the despair in her eyes had been replaced by a look of resolve. There's a toughness to her. She's been through so much, I guess it's tempered her. 'I've worked it out,' she said. 'Perry is on board. I rang Vincent, and he thinks it makes sense. We'll close the place for a couple of weeks, get it in order, and reopen when I get back.'

'Back from where?'

'I'm going to see my father.'

'Your mum told you who he is?'

'Yeah, she finally cracked. Said I'm eighteen and I have a right to know. Said she's legally bound not to tell me, but now he's stopped our allowances she doesn't give a shit. Anyway, that's why I want to borrow money. For the fares. So I can go see him, beg him to re-float us.'

'He's rich?'

'Fuck yeah. Unbelievably. We're not even a rounding error to him.'

'Sounds like a monster,' I said.

'Doesn't matter. He's my father and he's got money.'

'Where does he live?'

'The west.' She smiled, and I couldn't believe how brave she was. 'Any chance you could drive me to Broken Hill? It's about six hours from here. I can catch the bus from there.'

'So who is he? Your father?'

She shook her head. 'Can't say. I figure I'll have to do the same as Mum, sign some sort of non-disclosure agreement. Promise him I won't tell anyone.'

'You reckon he'll help you?'

She shrugged. 'Depends on how much of a bastard he is. Common or garden, or industrial-strength. He can't just fob me off, though. He might have signed an agreement with Mum, but I'm an adult now, and I haven't signed anything. Not yet.'

And at that moment, I saw the steel in her, the determination. I can't express how much I admire her.

FRIDAY, 18 DECEMBER

I looked at the map—of course I did. After dropping Maz in Broken Hill, I calculated I could make it to Melbourne in a day. Eight hundred and fifty kilometres. Ten hours, plus breaks. I thought about it the whole way, driving Maz to Broken Hill. I tried not to, but I wasn't capable of compartmentalising, not like Roman. Not like Maz. The daydreams refused to die.

But reality kept seeping in. The memory of standing exposed, my feelings laid bare, outside the machinery shed at Tavelly Station, embarrassing Roman's brother and his girlfriend with my humiliation.

I wasn't going to drive all the way to Melbourne for a repeat dose. I wasn't that stupid.

SATURDAY, 19 DECEMBER

Now I really do feel stupid. I've returned to Longchamp for Christmas; not much point staying in Port Paroo with Maz gone and the pub shut. I arrived home only to find Roman's letter. It had been here all the time. The mail is delivered weekly, so it must have been at Eulo post office when we drove through on our way *back from school. Normally Dad would have stopped to collect it, but it was late in the evening when our bus got in and the post office was already shut for the night.*

I've read the letter a hundred times now, memorised it. I'd get the final lines tattooed above my heart if I could.

My dearest Chloe,

I'm writing you two letters, one addressed to St Hilda's, one addressed to Longchamp, as I'm not sure which might catch you first.

I've had a lucky break, an opportunity I can't knock back. It's an internship in Melbourne at a big farm management consultancy. I'll pick up so much more insight in three months here than a year at ag college. Really smart people, really switched on, operating in the real world. I'm sorry, but it's too good to pass up. I'm sure you'll understand.

I'll be back home before university starts. I can't tell you how much I'm looking forward to seeing you again.

All my love for now and for always,

Roman

The other copy of the letter was also waiting, the one he'd addressed to St Hilda's, and the school had duly forwarded it on.

I'd wasted weeks crying for nothing.

WEDNESDAY, 22 JANUARY

Roman will be back next week—not that I will see him, not that I would want to, ever again. This whole summer wasted, frittered away. I could have gone to the coast, instead of hanging around here waiting. The bastard. He's compartmentalised me again.

His last letter was formal, like he's a solicitor. Containing the most brutal sentence in the English language: 'I've met someone else.' How many souls have been destroyed over the years by those four words? She's in Melbourne. Of course she's in Melbourne. I can just imagine them, strolling along the Yarra arm in arm, the river full.

Life here is getting worse and worse. We're all despondent. There's no water and there's no money. Vincent finally summoned up the guts to tell Dad he wants to study finance, not agriculture. He asked me to be there, for moral support. Or maybe to hose Dad down if he lost it. But Dad didn't yell or scream or say anything at all. He just looked a little lost, a little empty. And finally he just nodded. I wasn't sure if he was signalling his permission, or his understanding, or just his recognition that it has come to this.

At least Maz has got what she needed: the titles to the hotel, a way of supporting her mother. Her fuckwit of a father came through after all. Insisted on a non-disclosure agreement, like she predicted. Maz says he's married, wants to protect his wife and two kids. Sounds like bullshit to me.

'I don't care,' she said. 'He's done the right thing. We're debt-free. That's all I wanted. We're free of him and he's free of us. And Mum doesn't get to piss it away this time.'

I went down to Port Paroo to help her reopen the pub. Vincent came too, to get the books in order. It seemed to cheer him up, give him a sense of purpose, or maybe it's just that he's got dad's blessing to study finance. It was good for Maz and me to have him around. Reminds us that not all men are complete arseholes. Just most of them.

I can't wait to start university. I can't wait to leave.

SATURDAY

chapter twenty-five
MARTIN

THE MORNING IS AS BEAUTIFUL AS THE EVENING BEFORE. IT'S AS IF THE solitude has entered Martin's soul. He regards the lake, mirror-smooth in the dawn light, a piece of sky fallen to earth. Kangaroos bound past and a curious emu examines him, tilting its head as if to get a better look. The heat will come, but for the moment the air is cool, almost crystalline. He considers staying here forever, or at least a day or two longer, knows he can't, but takes his time packing his tent.

It's still early when, a few kilometres out of Port Paroo, his phone pings. And pings again. The phone tower must be fixed. Not that it matters anymore: the whole world knows he's out here.

He's almost at the junction with the Bourke road when he pulls over. He's hoping the messages are from Mandy; instead there's one from Jack Goffing. It had to be one or the other: they're the only two with his number. Them and Ecco the ghostwriter.

The Daily Mail again. Call me.

He gets out his laptop, hotspots it off his phone, grateful that Goffing didn't fob him off with a dumb phone. He wonders how much data he has available, how stingy the authorities are with that sort of thing. While he's connecting, he wonders what new fabrication the *Mail* has come up with, but he's thinking water theft and exploding dams, nothing like what greets him on the newspaper's website.

JOURNALIST IN SEX SCANDAL

Blinking against reality, he reads: *Disgraced investigative journalist Martin Scarsden is embroiled in a new scandal—caught in flagrante delicto with scarlet woman Ekaterina Boland.*

The website has some lurid footage, floating black shapes imposed at a pretence at decency.

He searches the internet, finds the uncensored images, purportedly from a 'nanny' cam. They show Martin and Ekaterina going for it. There is no doubt it's his face, nor any doubt it is her, the woman he met at Longchamp, the one calling herself Ecco. But the footage isn't real. With a growing sense of dread, he realises it's a so-called deepfake. Some bastard has learnt he met with Ekaterina and whipped this up. He stares hard at the video, trying to discern where they have melded the footage of porn stars with AI-generated images of his face, but he can't see it. The technology is too good.

He conducts a more thorough image search. It's Ekaterina Boland for certain; no doubt. The name rings a distant bell. He's about to dig deeper when his phone rings. Jack Goffing.

'You've seen?' asks the ASIO man.

'I've seen.'

'It's fake, isn't it?' asks Goffing.

Martin is shocked he's even asked. 'Of course it's a fake.'

'It's a very good one. The footage of the sex; we can't find the original.'

'What does that mean?'

'I got our boffins to scrape the web, see if they could find the original footage. If we found it, we could put it out there. Discredit the forgery. And with luck, have some idea who's behind it. But we couldn't find the base footage. We believe it's been purpose-made. Incredibly well done; they've got the angles perfect.'

Martin doesn't want to think about the angles. 'Jack, what's going on?'

A lengthy pause. 'If I had to guess, someone is trying to discredit you.'

'No shit. And they're doing a good job. Any idea who it might be? And why?'

'I have no evidence, but it's possibly the same people who ordered the hit on you. They've switched plans; instead of trying to kill you, they've decided on character assassination.' Goffing takes a breath. 'Tell me, have you ever met Ekaterina Boland? Does this video have any basis in fact whatsoever?'

'Did I shag her? Is that what you're asking?'

'Do you have anything to hide; is there anything else that might embarrass you?'

'Jack, I just told you, it's not real. Ask her if you don't believe me. She's at Longchamp Downs.'

'Okay, okay. Calm down. I had to ask. Has anyone threatened you recently?'

'You mean other than blowing up the Port Silver community hall and strafing the main street, and advertising for a hit squad on the dark web? No, other than that, it's been just dandy.'

Goffing ignores his sarcasm. 'Apart from the mafia? Is there anything you've done that these people might threaten to expose to gain leverage over you? If there is, it's important you tell me. We can work through it.'

'You're discounting the mafia?'

'Not yet.'

Martin isn't sure how to interpret that. 'No, Jack. There is nothing I'm ashamed of, nothing to hide. If they had something on me, they wouldn't be producing deepfakes.'

'Okay. That's good. What I expected, but important I asked.'

'Of course. Tick the boxes.'

'How do you know Ekaterina Boland?'

'I don't. I met her briefly yesterday afternoon. I went back to Longchamp Downs, trying to find out what happened with the destruction of the causeway. She was at the homestead and I spoke to her, but I didn't know who she was. Seriously.'

'What's she doing there?'

'Said she's ghostwriting a history of the property and the Carmichael family.'

'And the room, the one in the video. Is that the real interior of the homestead?'

'I don't know. I didn't go inside. We sat outside, on the verandah.'

'Where people could see you.' It's a statement, not a question.

'Yes.'

There is another of Goffing's contemplative silences. Martin thinks through who might have seen them: Clay Carmichael, the young man Jamie. A couple of workers on a bobcat, further away. Who else might they have told about his visit?

'I'll do everything I can to find out what's going on,' says Goffing, 'but I have to be honest. As it stands at the moment, I have no firm idea. Stay safe and I'll get back to you when I have more.'

Stay safe. Great advice. Brilliant. But how do you stay safe from people keen to trash your reputation online, without a fact in sight? Whoever is behind this can continue to make stuff up. The destruction of the culverts under the track happened, he was there. Totally misconstrued, but based on reality at least. The fabricated porn is based, however flimsily, on the fact that he and Ekaterina Boland met. If he leaves, hides away in Port Silver, why wouldn't they continue to fabricate material? And in Port Silver, he'd be a thousand kilometres from the only clues as to who's behind this. Whoever it is, they're connected to Longchamp Downs. He was there when the makeshift dam was destroyed, appearing on the front page of the *Daily Mail* just hours later; he returns to Longchamp Downs, has a totally innocent encounter with Ekaterina Boland, and in no time flat a phoney porno is all over the web. The conclusion is unavoidable: someone at Longchamp is either his tormentor or is feeding information to his tormentor.

Try as he might, he can't think of any reason why the owner of Longchamp Downs, Clay Carmichael, would wish him harm. Who then? Something Ekaterina said comes back to him. Clay wanted the history written because he was in the process of selling up: there was a new owner in the wings. Martin thinks of calling Goffing back, is about to dial, when he reconsiders. He doesn't want to become completely reliant on Goffing. After all, it was the ASIO man who sent him out here, directed him towards Port Paroo, with its broken phone tower and promises of anonymity. Goffing was quizzing him about the possibility Martin has been compromised, but who is quizzing Goffing and his colleagues at ASIO and the AFP?

He gets out of the car, walks towards the river. Still dry. Surely the flood will reach it today. The heat is starting to build and the flies are back on duty, bossing and nipping and seeking the moisture in his nostrils and in the corner of his eyes. He swats them away. They'd better get used to him. Hiding is no longer an option. Neither is running.

He calls his old colleague at the *Sydney Morning Herald*, Bethanie Glass. She doesn't answer. He realises she won't recognise his number. He sends a text. *It's Martin. Burner phone. Please call.*

While he waits for Bethanie to ring back, he starts pulling up articles about Ekaterina Boland. And there it is, all laid out in front of him: the perfect marriage, the glowing bride, the betrayal, the scandal, the condemnation. If someone wanted to smear Martin, they couldn't have chosen a better person to weaponise. He tries to recall their encounter. She seemed smart, self-contained, fierce.

The phone rings. Bethanie. 'Hi, stud,' says the familiar voice.

'It's not fucking funny.'

'Sorry. Couldn't resist.' And then she drops the banter, replacing it with something approaching compassion. 'You okay?'

'Been better. Been a lot better.'

'I'm assuming that's not you in the video?'

'No. A deepfake.'

'Can I quote you as categorically denying that it is you?'

'Quote? I didn't ring to give you a story.'

'What then?'

Martin reconsiders. 'Actually, yes. Do write the story. And yes, quote me as categorically denying having had sex or any intimate relations whatsoever with Ekaterina Boland. And say that the video is bogus.'

'Excellent,' says Bethanie. 'Now, why did you call me?'

Martin tries to make it as concise as he can. 'Okay. We're off the record now, right? Not for publication. It's possible someone is trying to blacken my name. Character assassination. I don't believe the porno is random; they're deliberately targeting me. And it's somehow connected to this grazing property in Queensland called Longchamp Downs. Can you sniff around, find out where the two stories first appeared—the dam raid and the bogus porno? See if it's the same outlet, the same journo. Maybe we can work backwards, figure out who their source is.'

'Who has it in for you?'

'Exactly.'

Bethanie sighs. 'Determining where the stories first appeared should be easy enough. But getting a journo to reveal their source? That's not so easy.'

'I'd be grateful for anything you can dig up.'

'Anything else?'

Martin searches his mind. 'One thing. This property, Longchamp Downs. Owned for generations by a family called Carmichael, but about to be sold. Can you find out who the prospective owner is? Not just the front company, but the beneficial owner.'

'You reckon that's who's targeting you?'

'Could be.'

'Why would they do that?'

'For no good reason I can think of.'

'So this is a fishing expedition?'

Martin smiles to himself, admiring Bethanie, practical and unsentimental. 'Yes. I'm desperate.'

'In that case, I'll see what I can do.'

Martin has just thanked Bethanie and ended the call, when his handset chimes again.

'Jesus,' he says, recognising the number. It's Mandy; she must have seen the video.

chapter twenty-six
ECCO

I STARE AT THE SCREEN IN DISBELIEF, MOUTH OPEN, STRUGGLING TO comprehend. I'd come over to the homestead early, riding the quad bike along the partially repaired road, all fired up, keen to progress—only to log on and see the messages from Emma, alerting me. And now I sit, immobilised. Emma warned me to brace myself, told me it's bad. Bad doesn't get close. Try traumatic. Try triggering. Try enraging. All the past comes rocketing back at me, the memory of that other sex tape, the one that destroyed my life. And now this. Not even real, but oh so convincing. And eternal, I know that: it will roam the internet for ever, spreading its poison until the end of time. Who could possibly have done this? Who could still bear such ill will towards me after all this time? After all I have done to reinvent myself? Some ally of my bastard husband, someone getting their jollies at my expense.

I've seen enough; I close the laptop. But still the images play before my eyes, lurid and startling. I know how this story will pan out, how I will be demonised. I've lived it before. This time I won't stand accused of bringing down a saint—instead I'll be

sneered at for wallowing in the mire with some low-life journalist—
but that makes me feel no better. I can almost read the script: he
will be forgiven, while I'll be characterised as the wanton harlot
who led a married man astray.

I try to shake off my despair, clawing back towards reality,
reminding myself that none of it is real. Scarsden is as blameless
as I am. But who will ever believe that? Me, Scarsden, the people
who created the deepfake. And who else? Emma? Or maybe
Emma won't care if it's real or not; she supported me when she
knew it was real. Saint Emma.

I think of my parents. They still refuse to speak to me after all
these years, unable to forgive my transgression. They had ridden
so high on my coat-tails, relishing the envy of their friends, so
that when it all came crashing down, they chose to support him.
I know them: they will believe what they want to believe, that this
new tape is real, confirming that they'd done the right thing by
casting me out. I realise that any chance of reconciliation, however
thin, is now gone forever.

I don't cry; it's a rule of mine. I've done enough of that. But
the thought of never seeing them again almost does it. The only
way to fight the impulse is to tap into the fury burning in my
heart. Right now, it's volcanic. I've done nothing to deserve this.
It must be admirers of my former husband. But why now, after
all this time?

As I search for an answer, I consider for the first time the
possibility that Martin Scarsden is the target. What had he said
out on the verandah? Hadn't he suggested that someone was
attempting to smear him? Shit. Maybe this isn't about me. Maybe
he was right. Someone found out we'd met and used my notoriety
opportunistically. Weaponised me and my past and my reputation.

Used me to hurt him, careless of the damage done to me. A means to an end? Disposable? Or what I accused him of being: collateral damage.

For a moment, I allow myself self-pity. Then I think: stuff that. I'm not going back there, to that black hole of despair and self-recrimination. This time I've done nothing to be ashamed of. Fuck them. I did the crime, I did my time. I'm not taking the rap for something I didn't do.

I open the laptop, examine the vision more closely. It's hard to do, that pulsating flesh, the kinkiness, the glistening sex toys dripping, but I suppress my emotions, look beyond the heaving bodies, hunting for clues as to who might be behind this. And almost immediately, I notice the setting. The room. Someone has gone to quite some trouble: it looks remarkably similar to the homestead's sitting room. Could that be right? I walk from the library to the sitting room, carrying my laptop with me. It's not similar: it's identical. The same room. I'm gobsmacked, not knowing what to think. I work out the camera angles, and I find it, the camera. A real camera, small and inobtrusive, mounted high in the wall opposite the fireplace, the fireplace in front of which the video has the fake Martin Scarsden cavorting with the fake me. A security camera. Not new by the look of it, not installed recently. Why would there be a security camera all the way out here? Longchamp Downs isn't even on a highway; the driveway from the Sundowner Track is kilometres long.

So what is it they've done, these fabricators? Smuggled porn actors in here, filmed them on the security camera, and then digitally attached our heads to the bodies? When? No, the idea is ridiculous. I only met Scarsden yesterday afternoon. And they've done what, bring actors into the house overnight? A chill envelops me. They were in this house, where I am now? Where Clay sleeps? Where Mrs Enright comes and goes?

I play through the video once more, holding the laptop, looking from the screen to the room. The light is different: the video was made in the evening. The windows are dark, not backlit. I steel myself, look at the avatars, Scarsden and me, disporting themselves so acrobatically. They look too real to be animated, the movements too fluid, too realistic to be AI. I try to ignore them, to study the image more closely, peering at the laptop and then back at the room where I am standing. The floor is the same, the walls, the bookshelves, the curtains. But no, not everything is identical. The settee is different, and the video has a glass-topped coffee table, whereas the real room has a solid wooden table.

I'm beginning to understand. Someone has built a virtual set, all green screen, based on an image taken from the security camera. Everything is the correct dimensions to match the real room. Only the settee, the coffee table and the bodies are genuine, superimposed onto an image of the actual room. Not so very difficult: only the bodies are moving. And all they would need is that one background image. Everything else could have been done on the other side of the world. I breathe a little easier; they weren't here, not in the house.

Easy enough to accomplish if you know what you're doing. And provided you have the money and the resources and the tech skills and access to the right facilities. It can't be friends of my ex-husband—or not just them. They're footballers, not tech geniuses. There's too much money here, too much expertise. It's been produced too quickly, overnight. It's like the news coverage of the dam blowing—mere hours. How could it be possible to turn it around so quickly?

And it still needs someone here, I realise. Not making the video, but someone feeding information, someone who knew Scarsden and I talked yesterday. Clay. Jamie. Not Mrs Enright, she was in town fetching supplies. There were a couple of workmen helping repair the causeway. I can think of no one else.

I return the laptop to the library and go hunting for Mrs Enright. I find her in the kitchen, preparing breakfast.

'Good morning,' she says. 'You're up early.'

'There's a security camera in the sitting room.'

The old woman looks perplexed. 'Doesn't work. Hasn't for years.'

'You're sure about that?'

'Of course.' She looks bewildered. If she's the informant, she's a good actor.

'Why is there even a camera there?'

She studies my face, as if debating whether or not to answer, but she relents. 'There was a robbery. Years ago. Decades. Some very valuable paintings were stolen. Mr Carmichael put in the cameras. See—there's another one up there.' She points and, sure enough, up in a corner overlooking the back door is another camera. In the clearer light of the kitchen, I can see it's old, its lens dust-covered, a cobweb adorning it. 'The thieves never returned. At some point the cameras stopped working. Why are you asking?'

'You don't know?'

'Know what?'

'Can you show me where the recorder was? For the camera?'

Mrs Enright shrugs. 'I don't know. In your library, I guess.'

Back in the library, I find it. Ancient, using VHS tapes. It's unplugged, with no sign of it being used recently. I pick up the laptop again, return to the sitting room. The footage, the background. It's identical to how it looks now; only the couch and the coffee table are different. So when was it filmed? Last night, after I returned to the foreman's cottage, most likely.

I wait until I hear Clay return to the house. Clay. I wonder how I should approach him. When I hear him walking through to the kitchen for morning tea, I follow. Mrs Enright is there, hovering, curious.

I ask Clay about the cameras in the living room. He looks dumbfounded but answers readily enough. 'Yes, some paintings were taken. Many years ago. Originals. Very valuable, dating back to before we arrived, from when the Abbotts owned Longchamp Downs, I believe. A famous colonial artist spent three months out here, painting landscapes. Percival McEwan Fitzroy. Well known among collectors.'

'So you put security cameras in after the paintings were stolen? Were there more paintings that you wanted to protect?'

'Is this for the book?'

'Possibly. It sounds quite dramatic.'

Clay looks upset. 'No. That wasn't it at all. They took all of the paintings; there was nothing of value left.'

He peers about as if seeking guidance, finding none. Mrs Enright is busy at the sink, but I have no doubt she is listening.

Clay continues. 'The thieves came when they thought no one would be home. Vincent and I were holidaying at the Sunshine Coast, but the house wasn't empty. Chloe was desperate to come back here for some reason. She said she had left something important behind. More likely she was desperate to see that fellow. Roman Stanton. She was here when it happened. Heard a noise, came through to the sitting room to investigate. They belted her in the back of the head, knocked her out. Scared the hell out of her. Scared the hell out of me, too. So I installed the cameras.'

He looks across at Mrs Enright, then back at me. 'It was really to reassure her, not to prevent robberies or capture thieves.'

'And what year was the robbery?'

Clay doesn't hesitate. 'Late January 2005.'

That makes me think. 'So about six weeks before Roman Stanton died and Chloe went on the run.'

'What are you suggesting?' He's looking pained; I can see the memory is not a good one.

'Nothing. And you didn't recover the paintings?'

'They were never the issue.'

Mrs Enright has given up pretending; she's standing at the sink, watching us. I say to Clay, 'The paintings might be good for the book, if this artist Fitzroy was such a big deal. You don't have any copies, do you? Photographs of the paintings?'

'No. Not that I know of. You can search the files. There might be something there.' And he takes a breath. 'Chloe liked them. She was very upset when they were taken.'

'Can you remember what they showed?'

'The homestead here, when it was first built. Lake Murdoch in flood. The back country, out beyond the ridges, dotted with mulga. And a rock formation, the Camel's Head.'

I start. 'Sorry?'

'And another one, quite eerie . . .' He looks at me, gaping at him. 'Are you okay?'

'Sure. Sorry. The paintings. I'd love to see copies, if they exist.' My mind is whirring. The Camel's Head. A stolen painting. My past. The fraudulent porno.

'Clay, who gave you the idea for the book?'

He looks genuinely puzzled. 'No one. It was my idea.'

'And how did you find me? Settle on me to be the author?'

He shrugs. 'I just googled. Found your agent.'

I look at Mrs Enright. I wish she wasn't here, but it can't be helped. It has to be said. 'You must have been aware of my reputation before you hired me.'

'I was. But everyone deserves a second chance.'

'Look, I'm sorry, but something awful has happened.' And I tell him about the video of Martin Scarsden and me, the one currently breaking the internet, emphasising it is a fake, that the technology is widespread, that Scarsden never set foot in the house. Clay listens impassively, mouth tight, brows cast down. Mrs Enright looks as if a witch has taken a seat at her kitchen table.

chapter twenty-seven

RETURNING TO THE LIBRARY, I GET BACK ONLINE. CHANCES ARE THAT CLAY will evict me as soon as he sees the video, reads what's being said about me. Whatever he chooses to believe, he still has a standing in this community, a reputation to uphold. I know what I would do if I were him.

I search for Percival McEwan Fitzroy and Longchamp Downs and the Camel's Head. And almost immediately I'm rewarded. Not just a text reference, but an image, from the Queensland Art Gallery. Part of their collection. *The Camel's Head at Dusk*, by Percival McEwan Fitzroy, circa 1893. Could that be it? The stolen painting is residing in the state gallery in Brisbane? Surely not.

I search on, find a report of the robbery at Longchamp Downs and realise my error. According to two separate sources, the painting stolen the night Chloe was here was called *The Camel's Head at Dawn*. A companion piece to the one in Brisbane.

I return to the gallery website, locate the image once more, magnify it as much as possible. The painting is of a low ridge of rocks, dark red, almost black, silhouetted against the still-glowing sky, the sun already set. So the artist was looking west. It reminds me of the expanse out beyond the ridge, the far side of the airstrip, the way Jamie led me yesterday. The formation isn't so very remarkable, just rocks on top of other rocks, the hump of a camel, nothing more than the suggestion of a head. The Camel's Head. It takes a good dose of imagination to see it. It could just as easily be called the Dog's Head, or the Fishtail, or the Mule's Belly. Or Collection of Rocks, Randomly Stacked.

I think again of Hentig and Stuart. Searching for treasure out beyond the boundary, searching for exactly this. In 1848. The painting in the gallery is dated 1893, forty-five years later, when Patrick Murdoch was dead and the Abbotts owned Longchamp Downs. This is what the two explorers sought, this place, painted by Fitzroy so many years later, unaware of their existence, of their passing. This is it. I can feel it. Redemption beckons. For a moment I allow myself the freedom of daydreaming, of forgetting the vileness flooding the internet. Momentarily, I float free above the putrid tide.

The sound of a quad bike brings me back to the here and now. I walk out onto the verandah; I'm not going to skulk.

The moment I see Jamie walking up the path, I can tell by his face that he knows, that he's seen the video. He looks as white as a sheet, despite his years in the sun. It brings reality rushing back, my predicament, the scandalous smear.

'What do you want?' I say to him quietly as he comes up the stairs.

'To check if you're okay,' he stammers.

My hackles rise. 'What do you reckon?'

He looks like a scolded schoolboy. 'I know it's not real.'

Anger flares. As if that is meant to console me, that he knows the porno is fake. I stare at him, see him wilt beneath my contempt.

'The sitting room,' I say. 'How did they get the background image? The CCTV isn't working.'

He's shaking his head. 'It's not like that.'

'So what it's like?' I ask, and I taste the venom in my whisper.

'I swear I wasn't in on it. I just took the pictures. Sent them through.'

His use of the plural stops me just in time. 'Pictures. The sitting room. What else?'

'All the cameras. They wanted to check all the angles the cameras covered. Whether they should just replace them, or resurvey the whole place. That's what they told me.'

'Who, Jamie? Who asked for the pictures?'

'The buyer's agent. Dermott Brick. He works in Cunnamulla. Real estate, equipment hire. Labour contractor.'

I recall the name; Jamie had mentioned it to Clay in the conversation I'd overheard on the verandah. 'So this Dermott Brick, he rings you up and asks you to send through images? Last night? What time?'

Jamie is shaking his head. 'No. He didn't need to ring. He was here, helping us fix the track. Asked me before he left for the evening. You'd already headed back to the foreman's cottage or you would have seen me do it. I wasn't hiding anything.' He sounds pathetic yet guileless; his words hold the ring of sincerity.

I think that through. 'So he was here when Martin Scarsden was here?'

'Yeah. Working on the track. His bobcat.' The white has bled from Jamie's face. Now, if anything, he looks like he might be blushing.

'Listen, Jamie. This doesn't end here. You understand that, don't you? I won't let it. This journalist Martin Scarsden won't let it either.' And as I say it, I sense the veracity, the power in the assertion. Scarsden. He's a high-profile journalist, practised in digging, in finding things out. In writing the truth, getting it out into the world. He might be able to help me. We might be able to help each other. And suddenly I feel better. I have a course of action. I have a target.

Jamie is looking like he wants to scurry away, but I'm not about to let him off the hook. Not yet, anyway. 'Was he here the other night, this Brick? When you blew the road?' I already know the answer from the eavesdropping on Clay and Jamie, but I want to hear him say it.

He looks at me, and I can see the internal conflict, some misplaced loyalty. Or some vested interest. 'You won't dob on me?'

I regard him with despair. Dob. Such an adolescent word, such an adolescent concept. 'Not if you tell me what you know.'

'Yes. He was here.'

'It was staged, wasn't it? The Stantons didn't blow up the road. This Dermott Brick did that. With your connivance.'

Jamie doesn't have to answer. He just hangs his head. I can read the guilt on his face like an open book. 'It had nothing to do with Martin Scarsden,' he says. 'I didn't even know he was here until we were filming them.'

'Brick never mentioned him?'

'No.'

'Did you give the videos to the newspapers?'

'Me? No. How could I?'

'So it was Brick?'

'I guess.'

'Listen, Jamie: Dermott Brick has done a terrible thing to me, an unforgiveable thing, and to Martin Scarsden too. You know that now. And he's played you like a fiddle. So you need to make a choice. Whose side are you on? Because I'm going after this fucker and I'm going to bring him down. There is no middle ground. You're either on my side, or you're on his. And let me tell you, his side will end up getting very messy indeed.'

Jamie stares at me, forlorn. 'You didn't fight back last time,' he says.

I explode, all the self-control, all the discipline, all the constraints bursting. I slap him across the face, as hard as I can, feeling the tears pressing hard behind my eyes. To think I was beginning to like this idiot, to trust him. How stupid can I be?

Slowly, he raises a hand to his cheek, touches the red mark. He turns, walks away, and I am left to fold in on myself, telling myself through my tears that I never cry.

—–

Later, when I'm back at work in the library, Jamie returns, contrition etched on his face.

'What now?' I say, the anger subterranean but still there.

'I want to apologise. Tell you what I know.' He offers a wan smile. 'Be on your side.'

'I'm listening.'

'When Clay decided to sell, once most of the cattle were gone, the manager and the other hands left. Only Mrs Enright and I stayed. Clay asked me to keep the place running while he found a buyer. I thought a new owner would appoint a manager, restock. Hoped I might get the job.'

'Is that why you were happy to accommodate the wishes of Dermott Brick?'

'Yeah. I guess. So he'd put in a good word.'

'Tell me what you know.'

'I can't see how they could have planned it. Scarsden, I mean. We started building that road weeks ago. Scarsden was nowhere near here, as far as I know. Neither were you. It has to be a coincidence.'

I think on it for a moment. 'The work on the airstrip road. Was that before or after that big rain event up north?'

Jamie's eyes widen. 'About the same time, I guess.'

'The flood that's just reaching us now?'

'Yes.'

'So Clay wanted the culverts, allowing the flood to flow through, and it was Brick's idea to block them?'

'Yes. To spread the water, make the place green. Then he got word the Stantons were heading our way, so we thought we'd frame them. It was spur of the moment, but it worked a treat.'

'Except you didn't know Scarsden was coming?'

'No. I told you that.'

'And yet all the online coverage, it's all about him.' By now, the fury has gone out of me. I'm even feeling sorry for Jamie. God knows why, but I can see he's been played. 'Before you go. One last thing. The Camel's Head. Ever heard of it?'

Jamie looks puzzled. 'Yeah. Out west. A long way. Past the ridge lines.'

'You know where, exactly?'

He shakes his head. 'You'd have to ask Clay.'

chapter twenty-eight
MARTIN

'YOU'VE SEEN IT THEN?' MARTIN ASKS MANDY.

'Everyone has seen it,' says Mandy. *'Everyone.'*

'It's not real. It's a deepfake.'

'Obviously,' says Mandy. And she laughs.

Martin's relief flows like cool water. 'Obviously?'

'Well, it's your head all right. Amazing technology. But that body they've stuck it on: far too buff. That guy works out.'

'Seriously?' asks Martin, involuntarily sucking in his stomach.

'Sure. And you know. Well endowed.'

'What are you saying?'

But she responds with laughter. 'Relax, big boy. I'm only joking.'

'Right.'

'I know it's not you. And not just because of the abs. I know you wouldn't do that to me.'

'Thank you,' he says. 'Thanks for believing in me.' He feels a well of emotion, realising how much he is missing her. 'How are you? You and Liam?'

'He's good. Tougher than me. He asks after you.'

'What do you tell him?'

'That you're on one of your adventures.'

Martin laughs at that, loves the idea of Liam being unaffected. He doesn't want the phone call to end; it's like a lifeline to a saner, more normal world. 'And you, Mandy? How are you coping?'

'Okay, I guess, but I worry, Martin. I worry.'

'No need. You should be safe. Provided you're not with me.'

'I'm worried about *you*,' she says softly. 'Tell me what's going on.'

He explains, outlining his theory that someone is trying to destroy his reputation: first implicating him in the destruction of the road, then the deepfake of him with Ekaterina Boland.

'But why? Why now? Why there?' Mandy asks.

'I don't know. I'm starting to suspect it's part of some elaborate plan. I think that whole story about the contract on my life was bullshit, all designed to split you and me up, to get me out here by myself.'

'The explosion? The gunshots?'

'I know it sounds crazy.'

'All to place you in that flyspeck town?'

'Maybe.'

Mandy doesn't speak for a few seconds. 'You think Jack is involved?'

'I can't rule it out. I think there's a possibility that he's being manipulated somehow.'

'But, Martin, he's ASIO. And he's smart and he's tough.'

'Nothing is impossible.'

She is silent for a long time. He's thinking that the line has cut out before she finally speaks. 'Martin, I'll have to call you back. There's a car coming up the drive.' And then. 'It's okay. Police.

They might have news. I need to go. I'll call when I know what they want.'

'Wait,' he says. 'Where are you?'

'Back home. Port Silver.' And she ends the call.

The police. At their house on the clifftop. Why? He tries calling back, but the call rings out. A sense of trepidation grips him. He feels powerless, conscious of every one of the thousand kilometres between Port Paroo and his home. He considers ringing Jack Goffing, his friend and defender, but finds himself hesitating. Doubting the man, and hating the idea he is doubting him. He loathes what his invisible tormentors are doing to him.

He's still holding his phone, trying to decide if he should call Goffing, when it rings in his hand, taking him by surprise. An unknown number.

'Yes?' he says tentatively.

'Martin Scarsden?' A woman's voice.

'Who's asking?' He is terse, on edge.

'Ekaterina Boland.'

Now she says her name, he recognises the voice. 'Where are you?' he asks.

'At Longchamp Downs. We should talk.'

'Right,' he says, unable to keep his voice free of suspicion. She's a fellow victim, but he's not sure how far to trust her.

'Martin, we need to get these fuckers. You and I know the truth. We need to make sure the world does as well.'

'What are you suggesting? Some sort of denial?'

'What? A press release? Fuck that. No. I'm suggesting we find out who has set us up and expose them. Isn't that what you do, Mr Journalist?'

For a split second, Martin feels embarrassed at being told how to do his job. 'I agree,' he says. 'I think it's me they're targeting, not you.'

'That's what I think too,' she says. 'But it doesn't mean the harm to me is any less.'

'Can we meet?' he asks. 'Somewhere private?'

'Not possible. But I have some information for you.'

'I'm all ears.'

'The explosives weren't set by Clay Carmichael or Jamie Stubbs or the Stantons. There was another man involved. A real estate guy, based in Cunnamulla. His name is Dermott Brick. He's also the one who commissioned the photograph of the Longchamp Downs sitting room, the background in the fake video. And he's the buyer's agent representing this Scottish multinational that wants to buy Longchamp Downs.'

Martin feels a surge of hope; finally, a lead to follow. 'Okay. That could prove useful. Thank you.'

'You're welcome,' says Ekaterina, all business. 'And do you have anything to tell me?'

He thinks of confiding his suspicions about Jack Goffing and ASIO, but demurs. He owes Goffing that much. 'Whoever is behind this must have money and clout. To produce a video like that overnight? That takes expertise and connections. And I think there are other, institutional players involved.'

'Institutional? What does that mean?'

'The police. Maybe the intelligence services.' And as he says it, he can't help but think of Mandy, the unexpected visit from the police at Port Silver.

'That's it—I can't have anything more to do with you,' she says. 'Not publicly. I can't afford to be seen to be participating in any of this.' She takes a breath. 'But I will do anything I can to help. I want my name cleared and these fuckers to pay.'

'Understood. As I said, I think I'm the target, not you. I'll keep you posted if I learn anything more.'

'Thanks, Martin.' And then, something like remorse, or concern. 'Good luck. And take care. I'll be in touch if I learn anything else.' She ends the call.

Dermott Brick. The name means nothing to him. Yet if the man instigated the dam explosion, and especially if he requested the photograph of the sitting room, then he's the link to whoever is behind this, the man on the ground. Martin googles him, finds a business in Cunnamulla. Real estate, labour hire, earth-moving equipment. Quite the operation. There's a photo of a group of a dozen workers, all in high-vis and workwear, standing in front of a warehouse, arms folded, like a footy team. Martin clicks through to a staff page, where he finds a photo of Brick. He's not the owner or managing director but the operations manager. He's a large man, a ranga with a head like a house brick, solid, with corners. Brick by name . . . In the photo, he's smiling. It's a mistake: it makes his face look distorted, like he's reflected in a carnival mirror. Or a hubcap.

Martin thinks again of seeking help from Jack Goffing, but instead googles the telephone directory, rings through to Dubbo police station, asks to be put through to Detective Sergeant Ivan Lucic. He gives his name as Jake Solander and hopes Ivan doesn't give him the flick.

'Lucic here.'

'Ivan, it's Martin Scarsden.'

Martin can hear the sharp intake of breath. 'Martin?' A short pause. 'Whose phone you using?'

'A burner.'

'Mate, I'm not sure I can talk to you.'

'Ivan, the porn's a fake. And I wasn't part of destroying that track; it was a setup. Someone is trashing my reputation.'

Another, longer pause. 'That's not all,' says Lucic ominously. 'You haven't heard?'

'Heard what?'

'The fraud squad are after you. Planning on raiding your house, if they haven't already. Where are you?'

'Out west.' Martin thinks immediately of the police arriving at the Port Silver house, Mandy there. 'The fraud squad? How do you know about it?'

'They're coming here to interview me about our relationship. Them and Professional Standards. I'm not thrilled.'

'Shit. I'm sorry.'

'I'll have to tell them about this conversation.'

'Of course. But tell me, is there a warrant for my arrest?'

Martin can hear Ivan tapping on his keyboard. 'Not yet. Might depend on what they find at your house. But why are you calling me?'

Martin goes to the heart of the matter, grateful Lucic is willing to hear him out. 'There's a man based at Cunnamulla, name of Dermott Brick. Can you check to see if he has a criminal record? Known associates, that sort of thing.'

Martin hears the tapping of a keyboard.

'No. Nothing.'

'Really?'

'But then again, Cunnamulla is in Queensland. I'm New South Wales police.'

'Of course. Well, thanks anyway.'

'Just hang on a moment.'

Martin hears more tapping.

'Interesting,' says Ivan.

'What's that?'

'The only Dermott Brick I can find died seven years ago in a mining accident in the Pilbara.'

chapter twenty-nine

DERMOTT BRICK. JUST A NAME, A FACE ON A WEBSITE. MARTIN SEARCHES further online, finds nothing. It's as if Brick appeared in Cunnamulla four or five years ago with no history. Maybe he's an imposter, an identity thief, assuming the name of a man who died seven years ago on the other side of the country. Surely, he can't have been here for years preparing for this attack on Martin's reputation. More like a hired hand. Dirty deeds done dirt cheap. Maybe he scouts for jobs on the same app used to recruit the B-team. A side hustle.

Martin's phone rings. Another unknown number. For an anonymous burner, it's sure getting a lot of traffic.

'Yes?' he answers, hesitant about identifying himself.

'Martin? Is that you?'

'Who is this?'

'It's Nick. Nick Poulos.'

Martin recognises the voice, immediately puts a face to the name. Nick Poulos, their lawyer and friend from Port Silver, last seen cowering from the destruction of the community hall.

'Nick. Yes. It's Martin.'

'Mandy gave me your number. You still out west?'

'That's right.'

'Listen, I'm with her now. In town, at the police station. She's not under arrest, but they have detained her for questioning. I'm representing her until her Melbourne solicitor gets here.'

'And Liam?'

'At school. Doesn't know anything is wrong. We'll pick him up, bring him to our place. A play date.'

'Thanks, Nick. We owe you. How's Mandy?'

'Holding up. She'll give you a call when she can.'

'What is it? Why are they holding her? I heard something about the fraud squad.'

'Martin, it's bad. I'd advise you to come back here as soon as you possibly can. Better optics. Otherwise they'll issue a warrant for your arrest. You'll be in the papers again, photographed in handcuffs.'

'This is bullshit, Nick. I haven't done anything wrong. *We* haven't done anything wrong. Who is it we're meant to have defrauded?'

'They've confiscated your hard drives. Going through them.'

Martin thinks of all the information, some of it sensitive. Some encrypted, some not.

Nick continues. 'You have your laptop with you?'

Martin hesitates, then rebukes himself. Nick isn't just trustworthy, he's protected. 'You're acting as my lawyer, aren't you, Nick, asking questions like that?'

'Absolutely. Your lawyer and Mandy's. Privileged.'

'Good. Thank you. And, yes, I have my laptop.'

'Okay. My advice is back up anything you don't want to lose. If they confiscate it, they might keep it for months. But whatever you do, don't erase anything, no matter how tempting, no matter how damning, no matter how innocuous. They'll be able to tell.'

'You're taking this very seriously, Nick.'

'Too right I'm taking it seriously. This is no casual investigation. There are half-a-dozen detectives here, state and federal. You think they're going to fly them all up here for a few missing tax receipts? My professional assessment: you're in deep shit.'

Martin runs his hands through his hair, trying to think through the implications. 'There's stuff on those drives I don't want made public—investigations, past and current. I want you to do your utmost to ensure none of that is released. There's no reason it should be; none of it reflects on Mandy or myself. And there is nothing on the drives or in the notebooks or the files that would incriminate Mandy or myself.'

'That's not what I'm hearing.'

'What?'

'It's not just fraud, Martin. They say there are images. Thousands of them.'

Martin feels the earth sway, like gravity itself is betraying him. Images. Blowing up a dam, a fabricated video of him shagging Ekaterina Boland, accusations of fraud. All bad, but all eventually survivable.

'What?' he asks, a tremor in his voice.

'Child abuse.'

'No,' says Martin. 'No. It can't be.' And his mind is writhing, a medusa of horror. The story of the hit squad. Goffing sending him west, sending Mandy overseas, the house on the clifftop left unattended, all those working documents, the filing cabinets, the notebooks, the hard drives, all there for the taking, unguarded for days. All there to be corrupted.

'Come back, Martin,' says Nick. 'You can't outrun this, you can't hide. When they issue a warrant for your arrest, they're sure to publicise it. I'll be in court seeking a suppression order, but that's not much use if it's already been leaked. The media will have a field day. They'll crucify you.'

Martin hears himself laugh, a disembodied scoffing, bitter and hollow. In the past, he's campaigned with other journalists to rein in the number of suppression orders. 'It'll be all over the *Daily Mail* whatever I do.'

'Martin.'

'Yes. I'll come back. And Nick, we need our own forensic expert. Someone who can examine the drives, determine where the images came from, when they were planted.'

'I'm on it.'

'Thanks, Nick. Good to have you onside.'

'Take care, Martin.'

Martin stares into space. This is it, he decides, the coup de grâce. An allegation of paedophilia or trading in child abuse material will cause irredeemable damage to his reputation. Even if Nick works some unlikely magic and the case collapses, there is no such thing as a finding of innocence. Not with this. The allegation will stick to him forever. He feels his mind losing its discipline, begins ploughing through scenarios, each worse than the one before. He will need to leave Mandy and Liam, for their own good, distance himself from the people he loves the most. Vern, the extended family. He can't allow them to be tainted.

For a dark moment, he's like a man swept from shore in a rip. At what point do you stop swimming, let yourself sink, breathe in the water? End it? Maybe that's what he should do now. Walk off into the desert. Drive the Subaru west, head off road, keep driving until he gets bogged or runs out of petrol. A final act, a noble death, protecting the ones he loves. If he's dead, the police won't pursue the investigation. There'll be no court case. They'll be safe.

His handset rings. He doesn't answer. What's the point?

It rings again. Insistent. This time he takes the call.

'Martin? It's Bethanie.'

Bethanie Glass, chief crime reporter for the *Sydney Morning Herald*. The police must have already started briefing; they must be very confident of the evidence they have.

'Bethanie. That didn't take long.'

'Well, I do have other work besides your research.'

Martin regroups, realises she doesn't yet know about the raid in Port Silver, the gathering storm.

'Sorry, Bethanie. Not how I meant to phrase it. What have you got?'

'The placing of the two news stories. The raid on Longchamp Downs and the fake pornography. Dropped to multiple news outlets simultaneously. A national PR company, Packlehurst and Glee. The *Daily Mail* was first only because they didn't bother checking anything.'

'Packlehurst and Glee? Never heard of them.'

'Corporate. Finance-focused. Stock market announcements, glossy annual reports, corporate videos, that sort of thing. Offices in all the state capitals.'

'So not some random source in the outback?'

'No.'

'Thanks, Bethanie. That proves it: this campaign against me is no accident. It's well resourced and well coordinated and deliberate.'

'I couldn't find anything on the prospective buyer for Longchamp Downs. Looks like it might be offshore.'

'A Scotland-based multinational?'

'Could be.'

'Thanks, Bethanie. I owe you one.'

She laughs at that. 'You already owe me several.'

'Put it on the tab, then.'

The call ends, and takes all thoughts of wandering off into the desert with it. The campaign against him is being run through a professional PR outfit that is planting the stories far and wide. Could they possibly be involved in installing the images on his hard drives? Probably not. For the first time, he sees not so much a glimmer of hope as a potential for agency: he can stop being the hunted; he can again become the hunter. Because the only way to prove his innocence will be to demonstrate that someone else is responsible. He thinks of calling Ekaterina; he'll need her evidence about the detonation of the dam, about the fabricated video. But he knows he'll need more, much more.

First thing, he must back up some sensitive files to the cloud. He taps away at his laptop, gets the process underway, wonders how long it might take with only the phone hotspot to transmit the data. As the files upload, he considers his next move. Maybe drive back up the Sundowner Track and on to Cunnamulla. Pay Dermott Brick a visit.

His phone rings. Jack Goffing.

'Jack. You heard about Port Silver? The police?'

'Don't worry about that. Get moving. Disappear.'

'What?'

'Melbourne. There's been a hit.'

'Shit. The B-team?'

'No. Worse. While the surveillance team was concentrating on them, two other gunmen took out one of Enzo Marelli's grandsons. Shot sitting in a cafe. It's going to kick off, a full-scale gangland war.'

'Why so urgent I disappear?'

'Don't you see? They knew all eyes were on the B-team. It was only a decoy.'

'They knew? How? An informant?'

'Most likely. We suspect a source inside the police has been feeding them information. And if the B-team was a decoy for killers targeting Marelli, they could just as easily be playing the same role for you.'

'Shit.'

'Get going. Disappear. Into the desert if you have to.' And Goffing ends the call.

But it's too late. As Martin has been talking to Jack Goffing, he's been watching a cloud of dust. A big twin-cab, coming from Port Paroo, across the bridge. But not going on to Bourke. It turns onto the Sundowner Track. He hopes the driver will think nothing of him, just drive on past. But instead it pulls up next to him. Before he can do anything, a man emerges, walks up to the Subaru, smiling broadly. He opens Martin's door. He has a gun.

chapter thirty
ECCO

THERE'S THE SOUND OF THE FRONT DOOR OPENING, BOOTS ECHOING ON THE hardwood floorboards. I'm leaving the library when I come face to face with Clay. His mouth is pursed like a cat's bum, his forehead furrowed, his eyes curdled with offence and distaste.

I sigh. 'You've seen the video?'

'How could you?' he sputters. 'My family home. Desecrated.'

I keep my voice even, emphatic. 'It's not real, Clay. I told you that. Scarsden was never here at night. He never came inside the house. We sat out on the verandah.'

I can see he doesn't want to hear, doesn't want to consider alternatives. Doesn't want to believe me.

I speak before he can form new words, my anger and indignation lending me authority. 'Take another look at the video. And instead of focusing on my fake arse, look at the settee. At the coffee table.'

I hold his gaze until he breaks eye contact. I can see he's listening now. I'm getting through.

'Come and see me when you're ready to apologise,' I say. 'I'll be in the library.'

— —

It's not until late afternoon that Clay returns. This time he doesn't barge in. He takes his boots off, leaves them on the verandah, knocks on the library door. He's holding his hat in his hands as if he's entering church, as if seeking atonement.

I walk past him without a word, leading him to the sitting room. He studies the settee and the coffee table, confirming what he already knows. I see him look up at the camera mounted across from the fireplace, nodding to himself.

'I believe you,' he says.

'Thank you.'

'I don't understand how they can do that,' he says.

'Not so difficult. Today's technology. They call it a deepfake.'

'Not the technology,' he says. 'I don't understand how they could do that to you. To anyone. Slander you like that. Why? Some cruel joke, some sadistic titillation. Because of your past.'

I wonder at his old-school decency. His naivety. 'No, Clay. It's not just some random internet trolls. Think of the effort involved. How quickly it was produced. All the effort to make the scene match this house.' I let that sink in a moment before continuing. 'It was considered and it was targeted. Possibly planned in advance. Someone who knew my reputation, and decided to deploy it to damage Martin Scarsden.'

'Scarsden?'

'Yes. What I can't work out is whether I was deliberately lured here to discredit him, or it was just opportunistic.'

Clay looks doubtful. 'No. I told you. The idea for the book was mine. I found your agent, she recommended you.'

'When was this?'

'A day or two before you agreed to come out. After I had the approach to sell, after I'd discussed it with Vincent and he decided once and for all he didn't want the place, that he'd prefer the money. That we were better off selling.'

'Was he pushing you to sell? Encouraging you?'

'Vincent? No. Only after he heard there was a buyer in the wings. But he'd made it clear many times that he wasn't interested in becoming a grazier, that his long-term plan was to employ a manager. So he supports the sale, says the money would be useful. Allow me to retire. Help with his mortgage, the school fees. Nothing wrong with that.'

'What about Chloe?' I feel bad saying it, see the anguish her name evokes.

'She will be looked after, of course. Makes it easier in some ways. They can split the inheritance fifty-fifty.'

'And you?'

'Like I told you: I want to stay here. Move to your cottage. Until she comes back.'

I'm not sure what to say. The poor guy. I don't know where his daughter is, but I can't see her returning after all this time. 'Clay, I want to clear my name. Will you help me?'

'If I can.'

'Tell me what you know about Dermott Brick.'

'Brick? He's been out here helping fix the track across to your cottage.'

'He's more than just a contractor, though, isn't he?'

Clay frowns. 'You think he's behind this?'

'I suspect so. The fake porn video as well.'

Clay looks troubled. 'It can't be him. He must be working for someone. He wouldn't know you, wouldn't know Scarsden. Employed by a reputable company. Go to for labour hire, work teams, equipment. I can't think of any reason for him to be targeting you or Scarsden.'

'He's also been acting as a buyer's agent for the company acquiring Longchamp Downs, hasn't he?'

Clay looks around, as if making sure we can't be overheard. 'That's right.'

'I heard it's a multinational, headquartered in Scotland.'

'Yes. Can't see how they could be involved.'

I can't either. 'Do you have any solid evidence that they're the buyer, or do you only have Brick's word on that?'

That gives him pause for thought. 'I've seen documents. Letters. Emails. They've looked genuine. My solicitor will check them out, of course.'

'Might be a good idea.'

'What will you do now?' he asks. 'Try and chase down Brick?'

I grimace. 'No. I'll leave that to Martin Scarsden. I want to finish your book. I need the money, but I also want to honour the place. I'm beginning to appreciate why you want such a book, a record of your time here, what it might mean to Vincent and Chloe and the following generations.'

'If you wanted to leave, I'd understand,' Clay says. 'You could keep what I've already paid you.'

I shake my head. The forty thousand down payment won't last long, won't secure my apartment. 'No, I intend to finish your book. And you saw the video. I don't want to be anywhere near Brisbane. I think staying here is a better option for me.'

Clay sighs. 'Fair enough. Let me know if there is anything I can do to help. To make things easier.'

'There is one thing. No, two. First, can I access Chloe's diaries, like I asked? I want to include her. She belongs in your story, the story of Longchamp Downs.'

'Very well. Let me have a look at them first, though. What's the second thing?'

'The Camel's Head. The place in the stolen painting. Do you know where it is?'

Clay says nothing, but I can see the astonishment in his eyes, a kind of shock.

'What is it?' I ask.

'Chloe . . . Chloe asked me that.'

'She did? When?'

'The week before she shot Roman Stanton. Not long before she went on the run.'

chapter thirty-one
MARTIN

THE MAN WITH THE GUN IS LEERING. A SECOND MAN IS STANDING BEHIND HIM, out of sight, but Martin hears him laugh, as if this is all just a jolly jape. The man with the gun is wearing a red trucker cap with a prominent letter 'A' in yellow relief.

'Hello, Martin. We're the A-team,' he says, with a reptilian smirk. 'We've come to kill you.' And he laughs, a high-pitched cackle, sounding like he's teetering on the edge of insanity.

Martin looks at the gun. It's chrome-plated, shimmering in the morning sun, the barrel dark with use.

The laughter subsides, replaced by a manic grin. The man has a crown on one of his teeth, chrome like his gun. Gangster bling, matching. 'You'll be coming with us.' The barrel is pointed directly at Martin's chest.

'No,' says Martin and tries to wrench the door closed.

'For fuck's sake,' says the man, his leg firmly wedged against the door. His companion, a large bulk of a man, still chuckling with the fun of it all, leans over his colleague's shoulder and shoots Martin in the chest.

Martin only has time to look down, see the dart, before his vision starts to tunnel. He tries to yell but can only summon a wheeze. Before losing consciousness, he wonders what a death rattle might sound like.

'Night-night,' says the shorter man.

——

Martin awakes in a sea of nausea, opening his eyes to a blinding whiteness, disorientated. It takes a moment for his eyes to adjust, for his brain to shuck off its confusion. He remembers the men in the red caps, the gun, the dart. A surge of adrenaline, a wave of panic, lifts him from his stupor. He's in a car, the front passenger seat, constrained by a seatbelt. His wrists are bound by cable ties that are in turn threaded through the side doorhandle. The car is familiar: Mandy's Subaru. He looks across. The younger man, the shorter, slighter one, is driving. The boss. Martin twists around, expecting the larger man to be in the back seat, but it's empty. He looks out the window. They're in the desert, not even on a track, driving slowly, threading their way through low-lying bushes.

'Where are we?'

'Oh, hello, it's Sleeping Beauty. Welcome back to the land of the living. Temporarily.' The man smiles, chrome tooth aglow.

For a moment, Martin thinks they're alone. Twisting around to see behind him again, through the trailing dust he catches a glimpse of another vehicle, someone following them. It must be the man's companion, the other half of the A-team.

'Where you taking me?' he asks. His throat feels dry and ragged. He could do with a drink.

'Road less travelled,' says the man.

'You're going to kill me?'

'That's the idea.'

'Who is it?' Martin asks. 'Who's paying you?'

'Fucked if I know. Deep pockets, though. Know what they want.'

Martin looks out at the wasteland. Across at the dash. It says the outside temperature is thirty-six degrees, and that it's 11.30 am. He's lost three hours. 'Why out here?'

'What do you reckon?' asks the man. His tone is conversational, like they're having a chat to pass the time.

They drive on, into the miasma of heat.

'Can I have something to drink?' asks Martin.

'Nah.' The man laughs. 'Defeat the purpose.'

They continue without talking, another half an hour, the man whistling tunelessly, seemingly enjoying weaving in and out of the random clumps of vegetation. Martin is starting to grow drowsy again, perhaps the after-effects of the tranquilliser dart. They hit a bowl, soft sand. Martin thinks they might bog, but before that can happen, the engine cuts out. The man tries to restart it, but the engine turns over without catching, the starter motor frustrated. 'Out of gas,' says the man.

Martin is about to protest that the tank was almost half full, then realises the futility of the assertion. Either they've been driving for longer than he first thought, or the A-team has partially drained the tank somewhere along the way while Martin slumbered. Eleven thirty in the morning. Jesus, they could be hundreds of kilometres into the wilderness.

'We're going to leave you here,' says the man, staring at the dashboard, seemingly unwilling to meet Martin's eye. At least the faux good humour has gone. 'It'll get near enough to forty-five degrees today. Maybe more. Hotter inside the car. You might last to nighttime, you might not. Even if you do, you'll die sometime tomorrow.'

'Without a mark on me.'

The man smiles. 'Not by the time they find you.'

The man cracks the door open, and the rush of heat feels like he's opened the gates of hell. Martin hadn't realised the aircon had been working.

'There's no water out here,' says the man. 'None in the car. We checked. Just in the radiator. But I wouldn't drink that. Coolant's nasty stuff.' The smile returns, and then the cackle, the unhinged braying. 'Something for you to think about.'

Martin says nothing, can only watch as the man retrieves a brown bottle, pours liquid onto a cloth. Martin catches the smell of something pungent, then the cloth is being held over his face. He passes out.

chapter thirty-two

WHEN HE COMES TO AGAIN, HIS HEAD IS POUNDING, HIS MOUTH DESERT-DRY, his tongue swollen. The heat is unbelievable. They've moved him across, sat him in the driver's seat. Presumably in case he never regained consciousness. He looks at his hands. They're no longer bound by the cable ties, and the marks around his wrists have vanished. He looks at the dash, but it's switched off. He tries the starter. It kicks over, but the engine doesn't start, of course it doesn't, although the battery isn't dead. The dash tells him the time has advanced to just past two o'clock. Before the electrics return to sleep he punches up the sat nav. It shows the car is in the middle of a featureless green swathe. He zooms out, and out again. A horizontal row of dots appears: the Queensland border. He zooms out further until, finally, he has a position. The middle of fucking nowhere. The nearest road of any description is seventy kilometres south, the Port Paroo to Tibooburra road. It's the only discernible feature.

The car is an oven. He opens the door. Gets out. The heat is searing, but somehow cooler than inside the car. He cracks the bonnet. The water reserve for the windscreen wipers has been emptied. He sees the coolant reservoir, knows its contents are toxic. Nevertheless, he wrenches the cap free, removes his shirt, soaks it. He might not be able to drink it, but it can help cool him. He puts the shirt back on, feels the fleeting relief. He lies flat on the ground, rolls under the car, into the shade.

He has one idea and one idea only: survive until dusk.

He recalls the rain. Heavy enough to close the roads. The story of the tin-roof country in Queensland. Surely it can't all have evaporated or soaked into the soil. Some of it must have gathered, not out here on the empty plain, but perhaps on one of the rocky ridges. Some crevice.

He considers it. If he can make it to sunset, he can start walking, head towards a ridge line. Or maybe he can find a creek bed, dry by now, but with water still preserved below the surface. He wonders what he might have in the car, some tool to dig with.

He wants to get up, search the back of the car. Find something to write with, something to deny his guilt, deny he has voluntarily headed out here, suicided. He wants to finger the A-team, so they can't get away with his murder.

But he doesn't move, stays in the shade, tries to slow his breathing, conserve his strength, conserve his moisture. Tries to switch off, to stop obsessing about water. He thinks of Mandy and Liam. He needs to live, to clear his name, to see Mandy released from custody, to remove any guilt by association. They need him. He has to survive. To endure. For them.

Time moves like treacle, measured by the shade cast by the car, creeping across the ground. He sleeps, wakes, the thirst becoming more and more intense.

Eventually the light turns golden, the sun dipping behind the western ridge, a moment he'd feared would not arrive. Martin rolls out from under the car, tries to stand. His knees buckle at the first attempt, and he almost faints at the second, the blood running from his head. He knows he's badly dehydrated. Knows his blood will be thickening, threatening cardiac arrest. But this is his one chance. He needs to harness the last of his energy, marshal his diminishing fluids. He eases himself onto the bonnet of the car; the metal is no longer hot to touch, the sun has lost its potency. He makes his way onto the roof, then stands. There is a ridge line to his west, silhouetted by the setting sun, and another to the east. The boundaries to his existence. The one to the west looks marginally closer. He tries to think, but his brain is sluggish, defying his attempts to concentrate. He wants to work out which ridge holds a better prospect of water, but can't decide. He'll try for the western ridge, the nearer of the two.

He's about to clamber down when something catches his eye: a straight line challenging the irregularities of nature. He peers at it, squinting. It looks like some sort of vertical tower. It's sitting below the western ridge line, but further to the north.

He eases down off the car. He searches around, finds a suitable rock. He scrapes a message into the bonnet of the car: *Abducted. The A-team. Murdered. Not suicide.* He adds his initials, *MS*, and the date. He wonders if it's a futile act, a waste of energy.

He starts walking. He is so very thirsty. His head is pounding and shapes are floating unbidden into his vision. His skin feels parchment-dry, like wrinkled paper. He's not sweating, not enough. Earlier, lying under the car, he'd been willing himself not to perspire; now he knows it's dehydration. He needs to take it slowly and steadily.

He reaches the ridge. Nothing. Just an outcrop of rocks. For the first time, he accepts how remote are his chances of survival. The defiance has leached out of him along with his moisture. He sits to regather his strength.

When he awakes again, it is almost fully dark, the stars replacing the sun. He sleeps again.

When he awakes again, the moon is up, a shining beacon, almost full. He's not dead yet. In the distance, under the moonlight, he can see the tower.

He makes his way towards it, walking on the smooth rocks easier than across the gravelly sand. The night is cool; he is grateful. The fatigue is overwhelming. All he wants to do is rest, to sleep. But if he stops now, he will survive the night only to die sometime tomorrow. If there are people searching for him, then staying still, preserving his strength would be the most sensible thing to do. But no one will be looking for him. Not yet. Except maybe the police. And they would have no way of knowing where to look. They'll find him eventually, no doubt. What's left of him.

He gets to the windmill, what's left of it. The tower, the broken metal sails, fallen to the ground. He's heard of the springs, the Great Artesian Basin. Knows that somewhere beneath him lies a vast and bountiful ocean of fresh water. As unattainable as the Antarctic ice cap. He examines the windmill under the light of the moon, but the bore is capped. Is it possible he can smash it open?

He staggers back to the ridge, finds a rock, returns to the windmill, bashes away. The sound of rock on steel, his hands jarring. Finally, he succeeds, bashes a pipe free from its bracket. But there is no water. The bore is dry. He collapses then, onto his back, staring up at the sky, the baleful moon. And he cries.

Feels himself cry. There are no tears; his body cannot afford that luxury. It's closing down, retaining what moisture it can.

He needs to get to the ridge, find shelter. He can't afford to be caught out here in the heat of the day. He shuts his eyes momentarily to regather his strength.

— —

He is woken by the first rays of the sun. Panic runs through him. He has slept. Slept through the night, slept through the coolness, breathing his residual moisture out into the night air. He shivers, cold. And yet now the sun is returning, bringing death with it. He has missed his chance.

He looks to the tower, for a prop to help him stand. And sees the moisture glistening on the metal. Dew. Gathered in the chill of the night. He licks it, licks the metal, tastes the steel, tastes the dust, tastes the life. Down along the blades are small deposits where the dew has trickled and gathered. He licks at it greedily, sucks at it. Licks more. Down at the bottom of the tower legs the drips have formed a tiny pool. He laps up as much as he can. It's not enough, he knows it's not enough, but it's something. If he can find shelter, shade, survive the day, perhaps he can return at dawn tomorrow, lick more moisture. Could it possibly be enough to sustain him until a search party arrives?

He starts rearranging the metal, trying to angle some of the looser blades in such a way as they might better collect the dew. He works for a few minutes, does what he can. But he can't stay out here, not with the sun coming.

He wonders if he might bury himself; whether that would offer protection from the sun. He decides against it. The ground is too hard, the effort required too great. He would be building himself an oven, not a shelter.

He heads back to the ridge, only a hundred metres away, reaches it. What he needs is shade. An overhang of some sort would be ideal, but he can't imagine finding one. The land is too old, too exposed, too eroded, the sharp edges taken from it by the aeons. But perhaps he can find a boulder that might shade him in the morning, another in the afternoon. If he can survive through the middle of the day, maybe he can last to another nightfall.

The sun is beginning to peek above the eastern ridge. He has another idea. He returns to the windmill, works two of the blades free, then a third, drags them to the ridge. He may be able to use them to construct a cover, if he can find a suitable location. And then, in the evening, he can position them to collect the moisture, run it at a gentle slope.

He feels so tired, so very tired, but he pushes on, slowly climbing the ridge, looking for a rock outcrop. Anything. Two-thirds of the way to the top, he finds it. Two boulders, waist high, a shelter between them, a natural hollow, lined with dirt and dust. He positions the blades above them. Shade. Not just in the morning and afternoon, but hopefully throughout the day. He lowers himself into the hollow, praying it doesn't become his grave; closes his eyes, hoping he gets to open them once more.

2004

SATURDAY, 9 OCTOBER

It was a shock to see Roman again. We were at the funeral for Maz's mum, held in St Stephen's, the little church in Port Paroo that I'd thought was shuttered for good. I was wrong: it hosts a service on the second Sunday of every month, the priest out from Bourke. His name is Paul, a Filipino with a constant smile who drove across for the ceremony. Perry was there, wearing a shirt with a collar, which looked like it might choke him. It was a good turnout; maybe eighteen or twenty. Not bad when you consider the town's population is an even dozen. A bunch of local graziers came in for it. I recognised some of them from serving behind the bar. Roman was there with his mum and dad. His dad was in a wheelchair, all shrivelled up, breathing with an oxygen bottle. He looked like an old man, skin stretched over his skull, while their mum still looked trim, except for the lines on her brow and the curve of her shoulders. It seemed unfair.

Merriman was there too, already married to that pretty girl, Gloria. She showed me her rings, seemed really proud of them, really happy.

I felt envious. Not because she was married, but because she was happy. I wouldn't want to swap places. She's the same age as me and already talking about babies. God, there's so much time for all of that, why not see the world first? Why condemn yourself to life out here so soon?

Afterwards, Maz hosted a wake at the pub. There were sandwiches and cakes, some made by Vincent, Maz and me, some supplied by the wives of the district, the CWA sub-branch helping according to tradition. There was an open bar, which Vincent and I ran, but for the most part people were happy to drink cold water or non-alcoholic punch. I guess there wasn't much enthusiasm for getting on the piss, given what it had wrought on Mrs Gingelly. Perry took charge, like a master of ceremonies, giving some shape to proceedings. He gave a generous speech, eulogising Maz's mum, casting her in a light so flattering it was hard to recognise the real person, but no one thought less of him for that.

When it came to Maz's turn to speak, she seemed hesitant, if dry-eyed. She'd been subdued ever since Vincent and I had arrived two days before, lacking her normal verve and energy. She thanked everyone for coming, expressing how important community is, how people need to stick together, especially out here. She thanked Perry, singling him out for praise, and me and Vincent and the priest, and the ladies of the CWA. She only mentioned her mother towards the end, saying that she'd had a hard life, had always done her best, had fought her demons and was now at rest. Maz finished by assuring everyone the pub would remain open into the future, serving the needs of the district.

When the speeches were over and people started to mingle, I saw him across the bar. Roman. He was crouched down, speaking softly to his father. He appeared much the same, maybe a little stockier, shoulders broader, but he moved with that same lithe grace, the same confidence. He looked up and our eyes met. I was older than the last time I saw him, more experienced, more worldly. I'd had other boyfriends, some serious, some less so. But my body responded when our eyes locked. I could feel it, that animal reaction, the magnetism, as if your first love leaves an imprint that never fades, like it's been inserted into your genetics, a permanent change at a cellular level. Inside your soul.

He walked over.

'Chloe.'

'Roman.'

'I was hoping I might see you here,' he said, setting off an internal conflict: his words sounded smooth, rehearsed, but his eyes were sincere.

'Why's that?' I asked coolly. My days of being exposed as a fool were over.

'I wanted to apologise,' he said. 'I treated you badly.'

'Thanks,' I said, trying to sound unconcerned. 'You met someone else. It happens. We were younger.'

'It's important to say it, nevertheless.'

'Thank you. I appreciate the gesture.'

He looked across the room to where Vincent and Maz were talking, Maz seeming relaxed at last, even laughing a little.

'They seem happy,' Roman said.

'It's her mother's funeral,' I said. 'He's cheering her up.'

'Of course.' He took a sip of his beer. Then he looked me straight in the eye. 'You seeing someone?'

'I am,' I replied calmly, even as my heartbeat betrayed me. 'An architect. Has his own practice. He's twenty-eight.'

He cocked an eyebrow. 'Well, I guess I'm outgunned then.'

'I'm sure you're not short of offers,' I responded, a little bitchily.

'Comes a point when that's not enough,' he said, looking right at me, right into me. 'Comes a point when you need more.'

'This is true,' I replied, reminding myself to keep my guard up. I might have been the centre of his world right then, at that moment, but the next day his focus would be elsewhere, in a different compartment.

'How long you back for?' he asked. 'You must be more than halfway through your degree.'

'He's married,' I blurted. 'The architect.'

He said nothing then, just considered me, his eyes on my face, those hazel eyes flecked with green. He looked sympathetic. Empathetic. Eventually he smiled, a gentle sort of an expression. 'I'm not married,' he said. 'Don't even have a girlfriend.'

FRIDAY, 26 NOVEMBER

The land is blighted. The drought is deepening day by day, week by week, year by year. It's not even summer yet and the heat is like an army, coming in waves out of the desert. Even the slightest breeze lifts the dust; the topsoil is blowing away. There are no clouds, just orange haze. Longchamp's manager has long gone, so have the farmhands, so have the sheep. There's a few scrawny cattle, watering from the bores and being hand-fed. Them and Mrs Enright.

Vincent told Dad he might as well be feeding the cattle twenty-dollar bills, that it's a complete waste of money. Dad said he didn't need some smart-arse with a half-finished finance degree telling him which way is up.

'I don't need advice,' he said. 'I need rain.'

'What rain?' Vincent replied.

'It will come,' said Dad. 'It always does.' It's become his mantra. I suspect the more he repeats it, the less he believes it.

'Not if the climate change predictions are correct,' said Vincent.

It's awful, hearing them at each other like that.

FRIDAY, 10 DECEMBER

I've been down staying with Maz at Port Paroo, and Roman and I are together again. It happened as if fated. I drove from Longchamp along the Sundowner Track, expecting it to occur, feeling none of the schoolgirl jitters I recall so well. He just sauntered into the pub, walked up to the bar where I was serving, and said hi. And that was that. We were back on, without even discussing it. Eye contact, touching, sex. One led seamlessly to the next. Discussion came afterwards, declarations after that. That night he stayed with me, out in the annexe. That night and the rest of the week, returning to Tavelly Station each morning to work on the property. It's so different now, like we're adults. I guess we are. He's kind and attentive and funny.

It feels so strange, to be in love in the midst of this disaster. The land is empty yet our hearts are full. Sometimes Maz sees me and laughs, ribbing me about the dreamy look on my face. But I can tell that she's happy for me, and I'm happy for her too. She's making a go of the pub.

Roman's finished his degree, plus a finance diploma, and has returned to Tavelly full-time. I have an entire two months before I need to be back in Brisbane for my final year. Merry's at Tavelly full-time as well, and already the brothers are effectively running the place. Their father is really crook. When Roman talks about it, it's obvious how gutted he is, how helpless he feels, how close he is to his dad. But it also reminds me of how he retains that ability to compartmentalise. When he's not talking about his father, he can be happy and light-hearted and seemingly not have a care in the world. I realise now that it doesn't mean he doesn't care. Once he thinks of his father, he's totally there, the distress palpable. I'm starting to think we're all like that, we all compartmentalise, it's just that Roman is better at it, that he can switch aspects of his life on and off, a conscious decision, whereas I lack that skill, that discipline.

Roman fetches fresh oxygen tanks once a fortnight from Bourke, two hours there, two hours back. I went with him on his latest run. We stayed overnight, spent hours at the public swimming pool. So much water, so luxurious. There is precious little in the Darling River, even with the weir. It's clogging up with blue-green algae, smells atrocious. Toxic. You can't even touch it, let alone drink it. Water restrictions are stage five; every lawn in the town is dead save a lucky few with bore water.

'Have you told your parents yet?' I asked Roman. 'About us being back together?'

He shook his head. 'They weren't so accepting last time round, but I would like to. You know, before it's too late.'

We put it off for a few days, but it started to hang over us, so Roman organised it. We went down for lunch. I put on my best summer dress, wore make-up for once. Mrs Stanton reciprocated, made an effort with the lunch, I could see that. Merriman and Gloria were there as well, so that helped.

'How's your father?' Mrs Stanton asked.

'He's well,' I said. 'Struggling with the drought.'

'He got any water?' Mr Stanton wheezed. 'Lake Murdoch?'

'No. It's been empty for years now. Nothing at all in the river. Waterholes are dry. Just the bores keeping us afloat.'

He coughed. An awful phlegmy sound. He was trying to say some-thing, but the coughing started and just kept coming. You could hear him gasping for air. The rest of us didn't move, frozen in the horror of the moment.

He tried again, looking directly at me with those rheumy eyes.

I still couldn't understand what he was trying to say. 'I'm sorry?' I asked.

'I said he's a cunt,' he managed at last.

And then he broke down again, coughing and wheezing, maybe laughing, maybe crying. He hacked and hacked, and there was blood on the napkin. Mrs Stanton gave him his nebuliser then wheeled him out of the room. Merriman was just staring down at his plate, Gloria's eyes were like saucers. We were all speechless. Eventually Roman laughed. Not a real, spontaneous laugh, but a conscious attempt to make light of the moment. 'So, that went well,' he said.

Merriman still didn't look up, and I was on the edge of tears, grasping Roman's hand like a lifeline under the table.

After a while, Mrs Stanton returned, a smile attached to her face like it had been stapled on. 'He's resting now. Should be fine.'

We finished the meal, no one referring to Mr Stanton's slur. Merry and Gloria did their best, recounting a story of a recent trip to Sydney, how odd the residents were, lining up in long queues for ice creams, drinking boutique beers, obsessing over real estate. I don't think I've ever felt so grateful to anyone in my life.

It was a complete disaster, of course, but as we were leaving, Mrs Stanton came out to see us off. No doubt she could see the strain on my face, hear the tremble in my voice as I thanked her for the meal. She smiled, a genuine smile, and when I held out my hand to shake hers, she hugged me instead. It was brief but it was real. 'I know you two will be happy together,' she said to us. And then to me, 'I see how Roman looks at you. How happy you make him. That's all that matters. You'll always be welcome here.'

MONDAY, 20 DECEMBER

It's almost Christmas. I need to get back to Longchamp, to be with Dad and Vincent. Roman and I will be separated, but it's not for so very long. A trial run for the year ahead.

Yesterday, we were lolling in bed in the annexe, when Roman asked, 'Is Vincent okay?'

'What do you mean?'

'He asked if he could borrow money. Said it was kind of urgent.'

I sat up, surprised, thinking maybe he was looking for a way to help Dad. 'Really? Did he say what it was for?'

'Said something about margin calls.'

I didn't know what they were, so Roman explained. Apparently, if you borrow money to invest in assets like shares or property, and the value of the asset falls, the bank can call in the loan, forcing you to sell the assets at precisely the time when the market is at its lowest.

'It can be disastrous,' said Roman.

'He hasn't mentioned anything to me,' I said. But thinking about it, I realised that my brother had fallen silent on the subject of money recently, whereas a few months earlier he'd been spruiking all sorts of fail-safe investments: options and derivatives and forex. 'I hope he hasn't asked our father,' I said. 'Dad's skint.'

'The entire district is skint,' said Roman. 'The whole of rural Australia has its arse hanging out.'

It must have reminded him of his own family's situation, because he started talking about his dad. 'The doctors say he only has months, not years. Mum is talking of taking him down to Dubbo. A nursing home. So he can get proper care.'

I reached out, stroked his hair.

'I am so sorry,' I said, and we sat in silence. I considered us then, Roman and Merry and Vincent and me and Maz. All of us so young still, yet all scarred by loss: Vincent and me, with our mum gone six years ago; both of Maz's parents dead, if you didn't count her biological father; and Roman and Merry watching their father die. Their mother is strong and healthy, mid-forties, but she'll soon be widowed, on her own like my dad. It's tough to be alone out here; hard enough if there's two of you.

'He apologised to me for what he said at lunch,' Roman continued. 'Said to apologise to you.'

'That's kind of him,' I replied.

'It is. Would have taken a lot for him to say it.'

I said nothing, just leant across and kissed Roman.

'I think we should get married,' he said.

'For them?' I asked.

'For us,' he said.

Later, after sex, while he snored softly, I tried it on for size: Mrs Roman Stanton. Mrs Chloe Stanton. Ms Chloe Carmichael-Stanton. The schoolgirl daydream coming true. I thought of my degree, my ticket to the wider world, the cosmopolitan world of art. I wanted to be with Roman, of course I did. Marrying him wasn't the issue; it was what came with it. I wished his father wasn't so sick, that he might live another ten years, another twenty, so that the two of us could go off and explore the world together, live in London, get it out of our systems. I'm not too young to commit to Roman, but I fear I'm too young to commit to Tavelly Station.

SUNDAY

chapter thirty-three
ECCO

JAMIE AND I DEPART BEFORE DAWN, SEARCHING FOR THE CAMEL'S HEAD. WE'RE
on the quad bikes, carrying food, fuel and lots of water. We say
nothing about what has passed before, the deepfake and his role
in it. But he's stiff, almost formal, as if not sure how to behave,
unable to make eye contact.

'We don't have to find it today,' he says. 'We can just go on
a recce.'

'You sure these bikes are the way to go? Not the truck?'

'Yeah. We take a truck, there's the risk of getting bogged in
a sand drift, or a breakdown. This way, if something happens to
one of the bikes, we both climb on the other one.' He looks about
at the landscape, as if perceiving danger. 'But as I say, this is the
first step. We find the way, then we can always return in a truck
if the terrain is stable enough.'

We head out. I'm feeling the part: still steampunk, plus a
good measure of Mad Max. I'm wearing goggles against the dust,
a bandana, an old slouch hat and soft leather gardening gloves,
like biker gauntlets. I take a selfie, that's how good I'm feeling.

We make our way along the track to the airstrip, but instead of heading north, we turn south, Jamie taking the lead. There's a track, or rather, there used to be a track, maybe used by cattle at some point. It's more an absence of low shrubbery and saltbush than a defined path. We run south for several kilometres, edging closer and closer to the far ridge, oriented north–south like a petrified dune. At one point it fades down towards the floor of the plain, just a few metres high. I can see where it rises again further south, so we take the opportunity to traverse it, heading west into a near identical landscape. It's another long flat plain, not really a valley but confined to the east and west by the same low ridges of red rock. It's featureless, without landmarks to guide the way: red dirt interspersed with sparse clumps of native grasses and saltbush. We pass a small group of feral goats, dominated by a black buck with a long beard, curling horns and eyes like pebbles. I can't understand how it can tolerate Australian temperatures with its thick shaggy coat.

We keep angling south and west. We traverse another ridge, this one more difficult. We need to get out of the saddles, throttle right down, moving as slowly as possible. But the bikes are capable, handling the rough terrain, the uneven surface of the rocks. I understand why Jamie decided against bringing the truck.

We take a break, the water from the canteens like a precious thing, tasting of life. Jamie sends up a drone, higher and higher, until I have trouble seeing it. The controller is connected to his phone. He shows me the screen. The world is laid out below, like an Indigenous dot painting, or a Fred Williams. I can see the long ridges, running north–south, the red land in between, dotted with dark clumps of vegetation. A little further to the north there's a clay pan, devoid of plants, and a little further north again a salt pan, white and pink. There is no sign of water.

'It's why they called it Longchamp,' says Jamie. 'These long valleys, between the ridges. It's French for "long fields".'

I laugh at that. 'Don't look like any fields the French would recognise.'

'Might be a line for your book,' he says.

'Yeah. Thanks.' He's right; I take a mental note. 'This land here, it still belongs to the Carmichaels?'

'Yeah. This and a lot more.'

'Is it good for anything?'

'Not much. Not most years.'

He brings the drone back down and we head off again. He must have decided on a route, because this time we edge a little north. We hit the clay pan—I'm not sure if it's the same one I saw on the drone footage—and we get to open up the throttles, speed along for a few minutes. Jamie uses the smooth surface to take us further west, towards the next ridge. There is no real gap this time, but the rocks are flatter and more uniform, easier to negotiate. It's tricky, and I'm still scared of rolling the bike, but I'm getting more and more confident. I feel pride in my ability to handle the machine, controlling it with the throttle, light touches on the brake, steering with gentle pressure. I'm enjoying it, despite the effort and the ache in my arms and shoulders. Jamie is ahead of me, he pauses at the summit. It's probably only twenty metres above the plain, but it feels like the alps. We drink more water, survey the way ahead, looking out across no-man's-land. There's not a lot to see, just another elongated plain, another *long champ*.

It's still early morning, but already the rocks are warming. I can feel their heat bouncing up at me. I'm dreading the return journey, understand now why Jamie cautioned about getting too ambitious on our first foray.

'Somewhere here is the boundary,' says Jamie. 'The next ridge or the one after.'

'Boundary?' I ask. I've latched on to the reference in Murdoch's diary, his meeting with Hentig and Stuart. I know the passage by heart: *Searching, they said, for a border, the line between east and west, a hidden road.*

'Yeah,' responds Jamie, unaware of my intensity. 'Longchamp Downs, the homestead, is on the Paroo, technically part of the Murray–Darling Basin. If there's a big enough flood—I'm talking once every twenty or thirty years, much bigger than the one we've got now—some of the water will wash all the way through the bottom of the flood plain and reach the Darling. But somewhere out here, these long flat depressions and the channels in them start running south-west, not south-east. Inland. A really big flood, it drains into the interior, all the way to Lake Eyre in South Australia. Kati Thanda.'

'Are there ever floods big enough to reach the sea?'

Jamie laughs. 'Impossible. The lake is below sea level. No outlet.'

'Right.'

'And some of these depressions, these ones where we are now, probably lie somewhere in between. Not the Murray–Darling, not the Lake Eyre system. Just nothing, literally the middle of nowhere.'

'So where does the water go?' I ask.

Jamie smiles. 'What water?'

'When it floods?'

'Nowhere. No floods here. Just a random bit of rain now and then. Either sinks into the earth or evaporates into the sky.'

As well as his phone, he has a hand-held GPS unit. He checks

it, then starts his bike, revs the engine and eases down the side of
the ridge. I follow him.

The next ridge has a gap, not so challenging to negotiate, and
the one after. Perhaps there is a route through for those who know
about it. Could this be the explorer's hidden road?

I wonder about the original inhabitants, the Parundji people.
Could they be aware of it? They must have done. How else could
any European have known what was out here? It seems unimaginable, venturing out here before mechanised vehicles. Could John
the Baptist really have wandered these plains? We've been out for
almost three hours, on motorbikes. I've already drunk two litres
of water, and the day is only just beginning to warm.

We've crossed four or five ridges, Jamie pausing to scan the
next one with his binoculars, when I see it: the vague echo of an
outline. A suggestion. The merest hint. I throttle down, descending
cautiously onto the floor of the plain, my angle of view lower, the
rise in the next ridge relatively higher. And the outline clearer.
Without having seen the image, the painting in the Queensland
Art Gallery, I never would have recognised it: The Camel's Head.

Emotions course through me, like a drug in my bloodstream.
The thrill of it, the excitement, the satisfaction. The vindication.
I'm on the threshold of something, I know it.

I stop my bike, climb off, raise my Mad Max goggles. The
glare is blinding, almost overwhelming, but soon enough my
eyes adjust. I extract my phone from my backpack, summon up
the image gleaned from the gallery website: *The Camel's Head
at Dusk*. It's the same formation, no doubt about it; the angle a
little different, the light a lot different, but similar enough after
more than a hundred years. I can't believe it. I look around, try
to work out where Fitzroy set up his easel. How could he even

have made it this far out? I take my own photo: *The Camel's Head Late Morning* by Ekaterina Boland, a companion piece for the state gallery's *Camel's Head at Dusk* and the stolen *Camel's Head at Dawn* by Percival McEwan Fitzroy.

Jamie has paused up ahead and now, seeing that I've dismounted, doubles back and pulls up beside me. He cuts the engine, climbs off. The world is silent about us.

'What?' he asks.

'This is it,' I say, pointing. 'That's what I'm looking for.'

He scans the desolate landscape, indistinguishable from the other plains we've traversed, his scepticism unmistakable. 'Why? There's nothing here.'

I laugh, show him the image of the painting. In my exhilaration, my residual resentment against him has evaporated.

He's looking at me as if I'm mad, a smile playing on his lips. He gestures at the bikes. 'All this, so you can check if a painting is real? That the artist didn't just make it up?'

I can't help myself; the euphoria of discovery loosens my mouth. 'Treasure, Jamie. There's treasure out here.'

He gapes at me for a fraction of a second, then erupts with laughter. 'Bullshit. There's nothing out here. Sand and rocks and bones, lizards and bush flies.'

'I found a note in one of the old journals in the library at the homestead. Recounting how two explorers came out here, said they were looking for treasure. Beyond the border. At the Camel's Head.'

'How could they know about it?'

'I don't know. Maybe they heard it from the Indigenous people.'

He's unconvinced, shaking his head. 'Blackfellas aren't stupid, you know. If there was treasure out here, why wouldn't they keep it for themselves? More likely they were taking the piss, sending these explorers of yours off on a wild-goose chase.'

'These explorers, they called past the homestead. They had two Aboriginal guides. Maybe they were all in on it, all four of them.'

'Yeah, maybe.' He looks around. 'Fucking hot out here. Going to get a lot hotter.'

He's right. Without the movement of the bikes, the day is sweltering. I drink more water. Jamie's not convinced, but he remains attentive, not ridiculing me and my quest. Nevertheless, his doubt is beginning to irk me. Perhaps because what he's saying is evidently true. I look about us. There's nothing, just emptiness as far as the eye can see. The vegetation is sparse, its cover thinner than back at Longchamp. I realise it's been becoming more scant the further west we've come, the more we've pushed into the interior. I haven't seen a tree, even the most stunted mulga, for more than an hour. An image comes to mind of Leichhardt, pushing on day after day after day, the weather getting hotter, the landscape growing ever more desolate, ever more hostile. The thought makes me unstopper my canteen, gulp more water.

'That ridge,' Jamie says, pointing at the Camel's Head. 'It's just rock. Nothing special about it. Not iron ore, not precious metals, not gemstones. Not gold, not silver. It's sandstone. Thousands and thousands of square kilometres of it.'

'So why did the artist come out here, all this way west of the homestead, to paint it?'

Jamie shrugs. ''Cos it looks good?'

He's not trying to be a smart-arse, but the comment deflates me. He's right. The idea that there might be treasure out here is absurd. I've always prided myself on being hard-headed, at least since my fall from grace, tempered by those events into something tougher, more robust. Yet here I am, hunting for treasure. Just like Hentig and Stuart. The thought of the two adventurers brings me back to myself, to my purpose: I'm not here to find treasure; I'm here to research a book, to find a story.

'Jamie, the men who came out here looking for treasure were never seen again after they left Longchamp Downs. We should search, see if we can find anything. A remnant. You know—a horse's stirrup, or a rifle. Something like that. It could be really important. Of historical significance.'

Jamie looks at me like he's about to say something, then thinks better of it. Looks away, looks back. 'Sure. Why not? Seeing we're here. Where do you want to start?'

I shrug. How would I know?

'Let's ride over,' he suggests. 'Climb it. See what we can see. Maybe they built a cairn at the highest point. Left something there. They might have been the first white men to climb it.'

I can't work out if he's trying to humour me, but even if he is, I'm grateful. He doesn't have to do this. Maybe he's motivated by guilt. It doesn't matter; I'm still thankful.

We ride over to the ridge line below the Camel's Head. There isn't a clear separation between sand and rock line, just some low scrub and saltbush patches. They must catch the run-off from the ridge on those rare occasions when it rains.

We edge our way through the vegetation and up onto the beginning of the ridge, but Jamie calls a halt soon enough. Perhaps he's being overly cautious. I'm pretty sure he could take the machine higher, but he doesn't want to risk me coming off. Given where we are, it feels like the right decision. So we go on foot, the rocks hot enough I can feel them through the soles of my boots, feel the radiant heat on my face, feel my skin reacting despite the layers of sunscreen and moisturiser. We scramble up. There's nothing. No, not nothing: there's a small pile of rocks. Jamie presents it to me with a theatrical flourish, as if he's unveiling it. I take a photo. Someone has gathered the rocks, maybe constructed a cairn, but that's all. I take another photo, before squatting down to examine them. But there is nothing more; they are covering nothing: no message, no tobacco tin, no button. I stand, look about, even such slight elevation opening up a vast panorama. The top of the ridge is a plateau, flat and featureless. There can't be treasure here. There's nowhere to hide it. I scuff at the rock with my boot, a solid sheet of sedimentary rock laid down millions of years ago. Ungiving and unforgiving. If Hentig and Stuart made it this far, how profound their disappointment must have been. They abandoned Leichhardt, their shot at glory, for this.

'What's that?' asks Jamie, pointing into the distance.

'Where?' I follow his finger. He's not indicating anything on the ridge; his gaze is fixed away to the south. I can see it as well: a blaze of light, a reflection, the sun bouncing off something.

Jamie has binoculars. Looks through them. 'Fuck,' he says. 'Take a look at this.'

'What? What is it?'

'A car. In the middle of nowhere.'

I look through the glasses. He's right. A white car, in the middle of nowhere. Not some ancient wreck. An SUV, the sun reflecting off the windscreen. 'You think we should check it out?'

'Of course. They could be in trouble.'

'What are they doing out here?'

'Fuck knows. We're a long way from any track.'

I take a last look around us at the top of the Camel's Head. I can come back some other time, maybe bring a metal detector, search the place thoroughly, but in my mind, I've dismissed the idea of treasure. I need to search for remnants of the two men, that's all. That's my treasure. But I'm starting to think even that search will prove futile. The most I might extract is a colourful passage for the book, the fruitless search into the deep desert.

'Poor fuckers,' I whisper to myself. I believe I know now why Hentig and Stuart were never heard of again.

Back on our bikes, we head south, towards the car. Along the way, we pass a derelict windmill, tower still erect but the blades long ago fallen. It seems absurd. I know about the bores, the Great Artesian Basin, but it stretches credibility. Could there ever have been water here?

Past the windmill, it only takes us another five minutes. Jamie gets there first. He's dismounting as I pull up. The car is new, covered in dust, but otherwise looking like someone has parked it for a moment. Only the location shifts it from the everyday to the exceptional. I shudder despite the heat.

Jamie approaches it, and I watch on in trepidation. Is something awful waiting for us inside?

Jamie eases the door open, then breathes a long exhalation of relief. 'Empty,' he says. He climbs in. I'm surprised to hear the starter motor kick over. He climbs out. 'No petrol left,' he says.

'Out here? Why would anyone drive here on half a tank? Without jerry cans in the back, at least?'

Jamie says nothing. His features are grim.

'How far to the nearest road?' I ask.

'Fifty kilometres, at least.'

'Lost?'

Jamie shakes his head. 'These cars. Sat nav is standard.'

I look at the number plate. New South Wales. I walk around the vehicle, wondering why someone would drive it deep into the desert, only to run out of petrol. There is a sense of horror creeping up on me.

'Hang on,' I say. I see markings on the bonnet, hidden under a thin layer of dust. I sweep it clear, read aloud what has been scraped there. *Abducted. The A-team. Murdered. Not suicide.* And the date. Yesterday's date. And the initials *MS . . .*' I gasp. 'Yesterday. Martin Scarsden.' Another shiver runs down my spine.

'Look,' says Jamie. There is another scratch. An arrow. Pointing back the way we came. He looks at me, then clambers up onto the car roof, sweeping the distance with his binoculars. He lowers them. 'He could see the windmill from here.'

'There was no one there,' I say. 'We would have seen him. Wouldn't we?'

'That's where the arrow is pointing.'

I climb inside the car, no longer intimidated, knowing there is nothing awful in there. I open the glove compartment. There are rego papers, some bills, a child's toy.

'It's him all right,' I whisper, getting back out. 'Scarsden was at Longchamp Downs the day before yesterday. I spoke to him on the phone yesterday morning.'

But Jamie doesn't appear to be listening to me. 'Look,' is all he says, pointing.

So I look. To the west, above the low ridge, there is a wall of swirling red dust, towering into the sky. 'Is that what I think it is?'

'Sandstorm,' says Jamie. 'Enormous. Never seen anything so big.'

'Can we outrun it?'

He doesn't answer immediately, just stares at the approaching wall. 'Doubt it.'

'The ridge. Can we find shelter?'

He shakes his head, but now he's smiling. 'The car. Your mate Scarsden might have saved our lives.'

chapter thirty-four
MARTIN

THE FIRST MARTIN KNOWS OF THE SANDSTORM IS BEING AWOKEN BY THE SHRIEK of metal on metal as one of the windmill blades is ripped away from above him. Suddenly alert, he has a sensation of being dropped into hell. The light is bright orange, diffuse, and tiny motes of dust float about him in his hollow, making it hard to breathe, hard to see. He eases himself a little higher, extends his hand, feels the sting of the biting sand. A sandstorm: a new misery come to torment him. He sinks lower, knowing to walk into the storm would be to die. He cringes, cowering, overcome by the roaring sound. Another windmill blade surrenders to the tempest, swept away into the howling nothingness. And now, without its protective shield, the sand is getting at him, not just the floating motes and errant grains, but needle-sharp filaments too, retaining the full force of the gale. He feels it shredding his face, intent on flailing the skin from his flesh and the flesh from his bones. He cringes lower and lower, devolving from man to some lowly mammal, a burrowing rodent.

And now something very strange begins to happen. For he feels that the earth has heard his pleas, has decided to accept him, and is beginning to give way, granting him ingress into its sheltering embrace. Surely he is hallucinating. And still the sand under him moves, then a few rocks surrender, and a few more, and he feels himself sliding downwards, lowered ever so gently down into the earth, a few centimetres, then a few more, and finally a few feet, until he reaches a point where relief begins to give way to terror: is the earth intent on swallowing him whole? Is this his grave, entered before he is dead? Or is he dead already; has it come to pass without his knowledge? He tries to hold fast, clawing with his fingers, but the hole continues to widen. He looks up at the diminishing orange glow of the sky, even as he continues to be sucked down, as if experiencing birth in reverse. His labouring consciousness is half in awe, but some more primal part of his cortex, some rudimentary urgency, tells him to hold on, hold on to anything. The rock beneath him settles further and as he reaches out in desperation, he moves his hand and finds it coming to rest on something wet. Something *wet*.

The landslip stops for a moment and he is at rest. Above him, seen through the narrowing passage, the sky still swirls orange, but the roar is muted, at a distance. Motes drift down, but they have been robbed of their power. He lifts his hand, places two fingers in his mouth. Water. He's sure of it. Salty. Gritty. But water. He reaches back, can feel it. A small pool, gathered in the rock. He raises his fingers; sees the water drip from them. Ever so carefully, ever so slowly, he twists his body, moving it little by little, until he is lying on his side and can see the extent of this miracle. The rain, he realises. The rain that drenched Port Paroo last week, the rain that closed the roads. It must have run from the ridge, flowed down through the rocks, collected here, underground. A week earlier, a week later, it wouldn't be here, couldn't be here. He twists a little more, gets around. More sand is sliding away from beneath him, but it doesn't matter; the pool is clear of the sand, above it. He kneels, grasping the stone on either side of his foxhole. And then, concentrating and cautious, he cups his hands and scoops water to his mouth.

Surely no benediction has ever been so sweet. He drinks another cupped handful, then lowers his head, suckling directly from the font. He drinks long and he drinks deep until it is gone. And still he licks the rock, eager for every last drop. A part of his mind, coming back to reason, says he should have rationed it, not drunk it all, but he couldn't help himself. It is a balm to his cracked and swollen lips, nectar to his parched throat, salvation to his desperate heart.

And then suddenly more of the sand shifts away from under him, and only by clinging to the rocks around him does he avoid being devoured in his moment of deliverance. But when the sand settles once more, he finds himself peering down into a darkness. The mouth of a cave. And there, twinkling in the darkness, the reflected light of the distant storm, bouncing back from the surface of half-a-dozen pools.

And as he beholds the water, he feels himself returning to the living world once again as freshly hydrated blood pumps out through his parched arteries, irrigating his imagination. And a new determination comes to him: he needs to survive, if only to write this story. For surely nothing he has ever before committed to paper can rival this.

chapter thirty-five
ECCO

INSIDE THE SUBARU, SITTING IN THE PASSENGER SEAT, I CAN FEEL THE CAR rocking more and more violently as the storm engulfs us. Jamie is in the driver's seat, grasping the steering wheel, looking straight ahead, as if waiting for a traffic light to turn green.

'Are we safe?' I ask.

'So far,' Jamie says. And then, only slightly more reassuringly, 'Should be.'

'How long will it last?'

'Don't know.'

I consider him then. 'You're a good man, aren't you, Jamie?' I don't know why I say it. Sometimes words can be like that; they arrive of their own volition.

He steals a glance at me. 'Try to be.'

We both turn back, look out the windscreen; now it feels like we're at a drive-in and we're waiting for the feature to start. There is no visibility, just a yellow glow, getting darker and darker. We watch as it turns a burnt orange, the light diminishing even as the crescendo of the wind grows louder and the car rocks more on its suspension, like a boat at sea.

I tell myself we will be okay. We had time before the wall of sand hit us to lift the water, the jerry cans of fuel, our food and other supplies from the bikes into the back of the car. We left the bikes hard up against the Subaru's leeward side. I wonder if they can possibly escape unharmed. Remain serviceable. Outside, the orange wind is screeching. Now I feel we are astronauts, re-entering the atmosphere, in danger of burning up.

'I saw a movie once,' I say, hoping conversation might divert us. 'These people, they were in the Sahara, caught in a sandstorm. Just like this. Sheltering in trucks. By the time it passed, one truck was completely buried. The people inside would have suffocated if their colleagues didn't dig them out in time.'

'*The English Patient*,' says Jamie. 'Good movie. Bit overwrought, but good.'

'Couldn't happen to us, could it?' I ask him.

He laughs, and the sound of it is like water. 'Not in a million years. Out in the Simpson or the Great Sandy Desert, maybe, but not here. Not enough sand. This place is so impoverished, we don't even have enough of that.' And I don't know why, but he reaches out, takes my hand. 'We'll be right. Just you see. We'll ride this out, be good as gold.'

Half of me wants to spurn his hand, the other wants to grasp it tight. 'What if the bikes are damaged? If we're stranded?'

'Nothing I can't fix,' he says with a ring of confidence, a ring of truth. 'Besides, we've got plenty of water. Some food. And our phones. Remember, in an emergency, they can send an alert by satellite.'

I'm reassured; he is right, of course. I feel a touch of irritation at myself for my feebleness. I peer through the windscreen, and as the car rocks, the illusion shifts once more. Now we're in a plane, flying through a storm, buffeted by clouds. I can't see the ground beyond the car, and the light seems somehow darker. A boat, a spaceship, a drive-in movie, an aeroplane. What image will my mind conjure next?

'What about him?' I ask, fear returning to my voice. 'Scarsden?'

Jamie says nothing, and we let the unsaid words blow away on the wind. There's nothing we can do, nothing we can say. I listen, but the wind might whisper or it might shout, but I can't understand it.

'Why'd you do it?' he asks, eyes back on the windscreen.

I'm taken aback. 'Here?' I retort. 'Now?'

He doesn't respond, just keeps his eyes straight ahead.

And to my surprise, I start to tell him. 'Footy fan?' I query, by way of a prelude.

'Big time,' says Jamie.

'So you know all about Dan Rackham then. Living legend. What did they used to say? Every bloke wanted to be him; every girl wanted to root him. Genius on the field, charming off it. Beautiful face, gorgeous body. Could have been a movie star if he'd possessed even a skerrick of talent. Did a few screen tests. Hopeless. But that didn't stop the advertisers; they loved him.' I take a deep breath, realise I'm dissembling, cut to the chase. 'He was a complete arsehole.'

Jamie goes to say something, then I see him hesitate. I think I know what's coming. And sure enough, I'm right.

'All those charities,' Jamie says. 'The kids with cancer. His foundation.'

'Raised a lot of money,' I say. 'Did a lot of good.'

'But?'

'Also made him look good.'

'Nothing wrong with that.'

'Nothing at all.'

'So?'

I sigh, wondering why I'm bothering. 'He was a root rat. Would fuck anything on two legs. Fucked my maid of honour on our wedding night. Put the hard word on her mother.'

'Seriously?' His mouth hangs open with disbelief.

I glare back. 'Do I sound like I'm joking?'

'Sorry,' says Jamie. 'It's just that . . . you know.'

'That wasn't the worst of it, Jamie. Infidelity. Neglect. Verbal abuse. Controlling my behaviour, controlling our money. I had to be perfect, even when he was anything but. And he hit me. Frequently. Not just when he was angry and out of control; even when he wasn't. When it took his fancy. He liked it, Jamie. Loved it. Got off on it. And he was untouchable. They knew what he was like. The team management. I found out later that was one reason they thought our marriage would be a good thing, that it might settle him. Not just a good PR opportunity, but it might actually calm him. So instead of warning me, protecting me, they knowingly fed me to him in the hope it might pacify him.' I swallow hard. It's not easy, never easy, no matter how much time has passed. Just talking about it takes me back there. 'He put my best friend Emma in hospital. He was angry—angry enough to hit her. Angry because she said no. Angry because she was more loyal to me than she was attracted to him. He fucking hated that.'

'Jesus,' says Jamie.

I can see he's recoiling, but I don't consider—can't consider—if it's a reaction to what I'm saying or the vehemence with which I'm saying it or because he's suddenly realising that his hero is abhorrent.

'I asked for a divorce. Demanded one. Begged for one. He laughed in my face. Said he'd divorce me when he was good and ready to throw me on the scrap heap. Get a new model. That's how he put it.' I paused then. The last barrier. Too late to stop now. 'That was the first night he raped me.'

And even as the sandstorm edges up a notch, my own pitch starts to fall.

Now Jamie takes a deep breath. I know what he wants to ask me. I expect it, anticipate it. Now it's here, I almost welcome it.

But he doesn't ask. Instead he says, voice penitent, 'That's enough. I'm sorry. You don't have to tell me anything more. It's not necessary.' And then: 'Forgive me. I shouldn't have pried, put you through it again. I'm so sorry.'

But I can't help myself. Here in this place, in this storm, this Armageddon, floating free of reality, I feel the need to unload, to confess, as if this is the end of days. 'I was stupid. So fucking stupid, even as I thought I was being smart. I thought I could get my divorce and my revenge all packaged up in one neat manoeuvre. So I fucked his best mate. And his best mate's best mate. And before you ask, no, I didn't know it was being filmed. Not until he published it, playing the victim. Saint Dan. Those tears he shed—he really could act after all. *Sixty* fucking *Minutes*, prime time. "The Saint and the Skank".'

The wind howls and the sand blasts away at the car, as if trying to devour it. Jamie is completely silent.

'I was only nineteen, Jamie. Nineteen. No one knew me, no one knew my name. I was just Mrs Dan Rackham, one of the WAGS, peroxide hair and low-cut gown on the red carpet at the Dally M awards. And then everyone knew my name.'

'It's enough,' says Jamie. 'I'm sorry. You don't have to go on.'

But I do; now that I've started, I do need to go on, to tell it all, so he knows, knows the whole of it.

'And then Dan got sick. And the whole world was on his side. He started the charities, and people gave millions. And then he died. The fucking cancer came back and he died. And everybody blamed me all over again, for the stress and grief and pain that I'd inflicted on him, as if I could possibly have had anything to do with that disease.' And now I'm crying, the dam bursting at last, the tears I haven't allowed myself all these years.

I wonder if Jamie wants to hear more, despite his protests, even if he's too shell-shocked, or too decent, to ask. About the rumours: that I had poisoned Dan, or injected him, or cursed him. But he doesn't ask and I don't volunteer, and we sit there. And the wind doesn't let up.

I feel an urge to pee, but suppress it. It's not possible to leave the car.

'Your turn,' I say instead.

'Hey?'

'Your turn. What are you doing out here, at the end of the road, on a dying property? A man like you, good-looking, capable, smart enough. Clay's selling it, everyone else has left, but you're still here, doing favours for Dermott Brick, hoping to ingratiate yourself. Hoping to stay on. What are you running from?'

He reaches into the back seat, takes a bottle of water, hands it to me, then reaches back and gets another for himself.

'Nothing,' he says.

'Bullshit. You've prised me open, heard my sins. Your turn.'

He can't meet my eye. He just sits there, staring at the orange swirl. I think he's clammed up, become resolute in his silence. But then he speaks. 'I was married too. Not to a bastard, not like you were. To the opposite: an angel. Her name even sounded like it: Angela.'

His gaze remains fixed on the oblivion beyond the windscreen. I wonder what he sees out there.

'We had a little girl. Jazz.' And he's rocked by a heaving gasp, a sob, like something subterranean has shifted in him. 'She died. They both died.'

'Jamie, no,' I say, without even knowing I'm saying it.

'My fault,' he says, and the sobs are coming as punctuation, powerful enough to rock the car, a counterpoint to the storm, his knuckles white on the steering wheel. 'In a boat. Down by Yamba. Coming in through the sandbar, I was steering. Beautiful day. Sun shining. We were laughing. Then we capsized.' He's crying now. 'I survived. They didn't.'

'Enough,' I say softly, placing my hand on one of his, covering it, even as he clings to the steering wheel. 'Enough now,' I say. 'Not your fault.'

'I was drunk. It was absolutely my fault.'

And now I am the one without words.

'I kept it together long enough to bury them. I pleaded guilty, went to prison. Deserved it. As soon as they let me out, I headed west, as far from the ocean as I could get. Ended up here.'

'Enough.'

And now it is, the two of us sheltering from the storm, ensconced in our grim camaraderie.

'What a pair we are then,' I say at last.

'Yeah. Look at us.' He laughs, a small and sorry laugh that somehow makes me feel better, not so lonely. And then guilty for feeling that way.

chapter thirty-six
MARTIN

MARTIN WAKES AND FEELS SOMEHOW REFRESHED, DESPITE A ROCK TRYING TO penetrate his spine. His right leg starts to cramp and he moves quickly to prevent it. Above him, the sandstorm is beginning to abate, the light growing stronger. It's still daylight. He peers down into the darkness, sees that more light is penetrating. He can make out the pools of water more clearly now, see how they have formed, the small channels in the rocks, the dripping from an overhang. He can see the white of calcium, maybe of lime-stone. So not just a hole but a real cave, formed over years, over centuries. A cave out here. It doesn't make sense. He's seen no sign of limestone. Never heard of it. Or was there something about opal mining? Weren't the opals set in among some sort of calcified layer? Isn't White Cliffs not that very far from here? Prehistoric lake beds, the opals formed by trapped water. He racks his memory, remembers visiting Finnigans Gap, can't decide whether he's imagining it. But he does remember the poster at the Port Paroo Hotel and its reference to an opal mine: *The Legend of the Hidden Road Hoard*. He gazes down, wondering if there might be opals.

Perhaps it's not limestone; maybe it's calcium lifted from underground along with water. Like that crusted onto the metal at the derelict windmill below the ridge. The Great Artesian Basin. He knows it lies under this land, under most of the state. There are natural springs and man-made bores. So could that be what this is—a natural spring? No. Not anymore, he decides. The water is from above, the sky, trickling down where the underground water once flowed. Whatever it is, it's saved his life. So far. That and the coolness of the cave, the shelter from the sun. He's not sure how long the water will last, though; how long it can sustain him. But surely days, not mere hours. Long enough for the car to be discovered.

And with that, a plan comes to him. The car. He'll return to it now, carve a new message on its bonnet, tell the searchers where to find him.

He waits another hour for the wind to die almost completely, taking the opportunity to drink from pools lower down. Then he eases himself out, careful not to slide back down into the depths, careful not to cause any further subsidence, careful not to send dirt tumbling into the magical pools of water.

Back on the surface, the day has calmed. The sky is still infused with dust, but high up. The easterly horizon is a solid orange cloud, while above him it's tinged with what in another world might be photo-chemical smog. To the west the sky is clear and the sun is blasting through. Judging by its elevation, it must be about 7 pm. He needs to be getting along; there's probably only another hour of sunlight. But first, he works to secure the remaining windmill blade, wedging it tight between boulders. If nothing else, it will signpost the cave's entrance for his saviours.

That done, he starts to descend the ridge. His legs feel rubbery, his balance unsure, despite the water from the cave pools. Fatigue still hampers him and his vision is grainy, bringing home to him how close to death he must have come. Perhaps he should have waited longer, rested more. Drunk more. But he's already at the base of the ridge. Easier now to stagger to the car. It's not so very far, yet time is bending in strange ways, making it difficult to judge how long he has been walking: slow minutes or rapid hours. And yet it seems to become easier the further he proceeds, the outlook growing clearer as the residual dust settles. He feels a sense of wellbeing, a quiet elation at the realisation that he is indeed alive. How beautiful the sandstone ridges look as they catch the late afternoon light.

His health is coming back to him and, with it, his imagination. He begins composing his piece in his mind, the narrative arc of his redemption. And so he's lost in his own story when, almost back at the Subaru, he sees it: the red flash of metal behind the car. A shudder of panic runs through him and he sways on his feet, the surge of adrenaline too much. The A-team? Surely not. He falls to his knees, overwhelmed. All of his effort, all of his luck, come to nothing.

And then the flash of colour resolves into a shape, the angles reveal themselves. A quad bike, half buried in sand, sheltered behind his vehicle. His rational mind reasserts itself. It's more than a day since the A-team abandoned him; why would they risk coming back now? He breathes deeply, makes the effort to stand. He is incapable of outrunning whoever is in the car, so he might as well confront them. He limps forward.

When he gets to the driver's door, the window caked in orange dust, he can just make out two figures inside. He takes a deep breath and knocks.

The door cracks open, sending sand cascading to the ground.

'Martin Scarsden,' says a man who looks familiar. 'You're alive.'

'I am,' says Martin.

The door opens fully and the man emerges. Martin recognises him now; it's Jamie: the surly young man on the verandah at Longchamp Downs, the one who kept interrupting, telling him to fuck off. Then the passenger door opens and Martin sees Ekaterina Boland. Ecco. He's overwhelmed by a sense of deliverance. 'You came looking,' he says.

Ecco blinks. 'No. Not for you.'

'My car,' says Martin. 'Why are you inside?'

'Sheltering from the storm,' says Jamie, as if it's self-evident. 'How on earth did you survive it?'

'I found a cave,' he says. He turns, points up along the ridge line.

'A cave?' asks Ecco, and he senses something urgent in her voice. 'Will you show us?'

chapter thirty-seven
ECCO

AS SOON AS I MENTION THE CAVE, I REGRET IT. JAMIE AND I ARE IN THE process of saving the journalist's life—and he should be thankful, should feel a debt of gratitude—but Martin Scarsden is still a reporter, and I know only too well what reporters will do for a story. And I've got the makings of a great story. A history-bending story.

'Do you have any water?' Martin asks.

'Of course,' I say, fetching a one-litre bottle from inside the car. He drains a good two-thirds of it.

'So will you show us the cave?' Jamie repeats.

'I can,' says Martin hesitantly, before gulping down the rest of the bottle. 'But shouldn't we be getting out of here while it's still light?'

'You should know that the police are looking for you,' Jamie responds. 'They called the homestead this morning; they've got a warrant for your arrest.'

'Why?' I ask Jamie, wondering what he knows that I don't. Perhaps Clay made a formal complaint about the trespass after all.

'Those allegations are bullshit,' retorts Martin. 'There is no fraud, there was no child abuse.'

'What?' I manage.

'Who said anything about child abuse?' asks Jamie. 'The report I saw alleged financial crimes.'

'Good,' says Martin. 'That means even the cops don't buy it.'

'Why should we believe you?' demands Jamie.

Now Martin appeals to me. 'There is no more truth in these allegations than there was in that video of us. I told you: someone is out to destroy me.' He walks to the front of the car, sweeps the accumulated sand away, revealing his message, carved into the bonnet. 'Look. First they tried to discredit me, blowing up the dam. Then the deepfake of us fucking. Now they've trumped up charges of fraud and abusive material, planted incriminating material in my home on the coast. And finally, they tried to kill me. Drove out here until the car was out of petrol, then abandoned me, so I could never disprove the allegations.'

'Who?' asks Jamie, looking at the message. 'The A-team?'

'Yes,' says Martin.

'Why?' I ask.

Martin shakes his head. 'The A-team are two hit men, hired for the job. I'm pretty sure they don't even know why themselves.'

'Someone doesn't like journalists,' I say.

'Thanks,' says Martin. 'That's helpful.'

Jamie says, 'Look, Martin, here's the deal. You show us this cave, we'll get you back to civilisation. Not only that, we won't hand you in.' Then he turns to me. 'You okay with that, Ecco?'

'Yes,' I say, impressed by Jamie taking the initiative. Then I speak to Martin. 'But first we need to establish some ground rules. You're a journo. I'm a writer. We both write books. The cave is mine.'

'What?' says Martin, and I can see the confusion on his face. 'You want a non-compete on the cave? It saved my life.'

I smile, knowing the cards I hold. 'That part you can use.'

'That part? What other part is there?'

'What's in the cave. How far did you go?'

He's frowning now, journo senses on high alert. 'Just the opening,' he says. 'It kind of gave way under me. I was trying not to fall in all the way. I just went far enough to drink some water.'

'There's water?' asks Jamie.

'Not anything permanent. Not a spring. Just rainwater from the storm the other night.' And then Martin addresses me again. 'What is it? What do you think the cave contains?' I can tell he's intrigued.

'I found a reference in an old journal,' I say, keeping it vague, not willing to share the story of Hentig and Stuart. 'It could be historically significant.'

Jamie interjects. 'Let's get going. Time is short. Once we know where the cave is, we can come back. Martin, if you stay at Longchamp Downs with us tonight, we'll bring you back here tomorrow with petrol for your car.'

The journalist nods his acquiescence. Well done, Jamie.

Jamie gets my bike started, extracts it from the sand that has built up around it. Then he kicks his over, makes sure it's functional. He takes the water and supplies from the Subaru, puts them back on the bikes. 'Climb on behind me,' he says to Martin.

'It's not far,' says Martin. 'I marked the entrance.'

It takes five minutes to get there. We leave the bikes at the bottom of the ridge, some way past the old windmill, the same ridge as the Camel's Head but further north. More like the hump. Martin is looking quite lively, given what he must have gone through. I guess survival and a litre of bottled water would do that.

As we climb, I see a windmill blade towards the top of the ridge, propped against some rocks. 'That it?'

'Yep,' says Martin.

'You put that there, or was it there already?' I ask.

'That was me. There were two others, but the storm got them. I was sheltering under them when the ground gave way.' He recounts the story again in more detail, trying to restrict himself to the briefest of facts, but I can hear the emotion laced through his description, get a sense of how frightening it must have been. It was scary enough in the Subaru.

'So the entry was totally blocked?' I ask.

'Seems like it,' says Martin.

'Okay, let me take a quick look,' I say.

'Five minutes, no more,' says Jamie. 'You got your phone?'

'Yeah.' I take my phone from my pocket, turn on the torch function, peer into the cave.

'Be careful,' says Martin. 'It's not stable, might give way further.'

I ease myself down, half sliding. I see the pooled water, dip my finger, taste it. Not bad. The faintest hint of salt, but nothing more. I take a couple of photos. The slide of sand comes to an end, and my feet are on rock. There is coolness here, but it doesn't seem at all damp. I go further, having to crouch. And then I am on a level, a kind of floor. I see small bones piled against a wall. Bats, trapped underground when the entry became blocked? I reach over to one of the lower pools, splash water on my face, then stand perfectly still. There is the faintest sensation of a breeze against my skin. There must be another opening deeper in. I'm encouraged. If that's the case, the air should be okay.

I should really head back up—not just because Jamie told me to, but because he's right: we can come back tomorrow, search it properly. Yet I can't resist. I keep going. The ceiling is low, I have to stoop, but the way forward is easy enough. There is a boulder, an outcrop, barring the way, maybe the result of some long-ago cave-in. But no, as I get closer, I can see a way around it. Promising myself this is as far as I will venture, just to determine if the passage continues or if it's a dead end, I move past it—and gasp.

A body. A skeleton, still dressed, in rough pants and a shirt, boots set aside, the bones of the foot still connected. Whoever it was, they died barefoot.

I cast my light forward but see nothing more. Is this Hentig, or is it Stuart? I move closer, scarcely breathing. I've found one of Leichhardt's lost lieutenants, I know it, but I need confirmation. And there, on a natural shelf in the rock, a hat. A pair of glasses. And a book. I approach slowly, my mind running ahead of me. Could this be the journal of Leichhardt's men, the story of how the expedition split, how the splinter party came south to seek their fortune? How they made it as far as this cave? I swing my phone torch about, as if it might catch the glimmer of gold or the sparkle of opals. But the rocks are dull.

I move to the book, which is somewhat modern-looking. I know I need to take care, that I shouldn't risk opening it, not here, lest I damage it. But I need to know.

I open it, but the name that greets me is not Arthur Hentig or Donald Stuart. It's Chloe Carmichael, and it's dated 2005.

chapter thirty-eight
MARTIN

THE SUN IS DOWN AND THE STARS HAVE CREPT ACROSS THE SKY FROM THE east, a celestial spray job. Martin can't help but be dazzled by its beauty, the reach of it. On the back of Jamie's quad bike, he arches his back, stares up into the heavens. The sight makes him feel the way it always does: insignificant. But on this night it also causes him to swell with life. He's coming back: back from the wilderness, back from the deep desert, back from the edge of death.

They pass by a windsock, emerging from the dark. They must be close to a landing strip. And now the headlights reveal they're on a formed track, Jamie accelerating. They pass through a gap in a final ridge and there is Longchamp Downs. By the beams of the bikes, he can sense rather than see the damage inflicted on the property by the sandstorm. There are sheets of corrugated iron flung about the place, and across the way he can see floodlights set up near a machinery shed, the figure of a man standing, waving to them. In the post-storm calm, he can hear generators rumbling. The power lines must be down.

Jamie pulls to a stop outside a small building, dark under the brilliant sky, and Martin eases himself off. Jamie stays mounted, engine running. Ecco pulls up next to him, cuts her own engine and joins Martin.

'I'd better go check on Clay,' says Jamie. 'Make sure he's okay. Let him know we're fine.'

'Of course,' says Ecco.

But Jamie hesitates. He switches off his bike's ignition. 'I'll need to tell him,' he says to Ecco. 'He deserves to know.'

'It can't wait until morning?' she asks.

Martin senses something akin to grief in the young man's bearing.

'I don't think so,' says Jamie.

'I understand,' says Ecco. 'Go help Clay, but don't tell him just yet. Martin and I will be over shortly. We'll tell him together. He'll want to hear it from me. I'm the one who found her.'

'Why not now?' says Jamie.

'The diary,' says Ecco. 'We'll need to give it to him, but I want to photograph it first.'

Martin thinks Jamie is about to object, but then the young man nods. 'Okay, but be quick.'

'And bring some clothes over for Martin, if you can,' yells Ecco, as Jamie starts his bike. 'He's beginning to stink.'

The farmhand waves an acknowledgement and keeps going.

Ecco turns to Martin. 'Sorry, mate. But after a couple of days in the desert, you need a shower.'

'Don't I know it,' says Martin. 'But I'd like a look at the diary as well.'

'All in good time,' she says as she leads him into the darkened cottage.

Inside, Ecco finds a lantern, some candles. Perhaps blackouts are common out here. Martin showers quickly; he doesn't want to miss anything. He emerges from the bathroom, a towel wrapped around him, to find Ecco standing at the kitchen bench, studiously photographing each diary page with her phone.

'Anything?'

'I haven't been reading. Just getting the images.' She clicks, turns the page, clicks again.

'You want me to turn the pages for you?'

She looks up. 'Sure.'

They move to the kitchen table. Martin sits opposite her and starts turning the pages as Ecco concentrates on her phone. Soon enough, they've established a rhythm.

'Can I talk?' asks Martin.

'Go ahead.'

'There's no doubt in your mind?' he asks. 'They were the remains of Chloe Carmichael?'

Ecco gestures towards the diary. 'None. It's hers.'

'She was on the run,' says Martin, turning a page. 'You know the story? She killed her fiancé and fled. There's still a warrant for her arrest.'

'Yes. The cops followed her trail to Nyngan and Dubbo. To Adelaide. But she slipped through their fingers,' says Ecco, and even as she completes the sentence, Martin can hear the doubt creeping into her voice. 'You think she went all the way to South Australia and then doubled back to hide in that cave?'

Martin thinks about it, but not for long. 'No. How did she get out there? How did she intend to get back? She would have needed an accomplice.'

'Perhaps they double-crossed her?' says Ecco.

Martin thinks about it, but not for long. 'No. I don't think she was hiding out. Or that she went to Adelaide and back. My guess is she was there all along.'

Ecco stops taking photographs, slides the book towards her, cautiously turns to the end, then works her way back to the last entry. 'Her entries. They're dated.' She keeps working her way back, scanning through each entry quickly before turning to the previous one. Finally she says, 'Here it is. The sixteenth of March.'

'The day Roman Stanton was killed,' says Martin.

'Not by her,' says Ecco. 'Listen to this.' And she reads: *I wonder what could be keeping Roman. My light has died, as I knew it would, so I can explore no further until he gets back. I wish he'd hurry up. I can't wait.*

'Jesus,' says Martin. 'How many more entries?'

Ecco sifts through. 'A lot. Pages and pages and pages.' She examines them more closely. 'But only five days' worth.'

They sit in silence then, the candlelight flickering about them, their thoughts centred on the young woman dying of thirst.

Eventually the sound of an engine disturbs their contemplation: Jamie returning.

'Let's crack on,' says Ecco. 'We might not see it again. The police will want it.'

And so they return to their production-line photography.

Jamie enters, carrying a bag, sees what they are doing. 'Some clothes for you, Martin. I can take over.'

Martin moves into the bedroom to change, as Jamie turns the pages. When he comes out, dressed in a large t-shirt and loose cotton trackpants, he's ready with questions, with theories. 'So she went there with Roman. He returned to the Stantons' place, Tavelly Station, to get torches and other supplies, leaving her at the cave.'

'Yes,' says Ecco.

'She didn't kill Roman Stanton?' Jamie asks, catching on immediately.

'No—she was already at the cave the day he was shot,' says Ecco.

'That's in the diary?' asks Jamie.

'Near the end,' says Ecco.

'You're saying she wasn't a fugitive?' the young man asks. 'She was searching for something?'

'The Camel's Head,' says Ecco.

'Which is what, precisely?' Martin interjects.

'The rock formation along the ridge where you uncovered the cave,' Ecco answers.

'And that's why you were out there? Looking for the cave, not me?'

'Looking for something.' She smiles at him. 'I'm glad we found you, Martin. Very happy we saved you. But yes, it was a coincidence.'

He returns the smile. 'Well, with all the shit luck I've had lately, that must just about square the ledger.'

'Same here,' Ecco says. 'Maybe our fortunes are turning.'

Jamie turns a page, Ecco takes a photograph.

'How much longer?' asks Jamie.

'Almost done,' says Ecco.

'I'll take over if you like,' Martin offers.

'Sure,' says the young man. He must be tired, riding all the way, not having the chance to rest, to shower.

Martin sits down, turns the next page in the diary, a dozen questions crowding his mind. He looks across at Ecco. 'You were very keen to set the ground rules earlier, lay claim to the story of the cave. Why? My assurance stands, so tell me: what were you looking for out there? It wasn't Chloe, was it?'

'No. Not her. But I think she was there looking for the same thing I was.' Ecco's head is still bowed as she continues taking photos.

'What was that?' prompts Martin.

She doesn't answer his question, not directly. 'We saved your life, remember? And we haven't turned you in to the police. You owe us.'

Martin stops turning the pages, on alert, unsure what is motivating Ecco. 'I promise, whatever is in the cave, whatever it is Chloe found or didn't find, it's yours. Your story.'

Ecco turns to Jamie. 'You heard. You're our witness.'

'He's a journalist,' says Jamie. 'Don't trust him.'

Martin can see her straining to make the right decision.

She takes a deep breath. 'I want to write a book. When you hear what I've got to say, you'll want to write one as well.'

'You want to collaborate?'

Ecco laughs, a temporary release of tension. 'I know how to write a book, thank you.' She keeps smiling. 'And I do think you should write a book. Absolutely. About what happened to you, how someone has tried to discredit you, smear you, kill you. The A-team. How you and the Stantons were conned. That's a great story. Particularly the section about me being collateral damage. You would be doing me a huge favour if you were able to convince the public I wasn't some raving nympho and that the video of the two of us was counterfeit. But the cave and what's in it, that's all mine.'

'Me sheltering there?' asks Martin. 'You and Jamie saving me?'

'No. That's okay. It will dovetail with my story.'

'Finding Chloe?'

She looks at him then, looks at him hard. 'I think we might need to share that.'

'Jesus, I can't believe you two,' says Jamie, shaking his head with what seems to Martin like part despair, part distaste. 'Like vultures, picking over the bones.'

Ecco ignores him, keeps her eyes on Martin. 'You should tell her story. The murder of Roman Stanton. Isn't that what you do? True crime? Exposés? Justice?'

'If I can,' says Martin, still cautious. 'I would like that very much.' He turns to Jamie. 'If that's okay with you?'

Jamie doesn't appear to be placated. 'Clay's waiting. We need to get over there before he goes to bed.'

And so Ecco tells Martin all about Patrick Murdoch's journal, about his encounter with Hentig and Stuart, members of Leichhardt's doomed mission, looking for the Camel's Head, seeking treasure. How the journal had probably lain unread for more than a century, until Chloe Carmichael found it and recognised the names of the explorers, and recognised the reference to the Camel's Head too, because there used to be a painting of it by a famous colonial artist hanging in the sitting room of the Longchamp Downs homestead.

'Chloe asked Clay if he knew where the Camel's Head was. Then she must have gone looking for the treasure, and for any trace of the men.' Ecco smiles wanly.

'It can't have been Chloe who killed Roman Stanton,' says Martin. 'We know that now.' And something more than curiosity, more than the chase of the story takes hold of him. It's an imperative, a sense of mission. Bad things have happened here; they need to be set right. 'I want to find out who was responsible for her death and who killed Roman. I want justice for them.'

'Good,' says Ecco. 'I will share anything I find in the diary that might help you achieve that.'

'Thank you,' he says. 'And if I find anything that might help your research, I will definitely share it with you.'

'We need to get back out there, with proper lighting, do a thorough search. To find out what, if anything, was in the cave and to see if Hentig and Stuart ever found it.' She looks at him, then to Jamie. 'We should go tomorrow morning. First thing.'

'Suits me,' says Martin. He feels the thrill of this new story coming on top of the thrill of being alive. He can see the same inspiration possessing Ecco, her quick laugh, her wide eyes, despite the rigours of the day.

But not Jamie. The youth has become more solemn, more pensive. 'We have to tell Clay,' he reminds them. 'It might be a big story for you two, but it's his daughter out there. He has a right to know. Tonight.'

And Martin is brought back to reality, recognising the truth in the young man's words.

Ecco, too, becomes sombre. 'Jamie is right, Clay needs to hear the truth,' she says, taking one last photograph. 'From me'—she holds up the diary—'and from his daughter.'

chapter thirty-nine
ECCO

WE HEAD OVER TO THE HOMESTEAD ON THE QUAD BIKES. I'D SUGGESTED MARTIN stay behind, so that Clay wouldn't learn of his presence, but he insisted on coming. Jamie makes sure Martin travels with him. I don't know if he's being gallant or protective or jealous, not wanting the reporter getting his claws into me.

We pull up outside the homestead. The lights are on, the hum of a generator coming from out the back somewhere. We dismount in silence, walk up the path to the verandah, remove our shoes, approach the door. Jamie takes the lead, using the brass knocker.

I'm no longer feeling so sure of myself. The excitement from finding the cave and the diary has faded, replaced by a sense of dread. Martin, to his credit, seems just as reserved. I can't imagine what's going through Jamie's mind, having lost a daughter himself.

Clay opens the door. I don't know what Jamie has told him, but he looks subdued; he must suspect it's bad news.

He flicks his head at Martin. 'What's he doing here?'

'It's important,' says Jamie.

'The police are after him,' says the old man.

'I'll be gone at dawn,' says Martin.

Clay looks from him to me and then to Jamie. Then relents, inviting us in.

We file into the sitting room. I can see Martin studying it, looking around, spotting the camera. But he doesn't say anything, knows it's not the right time.

Clay stands with his back to the empty fireplace, arms crossed. I sit next to Jamie on the settee, Martin in an armchair.

Jamie speaks. 'I'm terribly sorry. We're all sorry. But out in the desert, near the Camel's Head, we found her. We found Chloe.'

Clay says nothing, just looks at us, unseeing. Seconds pass; it feels like an eternity.

'How can you be sure?' he asks at last. 'After so many years?'

'I found her,' I say. 'In a cave.' I stand, give him the diary. 'Hers. It was next to the body.'

He takes it, holds it reverently, like a religious relic, the most precious, most fragile thing in the world. He seems like he might collapse. Jamie stands, moves across to help Clay to an armchair. The patriarch of Longchamp Downs seems to be ageing before our eyes.

'Tell me,' he says.

And so I do. I'm the one who knows the story best. The discovery of the entries in Patrick Murdoch's journals, the pencil marks in the margins. The mention of the Camel's Head, the painting in the Queensland gallery.

'That's why you asked about it,' says Clay.

'Yes.'

'Like she did.'

'Yes.'

And now he does look old. His back, always so ramrod straight, has become curved, as if bending under his grief. Chloe had asked him about the Camel's Head in the days before her death, but he had not made the connection after she disappeared. I can only imagine the self-recriminations starting to fire in his mind.

I continue, telling Clay how Jamie and I headed into the desert that morning, searching for any traces of the lost explorers out near the rock formation. Of finding Martin, who had stumbled across the cave. How I ventured down and found Chloe's skeletal remains, her boots and glasses and diary.

'Did you . . . ?' the old man starts to ask. He falters, eyes red; tries again. 'Did you take any photographs? On your phone?'

Now it's my turn to wilt. 'You sure you want to see them? It might be better to wait, to go there in person.'

'Why?'

'I don't know,' I say. 'A photograph seems so impersonal. At the cave, there was a feeling that she is at peace.' And as I say it, I mean it. 'Like a natural crypt.'

But Clay insists, and so I show him. The tears come then, the last inhibitions swept away by this final, irrefutable proof. 'I always felt it, you know. Deep down. She wasn't coming back.'

'She is now,' says Jamie, almost to himself. He has tears on his cheeks. Even Martin, the hard-arse journalist, looks like he might be tearing up.

We pass a silent minute, broken only by a sniffle from Clay. But then he gathers himself, sits straighter in the chair. He addresses Martin. 'We will need to notify the police about Chloe. They will come. You can't be here. They rang earlier. Told me to keep an eye out, that you could be dangerous. Possibly armed.'

'Do I look dangerous?' asks Martin.

Clay glares at him. 'You should go. Tonight, if possible.'

'Please, Mr Carmichael, hear me out,' says Martin, all deference. 'We're pretty sure your daughter was already out there in the desert, at the cave, when Roman Stanton was shot. She didn't kill him. She was innocent.'

Clay says nothing, but I can see he is interested.

Martin continues. 'I want to find out what happened. I want to find out who did shoot Roman. I want to clear Chloe's name. I want to find out who was responsible for her death.'

Clay looks to me. I nod. He looks to Jamie, who does the same. He turns back to Martin. 'Very well. Stay tonight. Leave tomorrow. I won't tell the police.'

'Thank you,' says Martin, but he's not finished. 'One thing I don't understand. If she was stranded out there, why was everyone so certain she was the killer?'

I think for a moment he has overstepped, asking Clay about this in his moment of heartache. Or maybe that's how journalists work, getting their questions in when people are at their most vulnerable.

If Clay is offended, he doesn't show it. Perhaps Martin's plea has struck a chord, his intention to clear Chloe's name, to find those responsible for her death. 'There were no witnesses to the shooting, but she was seen driving through Port Paroo around the time Stanton was shot. Then she withdrew money in Nyngan and Dubbo. Her car was found at the railway station there. Vincent got a message from her in Adelaide.'

'Who saw her driving through Port Paroo?'

'Maureen Gingelly, the publican's daughter. Testified at the inquest.'

'Maureen?' says Martin. 'You mean Maz?'

'That's her.' Clay looks at his watch. 'I'm sorry. I really should tell Mrs Enright. She was always so close to the children.' He stands, then catches my eye. 'Come with me. There is something you should have.'

He leads me down the corridor, towards the kitchen. From the back of the kitchen door he takes a key ring, then backtracks to the locked door. He opens it. Chloe's room. Clean, awaiting her return, maintained no doubt by Mrs Enright. Posters on the wall, remnants from her teenage years, soft toys from her childhood.

'There, on the shelf,' says Clay.

I see them now, Chloe's diaries, the same size and similar in style to the one I found in the cave.

'You should have them,' he says. 'Read them. Tell her story.' He walks over to the shelf, takes them down, and hands them to me, as if imparting something sacred. 'She's in your hands now. Treat her well.'

He leaves me then, goes to break the terrible news to Mrs Enright.

I look about the room. Feel her ghost. That young girl, barely a woman. And I think myself lucky, for the first time in a long while. I didn't deserve what happened to me, but I wasn't blameless. I'd done what I'd done. And yet here I am, alive. Unlike Chloe, only just emerging from her teens.

I open one of the diaries, see the writing, see the exclamation marks with their tiny circles instead of dots, recognise this from the notes in Murdoch's diary. I can almost hear her reciting the words.

So boring!! So unimaginably, utterly, irredeemably, brain-stewingly boring!!

335

I read a little more. The style is idiosyncratic, more like she's corresponding with a pen pal than addressing herself. I know it's ridiculous, but it feels almost as if she's writing to me. I recall her skeletal remains, and a profound sense of loss wells up in me. I close the diary and hold it close to my chest, knowing it is something to be cherished.

I give myself a minute, then return to the sitting room, where Martin is examining the broken security camera. 'I never realised how realistic the video was,' he says.

'Come on,' I say. 'Let's check the web.'

'I thought the lines were down?' says Martin.

'Satellite. Starlink.'

In the library, we check the news sites. They aren't good. We go to the ABC first. The national broadcaster is playing it straight, reporting official sources, nothing more. There's a warrant for Martin's arrest, police saying he is wanted for questioning on a number of matters, including financial irregularities as well as other lines of inquiry. They say he left the town of Port Paroo two days ago and hasn't been seen since.

He looks at me, shaking his head, a strange expression on his face.

We try the *Sydney Morning Herald* site, but Martin can't remember his subscriber login, so all we get is the front page. The story is a sidebar: MAN HUNT FOR HERALD CONTRIBUTOR.

Martin smiles wryly. 'That doesn't bode well—I'm a "contributor" now.'

We move on.

The *Daily Mail*'s headline pulls no punches: POLICE HUNT PERVERT, with a photo of a leering Martin, possibly digitally manipulated.

The real-life Martin looks like he's been hit by a truck.

We go to iView, the ABC news out of Brisbane. Martin is the lead story; it's uncomfortable viewing.

'Prominent investigative journalist Martin Scarsden is on the run this evening, with police voicing concerns for the welfare of the former high-flyer.

'The reporter went missing after police raided Mr Scarsden's home on the north coast of New South Wales.'

'Some raid,' observes Martin as the camera follows the police inside his house. 'More like a police-sanctioned hatchet job. They've tipped off the networks. Cameras all over it.'

The report includes an interview with a woman identified as Maureen Gingelly, Port Paroo publican.

'He was here, all right. Used a fake name. Jacob Solander. Last I saw him, he was very distraught. He left all his clothes. His phone and laptop. I'm worried he's done something impulsive.'

Martin looks bewildered.

And then the phone on the desk rings, the landline.

Martin regards it like he might a viper.

'Comes through the internet,' I explain, answering the phone, half expecting it to be for Clay, ready to make excuses on his behalf. Instead, I listen with amazement, then turn to Martin. 'It's for you. Someone called Jack.'

chapter forty
MARTIN

'JACK? IS THAT YOU?'

'Martin. Thank God. I was worried you were dead.'

'Almost was.' And before the ASIO man can respond: 'Just a moment.' Martin puts his hand over the receiver, speaks to Ecco. 'I'm sorry, but I need to take this in private.'

The ghostwriter looks pissed off, eyes narrowing, but she leaves the room, closing the door behind her.

'Jack, is Mandy okay? Last time I spoke to her, the police were coming up the drive.'

'She's fine for now. In custody at the Port Silver police station. Helping police with their inquiries. Liam is with your uncle and his family.'

Martin tries to breathe, to calm himself. 'Can you get a message to her? Let her know that I'm alive?'

'Of course. She'll be relieved.'

'And get her out of there.'

'I'll do my best.'

Martin runs a hand through his hair, not sure whether to feel grateful or stressed. 'How did you know to ring me here, Jack?'

'I didn't. Just covering the bases. Your car. Longchamp Downs is one of the nearest properties.'

'My car? How could you know . . . ?' Martin's voice trails off, his brain supplying the answer a tick or two before Goffing vocalises it.

'Satellite transponder. Pings every fifteen minutes. You didn't think I'd let you wander off completely on your own.'

'Fuck, Jack. Who else has access to that information?'

'Just me.'

'Why should I trust you?' Martin says the words without thinking, but doesn't regret it.

'What?'

'You're the one who sent me to Port Paroo.'

'Meaning?'

Martin pauses, wants to vent, not sure if he should, feels as if the tribulations of the past few days are clouding his judgement. 'Is this line secure?' he asks instead, aware he must be sounding paranoid.

'Very,' says Goffing. 'I've scrambled the signal at both ends, fully encrypted, locations disguised.'

Martin feels a little more reassured. 'What's going on, Jack? I'm being targeted and I don't know why.'

'Yeah, no doubt you're the focus,' says Goffing. 'The video of that track being blown up, the fake porno, the planting of fabricated evidence at the house in Port Silver. It all points in the same direction.'

'And the hit squad,' Martin adds quietly. 'You forgot the killers. The ones with the guns. They almost got me.'

'Killers?'

'A two-man crew took me out into the desert, left me for dead. Didn't disguise their intentions or their identities. Called themselves the A-team. Cute, right? Just to rub it in.'

'Seriously? They called themselves the A-team?'

'With the merch to go with it.' He describes the red trucker caps.

'Jesus, Martin. The B-team, the reason we sent you away, it was all a ploy to get you out there onto their preferred territory. Into their kill zone. Whoever the fuck is behind this, they didn't just play you, they've played ASIO and the federal police. Twice over: while we had all our resources focused on them, another team took out Marelli's grandson and tried to do the same with you. They've been pulling the strings all along. Still are, with all this confected nonsense about fraud and kiddie-fiddling.'

'No shit,' says Martin bitterly. 'Not just sourcing information from you and the cops, but feeding misinformation back in.'

Goffing ignores the jibe. 'Take me through it.'

Martin explains about his abduction, the drive into the desert.

'Jesus.'

'What happened, Jack? If you were tracking my car, pinging off satellites every fifteen minutes, why has it taken you so long to chase me down? The car's been sitting out there for a day and a half. I should be dead by now.'

There's a long gap, as if the line has dropped out. And then, at last, Goffing speaks. 'This next bit is never for publication.'

'You know you can trust me,' says Martin, crossing his fingers.

'I spent the last twenty-four hours in detention. Intermittently interrogated.'

'What? By whom? The intelligence services?'

'Yeah. There's a mole. We've been penetrated. This whole fuck-up with the B-team confirms it.'

'Wait,' says Martin. 'This mole, this penetration, it's connected with guiding me out here? The whole B-team, A-team strategy?'

'I'd say so.'

'Shit. You're sure this line is secure?'

'If it's not, I'm toast,' says Goffing.

'*You're* toast?' Martin feels his anger rising, tamps it down. 'After the bombing in Port Silver, you said no safe houses, that heading west, getting away from the phone towers, was the best strategy. You suggested Port Paroo. Who else knew? Who told the killers?'

'That's what they were interrogating me about.'

'And?'

'Not now, Martin. Not now.'

The two men are silent for a moment, Martin struggling to comprehend the scale of the conspiracy against him.

'I don't get it, Jack. It's so elaborate. Byzantine. If the mafia wanted me dead, they could just walk up and shoot me on the beach at Port Silver. Double tap, goodnight. Old school. What's with all this intricate plotting? I mean, infiltrating ASIO? That's batshit crazy.'

'I agree, it doesn't sound like the mafia. I'm thinking it's a psycho. Out for revenge. They don't just want you dead, they want you suffering and humiliated. Destroyed.' Goffing takes a breath. 'If you had been found dead, there would be no restraint. Every sordid unfounded lie would be out there, pumped into the world. They'd flood the internet.'

'Revenge for what?'

'Who knows? Might not even be real, just some imagined slight. People are weird. Take umbrage at what they read in the papers.'

'It's no lone wolf, Jack,' says Martin. He tells Goffing about Dermott Brick, his involvement in both destroying the road at

Longchamp Downs and the deepfake porno, recounting what Ivan Lucic told him: that the real Dermott Brick had died in the Pilbara seven years ago. And Martin tells him what Bethanie Glass has discovered: the media is being fed stories about Martin via a professional PR company, Packlehurst and Glee. 'Whoever is behind all this has money. And connections. And expertise. They whipped up that porn video in no time flat. And now you're saying they've infiltrated ASIO, the feds.'

Goffing's voice sounds almost embittered as he replies. 'You're right. Think about penetrating ASIO. How difficult it would be to place a mole within the intelligence community, and then be willing to burn that asset to prosecute a personal vendetta against a journalist.'

'Jesus. The more I think about it, the crazier it seems.'

'And you have no idea who it could be?'

'Dermott Brick has to be our way in. Him and this PR firm, Packlehurst and Glee.'

'Okay, I'll check Brick out: see if I can run facial recognition software, establish his real identity, start running surveillance,' says Goffing, like he's ticking off a mental list.

'You don't want me to confront Brick?'

'No. For God's sake. These people have tried to kill you once; let's not serve you up on a platter. See what I can find out first. What's your next move?'

Martin again finds himself hesitating, doesn't answer the question directly. 'I'll get my car back tomorrow, with luck. There've been some strange developments up here.'

'Such as? Connected?'

'I can't see how. Maybe tangentially.' Martin fills Goffing in on the cave and finding the remains of Chloe Carmichael.

'Extraordinary,' says the intelligence operative. 'Weirdly fasci-nating, but that all went down twenty years ago, Ludwig Leichhardt a lot longer ago than that. How could it possibly be relevant?'

'It saved my life,' says Martin.

'There's that. But you didn't answer my question about your next move.'

Martin sighs. 'I'm thinking of heading back to Port Paroo. I want to talk to Maz Gingelly, she's the publican at the hotel. She told the ABC I left my phone and laptop in my room, but I had them with me when the A-team abducted me.'

'What are you thinking?' asks Goffing.

'They put them back in my room. Planted them. She might have seen something. Got a look at those arseholes or their vehicle.'

'Go there and the police will arrest you. You know that.'

'I can't stay here. The police will be here tomorrow as well.'

'Okay. I'll see what I can do from this end.'

'Such as?'

And Goffing laughs, a humourless sound. 'All I can get on Brick. All I can get on Packlehurst and Glee. And find an escape route for you. Get you out of that district.'

2005

MONDAY, 10 JANUARY

I'm on my way back to Brisbane to prepare for my final year, and I don't want to go. I don't want to leave Roman; I already I miss him. There's something fundamental in my longing, I feel it deep inside, both physical and spiritual, this need to be together.

He proposed again and then for a third time, and I said yes. I always wanted to marry him, I was always going to consent, and on my last night at Port Paroo he asked for the final time, down on his knee. And by then we'd worked it through. I will marry him, but not to live at Tavelly Station. Not yet. Roman has come around, says he can put a manager on it, or ask Merry to run both properties, so that we can be together. I can't believe how happy I am!!

I'll miss him, but that's not the only reason I regret travelling east.

Dad set it in motion. I'd said goodbye to Roman at Port Paroo, spending a final night at Longchamp, packing my gear to head back to the city for my final year of uni. I was admiring the paintings scattered around the homestead. The portraits in the library, the landscapes in the bedrooms. And of course those four huge canvases in the sitting room and the dining room. I'd grown up with them, they'd always been there, literally part of the furniture, familiar and comforting. I guess they were an early influence, inspiring my love of art, guiding me towards my studies, and yet I had never closely examined them. The Homestead *and* Lake Murdoch in Flood *and* The Camel's Head at Dawn *and* The Mulga Plains. *I asked Dad about them, where they had come from. It was obvious all four were by the same artist.*

'They've been here ever since I remember,' he said.

'Commissioned by our family?' I asked.

'I guess. Or our predecessors. They're definitely local scenes. Lake Murdoch in Flood, *just up the river there.* The Homestead *is how this place used to look.* The Mulga Plains *looks like it might be the next patch over, where the airstrip is now. And* The Camel's Head, *the colour of the earth, the rocks on that ridge, that must be out west somewhere.'*

'Do you know who the artist is?'

Dad looked nonplussed. 'There'll be records in the library. All the old ledgers are in there. Journals from the early settlers. Patrick Murdoch and the Abbotts and my grandfather. Never really bothered with them myself. Too busy thinking about the here and now, planning for the future. But have a gander. It'll be there somewhere.'

And so I did. Took me hours to find it, a reference in the diary of Archibald Abbott. A visit by colonial artist Percival McEwan Fitzroy in 1893. I showed Dad. He agreed that must be it. I went to one of the paintings, held a torch light to it, found a murky signature in the bottom right corner: PMF 1893. So it was him, no doubt about it.

I returned Abbott's diary and, on a whim, started reading the journal of Patrick Murdoch, the first white settler on the Paroo. It's confronting. The way he viewed the blacks, the way he treated them.

Not the worst, perhaps, but still damning, that peculiar colonial mix of romanticism and brutality.

And then the strangest coincidence. Murdoch recounts meeting a couple of itinerants, Hentig and Stuart, white men wandering the outback. I would have thought nothing of it, except for the connection between that encounter of Murdoch's and the visit of Percival McEwan Fitzroy in 1893. Hentig and Stuart were searching for the very place that Fitzroy painted a generation later: the Camel's Head. It felt so unsettling, me encountering that same name, twice in the same day, over one hundred and fifty years after Murdoch's entry, like it was reaching across the years to tell me something. And the painting, still on our wall.

It's given me an idea for an honours thesis: Colonial Artist: The Works of Percival McEwan Fitzroy. *Roman can come to Brisbane; we can live together down there.*

TUESDAY, 18 JANUARY

Curiouser and curiouser. The most amazing discovery.

I'm back at university now, back in Brisbane, working a holiday job as a researcher for one of the professors, trying to save money for the year ahead. Take some of the financial strain off Dad. Hopefully, I can continue part-time when the term starts. The professor likes my thesis proposal, without promising me I'll get an invitation for honours.

The paintings have gotten under my skin; I want to get cracking on my research. I went to the state gallery yesterday in my lunch break and learnt that paintings by Percival McEwan Fitzroy are quite valuable. Not massively, but worth many thousands. I wonder if Dad knows. The gallery has some minor works of Fitzroy's from up on Cape York and around the Glass House Mountains. Nowhere near as grand as the ones at Longchamp. Apparently, he's popular with private collectors. Seems his specialty was expeditions to the frontier in search of the exotic. He's considered quite important, more for the places he captured so early in the spread of colonisation than for his artistic sensibilities and technical skill. It bodes well for my thesis.

It was only later, after I had seen the painting, that I asked the assistant about the two men, Arthur Hentig and Donald Stuart. She had never heard of them, but she pointed me to a register of Queensland explorers. I wasn't sure they were explorers—they sounded more like prospectors or swagmen—but I checked anyway. And I found them! They were members of Ludwig Leichhardt's lost expedition!

I can't wait to get back to Longchamp, find out what else is in those diaries. I've written to Roman, told him all about it, swearing him to secrecy.

SATURDAY, 22 JANUARY

I'm back on the train, the long slow trip home. It feels so strange, heading west, knowing that Dad is travelling to the Sunshine Coast for the Australia Day week, Vincent finally convincing him to take a holiday. I was meant to be with them. The plan was to break the news to Dad of my engagement to Roman, with Vincent present for support. I wish I could be in both places, but this might be my only chance to get home before uni starts, and I want to check Murdoch's diaries, see what else I can find.

It could be nothing, of course, because I didn't note down the date of Murdoch's diary entry. The two men could have visited years *before they signed onto Leichhardt's expedition. They could have been on their way to join it. Maybe they reached the Camel's Head, found nothing there, and continued north to the Darling Downs to meet up with the famous explorer. That is the most likely scenario, because if the men had wandered onto Longchamp after the last known sighting of Leichhardt and his companions, then surely Murdoch would have alerted the authorities; it would be on the public record.*

That is what I have been telling myself the entire way back. But soon I will find out for myself. Cunnamulla is the next stop, the end of the line. Dad has left me the car, keys behind the bar at the pub across from the railway station. I'll have the place to myself; even Mrs Enright will be on holidays.

SATURDAY, 22 JANUARY, LATER

Oh my god! I was right! I was right! I was right!! The entry in Murdoch's journal is dated July 1848, three months after Leichhardt and his expedition were last seen. They were here, Arthur Hentig and Donald Stuart. They camped by our river. This changes everything.

It's almost midnight and I'm exhausted, but I'm not sure I'll be able to sleep. This is amazing!

SUNDAY, 23 JANUARY

I've called the police. Dad will be on his way back, Vincent too.

They came in the early hours. I'd finally fallen asleep, so utterly exhausted from the travel and the journals and all the excitement. First,

I couldn't sleep; then I couldn't wake. But slowly, almost insidiously, the awareness came over me. Someone was in the house. I crept out. I remember standing there, realising I hadn't left the lamp on but that there was light coming from the sitting room. I went in and saw the blank spaces, the darker squares on the wallpaper where the paintings had hung for all those decades. That's the last thing I remember.

I regained consciousness, felt a pain in the back of my head. Touched it, my hand red with blood.

I raced to the window just in time to see a truck pulling away. Was I dreaming? I can't have been dreaming.

I called the police and then I called Vincent, told him what had happened and asked him to tell Dad. I tried to call Roman too, but he's not answering.

MONDAY, 24 JANUARY

Dad is home and Vincent came with him, bless them.

My brother was so calm, so understanding. So supportive. He's spoken to the police, who reckon they're doing their best. They say these sorts of thefts, on remote properties, aren't so rare after all. I told Vincent the same as I told the police, that I saw nothing, just the tail-lights heading towards the south gate.

He agreed it was strange that they'd leave that way. The thieves would have to travel two hundred kilometres to Port Paroo before they could even turn off the Sundowner Track. The police think it probably means the gang is based in New South Wales. Vincent has volunteered to head down to Port Paroo, ask Maz and Perry and the other locals if they saw anything. Put up a flyer in the pub.

THURSDAY, 27 JANUARY

Roman came up to Longchamp. Vincent saw him in Port Paroo and told him what had happened. I was so glad to see him. Dad wasn't at all happy having a Stanton on the property, wasn't sure why Roman was there, until I told him we're engaged. It wasn't how I planned it, but Dad took it well enough. He didn't say anything at first, didn't react at all, just that stoic persona of his. But over an hour or two he seemed to mellow, even opening some special wine to celebrate. I guess seeing us together has convinced him we're good for each other. Not that there's much he can do about it anyway.

I thought he would be more upset at the loss of the paintings, but he doesn't seem worried about that at all. Instead he's fussing over me, even though I'm fine. The cut to the head didn't need stitches and there was never any sign of concussion. He's blaming himself for being away, as if it is some sort of punishment for taking time off and spending money when the drought is so dire. He's talking about installing burglar alarms and security cameras, as if that would do any good now. I think he is just trying to convince himself he's doing all that he can. I tell him we can't afford it. And shutting the stable door won't do any good; the horse is probably in Sydney by now.

I told Roman all about the paintings and Percival McEwan Fitzroy, my idea for an honours thesis. We had our first big argument then, all about the extra year in Brisbane. I said things I regret, so did he. We ended up screaming at each other. It wasn't what Roman had been expecting; he'd thought we'd spend that year travelling before returning to Tavelly. But he calmed down after a while, put it in one of his compartments. After all, what's a year when we have a lifetime together? I suggested we could travel to Fitzroy's locations together while I was researching the thesis, like a pre-wedding honeymoon.

He liked the idea of that. I think maybe Vincent heard us fighting, but thankfully Dad was out with the cattle. I wouldn't want him turning against Roman when he's just starting to accept him as a future son-in-law.

Afterwards, I showed Roman Murdoch's journal and the printouts from the gallery and library, explaining what I had found. He listened intently.

'You should make that your thesis,' he said. 'Sounds fascinating. Groundbreaking.'

I do love him so.

And now I'm heading back to uni. I have Murdoch's journals with me. Reading them will be a good way to pass the time, seeing as it takes a whole day to get to Brisbane.

MONDAY

chapter forty-one
ECCO

I CAN'T SLEEP; I CAN'T STAY AWAKE. I STAY WITH CHLOE'S DIARY AS LONG AS I can, reading it off my phone screen, squinting in the night. But I keep losing concentration and falling into a doze, passing through imagined realities like passing through clouds. Could this book, this story, really be my path to redemption? Then why don't I feel more optimistic, more thrilled? Instead it haunts me, the memory of Chloe's body, reduced to a skeleton and memories. Lying out there still, in her cold, dark tomb, even as I lie safe and warm and secure at Longchamp Downs. I had disturbed her, like a grave robber. Or an Egyptologist, desecrating the tombs of the pharaohs, in thrall to my own ambitions.

And again and again my mind returns to Jamie in Scarsden's car, sharing his long suffering, his guilt over the death of his wife and daughter. And later, his insistence that our priority was to tell Clay, that the old man's right to know was more important than any ambitions of Martin Scarsden and me. It makes me feel ashamed, or self-obsessed or something. I ponder what it is I am really chasing out here. It occurs to me that perhaps the path home is not through restoring my public profile, proving the trolls wrong, but through nurturing my internal being. Maybe I can learn something from Jamie Stubbs. Decency. Generosity perhaps.

Eventually sleep does take me. I know, because one moment it was pitch-black outside my window, and now the sky is pale blue. Dawn is coming, but I feel no more refreshed than when I first closed my eyes. I dress, make coffee, but even while it's brewing, I hear the vehicles arrive. I step out to meet them. Clay is driving a big four-wheel drive, a Land Cruiser, with tanks of water and a winch and VHF aerials. Martin is in the passenger seat, while Jamie is on his quad bike.

'Why don't you go with Clay and Martin?' he says. 'More comfortable.'

'I'd rather ride,' I say. The thought of being confined doesn't appeal. I want to be in the open; I want to be with my thoughts. 'Is that okay?'

'Sure,' he says. His eyes are scanning my face, as if searching for something. 'I'll just check your fuel levels.'

After he has topped up my tank from one of the jerry cans in the back of the Land Cruiser, we head off in a loose convoy. Jamie first, me following, off to one side so I'm not chewing his dust, the big Toyota behind us. I'm not feeling so Mad Max today, more like a dispatch rider bearing bad news, or an escort at a state funeral.

We pass through the mulga plains, cross ridges, eventually coming to the long expanse leading to the Camel's Head and begin to track south, hugging the eastern ridge, still in its shadow. I've been distracted, not exactly sure where we are, trusting Jamie's knowledge. He must be confident; he hasn't paused the whole way except to give Clay time to traverse the ridges. And then, in the distance, I see the derelict windmill and I know exactly where we are, the landscape giving up its secrets as I reorientate myself, the Camel's Head to the west, still recognisable from this angle. We pass the windmill and a few minutes later pull up next to the abandoned Subaru. It looks none the worse for wear, except for the sand built up around its western flank from yesterday's storm. The bonnet is again covered with a thin layer of dust. Jamie brushes it aside with his gloved hand. The words are clear. No one speaks as Clay regards them.

'Fair enough,' he says, nothing more. I understand his mind is elsewhere.

'Let's see if we can get Martin going, then we'll head to the cave,' says Jamie. It's as if Clay has surrendered his authority to him, and Jamie has stepped up. He grimaces. 'These fuel-injected engines. Not meant to run out of petrol. Might not start without being properly primed.'

'Seriously?' says Martin. 'You're telling me this now?'

Jamie stares him down. 'Either works or it doesn't, mate. What can I say?' He empties two-thirds of a jerry can of fuel into the car. 'Okay. Secret is to take it easy. You want me to try?'

'Be my guest,' Martin says, still sounding a little surly. And then belatedly: 'Thank you.'

Jamie turns the engine over. The starter motor churns and churns. Nothing. After another attempt, he stops trying and gets out. 'If there's air in the fuel pump and I keep pushing, it could overheat. I'll give it a breather.'

He waits a couple of minutes, then tries again, turning the engine over once more. And still the car doesn't start. Another break of several more minutes. Martin seems calm enough, but I can see Clay is getting edgy. This is not why he's come here.

And now the sun is emerging over the eastern ridge, and the first heat pours down into the depression, a harbinger of what's to come. Jamie is beginning to look grim. He needs to get the car going soon, while it's still relatively cool. He tries again and, at the third attempt, the engine catches. It roars, then sputters, then roars again, before settling into a steady idle.

'Thank you,' says Martin, sincerity trumping any earlier irritability, as Jamie climbs out, leaving the engine purring. 'I would have ballsed that up for sure.'

'Learn something new every day,' says Jamie. 'Let's get some more petrol into it now we know it won't be wasted. I'll give you enough to get you somewhere you can fill up. Head south, stay within the ridges, and you'll get to the Port Paroo–Tibooburra road.'

'Are you sure you'll be okay?' I ask. 'Driving by yourself out here?'

'Car's got sat nav,' says Martin. 'I can't get lost.'

'And if you break down? Or get bogged? You don't have an emergency beacon. Is your phone set up?'

'No phone. They took it.' He looks unperturbed. 'I'll be fine. I'll call when I'm safe. Either that or you'll see me on the news being arrested.'

'Jesus,' I say, and before I know it I'm hugging him. I really must be fatigued. 'Take care,' I say. Only now he is leaving do I acknowledge that he's been an ally.

'You too,' he replies. 'I really hope it works out for you. The book and everything.'

'We'll meet again, I'm sure of it,' I say.

'Bound to.'

And Martin gets into his Subaru, plays about with the sat nav for a minute or so, then inches it out from the accumulated sand, turning in a wide arc before heading south.

'Can't make my mind up about him,' says Clay as we watch the billowing dust edge into the distance.

'Neither can I,' says Jamie, and I wonder if I hear a hint of jealousy in his voice.

— —

We drive back towards the windmill and Jamie stops below the ridge. I pull up next to him and cut my engine. Clay parks the Land Cruiser alongside. The sun is up, but the day is silent, as if out of respect for our mission. There isn't a breath of wind. We don't speak; there is no need. I clamber up the ridge, Jamie to one side, Clay following. He seems nimble enough, sure-footed in his worn riding boots, but we need to wait for him as we near the entrance to the cave. It's not that he's breathing hard, more like he's shouldering some invisible weight.

The blade from the windmill is there, marking the entrance. And still we don't speak, relying on nothing more than eye contact and shared expressions. I lead the way down, sliding on my arse, boots biting, trying not to set off a greater slide. Clay follows, Jamie remaining on the surface. This time I have a proper torch, a small backpack, leather gloves. I switch on the torch and the dimension of the subterranean space is simultaneously larger and smaller than the day before. I see the pools in the rocks, where the water has noticeably dissipated. Martin Scarsden is a very lucky man.

I inch downwards, get to the bottom, stand and wait for Clay. I hold out my gloved hand, help him the last little way, then move forward, forced to crouch by the low ceiling. The outcrop is just a few paces away, the boulder hiding Chloe's body.

'Just around there, behind the rock,' I say. 'You good?'

The old man looks grim but determined.

'You go ahead,' I say. 'I'll wait here.' All thoughts of bearing witness, of noting his reactions for my book, have vanished. Maybe Jamie is having an influence on me.

Clay moves forward, disappearing from view. I think that in the silence, the sound-eating silence of the underground, I hear a sob, maybe another, or maybe I'm imagining it. I wish Jamie were here, that we were waiting together for Clay to return. When he does, he's holding Chloe's glasses.

'It's her all right,' he says softly. 'Thank you.' His eyes are rimmed with red.

I guide him back towards the entrance. He seems frail, old. Jamie is there, descending most of the way to help Clay back out of the cave. I wait until they've returned to the surface and can no longer see me, then I re-enter the crypt. I pass beyond the outcrop, and I survey the mortal remains of Chloe Carmichael, boots neatly placed, skeletal toes outstretched. I bow my head in respect, not a conscious decision, just spontaneous, and mumble a prayer, directed to whom I can't say. It just feels like the right thing to do. I've read some of her diaries now, lived inside her head. To see her remains like this is heartbreaking. I can't begin to comprehend what Clay must be feeling. 'I'm so sorry,' I whisper to her, feeling inadequate, knowing she can't hear me. I pause for a moment longer, then I move past the body, keeping as much distance as I can.

Around me, the passage is dry, dusty, no evidence of water. A twist to the right and it opens into a cavern, tall enough for me to stand upright. There are more bones. It takes my breath away and I struggle to contain my speculation. What has occurred down here? I inch closer. On the walls, some ochre painting. Aboriginal. I wonder at the significance. Am I trespassing somewhere I've no right to be? Or is this place now as lost to Australia's First People as it is to the rest of us? I think of what I have read in the journals and what Clay himself told me. The 'dispersals': the ethnic cleansing of colonisation, the massacres, the survivors herded into missions. Was Indigenous knowledge lost? Might my discovery, the discovery of Martin, of Chloe, help rectify that in some way? Or is my presence here making it worse?

I sweep the torch beam over the bones. They're not human, even my rudimentary knowledge of anatomy is enough to glean that. My relief is palpable. They must be kangaroos. The torchlight catches a skull. It seems enormous, distorted by the close confines of the cave. I peer into the darkness, moving closer. And closer. The skull is not just big, it's gigantic. Too big to be a kangaroo or a wombat or any other animal I know. Could it be a camel? Down a cave? The Camel's Head? And then it comes to me, the obvious answer: it's the skeleton of an extinct animal, some part of Australia's distant past, when the interior was a more hospitable, habitable place. Long after the dinosaurs, but not so very long ago, not in geological time, in the time of the First People, just a few thousand years ago. Megafauna. Giant kangaroos, giant wombats. A treasure, to be sure. All perfectly preserved in the cave, cool, dark and dry, sealed off from the world. I remain transfixed for a moment, bewitched, full of wonder. Is this the treasure Hentig and Stuart were seeking?

It's only as I'm setting the torch down, moving to retrieve my phone from my backpack, intent on photographing the scene, that the reflection catches my eye, the torch beam penetrating a cover of dust, bouncing back from metal. I move to it, photos forgotten, careful not to disturb the bones. I brush the dirt away with my gloved hand. It's a lamp. Not a kerosene lamp; something more rudimentary. Older. I dare not lift it; instead I kneel closer, gently sweeping away the dust. Only then do I pick it up, examine it more closely. And on the bottom, an inscription. *Mahoney and Sons, Sydney. 1832.*

I handle it with reverence, photographing it, before replacing it exactly where I found it. With my torch I look around the chamber, searching for more evidence. And there, in the wall, an inscription, carved into the red stone with a knife blade. *AH. 1848.* I stare at it, disbelieving. So they were here. They found it, the cave of treasure, the cave of bones, hidden away under this remote ridge, the Camel's Head. I consider the bones of the ancient mammals. A treasure indeed. I wonder if the two explorers had any conception of what they'd found. Or were they gutted, disappointed not to have found gold or opals or some other glittering prize?

I edge my way back, past poor Chloe Carmichael who, trapped alone in the dark, probably never saw the treasure she'd come so close to finding.

chapter forty-two
MARTIN

MARTIN DRIVES, AND WHILE HE DRIVES, HE THINKS. ABOUT WHAT HAS TAKEN
place, about what his next move should be. He's taking it slowly,
trying to concentrate on steering, conscious that any mishap might
not be fatal but would severely limit his options. He has water on
the back seat, and the information screen on the dash tells him
he has enough petrol to last one hundred and ninety kilometres.
More than enough.

He's wary of dustbowls, wary of sharp rocks, grateful for the
all-wheel drive. He doesn't want to get bogged, doesn't want a
puncture. He weaves in and out of the sparse vegetation, picking
his way through. There's not much chance of getting lost, not with
the ridge lines to the east and west confining him, not with the
sun over his left shoulder, not with the sat nav. It tells him nothing
more than he is heading south, depicting the car as alone against a
featureless plain of green, but that's enough. Foreign software, he
supposes, assuming that open space should be rendered that hue.
There is precious little of the colour to be found in the landscape,
a few bushes, nothing more, more olive and khaki than a true

green, the plain dominated by reds and yellows and, above, the cloudless blue dome. And then, creeping into view on the southern edge of the screen, the Port Paroo–Tibooburra Road. He comes to it, eases up the shoulder, feeling the wheels grip, more assured on the graded surface. He stops the car, climbs out, stretches. There are tyre marks left in the bulldust. The road must be open; some traffic has passed through since yesterday's dust storm.

He can't go to Tibooburra, he decides. Jack Goffing wants him to leave the district, but what's the point? He would need to buy petrol. If the manager didn't recognise him, the EFTPOS machine would. He'd be arrested, detained, held incommunicado, deprived of agency and liberty. No, he decides to risk Port Paroo, see if he can talk to Maz. Maybe the police will be out looking for him and he can sneak in and out without being noticed.

He makes good time on the main road, and the town comes upon him with little warning. A wrecked car, a wire fence, a sign. PORT PAROO, POPULATION 12. Another of the Roads to Recovery signs, a relic of some long-forgotten election campaign. He sees the phone tower, passes the church, and then the pub. There's a police truck and a squad car parked outside. He can't go in, not with the police there. He can't even call Maz; he has no phone. So instead he turns south onto the Sundowner Track, following the right bank of the meandering Paroo River. There is water in the channel; the flood has reached Port Paroo, moving down-stream in an uninterrupted channel, not yet breaching the banks.

At Brown Water Creek, there is no flow, the watercourse under the bridge filled with dust and tumble weeds and empty bottles. He considers his agreement with Ekaterina Boland, the division of spoils: she will write a book about the cave, Ludwig Leichhardt and his lost expedition, Chloe's discovery in the old diary of one of the original settlers. But the rest is his. How Chloe came to die, who killed Roman Stanton.

He arrives at Tavelly Station, turning left at the steel robot and crossing the cattle grid.

He pulls up directly outside the house, enters the green swathe through the gate, the garden such a vivid contrast with the bare red dirt.

Gloria Stanton answers the door, eyes wide. 'Wow, you've got a gall,' she says, tone accusatory. 'Get off our land. I'm calling the police.'

'Mrs Stanton, Gloria, it's essential I speak with you and your husband.'

'Why would we want to talk to the likes of you?'

'Please, it's important.'

'Says you. Merry's off working with the boys. People do that out here, you know. Work.'

On the drive down the Sundowner Track, Martin had thought of ways of breaking the news gently but now concludes he has little choice. The woman is already reaching for the door, ready to close it on his face. 'We've found Chloe Carmichael.'

The door stops. Gloria doesn't move, as if snap frozen. 'Where?' she manages.

'She's dead. We've located her body. And evidence she didn't kill your brother-in-law.'

The woman stares a moment longer, aggression gone. 'Okay. You should come in then.'

She leads him into the kitchen, light-filled and smelling of recent baking. Martin feels almost guilty to disturb such simple domesticity. Gloria calls Merriman on the VHF, tells him to return to the house, insisting he should come immediately. She doesn't mention Martin's name, doesn't mention Chloe. He wonders about the VHF; it must be an open channel.

While they wait for her husband, Gloria Stanton brews tea, opens tins containing shop-bought biscuits and homemade slice, the time-honoured hospitality of the bush, the essential accompaniment to every encounter, the balm for every tragedy. Martin relaxes a little, confident that they will at least hear him out.

Fifteen minutes later Merriman bustles in, all business. 'What's this about, Gloria? What's . . .' He sees Martin. 'Police are after you,' he says by way of greeting.

'On my way to hand myself in,' Martin lies.

'Why stop here, then? Haven't you done us enough damage?'

Martin feels a spike of irritation. 'I didn't take you to Longchamp Downs, you took me. Remember?'

Merriman harrumphs. 'People are saying we helped you film that video of you and Ekaterina Boland going at it.'

'I'm here to clear your name then,' says Martin, wondering if there is any possibility of that proving true.

'They've found Chloe Carmichael,' interjects Gloria, and the bluff drains out of Merriman Carmichael like air from a balloon.

'What? Where?'

'Ask him,' instructs Gloria.

Merriman sits at the table, collapsing into a chair. He doesn't take his eyes from Martin's face as the journalist tells them of the discovery, a truncated version. Nothing about the A-team, nothing about his desperate fight for survival, nothing about the sandstorm, nothing about stumbling upon Ecco and Jamie, nothing about Ecco's search for Hentig and Stuart. He tells them simply that he and Ekaterina Boland and Jamie Stubbs found a cave out in the channel country where they discovered the body.

The couple listen in silence, grief-stricken.

'I was wrong. All this time I thought she'd gotten away with it,' Gloria says, pain in her eyes. 'Living the high life somewhere. I guess she got what she deserved after all.'

'Why come here?' asks Merriman. 'Why tell us? Why not Clay Carmichael?'

'He knows. He's out there now. We took him.' Martin takes a deep breath. 'Chloe had a notebook with her. A diary. It recounted the events leading up to her death. It almost certainly clears her of the murder of your brother, or any knowledge of it.'

Gloria holds her hands up to her face, as if in horror; Merriman keeps staring at Martin, assimilating this news.

'You're sure of this?' he asks. 'What does it say?'

'The diary? That she and Roman were at the cave together. He drove back to town to get some torches and supplies, left her there to explore. But he never came back. The dates fit perfectly, the day of his murder.'

Gloria stands up, then sits down again. Merriman extends his hand to her; she clings to it. 'But there was evidence Chloe had fled,' she says. 'A witness in Port Paroo, ATM withdrawals, her car abandoned in Dubbo.'

'But no witnesses to the actual murder,' Martin reminds her. 'Where was his body found? In Port Paroo or nearby?'

'Has no one told you?' asks Gloria, a touch of defensiveness in her voice. 'It's in all the police reports.'

'I'm sure it is,' says Martin. 'But I don't have access to police reports. I don't have my phone or my laptop. Can you tell me what happened, please?'

'I can,' says Merriman, and Martin can detect a change of attitude, as if the grazier has come to a decision, has decided to cooperate with Martin. 'Roman was found on the Sundowner Track between here and town. At Brown Water Creek. He was found lying beside his truck, keys still in the ignition. He'd stopped, gotten out, and someone shot him.'

'Why'd he stop?' asks Martin. 'Did the police ever find out?'

'No. Speculation was he was flagged down by his killer.'

'Someone he knew?'

'Who could say? Out here, someone waves you down, you stop whether you know them or not.'

Martin nods his acceptance of this obvious truth. 'And which way was his car pointing? Towards here or towards town?'

'Of course,' says Gloria, interrupting. 'It makes sense now.'

'Sorry, what's that?' asks Martin.

'He was driving back towards town,' she replies. 'There were signs he'd been here to Tavelly, collected some supplies. There were flagons of water in the boot of his car, plus ropes, and he had a couple of torches on the front seat. And a brand-new video camera, still in its box. The police could never work out the significance of the camera. Or the torches. Why he had them in the middle of the day.'

'He was heading back to the cave,' states Merriman.

There's a moment's silence then, as they imagine the horror of it: Roman on his way back to the cave but shot down in cold blood, leaving Chloe abandoned out there with little water and less hope.

Martin considers the evidence that convinced the police that Chloe was the killer. He can't say he can really blame them. 'And I'm guessing twenty years ago ATMs didn't boast video surveillance?' he asks.

'I never heard that they did,' says Merriman. 'The police would have checked, I'm sure.'

'Do you think Vincent Carmichael really believed it was Chloe he was sending money to?'

Merriman shrugs. 'Hope can do strange things, distort your judgement. Maybe he really did believe it. He told the inquest that Chloe and Roman had had a massive falling-out, a terrible fight, about six weeks before Roman's murder death. Maybe that convinced him.'

'Did he say what it was about?'

'No. Just that there was a lot of yelling and screaming and crying.'

'Right. But you didn't witness it?'

'Us? No. I gather it was up at Longchamp Downs, if Vincent was there. Or maybe at the Port Paroo Hotel.'

Gloria adds her own perspective, the hint of a tear in her eye. 'We saw none of that. They always seemed very happy together. They were engaged.'

'You supported Roman and Chloe getting married? Despite this decades-old feud between your family and the Carmichaels?'

Merriman looks dismissive. 'It wasn't such a big deal. Not for our generation. Even Mum came around when she saw them together, saw how in love they were. Roman and I even thought it would help repair things. Maybe end the feud once and for all. It almost did.'

'How do you mean?'

'Roman was worried about Chloe's father, Clay. He can be a right bastard. But Roman was confident of winning him over.'

Martin is trying to think. He sips some tea, already lukewarm in his cup. And brings the conversation into focus. 'I want to try and find out what happened. Now we know that Chloe didn't shoot Roman, we should try to discover who did kill him.'

'Yes,' says Merriman. 'All this time we've been blaming the wrong person.'

'Were you here when Roman came for the torches?' Martin asks.

'No,' says Merriman. 'I remember it like it was yesterday. I was in Roma, trying to sell the last of our cattle. Gloria was in Dubbo with my parents. The police contacted me in Roma.'

'So you didn't find the body?'

'No. It was a truck driver coming down from Queensland, taking stock further down the flood plain.'

'I guess you could speak to Maz,' suggests Gloria. 'Find out what she really saw.'

Martin thinks that's an excellent suggestion—but how can he avoid the police?

chapter forty-three
ECCO

WE DON'T GET BACK TO LONGCHAMP DOWNS UNTIL MID-AFTERNOON. WE'RE IN
no rush, Jamie and I riding slowly, outriders escorting Clay home,
a cortege without a coffin. The heat is like treacle, as if it has been
poured down upon us. I drink water, splash it over me; any relief is
fleeting. I'm starting to wish I had journeyed out with Clay in his
air-conditioned Land Cruiser. He's barely spoken since emerging
from the cave, Jamie and I respecting his silence. As we're crossing
the last plain, Jamie, who's been riding a little ahead, stops. I pull
up next to him. He has his goggles off. 'Look,' he says, pointing
at the eastern sky. I follow his finger and see it almost immediately: a light plane.

Clay pulls up and joins us. 'It's Vincent.'

'That was quick,' Jamie says.

'I rang him last night. After you told me.' He starts to walk
back to his vehicle, then stops and turns. 'I'll go and fetch him.
But thank you for today. Thanks to both of you.' And with slow
dignity, he resumes walking and climbs into the car.

'All class,' says Jamie.

—

Back in the cottage, I shower, change my clothes, get the air-conditioning powering. I'm not sure where Jamie is, whether he's supporting Clay and Vincent over at the homestead, back in the manager's house or working out in the heat, tidying up after the sandstorm. I'm feeling drained. Maybe it's the heat, the effort of riding back in the middle of the day. The lack of sleep. I should be excited, I know I should, and part of me is. I have the proof, incontrovertible, that Hentig and Stuart—or Hentig, at least—made it to the cave. The book will all but write itself. And yet my thoughts keep returning to Clay and Vincent. Those poor men, united by loss. United by self-recriminations, no matter how undeserved.

I'm making a sandwich when the knock comes at the door. I presume it will be Jamie, but when I answer it's a stranger, somehow familiar, silhouetted against the glare.

'Vincent Carmichael,' the man says, part introduction, part greeting. He's a formidable-looking chap with a strong chin and greying temples, tennis-court tanned, an expensive watch. The handsome lad of the paintings and photographs has turned into a handsome man.

'Ekaterina Boland,' I say. 'Please come in.'

He enters, casting his eyes around, assessing the cottage. 'Nice reno. Comfortable?'

It seems like a strange thing to say. 'Very, thank you.'

'Father is thinking he might retire over here,' he says, checking out the kitchen and shaking his head. 'Seems a little poky.' He turns back, pauses, sizes me up. 'He says you're the one who found Chloe.'

'Won't you sit?' I say. It feels awkward, the two of us standing like this.

'Yes. Thank you.' He takes a seat in the small lounge.

I sit opposite, before remembering my manners. 'Tea? Coffee? Something to eat?'

He smiles, holds his palm to his stomach. 'No, thank you. Mrs Enright has already put my blood sugar into the stratosphere.' The smile fades, leaving no trace it was ever there.

'How is he? Your father?' I ask.

'Difficult to say. Never been one to show much emotion.' Vincent takes a deep breath. 'Hopefully it will bring some relief. He's an old man, not so well. It should help, knowing what happened, that he won't die not knowing. What do the Americans call it? Closure?'

'What about you?' I ask, surprising myself with my concern. If the man is grieving, he doesn't show it.

He doesn't answer. Instead, he studies me imperiously, as if I've crossed some line, stepped into his personal space. He shapes to say something, then stops himself. His shoulders slump, and he closes his eyes, squeezing them shut. And in that gesture, I see his vulnerability. This is a man used to being in control, disguising his feelings, a trait learnt from his father.

The moment passes. Then he looks me in the eye. 'I stopped believing she was alive long ago. Father clung to the hope that she might still be out in the world somewhere, as if to accept otherwise was in some way betraying her. I knew she wasn't coming back.'

'How's that?' I ask.

He shrugs, as if stating the obvious. 'Chloe would have contacted me. We were close. She was my twin, you know. And after Mother died, and Father became distant, well, the two of us relied on each other. So it was unimaginable she would have left us in the dark all this time. For a month or two, if she was a fugitive, I could accept that. But not for twenty years.'

'Makes sense,' I say. 'Initially you did believe it, though. You sent money to Adelaide.'

He frowns. 'What business is that of yours?' And then he relents. 'I guess I was scammed. An easy mark. Like Father, I believed what I wanted to believe. Believed it for too long.'

'Your father has asked me to write a book. The history of Longchamp Downs. The history of the Carmichaels. Now, I guess I'll have to write what happened to Chloe.' And seeing his frown deepen, I add, 'It's his call, of course. Clay's. I'll write it in which-ever way he desires.'

'So you should,' says Vincent. And then another smile, more a punctuation mark than an expression of warmth signalling a change in direction. 'Tell me, though, what were you doing out there, in the middle of nowhere? How did you come across this cave?'

'Didn't Clay and Jamie tell you?'

'Not Jamie. Father. Except I was so overwhelmed by the news, I kept getting distracted. And he kept leaping between the present and the past, as if there aren't two decades between her disappear-ance and her discovery, theorising about what Chloe must have been doing. I couldn't follow all of it, but I didn't want to press him. Times like this, sometimes the best thing you can do is listen.'

I smile indulgently, even while my mind is racing, trying to determine how much I should tell him. Most of it? All of it? Probably. He's already been talking to Clay, and he knows the chain of events. And he has access to the diary from the cave. I haven't had a chance to read most of it yet, but no doubt it will contain her discovery of Murdoch's diary. And I feel I owe him some sort of explanation. I decide to tell him everything except for the evidence I found in the cave itself, the lamp and the initials carved into the wall.

'I was out there with Jamie, researching the book, when we stumbled across a lost man, the journalist Martin Scarsden. He'd found the cave purely by chance while sheltering from a sandstorm.'

'How far west?'

'Over two hours. West and south.'

'That's incredible,' says Vincent. 'Scarsden was lost all the way out there? He's a lucky man. Doubly lucky. First finding the cave, then you and Jamie. What was he doing out there?'

'Someone tried to kill him,' I say.

'Father says Scarsden doesn't know who it was. Or why.'

'That's correct,' I say, and realise that Vincent is quizzing me, comparing my recollections to those of his father. It makes me uncomfortable. What's he trying to discover?

The man smiles again, another punctuation. 'Indeed. But you still haven't explained what you and Jamie were doing such a long way from the homestead. How would that help you with your book?'

'I found references in the early journals to a place called the Camel's Head. And then I read about the paintings, the ones that were stolen from your family. You remember them? One of them was called *The Camel's Head at Dawn*.'

Vincent stares hard, unmoving. 'I remember. Go on.'

'Well, your father has requested that the book include pictures, family trees, illustrations. I thought it might be neat to find this place, take some photos. You know, match it to an image of the painting. Then and now.'

'You're putting that in the book?'

'I was exploring the idea. As I say, your father gets the final say.'

'So you weren't actually looking for this cave?'

It's a direct question. 'No, I was looking for the Camel's Head,' I answer truthfully. And I tell him about Murdoch's journal, Hentig and Stuart, the connection with Ludwig Leichhardt.

By the end of it, he's frowning profoundly. 'Intriguing. Do you think that's what Chloe was doing out there? Looking for these explorers?'

'Yes.' I describe the pencil marks in the margin of Murdoch's entry about them—pencil marks that I believe were made by Chloe. 'She never mentioned Murdoch's diaries to you?' I ask.

'Never,' he says, shifting in his seat, seemingly uncomfortable at being the one questioned.

'Murdoch doesn't mention a cave; Martin Scarsden stumbled across it by chance. I was intrigued. Thought I'd check it out. That's how I found her.' I take a breath, turn it back on him again. 'What would you have done?'

He again squeezes his eyes shut for a second or two. Another glimpse of vulnerability. And when he speaks, his voice is low. 'What impression did you have when you found her body? Do you think she was at peace?'

I find myself leaning forward, meeting his gaze. 'I do. There was a feeling of serenity. As if she had lain down and gone to sleep.' I'm speaking the truth, and yet I can't entirely escape a sense of horror: a beautiful young woman, just twenty years old, dying of thirst in the wilderness. There's not a lot of serenity in that.

'And she mentioned the paintings in her diary?' he asks.

'I haven't read her diary,' I say.

'Really?'

'Only enough to identify her,' I say. 'It's how I knew it was her in the cave; her name is inside. But I had no time to read it. Naturally, I'd like to. For my research.'

'Of course,' he says. 'Once the police are finished with it.' He stands. 'You must be very tired. Thank you for being so open. And for showing such kindness to my father.'

'He's more than welcome.'

'The police will come tomorrow,' says Vincent. 'They're sending a team in from Brisbane to retrieve the body. They'll want to talk to you. After that, it might make sense if you were to leave.'

'Leave? Why?'

'I'm sorry. This salacious video of you and the journalist Scarsden. It's appalling. I think it might be better all round if you weren't here. In case the media show up.'

'The video is a fake, Vincent. Ask Clay, he knows. And besides, isn't it your father's call if I stay or go?'

'Indeed.' He turns to go, then turns back. 'I don't hold anything against you. I'm grateful to you for finding Chloe. So is my father. But I don't want the memory of my beautiful sister tarnished by any association with you. With your reputation.'

'I need the money,' I say, blunt and unashamed.

There is understanding in his expression. 'We'll still pay you,' he says. 'You can write Father's book from back in the city. You can take the journals with you. You don't need to be here.'

'I was thinking I might dedicate it to Chloe,' I say.

He considers me for a long moment, and I feel he is reappraising me.

'Thank you,' he says at last. 'It will be my father's call.'

He leaves me then, and much as I try, I can't quite decide what to make of his visit. His grief is genuine, I have no doubt. And so is his desire to protect his sister's memory. Yet I can't help but wonder if that's the real reason he wants me gone from Longchamp Downs.

chapter forty-four
MARTIN

MARTIN LEAVES TAVELLY STATION, WHEELS VIBRATING ACROSS THE CATTLE grid, past the ever-smiling robot, and turns north towards Port Paroo. As he farewelled the Stantons, Gloria had taken his hand, a surprisingly warm gesture in light of her initial frosty reception.

'If you do find out what happened—to Roman, I mean—then we'd be so grateful. He was such a wonderful man.'

Her plea had been echoed in the pain on her husband's face. Martin had promised to do his best.

He's contemplating leaving the car just outside town, walking through to find Fergus White. The beekeeper owes him; he'd promised to help protect him. Maybe he'll honour his word and provide sanctuary, fetch Maz for him. But Martin's not sure which house belongs to White, and there's no guarantee the man will be home. He might be out with his hives, moving them in preparation for the flood.

Martin slows the car as he approaches a single-lane bridge. *The* single-lane bridge. The one crossing Brown Water Creek. The location where Roman Stanton was gunned down.

He pulls the Subaru over, gets out. The day is blinding. He tries to imagine it. Roman decelerating for the one-lane bridge, concentrating, seeing a car beside the road, someone waving him down. So he stops, of course he does. Gets out. And is shot. But not by Chloe Carmichael: she is waiting for him in the cave at the Camel's Head.

Martin looks about. The heat is appalling. There is a lonely gum, a raven in its branch, observing him with unblinking eyes. There's no evidence of what unfolded here all those years ago, there are no clues, just a pervasive sense of desolation, as if the crime has imprinted itself, as if the landscape recalls a life taken too early.

But why? He hasn't heard a bad word said against Roman. A suggestion from his brother that he may have been a ladies' man, that's all. And that was when Merriman was attempting to find a motivation to explain Chloe being the killer. Dead twenty years, and no one knows why. Two decades have passed, two decades filled with a falsehood, that Roman was murdered by his fiancée who then fled. But Chloe was only days from death herself, marooned in the cave.

Martin wonders if the killer knew, when they shot down Roman Stanton, that they were effectively killing her as well. If so, did they care? Is it possible they knew where she was, were content to leave her to die? Had Roman begged for mercy, if not for himself then for his fiancée? Or was that the whole point? Was Chloe the real target, not Roman? Martin thinks of the attempt on his own life, the A-team leaving him in the desert to die. Is that what happened to Chloe? What has happened before in Port Paroo? He recalls Perry, back on the day he first arrived, referring to people dying in the desert. The former publican for one. How many others?

He hears the truck before he sees its cloud of dust coming from the direction of town. For a moment his heart beats faster: what if it's the police? Could the Stantons have alerted them? Or what if it's some local busybody, someone who will see his car and recognise it as the same make and model as that belonging to the fugitive fraudster and alleged paedophile Martin Scarsden? He stands off to one side, turns his back, pretending to piss on the solitary tree, hoping the approaching driver might do the decent thing and look the other way.

Instead, an ancient-looking jalopy slows, a rust-red truck, paint faded and peeling, its brakes squealing and something loose knocking under the bonnet as it rattles to a standstill.

Martin tenses. Fight or flight? Or bullshit? But what story can he possibly concoct?

The truck door opens and Jack Goffing gets out. 'Hello, mate. Fancy seeing you here,' he says.

'Jack,' says Martin, the panic easing out of him. 'Top truck.'

'Best I could do. Hired a plane, flew into Bourke. Cash transaction. No records.'

The two men begin to shake hands but find themselves hugging instead. The raven caws, as if voicing its approval.

'Thanks, Jack. I'm glad to see you.'

'Glad you're still alive.'

'You still tracking me, then?'

'Lucky for you I am. Port Paroo is crawling with cops.'

The raven caws again and takes flight. Martin changes the subject. 'This is where it happened. Twenty years ago. Roman Stanton shot dead by a killer or killers unknown.'

'Here?' Goffing looks around, assessing the place, looking to the single-lane bridge, following the road with his eyes, perhaps coming to his own conclusions as to how the murder unfolded. 'You've totally ruled out Chloe Carmichael?'

'Yeah. It wasn't her,' says Martin.

Goffing grimaces. 'Fucking hot out here without a hat. You got aircon? My shit can is like a tandoori oven.'

'Sure.'

Inside the Subaru, Martin gets the engine going, kicks up the aircon. It doesn't seem to be working. He lowers the fan speed, gives it a chance.

'You check out Dermott Brick?' Martin asks.

'Interesting. Ivan Lucic was right. Dermott Brick died in Western Australia seven years ago.'

'So who's the guy in Cunnamulla?'

'Don't know. He's been there for four years. Before that, nothing.'

Martin is looking hard at Goffing. 'How likely is that? That ASIO can't trace him back any further than four years?'

Goffing looks like he's eaten something past its use-by date. 'I ran the photo on his website through facial recognition. Not a single hit.'

'He's had plastic surgery?'

Goffing laughs. 'No. Boffins reckon the photo's been manipulated, just enough. They're working on possible variations, but it's not something they've encountered before.'

'What about Packlehurst and Glee?'

'Working on it. Their expertise is corporate public relations. ASX 100 companies. Run a sideline on reputational protection.'

Martin thinks about that. 'Anyone shady among their clients? Mafia-linked?'

'We're checking it out.'

'Reputational protection. What about reputational destruction?'

'That too, by the look of it.'

The air-conditioner is starting to make inroads into the heat, and Martin turns up the fan. 'What's the game plan?' he asks Goffing.

'Not sure, to be honest. I haven't actually been sent out to help you. The DG dispatched me to see if I can determine how we were manipulated into directing you here. Any theories on that?'

Martin shrugs, a little disconcerted that Goffing is more interested in tracking down a leak than looking out for his welfare. 'Not really. They find the mole?'

'Not yet.' Goffing looks about, as if checking for eavesdroppers. 'But I've been given a clean bill of health.'

'That's something, I guess,' says Martin.

'If anyone asks, I'm AFP.'

'That's your cover?'

'Means I can carry a gun. Might come in useful.'

Martin swallows, finds it difficult, like the air is too dry. 'I'd still like to talk to Maz, the owner of the pub.'

'I'd like to talk to her too. But she's gone.'

'What? On the run?'

'Nothing so dramatic. Gone up to Longchamp Downs to pay her respects. Apparently she and Chloe were besties at school, and she's close to the brother. What's his name? Vincent?'

'Yes. That's him. He's there?'

'Yeah. Either there or on the way.'

'Maybe we should head up there too. Talk to both of them.'

'There'll be police around as well.'

'Will they care? Queenslanders?'

'Let me check,' says Goffing. Then holds up his phone. 'You mind?'

Martin shrugs and steps out of the car to give Goffing his privacy, into the wall of heat. He looks about. What a desolate place to die.

A minute or two later, Jack Goffing beeps the horn, loud in the silence, gives Martin the thumbs-up. 'Police won't be there until tomorrow morning now,' he explains once Martin is back behind the wheel. 'Special retrieval team. Forensics. Coming in from Sydney. We have a window.'

'Sydney? Longchamp Downs is in Queensland.'

'The cave is in New South Wales. Five kay south of the border.'

'Let's go to Longchamp then,' says Martin.

'You sure? I could drive you to Bourke, put you in a motel room, leave you with supplies.' There's a small smile playing on Goffing's lips, as if anticipating Martin's response.

'Fuck that. I'd be better off in custody, proclaiming my innocence.'

'You want to call your lawyer? Might need him.'

'Already have. He's advising me to return to Port Silver. Besides, I don't have a phone. The A-team took it.'

Goffing looks pleased with himself. He reaches into his backpack. 'There you go, champ. All yours.'

Martin takes it, the tattered cover instantly recognisable. Not another burner, his own phone, the one Goffing took with him to lay a false trail all those days ago when they left Port Silver. The one with all his contacts in it.

'I turn this on, it's as good as telling the police where I am, right?'

'Depends on how closely they're monitoring it. But you've got a point: I reckon as soon as you make a call, they'll be on to you.'

'Great. Thanks for nothing.'

'We should take your car,' says Goffing. 'I'm loving the aircon.'

'Mine doesn't have enough petrol,' says Martin. 'We'll need to leave it. Can't exactly fill it up in Port Paroo. But first you should photograph the bonnet.' He points through the windscreen.

Goffing looks horrified. 'You serious? Drive my shit heap all the way up there on a day like this? It's forty fucking degrees.'

Martin laughs, not sure why. Just the tough guy insisting on his creature comforts. 'Not exactly James Bond, are you?'

chapter forty-five
ECCO

I TRANSFER THE IMAGES OF CHLOE'S DIARY FROM MY PHONE ONTO MY LAPTOP, making them easier to read, and a couple of hours later I've reached the part where she has found the reference to Hentig and Stuart in Patrick Murdoch's diary. So Chloe first came across the mystery of the missing explorers in January 2005, as she was searching for information on the paintings. Her excitement comes through the page; it echoes my own thrill when I found the exact same reference, except with her exclamation marks in the margin.

I'm beginning to think I should personalise the book on Hentig and Stuart, so that it's not a dry, objective and academic work but more like a personal quest, recounting my own endeavours. Told through my eyes. And through Chloe's. I think it might work better; I think Clay might like that.

I wonder if reading her diaries now is the best use of my time, though. I should make sure I have everything I need in case Vincent evicts me. I have Murdoch's three journals and can take them with me. What else? The records of the Abbotts might be useful, if they set out in more detail Percival McEwan Fitzroy's tenure at Longchamp Downs. I know the artist was here in 1893, so that's one volume, maybe two. But I'm not sure how I could possibly carry enough material for the book Clay has commissioned. He wants images: maps, reproductions of paintings, documents, family trees. How can I do that remotely?

I hear an engine: Jamie. He looks hot, and exhausted. I invite him in, and the first thing he does, even before speaking, is make his way into the kitchen and down a glass of water, then another.

'You okay?' I ask.

'Sure. What about you? You've been through an awful lot.'

I hear a tenderness in his voice. It still feels unusual, almost unsettling, a man expressing compassion for me. Maybe we connected more than I've realised, out in that car, sheltering from the sandstorm.

'Vincent wants me to leave,' I say.

'Might be a good idea,' he says soberly.

'What? You too?'

'No. I like having you here,' he says, and there is a kind of modesty to his words, a shyness out of keeping with his bushman persona. He doesn't blush, but it's that type of awkwardness. I get the impression he is trying to be more open. More honest. That opening up to me in the desert felt good. 'Vincent and Clay are reading the diary,' he says. 'Arguing. Clay sounds very upset. You have any idea why?'

'I've been reading bits of it, but I haven't found anything likely to set them against each other. You sure it's the diary they're arguing over?'

He shrugs. 'No. I heard them shouting, but I haven't been eavesdropping.'

'Vincent came to see me,' I say. 'It was almost like he was trying to find out how much I knew about the circumstances surrounding his sister's disappearance.'

'What did you tell him?'

'Most of it.'

'Does he know you photographed the diary?'

'No,' I reply, fearing that Jamie is about to rebuke me.

'Might be a good idea to keep it that way,' he says instead.

We sit in the small kitchen, flicking through the images of the diary on my laptop, and I have to be honest: it feels good sitting so close to him, sharing with him. We get to the section where Chloe is describing the theft of the paintings.

I raced to the window just in time to see the truck pulling away. Was I dreaming? I can't have been dreaming.

I called the police and then I called Vincent, told him what had happened and asked him to break the news to Dad. I tried to call Roman too, but he's not answering.

'You think that's it?' asks Jamie.

'I don't know.'

'This all happened when?'

'Late January 2005,' I say. 'About six weeks before they died.'

'So the paintings were stolen,' he says. 'She thought it strange the thieves headed south. She confides in Vincent, and maybe Roman.'

'We could ask Vincent what she told him.'

Jamie is looking grave. 'No, let's stay clear of him. Like I said, it's probably best if you don't let on you have a copy of the diary.'

'But he was at the coast with Clay at the time. He can't have had anything to do with the robbery.'

'We don't know that,' says Jamie. 'Maybe he was the one who tipped off the thieves, thinking the house would be empty.'

'Why would he do that to his own family?'

Jamie considers this. 'Who knows? Money? The police will be here first thing. They'll want to see the diary, take it as evidence. It will shed light on how Chloe came to be stranded out there. Perhaps even give some indication of who killed Roman and why.'

'So you think Roman's death is connected to the robbery? The paintings?'

Jamie looks like he's thinking hard. 'I can't see how,' he concedes.

'Let's assume Chloe did confide in Roman, told him what she thought she saw,' I suggest.

'Maybe Roman found out something in Port Paroo, something connected to the robbery, and that's the reason he was shot?'

'Could be,' I say.

'Six weeks later?' Jamie sounds unconvinced. He stands up, starts pacing.

'Vincent went down there too. Remember? It says so in the diary,' I say.

'So what? He sent money to Adelaide. He obviously believed Chloe was still alive.' Then Jamie qualifies his own assertion. 'You think it could have been part of a cover-up? Creating an alibi?'

I look at him. 'I think you're right. I should leave. And we need to keep our copy of the diary secret. First chance we get, we back it up onto the cloud. Make sure it's safe.'

'You haven't already?' he asks.

'No internet over here. And I can't intrude over at the homestead.'

'My place,' he says. 'The manager's house. Let's go.'

——

The sun has set, the first stars appearing above the eastern ridge, and the temperature has dropped just a little, a breeze coming through at last. We take both bikes, cross the makeshift bridge over the Paroo. In the twilight, I can see it's still flowing, still full. Just as we're arriving at Jamie's house, I see an old truck coming through, a real clanger, blowing smoke, driving up from the south, not the main drive in from Eulo.

'Who was that in the truck?' I ask Jamie as we dismount.

'Don't know,' he says. 'Maybe word's out. Maybe they've caught Scarsden.'

Inside, Jamie's place is cool and remarkably tidy. Cleaner than my cottage, that's for sure. In other ways, though, it's a typical bachelor's residence: couch pulled close to a large television, DVDs on the coffee table, a games console, no ornaments or plants or anything decorative. Everything purely functional. The table in the kitchen is decades old, mid-century formica, worth a pretty penny in an inner-city op shop, nothing special out here. I figure it must have come with the house, like the rest of the furnishings.

We sit at the table, and I get on with backing up the images of the diary to the cloud. We talk as I work.

'What do you think Chloe saw the night of the robbery?' I ask.

'Not sure. Possibly just the fact that the van or whatever the thieves were driving was heading south.'

'Be interesting to know what happened to the paintings,' I muse.

'Hanging in Vincent's Gold Coast penthouse, you think?'

'I wonder,' I say, the germ of an idea forming. 'Let me check something out.'

The screen is telling me the upload is completed, the diary is safely on the cloud. I open a web browser, go to the Queensland Art Gallery page, explaining as I go. 'The state gallery has a companion piece to one of the stolen paintings. The one here at Longchamp was called *The Camel's Head at Dawn*, the one in the gallery is *The Camel's Head at Dusk*. But when Chloe visited the gallery twenty years ago, all she mentions seeing are smaller, more minor paintings by the same artist. *The Camel's Head at Dusk* must be a recent acquisition.'

I find the webpage, the digital reproduction of Percival McEwan Fitzroy's panorama.

'Wow, magnificent,' says Jamie. 'Just the way it still looks.'

'Here. There's a caption: *The Camel's Head at Dusk. Gift of Mrs Delaney Bullwinkel, April 2005*.'

'The month after Roman was murdered and Chloe disappeared,' says Jamie.

I search further. 'Mrs Bullwinkel's actual name is Floris. Husband's a mining billionaire. They're big collectors. Oh. Were. She died eleven years back.'

'Not much use then.'

'No. But let me check something else.'

I start googling, combining the terms 'theft' with 'Percival McEwan Fitzroy'. There are a couple of references to the robbery at Longchamp, old newspaper articles, a couple of social media ramblings. Nothing new. I almost miss it, but when I do see it, the story comes leaping off the screen at me.

'Holy shit,' I whisper.

'What is it?'

The search has found a reference to a robbery in Bowral, more than a thousand kilometres to the south. A newspaper article in the *Southern Highland News*: HEIST GONE WRONG. LOCAL MAN FIGHTS FOR LIFE.

> A prominent Bowral citizen and doyen of the arts is in a critical condition at Sydney's Royal Prince Alfred Hospital after a home invasion gone wrong.

And that's all. The rest is blocked behind a firewall.

'Oh, for God's sake,' I swear.

'Give me a moment,' says Jamie. He finds his wallet, gets his credit card. Five minutes later he's subscribing to a newspaper halfway across another state. We read on.

> Police believe local identity Akira Tennant disturbed a burglary in progress during the early hours of Tuesday morning at his estate, Plumbroke, three kilometres outside Bowral.
>
> They say Mr Tennant had arrived home unexpectedly earlier that evening after an event in Sydney was cancelled at late notice.
>
> It's alleged the well-known collector and patron of the arts was bashed and left for dead. He was found a short time later when neighbours raised the alarm.
>
> He was airlifted to Sydney on life support. *The Southern Highland News* can confirm Mr Tennant is in a critical condition in intensive care.
>
> Bowral police have released a statement: 'This was a brutal and unprovoked attack. We urge anyone with any information to come forward immediately, including any sightings of unusual activity after midnight in the vicinity of Mr Tennant's residence.'

Police say the thieves plundered more than a dozen canvases from Mr Tennant's private collection, including works by renowned Australian artists, including Arthur Streeton, Russell Drysdale and Sidney Nolan.

Mr Tennant owns one of the most extensive privately held collections of Australian colonial art, with paintings by Frederick McCubbin, Tom Roberts and Percival McEwan Fitzroy.

Mt Tennant lives alone at Plumbroke.

'Bashed and left for dead,' says Jamie.

'Look at the date,' I say. 'February 2005.' I search further. 'The guy died a fortnight later without regaining consciousness. It's murder. Just weeks before Roman was shot.'

'Do you think Chloe knew?' asks Jamie.

'Let's see,' I say, flicking through the diary. And find it. 'Here, the twenty-fourth of February. Roman found it, sent it to Chloe.' We read it together.

'*It was a newspaper report from Bowral in New South Wales, thieves targeting a collection of early twentieth-century and colonial Australian art, including another painting by Percival McEwan Fitzroy. The owner had been bashed, left for dead.*'

'About three weeks before Roman was murdered,' says Jamie. 'Let's get out of here.'

But before we can move the front door swings open and the way is barred. It's Vincent Carmichael. And he's brandishing a shotgun.

chapter forty-six
MARTIN

'SO WHAT ARE WE LOOKING FOR AT LONGCHAMP DOWNS?' ASKS JACK GOFFING.

'Who tried to kill me and why they needed to lure me out here to do it,' says Martin.

'Because killing you isn't enough,' says Goffing. 'They want to humiliate you. Discredit you. Make your name so toxic that even when you're dead, no one will want to buy the book. Or read it. Or believe it. Who would want to be seen with a book by an alleged paedophile?'

Martin stews on that for a moment. The sun is lowering towards the horizon and yet the heat remains unbearable. He and Goffing have towels wrapped around their necks. Every twenty minutes or so they stop to douse the towels and themselves with water.

'But why out here? Why the whole charade, driving me out into the desert?'

'To make it look as if you killed yourself.'

'Agreed,' says Martin. 'It can't be the mafia. They'd kill me in public, make a statement, let everyone know that if you cross them, you get killed. Like shooting Marelli's grandson at a cafe. In public, with witnesses.'

'So who then?'

'Good question.' More time passes before Martin elaborates. 'But I think you're right. It's about making me so toxic, as you put it, no one will ever want to read another word I've written.'

'Okay. That makes sense. Suggests something that's not already published. So what other book have you got in the works? If it's not the mafia, who else are you upsetting?'

'That's just it, I'm not working on anything else, controversial or otherwise.' He grins sheepishly. 'I'm hoping I might extract something from being out here. If I survive.'

Goffing is forced to brake suddenly, fighting the wheel, desperately trying to correct as the old truck slides perilously. And just manages to come to a stop without losing control. An emu is standing in the middle of the road, staring them down. Goffing toots the horn; the emu trots away, unbothered. Goffing hits the horn again for good measure. 'Fuck, it's hot!'

Now that they've stopped, they take the opportunity to repeat their ritual, soaking themselves and the towels.

Back in the car, moving again, Goffing asks, 'How much further?'

'Can't be far. No sat nav?'

'Lucky we've got an odometer,' says Goffing. And then swears, looking at the dashboard. 'Shit.'

'What?'

'Engine's starting to run hot.'

'Going to happen every time we stop. No air across the radiator. Just keep it moving. Not too fast. We don't have to stop to soak ourselves.'

They trundle along, passing through one of the creeks, water lapping. Martin can't be sure, but he thinks maybe the level is a tad lower, the flood peak passing.

'What about you, Jack? What exactly are you looking for out here?' The words land harder than Martin intended, but the proximity of death has stripped some of the polish from his persona.

'I told you. Looking for evidence of how ASIO has been compromised.'

'Out here?' All around them, there is a pervasive nothingness, the feeling of too much space.

'It's on me, Martin. I advised you to come here, to Port Paroo. But that advice was shaped inside ASIO. Someone was pushing to get you here. Squandered a lot of influence.'

Martin remains tight-lipped, staring out into the barren landscape. *Squandered.* He pushes Goffing. 'Your director-general must have some idea, assigning you to find out more. He knows enough to believe you're trustworthy.'

Goffing sighs. 'I don't know, Martin. I'm not sure I have anything useful to tell you.'

'Give it a crack. We've still got a way to go. You never know, something might resonate. Might end up helping both of us.'

'Yeah. Maybe.'

But that's all the federal agent has to say. Now it's his turn to stare out the window, to contemplate the vast emptiness.

Martin is deciding whether to keep prodding or give up entirely when some invisible thought process reaches a conclusion and Jack Goffing does speak. 'The mole. We think it might be the Chinese.'

'The *Chinese*?' Martin can't make any sense of that. Why would the Chinese target him? Why would they want to lure him to the Paroo? 'Can't be,' he says. 'I was never a China reporter. Went there a couple of times, but nothing controversial. Puff pieces, business and economics, travel articles. Mostly when the boss thought I needed a break. Last time was for the 2008 Olympics. Long time ago now. Most controversial story I wrote was doping in the badminton. No Chinese athletes involved. Why would Beijing give a toss about me?'

'Can't fault your logic,' says Goffing. 'We've been through your time there with a fine-tooth comb. Nothing.'

'Decent of you,' says Martin, his hackles rising at the idea the intelligence agencies feel entitled to monitor an Australian journalist. But this is not the time to voice his protest. 'I don't believe it. If the Chinese did succeed in placing a mole inside ASIO, they wouldn't waste it on me.'

'I agree,' says Goffing. 'You're not that valuable.'

'Thanks.'

They reach the section of road that Martin has twice circumvented, where the creek has cut the track.

'Slow up,' he says.

'How deep?' asks Goffing, braking.

'Don't know. I went around. But in a four-wheel drive.'

'What do you suggest?'

Martin isn't confident the truck will make it cross-country, out around the flooded clay pan. 'Let me out. I'll walk ahead. Anything up to my thighs should be okay. There's no current.'

He removes his shoes and socks. Out of the truck, the sandy surface of the road is burning hot, like walking on coals. He half runs, half hops into the water. Then he wades through, up to his knees, not much higher. He turns, gives the thumbs-up, and Goffing follows him across.

'You must have a working theory,' Martin says when he is back in the truck.

'I have a theory, but it's a long way from working.'

'I'm all ears.'

Again the lengthy pause, Goffing working through the implications. Minutes pass, minutes more. For a moment, Martin is distracted by something beside the road. He thinks it's a snake, but it's just a stick. There are no trees; he wonders how the stick got there. They've been trundling along at a steady pace, but the engine temperature shows no sign of dropping. If anything, it's crept a little higher.

Finally, Goffing speaks. 'It may not be the Chinese. Not directly. The DG thinks it's possibly domestic, an Australian. Someone who has gone to a lot of effort to place this source inside ASIO to funnel information to the Chinese, in order to curry favour with Beijing. But on this occasion they've reversed the flow, feeding disinformation back into the system to target you.'

'So the Chinese aren't the ones issuing orders?'

'Probably not even aware that their source has been jeopardised just to get at you.'

'That's unbelievable,' says Martin. 'Weirdly flattering, but unbelievable.'

'It is.' Now he's revealed the Chinese connection, Goffing seems less reticent about sharing his thoughts. 'There was a case in France, years ago now. The foreign intelligence service, the DGSE, were using a state-owned oil company called Elf as a cover for activities in Africa. Overthrowing governments, that sort of thing. It only emerged years later that rather than the DGSE running Elf, it was the other way around. Elf had infiltrated the foreign intelligence agency and was controlling it.'

'Before my time,' says Martin, 'but I remember a few of the old hands talking about it. Corruption at high levels.'

They drive over a sandhill. Martin has the sense they're finally approaching Longchamp Downs. 'So what's the relevance? You've lost me.'

'I think the mole is being run by an Australian. She's been feeding information to the Chinese at the behest of her Australian controller, either directly or indirectly.'

Martin doesn't reply, not straight away. He doesn't know the name of Goffing's boss, but he knows it's a woman. And he knows Goffing is here with the authority and knowledge of the director-general and no one else. He decides not to press too hard; his friend would have used the feminine pronoun deliberately. That was enough. Telling without telling. Martin takes it on board, progresses the conversation.

'So has this suspect admitted to anything? I assume she's being interrogated.'

'Not yet.'

'Not yet? They hauled you in, didn't they?'

'To rule me out.' Goffing changes down a gear then continues. 'They've got her under blanket surveillance. Trying to find out who's running her, if she's a lone operative or part of a cell.'

Martin is still having trouble comprehending the scope of the spider's web. 'So an Australian manages to recruit someone working inside our national intelligence system, and then starts feeding information to the Chinese. Why?'

'Money would be my guess.'

Martin smiles wryly. 'You're not talking cash in hand, are you? Brown paper bags at drop points?'

Goffing laughs. The sound comes from nowhere, unexpected, like a cloud burst in the desert. 'No. I'm thinking more like preferential trade deals, that sort of thing.'

'So a rogue corporation, something like that?'

'Yes.'

The ensuing silence is broken by the chirp of Goffing's phone.

'What? Out here?' says Martin, checking his own handset, seeing it has no reception.

'Satellite,' says Goffing, pulling the vehicle to a stop.

'Of course it is,' says Martin.

Goffing clambers out of the car, walks off into the heat. In the distance, the shimmering air makes the ground appear to be bubbling, like a lasagne fresh from the oven. Martin gets out as well, taking the opportunity to soak himself again. Goffing is not much more than twenty metres away, but Martin can't hear a sound, let alone anything comprehensible.

Goffing ends the conversation, waves to Martin to indicate he won't be much longer, makes another call.

Martin walks up a low rise. To the west he can see the river spreading out into a shallow lake, breaking the banks. The light is blazing back off it, like a mirror. There are a couple of cows in the distance, wading into the shallow water, their tiny figures giving the landscape scale. It's enormous, running on forever.

The horn beeps. Goffing is back in the truck.

'Anything?' Martin asks as he rejoins him.

Goffing starts the engine, gets moving, the air circulating once more. Both men regard the temperature dial; the engine is dangerously close to overheating. Finally, Goffing answers. 'Dermott Brick's real name is Raymond Penuch. Ring a bell?'

Thoughts and insinuations of thoughts trail through Martin's mind, tendrils of meaning, elusive, just out of reach. 'It's vaguely familiar. Who is he?'

'Used to be manager at a mine in Finnigans Gap. A tough nut, violent and criminal. Had a run-in with our friends Ivan Lucic and Nell Buchanan about four years back. I spoke to Nell. She reckons he was a bagman for a mining billionaire called Delaney Bullwinkel. Says they would have arrested Penuch, but he vanished.'

'Holy shit. Bullwinkel. That's it. I wrote a book, but it never got published. He could be the one behind all this. Exports to China.'

'Yeah, that's what I thought,' says Goffing, sounding unenthusiastic. 'He'd be a good fit. Except he's dying—if he's not already dead. In Switzerland, experimental treatment. He's got days, weeks if he's lucky.'

'Honestly?'

'We think Bullwinkel cut Penuch loose four years ago, about the time Ivan and Nell were chasing him.' Goffing tilts his head, one way, then back again. 'And also, we've confirmed that Packlehurst and Glee have a long and ongoing relationship with the Marelli family, and no known connection to Bullwinkel.'

Martin looks out the window. The country is too big, too stretched. He can't get his mind around it.

chapter forty-seven

THEY REACH LONGCHAMP NOT LONG AFTER SUNSET, AS NIGHT IS FALLING AND the first stars are appearing. A slight breeze has developed, taking the edge off the end of the day. The old truck rattles across the cattle grid as they make their way towards the cluster of buildings at the heart of the property. Martin sees the two red quad bikes left outside a modest-looking house, thinks maybe he sees Ecco and Jamie through the twilight. He considers asking Goffing to stop, but then sees the van from the Port Paroo Hotel parked outside the homestead. Maz Gingelly. Not exactly a titan of business, not likely trading with the Chinese, not likely to have infiltrated ASIO, but he still wants to quiz her about what she saw the day the A-team abducted him, and what she saw the day Roman Stanton died.

Goffing pulls his jalopy up next to the pub van. They've only just made it; the temperature gauge is red-lining and steam is starting to leak from beneath the bonnet.

Martin knocks on the door of the homestead, hears the footfall of stockinged feet.

Clay answers the door. 'You again?' says the old man. To Martin's eyes, he appears to have aged ten years in a day. 'We don't need you here.'

'I want to speak with Maz Gingelly. That's her van outside.'

'You came all the way here for her? Why?' He looks past Martin to Goffing. 'Who's this?'

Goffing badges him. 'Australian Federal Police. Mr Scarsden is helping with inquiries.'

'Police?' Clay echoes.

'Just so.'

'Investigating my daughter's death?'

'Assisting,' says Goffing. 'Primarily a state matter. But cross-border, you'll understand.'

'Right,' says Clay, looking a little confused. 'You'd better come in then.'

Maz is sitting in the lounge room, engrossed in a notebook that Martin immediately recognises: the diary found alongside the corpse of Chloe Carmichael. Maz is so engrossed she doesn't even notice the three men enter the room.

'Interesting reading?' asks Martin. 'Incriminating?'

Maz looks up, but her surprise is momentary, replaced by an expression of concern. She stands as if to greet him, but then surges across to him, hugs him. 'You survived! I'm so glad you're okay.' And she adds, as if her compassion hasn't been fully communicated, 'I was desperately worried.'

Martin can't tell if she's genuine or not, but he's not in the mood for small talk. 'You told the ABC I was distraught, implied I was suicidal,' he says. 'Why?'

Maz looks bewildered. 'Because I thought you were. You had every right to be.'

Martin is about to respond when Jack Goffing imposes himself. 'That's what you told the ABC, on the public record. You also told the police you saw Martin's car drive out of town, heading south towards Tilpa on the Sundowner Track, when in fact he was being driven west and then north.'

Maz glares at him. 'Who are you?' she demands. 'Police?'

'Correct,' says Goffing, flashing his badge again, looking like he enjoys it, the spook out of the shadows for once.

Now it's Clay who speaks, addressing Maz. 'Why did you do that? Were you in on it? Deliberately leaving someone out there to die?' There is a look of horror on the grazier's face and Martin can understand why.

Maz glares at him. 'This has nothing to do with what happened to Chloe.'

'What about your father?' asks Clay. 'Same thing happened to him.'

'I was six years old when that happened,' says Maz, visibly upset.

But Clay doesn't appear mollified. 'Why did you drive all the way up here?' he asks her.

Now Maz really does look offended. 'To check on you. To see Vincent. To see how I might help. To find out what happened. You know I was Chloe's best friend.'

Martin sees an opportunity to insert a wedge, to play on Clay's emerging suspicions. 'And because you wanted to read the diary, right? See what it said about you?'

Clay is staring at him, mouth open. 'What are you suggesting?'

'I didn't know the diary existed until I got here,' Maz asserts.

'You were her best friend,' Martin retorts. 'You knew she kept diaries, and that her last one had never been found.' He turns to Clay. 'What does it say? Does it reveal who left your daughter out there?'

Clay's mouth starts to move, shaping words, but nothing comes.

'Tell them, Mr Carmichael,' says Maz. 'They won't believe me.'

'It was an accident,' says Clay. 'It's all there. In her last entries. She and Roman were excited about finding the cave. He left her there to go and get torches and ropes. A simple, stupid mistake. They hadn't told anyone where they were going, wanted to keep it secret. But he never returned.' And then, as if to emphasise the point, 'It wasn't deliberate.'

'That's what the diary confirms,' says Maz quietly. 'It was a terrible misfortune.'

'No one knew she was there,' Clay repeats.

'Someone did,' counters Martin. 'Someone drove her car to Nyngan and Dubbo, withdrew money from ATMs using her cards. Someone close, someone who knew her PINs. Bought a train ticket to Sydney, left the car at Dubbo.'

Goffing addresses Maz. 'You made a sworn statement that you saw Chloe driving out of town, heading east.'

'That's right,' says Maz. 'That's what I saw.'

'Just you and nobody else,' says Goffing. 'Uncorroborated.'

'You're saying I made it up?' spits Maz. 'Why would I do that? She was my best friend.'

'Same reason you told police you saw me driving south when the A-team was driving me west?' suggests Martin.

'Who the hell is the A-team?' she says, but continues without waiting for an answer. 'It wasn't me who sent money to Adelaide,' says Maz. 'Don't forget that.'

'What are you saying?' demands Clay, anger overriding his sorrow.

'Vincent, that's what I'm saying,' says the publican. 'Open your eyes.'

But before Martin can probe any further, ask her what she means, the door opens. And coming into the room, guns levelled, are the A-team in their red caps.

'Did someone mention our name?' says the short man with the chrome tooth. And he lets out that high-pitched squeal of laughter, the cackle that speaks of borderline madness.

His colleague, the big man, doesn't speak, but he's all the more threatening for it. He's wearing a stocking over his head, underneath the red baseball cap. Martin's first thought is how stifling the disguise must be in this weather. His second thought is a flash of recognition: that strangely square head. 'Raymond Penuch,' he whispers, and immediately regrets it.

chapter forty-eight
ECCO

VINCENT LEVELS THE GUN AT ME, RIGHT INTO MY EYES, AND I CAN SEE THE barrels trembling, his eyes choked with desperation. The urbane exterior has gone.

'You armed?' he asks Jamie, who is standing next to me with his arms raised.

'Why would I be armed?'

'Unusual times,' says Vincent.

'No, I'm not,' says Jamie.

'Neither am I,' I say, somehow irritated he hasn't bothered to ask. 'Have you read the diary?'

Vincent stares, and I get the feeling he's affronted: he's got the gun, but I'm asking the questions. Nevertheless, he answers. 'Yeah, we did. Father and me.'

'And?'

He pauses, and some of his desperation seems to ebb. He allows the barrel to tip downwards. 'She lasted five days.' The pain is evident in his voice.

'Why were you and Clay arguing?' asks Jamie.

'Who told you about that?' Vincent asks, gun barrel back up. He's skittish, on edge.

'I could hear you from a hundred metres away.'

Vincent grunts, then again allows the barrel to lower, so it's now targeting my stomach. 'We were both angry that she died so needlessly. So senselessly. Father was angry that I had sent money, had encouraged him to believe she was still alive. As if that was my fault.' He pauses. 'I was angry that he didn't think to look for her. She says in the diary that she asked him about the Camel's Head and he told her where she might find it.'

That rings true to me. I recall Clay's surprise when I asked him where to find the Camel's Head.

'That's understandable,' I say, trying to sound as calm as poss-ible, trying to lower the temperature. 'The two of you being upset, I mean.' I'm thinking of the diary as well, the stolen paintings, Chloe confiding in Vincent. But I'm not about to utter a word; if Vincent believes we haven't read the diary, so much the better.

'I don't understand the gun,' says Jamie.

'I want you to come with me,' says Vincent. 'To the homestead. To bear witness.'

'Bear witness to what?' I ask.

'Maz Gingelly is over there, just arrived,' says Vincent.

'You don't need to threaten us with a gun,' I say.

He blinks. 'That's not what it's for.'

'What's it for?'

'In case things get volatile.'

I look to Jamie, who looks like I feel: jittery. Vincent hasn't just brought the gun with him: he's thrust it straight at my face. Even now, the gun would take off my feet if he accidentally pulled the trigger.

'Maz Gingelly,' I say. 'The one who reported seeing Chloe leave town, driving her car.'

'The car found in Dubbo,' says Vincent.

'All right,' I say. 'We'll come. Bring your gun, but please keep it aimed at the ground.'

We walk to the homestead across the open space between the cluster of buildings, Vincent a distrustful couple of paces behind. The night is fully formed, the moon yet to rise, the sky painted and shimmering, seemingly alive with stars and galaxies and the eternal. It occurs to me once more how very beautiful it is out here. Chloe must have seen it like this, venturing out of her shelter at night to marvel at the universe. To see the endless possibilities, even as her own diminished. It's a sobering thought.

'Look,' says Jamie. 'More company. That's Clay's Land Cruiser, and one of the farm trucks, but who owns the other three vehicles?'

'That one there, the van, belongs to Maz,' says Vincent. That much is self-evident: it has *The Port Paroo Hotel* stencilled on its door, together with contact details. 'Don't recognise the other two.'

One is a battered old truck, paintwork flaking and the suspension shot, so that it's listing to one side. There's tendrils of steam escaping from beneath the bonnet. Next to it is a brand-new jeep, a jacked-up can-do model, equipped with a battery of driving lights, oversized tyres and a roo bar of gleaming chrome.

'You don't recognise them?' asks Vincent.

'Not me,' Jamie replies.

We're almost at the vehicles when the front door opens and Martin Scarsden exits, hands raised. I turn to Vincent, knowing he still has his gun, when Jamie grabs my arm, hauls me down behind the farm truck. I'm about to protest when my brain catches up; something else is unfolding. I peer over the top of the tray. Scarsden is being shadowed by a man, a gun at the journalist's back.

Their movements trigger a motion-sensitive floodlight, and everything is laid bare, like stage lighting, harsh and revealing.

'You! Stop!' says Vincent, walking forward beyond the cars, into the open space before the gate. *Entitled moron,* I think. *Does he believe he's bulletproof?*

A gunshot, single and emphatic, proves he isn't.

I hear the thwack, the sound sickening, as it hits Vincent, spins him, drops him. I see him fall. The night is silent, the universe oblivious, the stars rendered invisible by the floodlights. I can see Martin's legs shaking.

'Keep moving,' the gunman barks at him. And Scarsden, arms still raised, begins walking once more. Towards us. I can see Vincent moving. Still alive. For the moment.

Another figure emerges from the house, another gun-wielding stranger, a big man, perhaps alerted by the first shot. I feel a desperate urge to scream out to Vincent, tell him to lie still, not provoke this second gunman.

'All good?' yells the second man.

'Never better,' replies the first man. And he laughs, a treble cackle that raises the hairs on my neck. He pushes Martin in the back with his gun barrel. 'Keep moving.' They walk forward, through the gate, past Vincent, a dark stain surrounding the fallen man, his gun useless by his side. He's stopped moving; I don't know if that's significant or not.

Jamie takes my arm again, points down, the gesture clear. I understand. I crouch, lie down, roll under the truck, the clearance high. I fight to control my breathing, fight against coughing or sneezing. Roll a little further, expecting Jamie to roll in beside me but not so far as to be easily visible to the approaching men. They're coming towards us, Martin and the gunman, coming to the truck, not the jeep. Holy shit. All I can hope for is that they don't see me, just get in and drive away. The boots of the men approach, backlit by the floodlight: the hiking boots of the journalist, the riding boots of the gunman.

'Get in,' I hear the gunman bark. 'You're driving.'

And then I hear the impact, the wallop, like a bricklayer slapping stonework down on fresh cement, and from beneath the truck I see the knees above the riding boots crumple, and I see the body fall. The man hits the ground only a metre from me, eyes rolling unseeing in their sockets, a cap still on his head, blood running into the gravel, the same colour as the cap. Jamie. It must have been Jamie.

There's no respite. A gunshot, then another. The gunman's accomplice, firing from the verandah. I curl into myself, hoping that the man won't direct any shots towards his fallen colleague. I hear Jamie and Scarsden scrambling, getting behind the truck.

Another shot. Am I imagining it, or is the man getting closer? Shit. If he comes out to the vehicles, we'll be sitting ducks, all of us. I look towards the fallen man, now motionless in the dirt, see his gun beside him. I swallow. Raise my head, peer out. I'm right: the second gunman is approaching along the path; he's almost at the gate. Fuck it, I have no choice. I scramble across, reach out and take the gun, hoping if the remaining shooter notices me, he won't fire, won't risk hitting his colleague.

The man does see me, puts a bullet into the car, just inches above my head. Another shot; the windscreen explodes.

I roll back, out the other side of the truck. And there is Jamie, hand outstretched, not to help me up but for the gun. I pass it to him. He examines it urgently, even as I get into a squatting position, cowering behind the rear wheel.

'Right, got it,' says Jamie to himself. He stands, levels the gun across the back of the tray. Fires once. 'Stop right there!' he barks.

He's too good a man, too decent. Too good for the likes of me. I would have shot the gunman without hesitation. Self-defence.

Two shots come withering past us. Jamie fires back, holding the gun above the tray but unable to aim, his opportunity lost.

And then, the roar of a totally different type of weapon. The emphatic exhalation of a shotgun, breathing death. Two shots in quick succession.

And then nothing.

'Jesus,' says Scarsden.

There's silence, as if the very landscape is holding its breath.

'Stay down,' says Jamie to me, voice gentle.

'Are we safe?'

'We're safe. But it's not pretty.'

I stand. Over by the homestead, Clay is standing over a ragged red pulp, the shotgun still in his hand.

chapter forty-nine
MARTIN

MARTIN RUNS OUT FROM BEHIND THE TRUCK, HE AND JAMIE. FROM THE HOUSE comes Jack Goffing, having regained his handgun. There is nothing to be done for Raymond Penuch. He lies profoundly dead, shredded by Clay Carmichael's shotgun blasts. What's left of him is sprawled just outside the front gate, inconveniently blocking the way.

Martin goes instead to Vincent Carmichael, groaning softly as he bleeds out, the red of his blood glistening brightly in the harsh floodlighting. Martin's hostile environment training kicks in; he knows these first minutes are essential, the need to staunch the bleeding. He pulls off his t-shirt, lent to him by Jamie just that morning. Ecco is with him now. He gives the t-shirt to her, kneels in the dirt, rips Vincent's linen shirt open, buttons popping.

Vincent groans, opening his eyes. 'Oh faark,' he gasps, eyes wide, taking in the sight of his own gore.

'Thank Christ,' says Martin. Consciousness means hope. He takes the t-shirt back from Ecco, wipes at the wound, which is

413

slowly pulsing blood. It's a clean shot, just below the rib cage on the right side of the abdomen. 'Vincent, you with me?'

'Hurts like hell,' the man gasps.

Martin is encouraged. Vincent isn't coughing blood, there's none on his breath. The bullet has missed his lungs.

Jamie is with them now. 'Shirt off,' Martin instructs him. 'We'll compress. Front and back.' And then to Vincent: 'We'll sit you up. Get a bandage on the entry and exit wounds.'

Vincent whimpers.

'Stop. Here.' It's an elderly woman Martin hasn't seen before, appearing from nowhere, like an angel. She's holding a medical kit the size of a suitcase: the sort required this far from the nearest hospital. She kneels, opens it. It has everything: bandages, snakebite antivenom, an array of syringes, drug vials, bottles of alcohol, antiseptics and disinfectants. Even surgical instruments: scalpels, needles, sterile thread, scissors.

'You're a saint, Mrs Enright,' Vincent whispers, managing a weak smile.

'The flying doctor's on the way,' she tells him. And then to Martin: 'An hour.'

Martin tries to think; this is far beyond his level of expertise. Should he try suturing? He has no idea.

'There's morphine,' says Mrs Enright.

Martin shakes his head. 'Not yet.' Then he addresses the others. 'We'll ease him up. Swab the wound with alcohol then try to plug it with sterile bandages. Bind them if we have enough to wrap around him, otherwise manually compress with the t-shirts. We need to stem the bleeding until the flying doctor gets here. Ready?'

'Inside,' says Mrs Enright. 'We have bags. Saline drips.'

'Oh yes,' says Martin. He feels like crying, he feels like kissing her. 'Please, get them. Hurry!' As she scurries towards the house, he looks at Vincent. 'You're going to be okay.' And for the first time, he believes it.

——

The flying doctor's twin-engine plane swoops over them in a graceful loop before coming in to land behind the western ridge. It seems to have taken no time and forever. Martin's perception of time feels warped, distorted by the violence and by his own narrow escape from death for the second time in less than a week. He feels threadbare, depleted by the heat of the day, reserves stripped away by the fragility of his own mortality, emotionally drained by the battle to save Vincent. The heir to Longchamp Downs is lying peacefully in the dirt, the morphine working its magic, blood still oozing from the bandages, but at a sustainable rate. Mrs Enright stands over him, holding the saline bag aloft, like the Statue of Liberty, while Clay is down in the dirt next to his son, mopping his brow and whispering softly to him.

Jamie and Ecco have taken a couple of vehicles and headed to the airstrip to collect the medical crew. Goffing is over by the gate. He has scavenged some rope to tape off a perimeter around the corpse of Raymond Penuch. Martin walks over to the other would-be assassin. He's motionless, still lying in the recovery position where someone has had the presence of mind to place him. His breathing sounds laboured. Martin wonders if the blow to the head has done more damage than he first thought. As he watches, the man convulses. 'Shit,' says Martin, reluctantly kneeling to help. Before he can do anything, the spasm ends, and the man lies still again. Martin checks his pulse; it seems strong enough.

Jack Goffing appears next to him, hands him some swabs and a bottle of alcohol. Martin grimaces but sets to work nevertheless. He tries to remove the A-team cap, gently at first, but it has become mired in the blood of the wound and the man's matted hair. Martin splashes some alcohol on the wound and prises the cap loose. He cleans the wound. It's still bleeding. Martin doesn't know how serious it is; he knows head wounds can bleed a lot.

The vehicles arrive, and suddenly the area is bustling once more, two medicos leaping out, Jamie unloading stretchers. The medical team looks incredibly young. One runs over to the gate, doesn't bother checking the dead shooter. Then she's over kneeling beside Vincent, talking to Clay. The old man points to Martin. The doctor looks across, nods a silent acknowledgement, then sets to work. Her colleague, a man, joins Martin and the wounded A-team leader. 'Head wound?' he asks.

'Blow to the head,' says Martin. 'Unconscious for more than an hour. Convulsing.'

'Right,' says the nurse, searching for a pulse.

Jack Goffing shows the nurse his federal police badge. Martin understands his friend isn't asserting his authority so much as explaining who's who. 'This man is dangerous. Extremely violent. A killer. He will need to be constrained in case he regains consciousness.'

'Okay. Understood.' The nurse bends down, opens the gunman's closed eyelid, shines a light directly into the eye.

Martin sees no reaction.

The nurse addresses Goffing. 'You help us get him into the plane, we'll do the rest. Restrain him. But I don't think he's going to be bothering anyone.'

Once the team is satisfied that Vincent is stabilised and strapped in, Jamie and Goffing help load his stretcher onto the tray of the truck. Mrs Enright hovers, wringing her hands; Clay looks almost catatonic. Martin and the nurse carry the gunman across; apart from the occasional convulsion, he still hasn't moved or regained consciousness. The nurse goes in the back with the two wounded men, Ecco and the doctor ride in the cab, Jamie behind the wheel. He drives towards the landing strip.

Martin stands with Jack Goffing watching them go, slowing to an absolute crawl as Jamie eases the truck over the repaired section of the causeway crossing the Paroo River. Neither man speaks. Martin feels too exhausted to unpack what has happened. It can wait for another day.

Clay joins them, hands smeared with his son's blood. Martin regards his own, sees that they're the same, blood and alcohol. He hadn't noticed. They watch the receding truck in silence.

'They say he will be okay,' Clay says.

'He's in good hands,' says Jack Goffing. 'The best.'

chapter fifty
ECCO

JAMIE AND I WATCH THE PLANE TAKE OFF FROM THE EDGE OF THE AIRSTRIP, the paint-tin cloths still alight, the air pungent with kerosene and av gas. The moon is edging over the horizon, no longer full. Late to the party.

We stand together, looking as the lights of the plane merge with the stars, the sound of its engines already wavering in and out of the evening calm.

'He'll survive,' says Jamie, as if to convince himself. 'The doctor reckons there's every chance. Bullet straight through his liver, in and out. Should make a full recovery.'

'Let's hope so.'

I watch the torches burning in the night and wonder if we should make the effort to extinguish them. When we'd heard the flying doctor was on the way, the two of us raced across, setting them alight, lining the runway. Jamie had known what to do, finding the cans in the shed by the strip, filling them with kerosene, screwing on the tops with the ragged cloth wicks protruding. For emergencies only, the strip not rated for night landings.

'Let them burn out,' says Jamie, apparently reading my thoughts.

'That was brave,' I say. 'Taking on that gunman. Knocking him out.'

'Brave? Me? You're the one who retrieved his gun. Under fire. That took real guts.'

'Yes,' I say. 'We did well. All things considered.'

The lamps burn. That old expression comes to mind: a torch song. I wonder where it comes from, what it means. The makeshift landing lights flutter in the slight breeze.

'Do you think it's over?' I ask him.

'The violence?' Jamie sighs. 'I hope so. But the rest? No, it's not over.'

'No, I guess you're right.'

'We need to find out who those men were. How this all came to pass.'

'That needn't bother us,' I say. 'Let the police work it out. Let Martin Scarsden dig his way to another bestseller. Something hefty, something significant.' I look at Jamie then, at his face, serious and resolute, catching the light from the runway torches. 'Don't you see? We're free of it. I can write Clay's book, if he still wants it. And I can write another, all about the cave, Ludwig Leichhardt, the lost expedition, the megafauna. How we found it, you and me and Martin. It's the past; it's safe. The rest, the present-day stuff with guns and killers? That's dangerous. Martin can have it. We should leave Longchamp Downs and put everything in the past.'

'We?' he asks doubtfully.

'Haven't you spent enough time out here? Served your penance? If I deserve a second chance, then surely you must.'

He's silent after that, for a long while.

'I want a life,' I say, pressing the point. 'Not my old life. Not any life. A new life. Shaped by me. Surely you want something similar.'

He still says nothing, just stares at the sputtering flames.

I think he's working through it, seeing the possibility of a different existence, weighing it up. A new life. Together. But in the flickering light, I see the conflict in his eyes.

'We can go together,' I say, making it explicit. I reach out, take his hand in mine.

'I'm not sure I can,' he says, holding my hand but not meeting my eye. 'If it's not over for Clay, it can't be over for me.'

'Why not?'

'Last night he learnt that his daughter was dead, tonight he might lose his son. I can't just abandon him.'

'You can't stay here forever, Jamie,' I say gently.

'He saved me, Ecco. I'd be dead if it wasn't for him. I was lost, out here in my own personal wilderness. He took me in, gave me a job for which I had no qualifications and no experience. All I knew about was boats.' Jamie looks at me, making his point. 'He saved you as well. A lifeline when you needed it most.'

Jamie is right. Without Clay, without his compassion and generosity, I'm not sure where I'd be. Struggling at the very least. He gave me a second chance when so many others were all too ready to condemn me. But I'm not sure what Jamie is asking. Surely not to stay out here indefinitely? I can't do that; I just can't. 'You're not Vincent, I'm not Chloe,' I say to him. 'We can't be surrogates for his lost daughter and his absent son.'

I can't read Jamie's expression. He's looking at me with some mixture of affection and regret. 'Agreed. But we can't just desert him. I owe him more than that.'

'You won't come with me?'

'Not yet.'

I stare along the airstrip as first one and then a second of the flares sputter and die.

chapter fifty-one

JAMIE AND I RETURN FROM THE AIRSTRIP IN SILENCE, NOTHING LEFT TO SAY.
I can't tell what he is thinking. His face could be made of stone.

I'm consumed by a familiar hollowness. I bite my lip and chastise myself for ever daring to hope. It only serves to emphasise
how lonely I've been these past few years, despite all my denials,
pouring all my energies into re-creating myself, never taking the
time to pause and reflect. Perhaps if I had, I'd know myself a
little better than I do. I feel a tear leak from my eye. I'm unable
to stop it, yet I refuse to wipe it away, letting it slide down my
cheek. I don't know if it's for me, or for losing Jamie.

He glances across at me, the stone visage softening in the light
of the dash, lips pulled tight, eyes sad. He reaches a tentative hand
towards me.

'Don't,' I say, not even knowing if I mean it.

We pull up outside the homestead. I take in the floodlit tableau,
a stage where the play has finished but they've neglected to lower
the curtain or clear the set. The cars with their bullet holes and the

smashed windscreen. Discarded bandages. Bloodstained t-shirts. Vincent's shredded linen shirt. The body of the gunman lying just outside the gate where he fell.

We sit in silence. I don't want to open the door, I don't want to get out of the truck, I don't want to enter the future. Not yet. There is no new life to be found out there, just the same old one, damaged and compromised. I'm not sure I can endure an existence of perpetual punishment, of unending loneliness. I'm not sure I still care to try.

We're sitting motionless when I see movement: it's a woman skulking down the side fence, coming from the back of the house. She steps into the light, pausing to look around the deserted stage, an actor who's missed her cue. She moves towards the vehicles.

'That's Maz Gingelly,' says Jamie. 'The publican from Port Paroo.'

'Where the hell has she been?' I ask.

'She's got the diary,' says Jamie, cracking his door open as he says it.

'Shit,' I say. And suddenly I do care. I care very much. I'm out of the car, a pace or two behind Jamie.

'Stop!' he yells, getting to her van at the same time as Maz.

She swivels, turns, handgun aimed right at him. She fires the gun. Jamie stops in his tracks.

But nothing can stop me. The emotions swirling through me are too strong, carrying me on, sweeping me past Jamie, contemptuous of the consequences, too angry at life and what it has wrought. I hear a second shot but feel nothing except the impact with her, shoulder first, driving the woman hard against her vehicle, hearing the breath bellow out of her. And then we are down on the ground.

Then another shot. I look up to see Jamie silhouetted against the floodlight. He's holding the gun, saying something, but I can't make it out. It's difficult to breathe.

And then Martin's mate, Jack Goffing, is there, his own gun out, barking at Jamie to drop the weapon. For a moment, fear comes hard, the fear so absent when I charged the publican. Fear for him. Jamie moves slowly, deliberately, lowering the gun to the ground, stepping away from it, away from me and Maz. And now I see Martin. He's walking up next to Goffing.

Jamie has his hands up but speaks calmly and clearly. 'Ecco and me. We saw her leaving. Taking Chloe's diary.'

Martin speaks. 'Jack, that diary is critical evidence in the murder of Roman Stanton and the death of Chloe Carmichael.'

Goffing nods, and now he trains the gun on Maz. I stand, movements telegraphed, raise my hands. My breathing is coming easier. I check myself. No bullet wounds, just a pulsing pain in my shoulder where I collected Maz Gingelly.

'Who pulled the gun?' asks Goffing.

'She did.' Jamie and I say it in unison, pointing at Maz.

A smile comes to me, and I quickly try to suppress it. I look at Jamie. He's smiling too. On the ground, Maz is regaining her breath.

Goffing speaks again. 'Martin, go get the handgun. Secure it. Try not to touch the grip, if you can avoid it. And then, please retrieve the diary.' He keeps his gun trained on Maz.

Martin fetches the gun and the diary.

'Stand up,' says Goffing to Maz.

She groans as she rises, not bothering to raise her arms. She snarls at Goffing but says nothing comprehensible.

'Martin, frisk her, will you.'

'Like hell,' says Maz.

'Submit, or I'll cuff you,' says Goffing.

Maz raises her arms, allows Martin to search her. He declares her weapon-free.

Goffing breathes out, an audible sigh, but keeps his gun trained on the publican. 'Okay, everyone inside. Maybe Mrs Enright will have something to restrain her.'

We let the others go in before us.

'I love you,' says Jamie.

'Then come with me,' I say.

chapter fifty-two
MARTIN

MARTIN SURVEYS THE SITTING ROOM. CLAY CARMICHAEL IS SLUMPED IN AN armchair, head in his bloodied hands. Mrs Enright has fetched him a whisky, but it remains next to his chair, untouched. On the settee, Maz Gingelly sits upright and defiant, eyes blazing, staring up at Jack Goffing and Martin. Her wrists are bound with cable ties.

'Let me go,' she says. 'I've done nothing wrong.'

'Except steal a vital piece of evidence and attempt to abscond from a crime scene with it,' says Goffing, voice measured.

'Bullshit,' she says, almost spitting the word. 'I wasn't stealing it; I was borrowing it. Taking it to my car to read in peace. That's what I was doing earlier, when you two goons arrived here, if you remember.'

'You pulled a handgun and fired it multiple times,' says Goffing. 'Narrowly missing your intended victims.'

'Warning shots. Self-defence.' She takes a breath. 'I want that bitch charged with assault.'

'You sent police in the wrong direction when they were searching for me,' adds Martin, earning his own contemptuous glare.

'You've got nothing.'

'What's so important about the diary?' Martin asks.

Maz looks like she wants to kill him. 'Chloe was my best friend. Pretty much my only friend. Since school days.' She takes a moment to gather herself, anger dropping back a bit. 'I wanted to read her last words, before the diary is taken. The police will want it, the coroner.'

'The Queensland police are on their way,' Goffing says. 'We'll let them decide what to do with you.'

'No,' says Maz. 'You either charge me, or release me.'

Mrs Enright enters the room, bringing silence with her, pushing a trolley bearing a full tea service: bone china cups and saucers, silver milk jug, cut-glass sugar bowl. There are small plates, dessert forks, slices and cake and Anzac biscuits. It puts a stop to the discussion, Martin and Jack Goffing and Maz Gingelly staring in mutual disbelief. Martin can still see the blood on the old woman's hands from helping Vincent. She must be in shock.

The elderly housekeeper politely asks Clay if he would care for a cup and, when he doesn't respond, pours him one anyway. 'And you, young lady?'

Maz looks askance, then gestures with her bound wrists, communicating her inability to partake.

'Gentlemen?' asks Mrs Enright, unfazed.

'Black,' says Goffing.

'White, no sugar,' Martin responds, the scene becoming increasingly surreal.

After serving them, Mrs Enright retreats towards the kitchen, leaving the trolley, and reality begins again.

'You have to let me go,' insists Maz, anger replaced by resolve. 'You are breaking the law detaining me like this.'

'The police will charge me then,' says Goffing.

Martin hears the front door open and footsteps approaching. Goffing swivels, gun in hand, just in case. But it's just Ecco and Jamie Stubbs. Unarmed.

'What's she saying?' asks Ecco, taking in the tea trolley, the cups and the cake, brows knitted in bemusement.

'Not a lot,' says Martin.

'She hasn't finished reading the diary?' asks Ecco.

'Not yet,' says Martin. 'Thanks to you and Jamie.'

'Maybe we should read it together,' says Ecco, something teasing in her manner.

'While we wait for the Queensland police,' Jack Goffing chimes in, the slightest smile on his face, perhaps elicited by the antipathy spreading across that of Maz Gingelly.

'I've read it,' whispers Clay. 'Vincent and me.'

All eyes turn to him.

Clay is scowling, as if trying to dismiss some unwelcome thought. 'The paintings.'

Martin glances at Jack Goffing, but his friend looks none the wiser.

Ecco seems to understand. 'Where did it hang, Clay? Percival McEwan Fitzroy's *The Camel's Head at Dawn*?' She looks from Clay to Maz and back again. 'Stolen not so very long before the death of Roman Stanton and the disappearance of your daughter, Chloe.'

Clay has suddenly become more alert, prompted by Ecco's question. 'Over there. That wall. Look and you can still see where the wallpaper is less faded.'

All heads turn and they regard the empty space.

'Chloe saw something the night the paintings were stolen,' says Ecco. 'Something that bothered her. Enough for her to put it in her diary. The thieves were heading south towards Port Paroo.'

Maz simply stares. Defiant.

'But what really upset her was Roman Stanton's discovery of another robbery some weeks later. Down in New South Wales. Bowral. Another painting. *The Camel's Head at Noon,* also by Fitzroy. Except this time, a man was killed. Murdered.'

'Nothing to do with me,' says Maz.

A thousand questions rush into Martin's mind, but he bites his tongue, letting Ecco hold the floor, wondering what else she's uncovered.

'Within weeks, a third painting, *The Camel's Head at Dusk,* was donated to the Queensland Art Gallery,' she says. 'The owners must have been scared they'd be next.'

This time Maz says nothing.

'What owners?' asks Jack Goffing. 'We need to talk to them.'

'Delaney and Floris Bullwinkel,' says Ecco.

'What?' says Martin, turning to Goffing, who looks as stunned as Martin feels. Delaney Bullwinkel, erstwhile employer of Raymond Penuch, the billionaire's bagman and gofer, now lying dead outside by the gate. Delaney Bullwinkel: subject of Martin's unpublished exposé, *Opals and Dust.*

Ecco continues, apparently unaware of the fire of speculation she's sparked in Martin's mind. 'Chloe knew about Bowral. Had her suspicions. Shared them with her fiancé, Roman. And then he was murdered and she was left to die.'

Maz stares at them, defiance burning bright. 'Bowral wasn't me. That was Vincent. I'm not the killer—he is.'

2005

THURSDAY, 17 FEBRUARY

I think I'm finally getting over the robbery. I've seen a counsellor a couple of times now I'm back in Brisbane; she seems to think I'm doing okay. Dad's finished installing security at Longchamp. I'm not sure why. I haven't asked for it. The police have made no headway. I think we just have to accept the paintings are gone forever.

THURSDAY, 24 FEBRUARY

I should be getting stuck into my uni work, but there is plenty of time for that. I've been scouring Patrick Murdoch's journals. It's amazing. He actually found out who Hentig and Stuart were after reading their names in The Bulletin *and realised that he'd encountered them months after the last official sighting. But I'm increasingly confident he kept that knowledge to himself and I'm pretty sure I know why: treasure. The two men were seeking treasure!!*

I wrote to Roman, but in the meantime he sent me an email. The subject line was ho-hum: 'FYI'. The message read: 'Thought you should know. Available to talk it through anytime. Love, R xxx.'

I assumed it was something light-hearted, his message mock serious. But when I opened the attachment, I saw there was nothing funny about it at all. It was a newspaper report from Bowral in New South Wales, thieves targeting a collection of early twentieth-century and colonial Australian art, including another painting by Percival McEwan Fitzroy. The owner had been bashed, left for dead.

I wondered what Roman was thinking, just sending it to me like that. Like he didn't fully understand. Like he was in the wrong compartment.

MONDAY, 14 MARCH

I'm back at Longchamp, taking a week off uni. I really shouldn't be, but I can't help it. I'm a bag of nerves and no way could I wait for the next holidays. Roman and I are heading into the wilderness, searching for the Camel's Head, to see if we can find any trace of Arthur Hentig and Donald Stuart. What a discovery it would be, what a mystery solved!

Dad's being a worry wart. Not about me, mind you. About Vincent. It seems Dad has been sending money to my brother for his rent in Armidale, but now Dad has received a call from the landlord saying money is still owed from last year. We tried calling, but Vincent's share house doesn't have the phone on. When we finally got hold of him he said it was a mix-up, and the money has been paid. So at least that's settled.

*I asked Dad about the Camel's Head. He thinks it's a rock forma-
tion way out west near a capped spring with an old windmill. I've
told him it's part of an art assignment for university, based loosely
on our stolen painting. I didn't want to worry him, so I didn't let on
that we intended finding it. I don't think he suspects anything; he's
convinced that 'book learning' has no association with the real world!
Roman and I have decided the best route will be to approach from
the south. We'll head out on the Tibooburra road, then carve north
cross-country from there. Hopefully, that way we can avoid most of
the ridge lines we'd have to traverse if we tried to follow the route
Hentig and Stuart must have taken from Longchamp Downs. I'm
heading down to Port Paroo tomorrow and we'll go from there.*

TUESDAY, 15 MARCH

*My car's been running hot, which is a bit of a worry, and when I filled
up at Port Paroo, Perry checked under the bonnet and confirmed the
fan belt is slipping. He tightened it, said it should hold for a week or
two while he orders a new belt, but there's no way I'm going to take
it off road. We'll have to go in Roman's truck.*

*While I was in town, I dropped by the pub to see Maz and ask
her if I could stay the night in the annexe. I think I caught her
by surprise, dropping in without ringing first, but she laughed it
off and gave me the most humungous hug. She'd heard about the
robbery, wanted to make sure I was okay. I said I was fully recovered
and that she shouldn't worry. I told her my visit was spur of the
moment, that I was meeting Roman. She asked about him, about
us. As we talked, I gained the impression that not everything was
okay with her; she seemed distracted, unhappy. She's older now, but*

in some ways she's just like the girl I first met at school: not quick to share her troubles.

'What is it?' I asked. 'Are you okay?'

'Sure. Just a bit envious.'

'How so?'

'You've got Roman. His brother's already married. Not many suitable candidates out here.'

'How about Vincent?' I asked, half joking.

She shook her head. 'Nah. He's heading for the city, we both know it.'

'I thought you might sell the pub, move down there yourself.'

'And do what? Reckon I'm stuck here now.'

I must say, I admire her, after all she's been through. The pub is back on an even keel. It's a credit to her.

'Maz, did Vincent ever ask you for money?'

'Vincent? No. Why?'

'Sounds like he's overspent his budget at uni in Armidale.'

'No. He told me one of his investments was looking a bit shaky for a while, but it's come good. You know how much he likes that shit.' She changed the subject. 'You and Roman have made up, then?' she asked.

'Made up? What do you mean?'

'Vincent told me you'd been fighting.'

'Really?' I thought of the argument Roman and I had up at Longchamp when I told him about my plan to spend an extra year at uni in Brisbane. Vincent must have overheard us. 'It was nothing,' I told Maz. 'Just a tiff. Weeks ago. Everything's good now—I just miss him.'

I didn't mention the real reason I've come to see Roman, the search for Hentig and Stuart and the Camel's Head. Maz is a terrific friend, but she runs a pub—gossip is part of the job description. If I told her what Roman and I are looking for, she'd tell Perry, and then the whole district would know.

TUESDAY, 15 MARCH, LATER

Roman drove up from Tavelly and we ate down by the empty river. The stars were out and the air was warm. He asked what I would do if we do find some trace of the lost explorers in the desert, what I planned to do with Murdoch's diaries. And, inevitably, that led to us talking about the future again. And my suggestion of not one but two more years in Brisbane. I thought we'd settled it; apparently not.

'It's not just two years, is it? You never want to live at Tavelly Station,' Roman said. 'I realise that now.'

'Not never,' I said. 'But I'm twenty. You're twenty-three. Don't you want to do other stuff first?'

'Of course, but Dad doesn't have much longer,' he said. 'Mum took him down to Dubbo today.'

'Oh, Roman. I'm so sorry.'

We let the subject drift then: his father's mortality, his inheritance, his family responsibilities. Our future. But the issues were too big; they couldn't be compartmentalised for long.

'What about getting a manager for a while?' I said. 'Or let Merriman and Gloria take care of it. Isn't that what you suggested?'

'For a year. Longer than that, it's not fair on them. They've got their own life to build.'

I hesitated to respond. The conversation was heading down the same path as the one that led to the last argument. My desire to achieve something in the wider world; his obligation to his family.

'I'm thinking of selling,' he said, blindsiding me.

'What?'

'Why not? It will be mine to sell.'

'What will your parents say?'

'I'm not sure. Dad might be upset; Mum might be relieved.'

'What about Merriman?'

'He and Gloria will still have the spread down south. Dad has sorted that out.'

'Why?' I asked. 'What's changed?' I thought of our fight; how resolute he'd been about taking on Tavelly.

'I've had an offer. Above market rates. Drought like this, might never get another one like it.'

'There must be more to it than that.'

'Yes. You. Us. With that sort of money we can do whatever we like. Travel. Live in London. Isn't that what you want?'

'You'd do that? Give up the station? For me?'

'Why not? Just because I'm the son of a grazier doesn't mean I have to be one as well.'

He made light of it, making it sound like he was sacrificing nothing, but I knew Tavelly Station was everything to him. He loves that place. He'd spent three years at ag college preparing to run it. It was the most unbelievable gesture. I was so overwhelmed. The words to express how much I loved him in that moment don't exist.

THURSDAY

chapter fifty-three
ECCO

I MEET THE DETECTIVES IN THE FOYER OF DUBBO BASE HOSPITAL. IT'S BIG AND bustling, like a capital city hospital. It's three days since the shootout, and Jamie has driven me the seven hours from Longchamp Downs. Now he's off parking the car, seeing about organising our accommodation. The police have informed us he's not needed, just me.

They stand as I come in. Detective Sergeant Ivan Lucic and Detective Senior Constable Nell Buchanan. Homicide detectives, looking the business, both wearing suits, no ties. Lucic is regarding me sceptically, but Nell Buchanan welcomes me with warmth. She's not as old as I expected, not much older than me.

She smiles broadly. 'Thank you so much for coming all this way,' she says. 'We really appreciate it.'

'I'm still not sure why you want me here,' I say.

'It's not us,' says Detective Lucic bluntly. 'It's Vincent Carmichael. He insists. Either you're here or he won't speak.'

'And you're okay with that?' I ask. 'My reputation, I mean. It won't contaminate the evidence or something?'

'It's not ideal,' says Lucic. 'But he's promising to make a full confession. On the record. And anytime a suspect offers to sign a full and voluntary confession, that's a good day for justice.'

Nell's attitude is more inclusive. 'If he confesses, signs a statement, then that puts an end to it. There won't be a full trial, you won't have to testify.'

'Okay then. Let's get on with it.'

——

Vincent Carmichael is in a private room, propped up in bed, supported by a bevy of pillows. 'Ekaterina,' he says. 'Thank you for coming.'

Beside him is a young woman dressed in an expensive suit. Her watch is gold and her earrings are pearl. She introduces herself as his lawyer. She has a notepad and a voice recorder, but has positioned herself off to one side, giving the impression she intends to be an observer rather than a participant. The police and I pull up a seat each.

'Are you okay?' I ask Vincent. He looks terribly gaunt to me; he's pale and a little jaundiced. His tennis-player tan has been replaced by the pale sheen of a late-night gambler.

'I will be. They cut out a good part of my liver but they say it will grow back, that I'll make a full recovery.'

'Shall we start?' asks the lawyer. 'I don't want my client getting unnecessarily fatigued.'

'Just one thing before we begin,' I say. I turn to Vincent. 'Why do you want me here? The detectives say you insisted.'

'It's the book. The family history. I want to make sure you have it all, set the record straight.' He glances at the police. 'If these officers arrest me, I might not get another chance.'

Detective Lucic starts recording, stating the date and time and those present, then prompts Vincent. 'You have offered to confess to a crime or crimes. Can you set that out for the record?'

'Yes.' He looks at me, and I get the feeling it's me he wants to confess to, and that the presence of the police is almost coincidental. 'My sister Chloe Carmichael has stood accused of murder these past twenty years. We now know that's not the case. She didn't kill Roman Stanton. And neither did I.'

'Sorry?' says Lucic, exchanging a quick glance with his partner.

'We were under the impression you were willing to confess,' says Nell.

'I am. But not to the murder of Roman Stanton.'

'Bowral,' I say. 'Akira Tennant.'

Vincent looks almost grateful. 'Yes,' he says. 'Bowral. I killed him.'

There's a moment of confusion, or of repositioning. Nell stands, leaves the room without speaking. The lawyer asks if Lucic wants to break, but he declines, looks at me, then to Vincent. 'We're aware of the murder of Mr Tennant. The possible link. My colleague will be back soon with a brief and some questions. In the meantime, tell us who you think did kill Roman Stanton.'

'Maureen Gingelly. Maz. The owner of the Port Paroo Hotel. My sister's best friend.'

'And why has it taken you twenty years to make this allegation?'

'Because I believed the same as everyone else. That Chloe killed him. But that was before Ekaterina discovered that couldn't be true.' He looks at me and his mouth curves in what might be a smile on a healthier face.

I can't help it. I interject. 'You believed it, though. That your sister was the killer. How could you?'

That makes him pause. I see the self-recrimination in his eyes. 'Yes. I should have known it couldn't have been her. Not Chloe. But the evidence at the inquest. Reported sightings of her. The withdrawals from the ATMs. The message I received, sending money to Adelaide. If she wasn't guilty, why did she run? I'd heard her and Roman fighting, really slagging each other off, a month or two before she disappeared.'

'So you had no idea she was out in the desert, in that cave?' I ask. I glance across at Detective Lucic, fearing I may have overstepped, but he gives me an encouraging blink.

Vincent is beginning to look distressed. 'No. She never said anything about it. Neither did Roman.'

'Now that we know she didn't kill him,' says Ivan Lucic, voice calm, bringing the interview back on track, 'tell us why you suspect Ms Gingelly.'

'The paintings,' says Vincent. 'Bowral.'

I notice Nell re-enter, give Lucic a reassuring nod. She's holding a sheaf of papers. Vincent's revelation can't have come as such a surprise after all.

Vincent must see it as well. 'You have the file?' he asks her.

'I do,' says Nell.

'Tell us what happened,' I say. 'But first, maybe tell us about the theft of the paintings at Longchamp Downs. That took place before Bowral, right?'

'Yes, that's important.' Vincent looks to Lucic, as if seeking permission.

'Go ahead,' says the detective.

'I knew it was Maz straight away. We'd laughed about it, all those old colonial canvases that had been on the walls for so long no one even noticed them. How they were probably worth a pile.

And she knew that we were all meant to be away, Chloe and me and Dad, on the Sunshine Coast. The Australia Day week, in 2005. Chloe only returned to Longchamp at the last moment. What she saw convinced me it was Maz.'

'What did she see?' asks Ivan Lucic.

'The thieves driving away from Longchamp, but heading south. It would be much faster to go north to the paved road. More options, more directions from there. On the Sundowner Track it's not possible to turn off till you get to Port Paroo, two hundred kilometres away. A few out stations, but no through roads. So I volunteered to go down to Port Paroo, ostensibly to ask the locals if they'd seen anything, but really I was going down to warn Maz.'

'Warn her? Why didn't you confront her? Report her to the police?'

Vincent hangs his head. 'I needed the money. I was playing the markets. Doing very well, but taking too many risks. Not diversifying. Borrowing too much money, too highly leveraged. All the newbie mistakes. There was a market correction, I received a margin call. Calls. I was going to lose it all, have nothing left but debt. Years of investment, gone in no time.'

Ivan Lucic leans in. There is an intensity in his gaze. 'Did she know that before she took the paintings?'

'Yes. I'd tried to borrow from her.'

'Did she tell you she intended stealing them?'

'No, but when I got down to Port Paroo, she didn't deny it.'

'She gave you money?'

'She did.'

'Enough to pay off your debts?'

'No. Enough to buy some time. Bowral would see me debt-free.'

'She co-opted you?'

'Yes. But I can't blame her. I was willing enough. She'd taken the paintings from Longchamp. They meant a lot to my father, even more to my sister. If I could turn a blind eye to that, what did I care about some multimillionaire art collector? Maz said he'd be insured, that it was a victimless crime.'

Nell Buchanan leans across and whispers something to her colleague, hands him a piece of paper, points something out.

Lucic reads for a moment or two, then recommences his questioning. 'Bowral is important. Take your time. Tell us what happened.'

'We were in the house. It was all going well, we were almost done, then a light came on further inside and a man emerged. He had a gun, was pointing it at Maz. A shotgun. Told her not to move. I was in the shadows; he hadn't seen me. I reached out and grasped some sort of metal rod. A fire poker, something like that. He heard me, started to turn. I hit him once. Then I hit him again, and he fell. I killed him. I ran. We ran.'

No one says anything, the weight of the confession hanging in the room.

It's Nell who breaks the silence. 'And that's the crime you wish to confess to? The murder of Akira Tennant?'

'Yes. I killed him. I didn't mean to, but I did.'

'Manslaughter,' interjects the lawyer. 'You heard him.'

Another long silence. Vincent studying his hands, Nell writing, Lucic staring at Vincent with a laser gaze, his blue eyes alight.

It's left to me to push on. 'You still took the paintings? Why do that? Wouldn't they potentially link you with the killing?'

'I guess. But most of them were already in the van. We weren't going to put them back. We needed to get away.'

'Most of them?' asks Nell.

Vincent blinks. Frowns. 'There were a couple that we'd removed from the walls but they were still inside. Maz went to fetch them while I got the van. There was a big one she was determined to get.'

'*The Camel's Head at Noon*,' I say.

Vincent looks at me with a kind of surprised admiration. 'Yes,' he whispers.

I'm about to ask more, when Nell looks up from her briefing papers and says, 'Maureen returned inside for this last painting, *The Camel's Head at Noon*?'

'Yes. It was important to her.'

Lucic leans forward. 'You won't be aware of this, but there was evidence tendered at Tennant's inquest that was held in camera. In secret. The police requested it, because we didn't want it made public at that time.'

'What are you talking about?' asks Vincent, looking to his lawyer for guidance, but she seems as confused as he does.

'The post-mortem,' says Lucic. 'Akira Tennant was beaten between ten and a dozen times.'

Vincent stares at him. 'What? No.'

'Twice while he was standing, the rest when he was already on the floor.'

Now Vincent is lost for words, mouth ajar, eyes wide.

'The fatal blow or blows were landed when he was already down,' says Nell.

'What are you saying?' asks Vincent's lawyer, leaning forward.

'We don't think your client killed him,' says Nell. 'Maureen Gingelly did.'

'She'll never confess to that,' says Vincent.

Nell holds up the file. 'There is also CCTV. That's the other evidence withheld from the public at the inquest,' she says. 'Two figures in black. They leave. The smaller figure returns, moves towards where Akira was lying. Then this figure moves back into frame and carries the paintings out.'

Vincent says nothing for a long while, but there are tears welling. 'All these years . . .' is all he can manage.

'You need a break?' asks his lawyer.

'Let's finish it,' he says, setting his jaw.

Lucic continues. 'So after Bowral—you got your money?'

'Some. Enough. But that was the end of it. I went to the coast, didn't come back unless I had to. The sight of the empty walls. It was too much.'

'But you didn't tell the police either,' I say.

'No. She had that over me. I thought I'd killed that man.' He looks forlorn. 'I was weak.'

Lucic just stares at Vincent, blue eyes boring into him. 'What was special about the paintings by Fitzroy?' he asks.

'They're the key,' says Vincent.

I think the detective might snap. 'This is not a parlour game, Mr Carmichael. Why were the Fitzroy paintings so important to Maureen Gingelly?'

'She explained when I went to see her, when I warned her Chloe was suspicious. Maz wasn't interested in the paintings— her father was.'

'Her father?' asks Nell.

'Who's her father?' asks Lucic.

'I don't know,' says Vincent. 'She said it was her biological father. That he'd paid for her to go to private school, had given her mother an allowance until she turned eighteen. She told me that if she revealed his identity, he would disinherit her, but if she stole the paintings, he would help her buy Tavelly Station.'

'Delaney Bullwinkel,' I say.

'Who?' asks Vincent.

The detectives are looking at me expectantly. Even the lawyer seems spellbound.

'A billionaire mining mogul. He and his wife already owned a third painting, *The Camel's Head at Dusk*. He donated it to the Queensland Art Gallery just weeks after the murder of Akira Tennant. I thought at first it was because he was scared the thieves might target him, but now I think he'd asked Maz to steal the other two. But after Bowral, he offloaded the one he had. Made it look like philanthropy. Vincent?'

He looks around the circle and agrees. 'That's what Maz told me. She said her father collected stolen artworks. Had a basement full of them. She said it was a test he had set her. If she got the paintings for him, he would acknowledge her.'

'She believed that?' I ask.

'I guess. But after Bowral, her father disowned her. He no longer wanted the paintings, was scared he would be implicated. So he cut her free. The offer to buy Tavelly was withdrawn.' Vincent looks down. 'I don't think she ever really wanted it. Not then, not during that terrible drought. Rather, she thought if her father bought it, then it would set Roman and Chloe free. They'd have the money they needed to go travelling, see the world.'

'Bullshit,' I say. 'She shot him, left Chloe to die.'

'Because of Bowral. It's in Chloe's last diary. She told Roman that the thieves who took Longchamp paintings must have passed through Port Paroo. Then Roman heard of Bowral; I guess he made the connection. Maybe he kept his mouth shut, because he wanted Maz's father to buy Tavelly. And so that day, when Maz killed him, I think she'd come to tell him the offer to buy Tavelly had been withdrawn. He would have been pissed off, for Chloe's sake, threatened to expose Maz. She must have been infuriated to have her intention to gift them the property turned back on her. So she shot him. Maybe she panicked, same as at Bowral when she was backed into a corner,' says Vincent. 'She wasn't getting her inheritance, but she wasn't going to prison.' He looks down at his hands. 'Just like me, I guess.'

'She knew Chloe was out there and left her to die,' I say. 'She lied about seeing her leave town. A perfect scapegoat.' I can't hide my contempt. 'She's just like you. The pair of you were thinking only of yourselves.'

'You're right,' he says. 'We all like to think of ourselves as good people. And we are. Until we run out of options, when it's us or the other guy. It's only then that you truly know what you are capable of.'

Quiet fills the room, only broken by Vincent's laboured breathing.

'Enough?' asks Vincent's lawyer.

'For now,' says Ivan Lucic.

chapter fifty-four
MARTIN

SIX HUNDRED KILOMETRES NORTH, IN CUNNAMULLA, JACK GOFFING ENDS THE
call and turns to Martin. They're in the pub, drinking zero-alcohol
beers.

'Ivan Lucic. Making considerably better progress than we are.'

'Good to hear it. What's he got to say?'

'Your suspicions seem to be on the money.' And Goffing conveys
to Martin what the detective told him about Delaney Bullwinkel.

'That's something, I guess.' Martin takes another sip of his
alcohol-free beer. The first schooner had been refreshing, and
the second tasted good enough, but a third seems pointless. 'You
reckon we're going to get anywhere? I can't see Maz Gingelly
telling us jack shit now she's lawyered up.'

'Quite the suit,' says Goffing. 'You been able to place him?'

'Cyril Flange. Bullwinkel's corporate counsel.'

Goffing scans the near-empty bar, before replying. 'You're right.
We should go, Martin. We're wasting our time here. Leave it to
the Queensland police.'

Martin pushes his glass away from him. 'What's happened with the mole?'

'Still under surveillance. We lack any concrete evidence.'

'She might get away with it?'

'She'll lose her job, one way or another.'

'Working for Bullwinkel?'

'That's what we suspect.'

'And what about the mafia? The Marellis and the Melbourne underworld?'

'The B-team and the contract on the app was just a ploy to send you west. Then, when a real mafia hit squad arrived in country, our mole saw an opportunity, planted the idea they were targeting you. Truth was, they were imported to target Marelli's enemies; they never did call themselves the B-team. Then she tipped them off, them and their employers, so they went to ground, soaking up our resources while the A-team targeted you. Then another team took out Marelli's grandson.'

'So the mafia wasn't after me?'

'Never.'

Just then the suit enters. Cyril Flange. Well dressed, a distinctive cologne, wearing an immaculately cut suit with French cuffs. Silver cufflinks. Carrying a razor-thin briefcase. He wouldn't look more out of place in a rugby scrum. He acknowledges Martin and Goffing with a finger to his nose, goes to the bar, orders himself a glass of wine from an amused-looking barman and joins them.

'Cheers,' he says, raising a glass.

Goffing looks unimpressed. 'Don't tell me, your client's not talking.'

'Of course not. Not in her interest. It would be unethical of me to advise her otherwise.'

'So you've come to gloat,' states Goffing with an air of resignation.

'I've come to talk.' The lawyer raises his glass, takes a sip, curls his nose with distaste.

Goffing looks to Martin, then back to Flange. 'If you're talking, we're listening.'

'This is off the record,' says Flange. 'Or more precisely, it's privileged. I'm Delaney Bullwinkel's corporate counsel. I'm also his personal attorney. You understand what that means?'

'You can't testify against him,' says Martin.

'Not even if I wanted to. Such testimony would automatically be adjudged inadmissible. No court would hear it. And I'd risk being convicted of contempt and disbarred.'

'So why talk to us?'

Flange smiles, a self-knowing, world-weary expression. 'You're a spook, Jack,' he says to Goffing. 'You don't care whether it's admissible or not.' Then he turns to Martin. 'And you're a journalist. Yours is the court of public opinion. The rules of mud-wrestling apply, not jurisprudence.' He samples the wine for a second time, winces theatrically. 'I rest my case.'

'What is it you'd like to tell us?' asks Martin, suspecting the man is toying with them.

'Delaney Bullwinkel is dying.'

'We know,' says Goffing. 'Switzerland. Weeks to live. At most.'

'And when he dies, I'll be out of a job,' says Flange. 'Reduced to penury, drinking cheap wine.'

Goffing can't help himself, emitting a small chuckle. 'I find that hard to believe.'

'The gravy train is pulling into its final station. Time for me to get onside with the authorities. Cut a deal. Immunity. Make the platform safe and comfortable.'

'I don't have that sort of authority,' says Goffing, serious again. 'You must know that.'

'I do. But I also know you have a direct line to the director-general of ASIO and the commissioner of the Australian Federal Police.'

'What are you offering?'

'Full disclosure of Delaney's activities, legal and illegal.' He goes to sip more wine, thinks better of it and rests the glass on the table. 'Including the identity of the mole Delaney has placed inside ASIO.'

'You can supply evidence?'

'I can.'

Goffing is perfectly still, eyes locked on Flange. 'I am sure there will be interest. And in return, you will be seeking . . . ?'

'Anonymity. Immunity. Security. And no attempt to garnishee any of the wealth I've accumulated in the service of Mr Delaney.' He holds his hands wide. 'I assure you, it will be a very rewarding deal.'

Martin runs his finger round the top of his glass, knowing he has little to put on the table, that this is Jack Goffing's play.

'I'll see what I can do,' says Goffing. 'Perhaps, to demonstrate your sincerity, you might identify now the person who has infiltrated the intelligence community?'

Flange smirks. 'I fear that card might be a little too high in value to simply surrender. You understand, I'm sure. But as a sign of my good faith, I am willing to reveal Delaney Bullwinkel's role in your recent trials and tribulations.' He turns to Martin and winks. 'You'll be interested, I'm sure.'

'You're suggesting he played a role?'

'Instrumental. He hired Seamus Toole and Raymond Penuch.'

'Who are?' asks Goffing.

'Known to you as the A-team. Penuch is the dead one. Toole is the vegetable.' Flange smiles, picks up his slimline briefcase, flicks the catches. He withdraws a dossier, A4 paper in a clear plastic sleeve, and hands it to Martin. 'Their backgrounds. Criminal records.'

Martin can't resist the temptation. He accepts the file. 'Jack?'

Goffing nods. 'We'd be grateful to hear what you have to say. I'm open to making representations on your behalf, if you can convince us that you're on the level.'

Flange frowns, regarding his glass. 'You think if we bought a bottle, it might be more palatable?' he asks.

Martin stands. 'Let me try.'

He goes to the bar and brings back the hotel's token bottle of riesling and three glasses.

'Best you could do?' asks Flange, resignation in his voice.

'Either this or sav blanc with ice cubes,' says Martin.

Flange grimaces, Martin pours the wine. He has no intention of drinking more than a mouthful; he knows Goffing will be the same. Without note-taking or recorders, they will need concentration, smart wits and good memories.

Flange tastes the wine and raises an ironic eyebrow. 'As I said, Delaney Bullwinkel is dying. Lawyer–client privilege will survive him. Defamation protection will not.'

'Of course,' says Martin, and has an inkling where this is heading.

'A number of years ago, you wrote a book highly critical of the affairs of Mr Bullwinkel and his activities in a town called Finnigans Gap. *Opals and Dust*, wasn't it? Based largely on information you obtained from the Homicide detective Ivan Lucic and

453

from Mr Delaney's former partner and arch rival, Bullshit Bob Inglis. Quite the page turner.'

'You read it?'

'Indeed.'

'It was never published.'

'Of course not. We quashed it. Convinced the publishers it was too contentious, that they risked a multimillion-dollar libel suit.'

Now it's Martin's turn to look scornful. 'Not that it would have mattered. By the end so much had been cut out that it wasn't worth publishing.'

'Yes. Innocuous. Emasculated.'

'But now?' asks Goffing.

'Well, that's the point, isn't it?' says Flange. 'When Delaney dies, Martin here can publish whatever he likes. Defame Delaney till the cows come home. Doesn't even have to be true. The dead can't sue.'

'So he tried to kill me to stop the book being released?' says Martin. 'That seems extreme.'

'Now you are gaining an insight into his character. He loves to be extreme. To flout the law, to position himself above it. So he didn't just want to kill you but discredit you so thoroughly that no publisher would touch it, no newspaper would run excerpts, and no reader would buy it.'

'Why would he care? If he's dying?'

Flange twists his mouth into something akin to a smile. 'He cares what people think of him. Wants to protect his legacy.'

'He might still succeed,' says Martin. 'I'm facing some very damaging allegations.'

'Yes. And you would already be dead in the desert, having died in abject disgrace, if it wasn't for the remarkable coincidence of being found by Ekaterina Boland, of all people.'

'Was she part of the plan?'

'No. She was part of the improvisation by Maureen Gingelly.'

'Is it true that she's Bullwinkel's biological daughter?' asks Goffing.

'It is.'

Martin is experiencing something akin to information overload. He involuntarily sips some of the wine, not even tasting it.

Perhaps Jack Goffing is experiencing something similar. 'Maybe you'd like to step us through it,' says the ASIO man. 'Start at the beginning.'

'A very good place to start,' says Flange, smiling. He raises an eyebrow and Martin tops up the lawyer's glass.

'Many years ago, forty years or so, before my time, Delaney was prospecting out in the Paroo Basin. Not with a geology pick, but visiting prospective tenements. He stayed at the Port Paroo Hotel, where he cuckolded the owner and impregnated his wife. He denied paternity, but to keep it under wraps, he reluctantly agreed to support the girl—pay her school fees and whatnot. All on the strict proviso that the mother never revealed his identity. A non-disclosure agreement was drawn up and signed. He wanted nothing to do with his daughter.'

'But she found out anyway,' says Martin.

'Yes. Serves Delaney right. Stingy bastard. He cut them off as soon as the daughter turned eighteen. Washed his hands of them. Which meant the mother no longer had any reason to honour the NDA. She told the daughter, who proceeded to turn up in Perth. Managed to get into a cocktail party at his home and confront him.'

'He softened?'

Flange laughs. 'Soften? A foreign concept to the man, I assure you. But she impressed him. It's my opinion he saw something of himself in her, a ruthless streak. He had two legitimate children he despaired of. She was different.'

Martin is intrigued. For a lawyer, Flange is a good storyteller.

'I was there. I witnessed the encounter. He had a painting hanging on his wall. It was big and impressive and old. I always thought it somewhat lacklustre, but there you go. He's a mining billionaire, not an aesthete. *The Camel's Head at Dusk*. She said she knew of another quite like it, the same view at dawn. She offered to ask if the owners wanted to sell. Delaney suggested instead that she should acquire it for him, as a gift, a sign of her fealty. Her thanks for all he had done for her.'

'Jesus.'

'He was toying with her, of course. She said she had no money, could not afford it. Which he knew.' Flange offers a sad little smile. 'Delaney could buy a thousand paintings like that, but that's not what he wanted. He wanted her to steal it. That and another companion piece, *The Camel's Head at Noon*, held by a collector in Bowral. And in return, he would consider some sort of endowment.'

Martin is shaking his head. 'But they'd be stolen. He could never display them.'

Flange smirks. 'And therein lay their appeal. He would have his legitimate piece up where he entertained his guests, and the two stolen pieces secreted in the basement. Along with the rest of his hoard. You should see it. Perhaps you will. It's obscene. Worth a chapter in your book, Martin.'

'A stolen hoard?' says Goffing, sounding incredulous.

'Quite the thing among the uber rich,' says Flange. 'Russian oligarchs, Saudi princes, African despots, Trump loyalists. I mean, after the palaces, the private jets and the mega yachts, what's left? There's a huge black market: antiquities plundered from Middle Eastern battlefields, treasures looted by the Khmer Rouge, French impressionists stolen by the Nazis. Or works stolen to order. Maureen Gingelly had no way of knowing, but she'd stumbled upon his fetish. A way to get to him. So he commissioned her.'

'With no intention to honour his word?'

'Ah well, it's difficult to say. That's his other fetish, manipulating people. And having someone like her in his thrall, beholden to him, someone with guts and initiative, I think he found the idea attractive. He could have his legitimate children on public display, like his legally acquired artworks, and then he would have her in the shadows, lurking in the basement, like his stolen treasures.'

Martin can't help but squirm. 'Quite the unit, your boss.'

'You don't know the half of it.' Flange sighs. 'Mad as a March hare, but not half so pleasant.'

He drinks some more wine; as far as Martin can tell, the alcohol is having no effect. Despite his slim build, Flange must be quite the practitioner.

The lawyer continues. 'So she agrees. Heads off to steal the paintings. No idea what she was doing, of course. Amateur hour. She gets away with it the first time, at Longchamp Downs, but then she goes to Bowral and it all goes pear-shaped. Maureen and her accomplice killed the collector. Delaney cut her off, told her never to contact him again. Gave her some walk-away money and threatened unholy retribution if she ever spoke a word of it. Said he'd kill her if she so much as contemplated doing so. And there you have it.' Flange rubs his hands together, then holds them out, as if serving a delicacy for their enjoyment.

'Did Bullwinkel have anything to do with the death of a man called Roman Stanton?'

'No, that wasn't him. Not directly.'

'How then?' asks Martin.

Flange hesitates.

'This is very valuable information,' Goffing assures him. 'Useful. Tell us all you know about the relationship between Delaney Bullwinkel and Maureen Gingelly, and you have my word I will do all that I can to cut a deal.'

'Very well,' says Flange. 'I'm not entirely sure what unfolded, but I know the catalyst. When the daughter delivered the first of the paintings, including three more by the same artist who painted the *Camel's Head* series, Delaney was delighted. Delighted with the art, and delighted with her. A chip off the old block. So he promised her something. If she secured the third painting in the series, *The Camel's Head at Noon*, he said she could name her price. Her price was a nearby grazing property. She could join the squattocracy.'

Martin leans forward, sensing a connection being made. 'Any property, or one in particular?'

'She'd identified one close by to where she lived. A young grazier who wanted to sell up.'

'Roman Stanton?'

'Indeed. His father was ill and he was about to inherit. He wanted to sell. Something about running off to London with his fiancée. Maureen knew about it because she was best friends with the fiancée.'

'Chloe Carmichael,' says Martin.

'Delaney had it investigated. Another predilection of his: hiring private detectives to poke about in people's lives without their knowledge. It checked out, appealed to him in all sorts of ways.'

'Such as?'

'Well, there was bad blood between the two grazing families, the Stantons and the Carmichaels. Maybe that was why Roman wanted to sell; so he and Chloe could get away from there, leave it all behind. Delaney liked the idea of stirring the pot. He doesn't like old money. And then installing his bastard daughter into one of these old grazing properties, that appealed to him as well.'

'So you think he would have honoured the agreement with Maz?'

Flange laughs. 'Who knows? He's a capricious bastard. Loves to appear unpredictable. But probably. Money means nothing to him. A nightmare to work for.'

'Must pay well,' says Martin, unable to help himself.

'Indeed,' says Flange, apparently unruffled. 'Why do you think I sully myself?'

'So what went wrong?' asks Goffing.

'Well, I can't be sure,' says Flange. 'Like I said, the deal was off. Delaney cut Maureen adrift after Bowral. I think maybe Roman got wind of her role in the thefts and threatened to expose her, so she killed him. As I say, her father's daughter.'

'Jesus,' says Martin.

'And so nothing happened for twenty years,' says Goffing. 'What changed?'

'Delaney discovered he was dying and started worrying about his legacy. So he did what he always did: paid someone to find out if there was any threat. And it all came down to one thing really. You, Martin.'

'Me?'

'Yes. There were all sorts of people who had it in for him, but they could either be bribed or threatened with mutually assured destruction. You were the only loose end. You had all that unpublished information, including his commissioning of murders at Finnigans Gap. We war-gamed it. The first book would be bad enough, but then everyone would come out of the woodwork, feeding you more and more destructive information. And with Delaney dead, there would be no law of defamation to restrain you. He particularly resented the idea that you would get rich doing it. So he decided to kill you.'

'Right.' Martin moves uncomfortably.

'I advised against it, you'll be pleased to know. If you died, and he died, the publishers would simply hire a ghostwriter to update your book. So he settled on a plan to discredit you, and we started drawing up a strategy. Thought child abuse was best: there's no coming back from that. Then we'd fake your suicide.'

Martin feels ill. Goffing looks horrified.

If Flange notices, it doesn't stop him. He's on a roll. 'And who should reappear as if on cue but Maureen Gingelly. In the interim, Bullwinkel's two legitimate offspring had proven themselves worthless. One was dead, the other has transitioned and is unable to have children. Which is the other thing the uber rich hanker after: a dynasty.'

'Good timing on Maz's part,' says Martin.

'Very good timing. She's been trying to get pregnant.'

'Shit,' says Jack Goffing.

'Who's the father?' asks Martin.

'Anonymous sperm donor; she needs a child, not a husband,' says the lawyer. 'Delaney knew she'd killed Akira Tennant. Suspected she'd killed Roman Stanton. So they teamed up. She even suggested the method: leaving you out in the desert to die. Apparently, that's what her mother did to her stepfather. Got him dead drunk and left him there with no water.'

Martin shivers involuntarily. He remembers how close he came to dying in the same way.

'Delaney loved it. You wouldn't just die; you would suffer. So he agreed. As a down payment, he said he'd buy her a property just as she'd wanted first time round. Not Tavelly Station—another one.'

'Longchamp Downs,' says Martin.

'It was to help out her friend Vincent Carmichael,' says Flange.

'How did they orchestrate it?' asks Jack Goffing. 'Getting Martin to Port Paroo?'

'Through the good offices of Delaney's plant in ASIO, combined with some useful former soldiers to blow up the hall in Port Silver.' Flange smiles.

'And you'll give us their names?'

'That's what I'm offering.' Flange drinks more wine, more of a quaff than a sip. Martin doesn't know why, but he suspects when the bottle is finished, Flange will stop talking. Like an hourglass. Or billable hours.

'What about the mafia?' asks Goffing. 'Were they even involved at all?'

'No, not directly,' says Flange, smiling slyly. 'Delaney's ASIO mole got wind of organised crime bringing in a hit squad to take out Marelli's grandson. The mole tipped them off, warned there would be wall-to-wall surveillance. So the B-team became a decoy, while another team did the business. In return, the anti-Marelli faction agreed Delaney and his dirty-tricks department could use the app to pretend the B-team was targeting someone else.'

'Me,' says Martin.

'You,' says Flange.

'The DG will go ballistic when he hears this,' observes Goffing.

Flange raises his glass, a silent toast, eyebrows lifted and a smile playing on thin lips.

'Just clarify one thing for me,' says Martin. 'The explosion at Port Silver, manoeuvring me into the outback, hiring the A-team to kill me: I can see how you could organise that. But blowing up the road at Longchamp Downs, the timing with the flood, the presence of Ekaterina Boland on the property, the deepfake porno—how could you possibly plan that in advance?'

And Cyril Flange laughs with delight. 'Yes. Superb. Don't you see?'

'Tell me.'

'Maureen Gingelly. Improvising. Making it up as she went along. Demonstrating to Delaney just how inventive she is, how adaptable, how capable. How utterly ruthless. How deserving to be his heir. His sole heir.'

'And the stories placed in the media, that was her too?'

'Penuch was following her orders, yes. But she also had Delaney's dirty-tricks brigade to call on. Skilled practitioners of the dark arts. The fabricated video was their work. She wasn't flying solo.'

'Packlehurst and Glee?'

'Head office told Penuch where to send the material. Same dirty tricks brigade that planted those images in your house in Port Silver.'

'How fucking evil,' says Goffing.

Flange drains the last of his wine. 'She's helped make a dying man very happy.' He addresses Martin, 'He's loved putting you through the mangle.'

SATURDAY

chapter fifty-five

THE SUN IS PITILESS. MIDDAY AND IT'S BORING DOWN, THE AIR-CONDITIONING struggling to cope. Martin stops at the bridge over Brown Water Creek. Where Roman was shot down. Where Chloe Carmichael's fate was sealed. It's no different. Timeless. Uncaring and unaffected. There's still no water; the flood hasn't pushed this far up.

He continues to Tavelly Station, past the glimmering robot, over the cattle grid, carrying the news from the east, of the arrest of Maz Gingelly, the pointless warrant for Delaney Bullwinkel, the formal laying of charges.

The lads, Lachie and Punt, come towards him on horseback, looking the part under their well-weathered akubras. 'You good, mate?'

'Your mum and dad in?'

'In the house. You'll just about catch them.'

'Thanks.'

Martin walks through the gate, up to the house, the lawn as verdant and immaculate as ever. Merriman and Gloria have seen him coming and are standing on the enclosed verandah, waiting for him.

Merriman shakes his hand; Gloria looks incurably sad.

'Thanks for coming,' says Merriman.

'Least I could do,' says Martin.

Gloria offers him a seat, says she can rustle up tea, some food.

'That's very kind of you, but I won't stay long.' But he does take a seat. It feels too formal standing.

'We saw on the news. Maz Gingelly. Helping police with their inquiries. What does that even mean?'

'She'll be charged with murder,' says Martin. 'But she has extremely good lawyers, the best money can buy. All the inheritance in the world won't do her any good in prison, though.'

'Closure,' says Merriman. 'You're writing a book? That's why you've come?'

'Yes. In part. Tying up loose ends.'

'We're very grateful to you for finding out what happened to Roman,' says Gloria. 'And to Chloe. Seeing that justice is done.'

'A viper in our bosom,' says Merriman. 'How long will she get?'

'Hard to say,' says Martin. 'It's intriguing, though. She's confessed to the murder of Akira Tennant. Her lawyers are arguing it was manslaughter, unintentional, but I don't like her chances. She's staring down the barrel of a lengthy stint in prison.'

'Good riddance,' says Gloria, voice ripe with condemnation.

'But she's still denying killing Roman,' Martin says. 'The police believe it's because the Bowral case is impossible for her to defend. There's CCTV and a witness, Vincent Carmichael. But there were no eyewitnesses at Brown Water Creek. No CCTV. The weapon was never found. So it's a purely circumstantial case. Hard to convince a jury, prove beyond reasonable doubt.'

'But surely, if they know everything else she's done,' says Merriman. 'Bowral. Her part in trying to kill you.'

'No. None of that is admissible if they bring her to trial for killing Roman. It's prejudicial. The trial must rest entirely on relevant evidence. And, as I say, the only evidence is circumstantial.'

Merriman Stanton looks disgusted. 'So she gets away with it?'

'Unless the police find new evidence connecting her to the crime,' says Martin. 'But twenty years on, that seems unlikely. And as I said, she'll soon have the money, the resources, to hire the very best lawyers.'

'That's outrageous,' huffs Merriman.

Martin sizes them up. Merriman in his disgust and turmoil, Gloria looking profoundly unsettled.

'Here's the thing. What's really giving the police pause is that the day after Roman was murdered, Maz gave a formal interview to New South Wales detectives claiming to have seen Chloe driving at speed past the hotel, over the bridge and on towards Bourke. A newly minted sergeant, Morris Montifore, recorded the interview. A very thorough officer, quite the young gun back in the day.'

'So?' asks Merriman, forehead creased, the smile gone. 'She was obviously lying. She drove the car herself.'

'It's not what she said that has the police flummoxed. It's the existence of the interview itself. It's time-stamped. It was conducted at exactly the same time that Chloe Carmichael's debit card was withdrawing cash from an ATM in Dubbo.'

Martin has his eyes on Merriman, sees the confusion, the attempt to reconcile the conflicting facts.

'Why didn't the police realise that at the time?' he asks Martin.

'Why would they? They assumed Maz Gingelly was a reliable witness, and that Chloe had killed your brother and was in Dubbo. Maz giving an interview at the same time the ATM was used was totally consistent with that scenario.' Martin sighs. 'So who was it in Dubbo? It wasn't Chloe. And it wasn't Maz. It was an imposter. Ironic, isn't it? For once in her life, Maz Gingelly was telling the truth.'

Merriman looks aghast, eyes squinting with concentration; Gloria saying nothing, lips pursed.

'Something else to consider,' says Martin. 'The imposter would only attempt such a thing if she knew that the real Chloe wasn't about to reappear.'

'Jesus,' says Merriman.

'The police have checked your alibis. Merriman, yours holds up well. You were at the sales in Roma as you claimed. Plenty of witnesses. But Gloria, they're not so sure about you.'

'Rubbish,' says Merriman. 'She was in Dubbo with my parents. Getting them settled into a retirement home. My father was ill.'

'That's right,' says Gloria. 'The police know that.'

'How did you get there?' asks Martin. 'To Dubbo?'

Gloria stares. 'I drove down with them. Merriman picked me up and brought me back after we heard about Roman.'

'Big detour,' says Martin. 'Roma to Dubbo then back here.'

'Had to be done,' says Merriman, but he's sounding less convinced. 'I wasn't just picking up Gloria. I needed to tell Mum and Dad what had happened to Roman.'

'They must have been distraught.'

'They were. Very.'

'Your mother: she's in her late sixties now,' says Martin. 'Still in Dubbo.'

'Yes,' says Merriman.

'She told the police that Gloria drove her own car to Dubbo. Met them there. She's certain of it.' Martin lets this sink in. 'Yet when you drove Gloria home, her car was already here at Tavelly.'

Merriman stares at Martin a long time before turning to his wife, as if afraid to behold her in this new light. 'Why?' he asks her, face starting to crumble, his life beginning to unravel. 'He was my brother. Our own blood.'

And finally she turns on him. 'You stupid man. He was going to sell us out to that billionaire. Take the money and go gallivanting off to London. Spending all our money on that hussy. A Carmichael. Squander our legacy. Leave us high and dry down on that borderline pasture at the end of the flow, in the worst drought this country has ever seen. We'd be there now, if we'd survived the drought, still praying for the water to make its way down to us. Us and the boys. I did it for them. Our boys.'

'How could you know that? That Roman would sell? He never told me.'

'He told me. I drove back here to fetch some medicine for your dad. We'd left it behind by mistake. Your mother didn't know; we didn't want to stress her. I passed Chloe's car; she'd left it by Brown Water Creek. I stopped to check it out, make sure she was okay, but she wasn't there. The bonnet was cool, so I knew it had been there for some time. I got back to Tavelly, and Roman was here. He told me he and Chloe had found something out in the wilderness, so he'd come to collect supplies.

'We had tea. He was so full of himself, bouncing around like a schoolkid. I'd been in Dubbo looking after his parents, your father at death's door, and you were in Roma trying to extract a few paltry dollars for the last of our cattle, and he was out playing explorer. That's when he told me he was going to sell. That he and Chloe didn't want Tavelly. That they would travel the world. Live the high life. And I thought of us, condemned to a subsistence life, scrabbling to stay afloat.

'So I offered to collect Chloe's car, bring it back here, if he dropped me at Brown Water Creek. I took my gun, the handgun. We stopped by the bridge, and I shot him. And I didn't regret it. I had her car, had her credit card. She'd given it to Roman, PIN number on a piece of paper wrapped around it.'

Merriman slumps in his seat. 'Our boys,' he whispers. 'What have you bequeathed them now?'

2005

TUESDAY, 22 MARCH

The stars are so bright tonight, the universe awash.

*I clambered up here, fought my way up one last time. I almost
didn't make it. I feel so weak, so tired, deep in my bones. So thirsty.*

There is no water. No hope.

*And yet there it is, all the wonder of creation spread above me.
The universe so deep and mysterious. I feel I could dive into it, go
swimming through the galaxies. Drink from its source.*

*I'm at peace now. I only regret having to die with so much still
left to live for.*

*I know Roman hasn't forsaken me, that something terrible must
have befallen him. Perhaps he has died before me, is waiting for me
even now. I wish I believed that.*

*At the end, you know certain things. They come to you with
clarity, as if from some universal truth. I know that he loved me.
And I loved him. And isn't that everything? Shouldn't it be enough?
To love and be loved?*

THURSDAY
TWO WEEKS LATER

chapter fifty-six
ECCO

JAMIE AND I ARE IN BRISBANE; I WANTED TO SHOW HIM THE APARTMENT. WE stand looking out at the view. The river is gleaming, the city is shining, freshly washed by a passing storm. It has never looked so good.

We drove up from Port Silver, where we went to Martin's book launch, the one about the Melbourne mafia. It's been out for weeks already, a bestseller, but Martin wanted to have an official launch, to demonstrate that he's alive and has nothing to be ashamed of. His partner was there, Mandy, who was so welcoming, and their son, Liam. They're lucky; they live in such a supportive community. Jack Goffing was there, and so were the Homicide detectives I met in Dubbo when we interviewed Vincent Carmichael, Ivan and Nell. Ivan is nowhere near as intimidating when he's off the clock, and Nell seems far too nice to be such an accomplished detective. They all know each other, go way back. No wonder Martin gets such good stories.

Martin's agent and publisher were there too, buzzing with anticipation for his next bestseller: the sorry saga of murder and dynastic feuds in the outback. And soon, a comprehensive exposé of Delaney Bullwinkel. They will be busy indeed. But not too busy to ignore a blockbuster new book containing amazing revelations about Ludwig Leichhardt's doomed expedition. Emma was with us; the three of them were quaffing champers and enjoying the moment, like a horseracing syndicate that's just won the cup. I'm so glad this has worked out, that I can repay Emma for her loyalty.

From the apartment, Jamie and I watch the CityCats ply the river and the shimmering clouds reflected in the glass towers of the CBD.

'It's really something,' he says.

'Isn't it?' I say.

'You sure you want to sell it?'

'Positive.'

And I do. It's not for me, not anymore. I wonder if it ever was. It was a goal, an imagined sanctuary, hermetically sealed, clean and glossy, nothing old or second-hand or shop-soiled. A contrast to my messy and sordid life. But I don't need it now. My life is fine.

'Lot of water out there,' he says.

'You okay?' I ask.

'Never better,' he says. And he kisses me. So I kiss him back.

We're off to London tomorrow. The world beckons.

AUTHOR'S NOTE AND ACKNOWLEDGEMENTS

FIRST, A CONFESSION. I'VE DEPLOYED A BIT OF POETIC LICENCE IN THE TELLING of this tale. It is, after all, fiction.

The explorers Arthur Hentig and Donald Stuart were indeed members of the last expedition led by Ludwig Leichhardt. And as recounted in *Legacy*, that expedition was last seen departing the Darling Downs on 3 April 1848. However, the two men couldn't possibly have encountered Patrick Murdoch on the Paroo soon after this date, as European settlement had not yet penetrated that far into the interior. The Paroo wasn't settled until the 1860s.

I have also reimagined the landscape around the Paroo to some extent, particularly the prominence of the ridge lines. But go have a look for yourself—it's an amazing landscape.

Now to the good bit: acknowledging all the people who have helped me in the production of this book.

A huge thanks to the Australian editorial team who have guided the editing and production of *Legacy*: Cate Paterson, Christa Munns, Ali Lavau and Kate Goldsworthy. Immense gratitude to publicist Bella Breden and marketing whiz Shannon Edwards. And to all the other members of the amazing Allen & Unwin team.

Thanks to Wavesound, who produce the audio books for Australia and New Zealand, and their amazing narrator Dorje Swallow. And to UK counterpart, Lockie Chapman, who narrates the international audio books.

I'm hugely indebted to everyone at Wildfire Books in the UK, including Rachel Hart, Alex Clarke and Caitlin Raynor.

No writer has a better team of agents: Grace Heifetz in Sydney, Felicity Blunt in London and Peter Steinberg in New York, plus page-to-screen agents Orly Greenberg and Gemma Craig. Thanks as always to the enthusiastic team at speaker's agency Booked Out and to all the translation agents, particularly Nerrilee Weir at Bold Type, Gray Tan at the Grayhawk Agency and Jemma McDonagh at JMA.

Thanks to Ian Collie, Rob Gibson and the crew at Easy Tiger, and to Martha Coleman at Third Act Stories, for so successfully bringing the Martin Scarsden books to the screen. A special shout-out to Felicity Packard, writer and producer extraordinaire.

Luke Causby at Blue Cork has produced yet another stunning cover for *Legacy*, and Aleksander Potočnik has created yet another extraordinary map. Thanks to my dear mate Mike Bowers for all his author portraits and publicity shots.

Thank you to my immediate family: Tomoko, Elena and Cameron; to my wider family including my mum Glenys, my brother Brendon and sister Gwyneth and their families; and to my extended family of fellow crime writers—what a wonderful bunch you are!

And my deep gratitude once again to the wider writing community: the critics and bloggers and book clubs and libraries and booksellers and festivals, with their dedicated volunteers and over-worked directors. And finally, of course, to you: the reader.